WRITTEN IN BLOOD

A.D. WILDE

SWEETWATER SERIES BOOK 2

Cover Designer: Dark Woods Publishing

Developmental Editor: Kim Deacon

Editor: Kylie MacDougall

Third edition 2025

Author Website: www.authoradwilde.com

CONTENT WARNING

This story contains content that may be triggering to some readers. Please consider the following trigger warnings before reading. YOUR MENTAL HEALTH MATTERS.

This story is a dark military romance novel containing morally gray characters. There are scenes of graphic violence and gore, death, dismemberment, torture, human/sex/child trafficking, child abuse and neglect, graphic domestic abuse and rape, alcohol abuse, and mentions of drug trafficking. If any of these things give you the ick or may trigger you, please reconsider whether reading this book is right for you.

To all of you good little sluts who want a gentleman in the streets, but a pierced, possessive, spitting, filthy-talking alphahole between the sheets. I've got you.

One

Zak

I STARE DOWN AT the naked heap of flesh and blood that reeks of piss, shit, and decay. Most of his teeth are missing and one eye's completely swollen shut. I count his fingers and toes. There are less than half of them still attached to his body, courtesy of Liam's twisted desire to quite literally pick these sick fucks apart one limb at a time. Like a child plucking the legs and wings from a fly.

I take a step forward and nudge our captive's leg with my booted foot, startling him awake. He stares up at me, his good eye wide with terror and leaking bloody tears as he takes in his surroundings.

He mutters a string of garbled Spanish—a prayer. But God won't take mercy on his soul, and neither will we.

I drop to my haunches and flash him a sadistic smile. "You must be Diego."

"Who … who are you?" he wheezes out.

Angling my head at him, I respond with disappointment, "You don't remember me?" I gesture to the sling my arm is cast in. "I took a bullet for you, Diego. I'm the man who saved your life. You should be grateful you didn't die in that hellhole." *Instead, you'll die here.*

Diego rears back and spits, a glob of bloody saliva lodging itself onto the toe of my boot.

I tsk. "And here I thought we could be friends."

"Vete a la mierda." *Fuck you.*

Choosing to not acknowledge our guest's rude behavior, I cut to the chase. "You're going to give me a name, Diego. The quicker you do that, the quicker we can all go home." I stand to my full height, towering over Diego. "Well … not all go home," I add with a hint of amusement.

A manic laugh bubbles from Diego's chest, but all humor vanishes the second Liam wraps his hand around his throat and squeezes until Diego's good eye begins to bulge from his head. When I'm satisfied that he's going to take us more seriously, I pat Liam on the shoulder and he releases him, swiping his bloody palm on his thigh.

"Let's try that again, shall we?" Glancing at my watch, I add, "And please make it quick, Diego. I have a party to get to and I'd hate to be late."

When Diego doesn't respond, I release a long, dramatic sigh, nodding once to Liam. Before I know it, the Colombian is squirming beneath my teammate's favorite switchblade, a fresh sheen of sweat and blood coating his body like a second skin. When he finally caves and gives us the information we need, I stand behind him, grip his skull on either side of his head, and snap his neck, gifting him the sweet release of death. If I had left it to Liam to finish him off, it would have taken days.

Diego was as good as dead the moment I spotted him huddled under a table while the rest of his men took aim and made a half-decent effort at trying to stop us. I have to admit, I pegged the sick Colombian prick to be a little more badass than that. But as it turns out, Diego was not only a few chain links of command down from the head of the Colombian cartel, but he was also a fucking coward, seeking his own refuge while others took our heat.

But in the end, he was a coward who gave us something we didn't have before. A name.

Santiago Ortiz.

Whether Ortiz is the head of the cartel or if he's just ranked one level up in the hierarchy of the outfit remains to be seen. Either way, he's next on our shit list.

I change into a clean pair of jeans, cleanse the remnants of Diego's blood from my hands, and within an hour, I'm standing in my best friend's living room with a bottle of beer, watching in awe as a group of three-year-old girls dressed in unicorn costumes ambush a six-foot-six Navy SEAL mercenary. Joel finally gives up and collapses into a heap on the floor, swallowed whole by a monsoon of high-pitched squeals and giggles.

They're tiny monsters.

Stella, Joel's wife, appears beside me a moment later, playfully bumping me in the shoulder and smiling sweetly up at me as she strokes her growing baby bump. If my memory serves me well, she's about four months along now with her second child.

"Hey, Zak," she chirps. "I might have to send you in for an extraction shortly." She gestures to the herd of unicorns piling on top of her husband. "I'm afraid he might not make it out alive with all those tutus and glitter suffocating him."

I swipe my thumb over my mouth and smirk. "I say let him suffer a little longer. It's about time the big grump is taken down a peg."

Stella laughs, her smile stretching all the way to her eyes as she watches Lainey, their three-year-old daughter whose birthday we're currently celebrating, lead the pack to victory.

"So the new guy ..." Stella drawls, peeking back up at me. "How's he doing so far?"

"Seems to be fitting in alright," I tell her over the top of my beer bottle. "But it's a trial. Things could change."

I knew our boss, Mac, had intentions of expanding Sweetwater by another member for a while now, but it wasn't until three months ago that he announced he's made a decision. When Cameron Brooks's file slid across Mac's desk, boss man took his shot and offered him a one year probationary trial to see how he fares out on the team. So far he's been an asset and takes orders like a good little soldier, so there have been no complaints from the rest of us.

When I peer back down at Stella, I realize her gaze has stretched beyond my shoulder, the twinkle in her eyes brightening. I spin to follow her line of sight and discover the source of her excitement.

"Harper!" Stella chirps, bolting toward the leggy blonde whose sole mission in life is to irritate the shit out of me. She pulls her in for a hug, and I take a long pull of my beer and avert my eyes, forcing myself to not look directly at her. "You're back early," Stella observes cheerily.

"Of course I am," Harper responds, her voice sultry and sweet and as obnoxious as nails on a chalkboard. "I couldn't miss Lainey's third birthday. Where is she, anyways?"

Stella gestures to the living room and Harper huffs out a soft laugh when she spots the mountain of tiny humans swarming Joel. I take the opportunity to look directly at her. Long and lean with subtle, lithe curves. Sun-kissed skin from her recent trip to Costa Rica. Thick, blonde hair that falls in loose waves down her back, stopping just above the curve of her spine.

And those fucking eyes. The same vivid blue as the shallow shores of the Caribbean. The girl's a wet dream. When her mouth is shut.

Harper Hilton is a force to be reckoned with. She's feisty and loud. Smart and manipulative in the most dangerous kind of way. And she uses her body as a weapon, luring unsuspecting victims into her web, chewing them up and spitting them back out. In the four years I've known Harper, I've watched countless grown-ass men reduce themselves to blubbering babies over a piece of fucking pussy.

Idiots.

My gaze wanders north over the lavender dress that hugs every one of her curves, our eyes clashing when she catches me ogling her. Her blue orbs dart to my arm sling, something flickering behind her irises. But it's gone before I can tell what it is. I lift my bottle and tip my chin at her. I'd rather strap a steak to my dick and go scuba diving with sharks than spend any length of time in the same room as the hot piece of ass that grates on my last nerve. But here we are.

I peel my gaze from Harper and shift my focus to the door just as Brooks saunters into the house, his short, blond hair buzzed military style and sharp jaw clean shaven. Unlike myself who prefers to maintain a short, dark, well-groomed beard, Brooks is a golden retriever.

And imagine my surprise when Harper sets her sights on the newest team member of Sweetwater, batting her long, thick lashes and smiling sweetly at him. He's not her usual type. Harper typically prefers men in Armani. Wall Street sharks with fat wallets and skinny morals. The type who slip their wedding bands off before going out to a fancy nightclub and dipping their dick in strange pussy. But Brooks isn't a suit. He's a clean-cut Navy SEAL. A stark contrast to both the wealthy businessmen Harper dates, as well as the rest of us on the team.

Brooks's gaze flicks over Harper, sweeping his tongue over his teeth as he slides in beside me. Obviously he likes what he sees, because he can't be fucked to pay me any mind.

"Glad to see you made it," I tell him, but he's distracted, his focus pinned on Harper helping Stella peel small children off of Joel. I have to suppress an eye roll. This dumbass is as good as gone. I won't bother warning him. It wouldn't work anyways. Once Harper has something—someone—in sight, it's game over.

"Yeah," he responds lowly. "Me too."

Jesus. I can't watch this.

On cue, there's a small tug at the hem of my shirt. "Uncle Zakky," a tiny voice drifts up from my feet. I glance down to find a pair of giant, hazel eyes staring up at me.

I reach down and hoist Lainey into my good arm. "Hi, sweetheart." I tickle her cheek with my beard and she squirms and giggles.

"Mommy says I'm puhposed to ask if you can help daddy with the castle."

I glance over at Stella, who's staring back at me with hope in her eyes as she folds her hands in prayer and mouths *pretty please* at me.

"Well, who could say no to such a pretty little unicorn on her birthday?"

I leave Brooks alone to drool in solitude, sliding past him and heading out to the backyard. Setting Lainey on her feet, I suggest to the swarm of tiny terrorists, "Why don't you girls go find Uncle Liam and see if he wants to have tea." The little monsters disappear in a hurricane of pastel tutus and a pitch of laughter that I'm sure dogs on the other side of California could hear.

"Fucking thing doesn't work," Joel grumbles, raking a hand through his hair in frustration. "How hard could it be to suck in air and blow it back out?"

Shaking my head and huffing out a dry laugh, I stride toward the air compressor and lift the power cord. "Did you try plugging it in?"

"Jesus Christ. Ask me to take out an entire cartel … no problem. But inflate a plastic bouncy house?"

I plug the compressor in and power it up. Within minutes, we're staring at a bobbing, pink castle that eats up half of the backyard.

I catch movement out of the corner of my eye and swing my gaze toward the side of the house. And there stands Liam, his fists balled and jaw clenched as he glares at me. My eyes flash to the doll-sized apron tied around his thick, tattooed neck. He points a finger at me, draws a line across his throat with the opposite hand, then disappears again.

Joel chuckles and slaps me on the back, and I wince from the contact. It's been four days since I was shot in the shoulder, and my pain meds are floating somewhere in the city sewer. "Better sleep with one eye open, brother."

Just as I'm about to open my mouth to speak, soft laughter floats through the air and slams into me with the subtlety of a wrecking ball, rattling me to the very core. A shiver rolls down my spine as I turn to see where the demonic sound came from.

Harper.

She must sense me watching her flirt with her shiny, new toy, because our eyes lock for a brief second before she returns her attention to Brooks and begins twirling a lock of her glossy, blonde hair between her fingers while she stares up at him with little red hearts in her eyes.

I grit my teeth and look away. Brooks is in for a rude awakening. Wildcats with sharp claws were never meant to be domesticated.

Two

Harper

MY VERY FIRST BOYFRIEND lived two doors down from my house. His name was Trent. He was seventeen—one year my senior—and had sparkly, blue eyes and a killer smile. He was also tall, fit, and knew his way around the strings of a guitar. So naturally, I fell head over heels in love with him. The only problem with Trent was that he was hung up on some ditzy bitch named Carla. She was the captain of the cheerleading squad and had enormous boobs that she flaunted all over school. It didn't help that her parents had a pool and allowed her to throw parties when they were out of town. But like any good high school romance story, the cheerleader was in love with the captain of the football team and squashed poor Trent's hopes and dreams of ever bagging the hottest chick in school.

Shocker ... I know.

Anyways, Trent was the perfect gentleman. Respectful and tender in all the ways a boy should be when snatching up a girl's V-card. He had me wrapped around his finger. But when he went off to college that fall and returned during Christmas break with a giant hickey on his neck, he crushed my teenage heart to a pulp.

And just like that, I threw my walls up and refused to ever be vulnerable again. I went through a *meta-whore-phasis.* And now … I'm Harper *The Heartbreaker* Hilton. I date and dump. Rinse and repeat. It's safer that way. But *safe* has gotten me nowhere, and now I'm thirty-two with no rock on my hand and no bun in my oven. I don't own a house or have a stable career. Not that there's anything wrong with that lifestyle. It's just … I find myself yearning for more. Ever since Stella announced that baby number two is on the way, I've decided I'm sick of being left in the dust.

So I asked the universe for just a pinch of mercy, and boy did she deliver.

"Morning," Cameron murmurs as his sleepy, gray eyes crack open and peer down at me.

Twirling a finger over the light smattering of hair on his broad chest, I beam up at him and plant a kiss on his cheek.

"How are you always so damn beautiful?" he asks, his knuckles skimming over my bare arm and causing a flurry of bumps to rise in their wake.

Grinning up at him, I slip my hand beneath the covers and wrap my fingers around his morning erection. "And how are you always so damn hard?"

"Harper," he says warningly, his gaze darkening as I begin slowly stroking the length of him.

"Yes, Cameron?" I respond coyly, batting my eyelashes and feigning innocence.

When I roll my thumb over his tip and collect the bead of pre-cum, he releases a soft groan and tips his head back, closing his eyes and allowing me to take control of his body. And since I'm feeling extra generous today, I dive beneath the covers and slip his cock past my lips, circling the head with my tongue before taking him all the way into my mouth. It's moments like this where I'm mildly grateful for the fact that his dick is average and not something that will blow through the back of my skull.

Cam releases a hiss and fists my hair, driving himself further into my mouth until he's nudging my tonsils. It isn't long before warm jets of cum shoot to the back of my throat. I swallow every last drop of him and swipe my lips with the back of my hand.

"What was that for?" he asks as I climb back up his body and flop down beside him.

"For agreeing to meet my grandmother this afternoon?" It's a rhetorical question. Because I always get what I want. And my nan is the most important person in my life, so I know he won't refuse.

Rolling onto his side, Cam slides an arm under my pillow and stares back at me.

"Hmm," he hums thoughtfully. "Think she'll like me?"

I roll my eyes at that because it's the most ridiculous question I've ever fucking heard. "Of course she will. What's not to love?"

Cameron pops his dimples that could double as shot glasses, and I practically melt into a puddle of wanton goo all over my mattress.

"So if I'm meeting your grandmother, does that mean you're ready to meet my family?"

Warmth spreads in my chest at the thought of being introduced to his family. But that warmth is quickly stamped down by my rattled nerves. I've never met a man's family before, so this is a milestone for me. A crazy, huge, *terrifying* step toward finally settling down. "I'd love to."

Cam reaches around and gives my ass a firm squeeze. "We have a small job in a couple days. I won't be gone long, but when I'm back, we'll set up a dinner date."

"Can't wait," I respond cheerily shoving the anxiety of meeting my boyfriend's parents aside. Here's hoping I don't catch a nasty case of verbal diarrhea and end up failing miserably. It wouldn't be the first time my mouth has gotten me into trouble. *Or out of it.*

Cam sweeps a stray strand of hair from my face, the backs of his knuckles grazing my jaw and causing a small puddle to gather in my panties. *Christ on a cracker, he's handsome.*

Our lips barely brush as he gives me a quick peck on the mouth, avoiding taking the kiss deeper because ironically he's grossed out by his own semen. He crawls out of bed and tugs on a pair of jeans.

"I have a few errands to run, but I'll be back to pick you up later."

Then he's gone, just like that. It's become a routine of ours. Cam and I do our own thing during the day, reconnecting as early as possible and spending every waking minute together when neither of us are working. He picks me up, wines and dines me the way I love. Then we crash through the door of his place or mine, a frenzy of tongues and teeth and hands before falling into bed.

But I've never been a fan of routine or predictability, and deep down, I worry that I'll sabotage this just like I do everything else. I read somewhere that we self-sabotage because it's the easiest way for us to remain in control. Unfortunately for me, control isn't something I've ever been comfortable relinquishing. But my internal clock is ticking, and if I have even a shred of hope at making this relationship last, then I need to put my big-girl panties on and grin and bear it. I need to lower my walls and let Cameron in, because the clock waits for no one.

Tick. Tick. Tick.

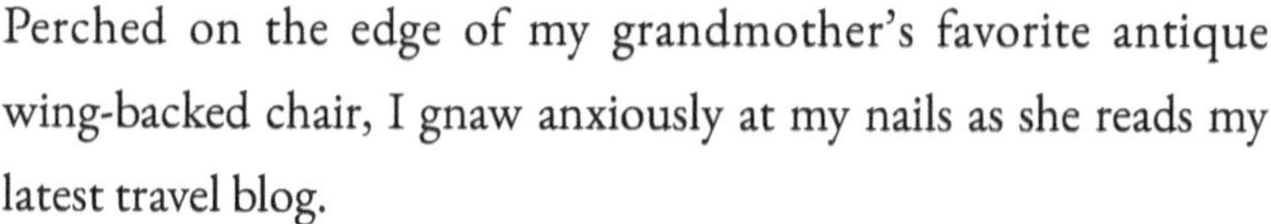

Perched on the edge of my grandmother's favorite antique wing-backed chair, I gnaw anxiously at my nails as she reads my latest travel blog.

Nan's blue eyes widen in horror as she brings her frail hand to her mouth and gasps. It's human nature to automatically begin defending yourself, so that's exactly what I do.

"I know, I know. But Nan, I—"

"Stripped down to your skivvies and went swimming in the dark with a group of strangers. Harper Rosalee Hilton," she chastises. I groan audibly, hating when she uses my full name. "Did I not teach you common sense?"

Rolling my eyes, I reassure her, "Yes, Nan. You did. But they weren't strangers. They were friends." That part's a hair fracture away from a lie. But who's counting?

Okay. I am. I'm counting. And that's at least the millionth lie I've told her. She's always supported my wild endeavors, but that doesn't mean I have to tell her all the nitty-gritty details of my globe-trotting adventures. She'd have a conniption.

Nan's weathered face pinches into a tight scowl, and I slide onto the couch beside her, clasping her warm, wrinkly hand in mine. Then I slather the sugar on extra thick.

"Nan, I promise I'm always careful. But this is my job. There are tons of solo female travelers out there. Practically everyone's doing it these days."

Her eyes narrow to thin slits. "You youngsters underestimate us old-timers. We've been around a lot longer than you." She pokes me in the shoulder. "You're forgetting that I raised you. I know when you're fibbing to me, missy."

I can't help but smirk because she's just so darn cute when she's mad. Deciding now's the perfect time to sweeten her mood, I tell her, "I brought something back for you."

"Oh, deary." She pats the top of my hand. "You don't need to bring me souvenirs."

I slip my hand from beneath hers and rummage through my bag to retrieve a small cardboard box, thrusting it toward her with a beaming smile. "Here. Open it."

She breathes out a sigh and accepts the box. Opening it with shaky hands, she unwraps the beaded earrings I purchased from a local artisan at one of the markets in Peru, my most recent blogging destination where I hiked Machu Picchu and filled my camera with pictures of rich, rolling acreage and fluffy, wild llamas.

"Do you like them?"

She smiles sweetly at me, her pretty eyes twinkling with delight. "They're beautiful, deary." She sets the earrings down beside her and reaches out for a hug. I lean into her and inhale her soft, powdery scent. She smells like home, and although it's only been two weeks since I've seen her, I've missed her. "I know money's tight for you," she says cautiously.

Retreating from her warm embrace, I face my grandmother head on, steeling myself for yet another lie.

"Nan ... I'm fine. I promise. My blog is growing like crazy and I get to travel for a living. What more could a girl want?"

A ring. A wedding. Babies upon babies upon babies.

My grandmother's lips press into a firm line. "You know I'll always worry, Harper. It comes with being your grandmother."

Nan may be my grandmother, but she raised me from the tender age of seven after both of my parents were killed in a car crash. She also believes she's gifted, claiming she can sense things others can't, read auras, see ghosts. Blah blah blah. I think it's just her growing old and senile, but then there are moments like this when she seemingly peers straight through my bubbly, outgoing exterior.

"Don't you think it's time to settle down with—"

I cut her off. "Actually, Nan ..." I clear my throat and straighten my spine, swallowing my nerves and mentally preparing myself for something I've never done before. "There's somebody special I want you to meet."

"Oh?" Her blue eyes widen, and all the earlier concern vanishes from her face, replaced by pleasant intrigue.

"His name is Cameron. He's really cute. And Nan ... he's so sweet. We've only been dating a couple months, but he's perfect." I gnaw anxiously on the inside of my cheek as my grandmother's eyes light with excitement. "He's waiting outside if you'd like to meet him."

Her smile stretches wide, reaching all the way up to her baby blues. Seeing my nan happy is always the highlight of my day.

"Oh, deary. Why didn't you say something sooner? You should have invited him in when you got here."

She tsks, then rises from her chair and begins pacing, her slippers shuffling over the old, worn-out hardwood as she clutches one of her special stones to her chest. I pull my phone out of my bag and fire a text off to Cameron. Moments later, he's sitting across from my grandmother, acting the perfect gentleman while I watch in awe as my grandmother falls head over heels in love with him.

I understand her appeal. After all, I hand-selected him myself. And it only helps that he's so attractive. I'm fairly certain my vagina has sprouted her own heartbeat. Sharp jaw, dove-gray eyes, deep dimples that pop when he smiles. He'll make gorgeous babies, no doubt. And a wonderful husband someday.

Nan's eyes slide to mine, and I know I have her approval. Cameron flashes me a panty-melting smile and I liquify into a mess of hormones on my grandmother's chair while my ovaries break into song and dance.

Nan saunters off to the kitchen, and Cameron and I sit quietly, competing in a staring contest and seeing which one of us can flash the cheesiest smile. The chatter of teacups snaps me out of my lust-filled daydream as Nan saunters back into the living room carrying a tray of tea and biscuits. She sets it down carefully on the coffee table in front of us, and a tiny piece of my heart chips away as I watch her trembling hands fumble with the sugar bowl.

Cam checks his watch and stands, catching me off guard. "I'm so sorry," he apologizes. "But we have a dinner date and should probably get going."

"Oh." Nan's disappointment slashes through me like a hot knife through butter. That twinkle in her eyes dims out, and I find myself feeling torn. "Well, that's alright," she says gently, patting me on the shoulder and smiling politely at both of us.

I stand and wrap my arms around her, sucking in one final lungful of her scent to take with me, then give her a quick peck on the cheek. I hate this part—leaving her. It never sits right with me.

"Will I see you in a couple days, deary?"

"Of course, Nan." I peer over at Cam, who's now hovering by the front door, his hands stuffed in his pockets. "I'll be by on Monday."

She nods, then plops down on the couch and begins rummaging through her bag of stones, searching for something specific.

"It was lovely to meet you, Mrs. Hilton," Cameron says politely, then ushers me out of the house.

The door closes behind us and I stop on the porch and frown. "What the hell was that all about?"

He angles his head at me. "I told you we had dinner plans, sweetie."

I recoil, because so-the-fuck-what if we had dinner plans. That was straight-up rude of him to end the visit like that. And nobody's rude to my grandmother. I will literally cut a bitch ...

He takes my hand and brushes his lips over my knuckles, the gesture causing a pool of lust to gather low in my belly as he mutters against my fingers. "I'm sorry if I upset you, Harper. I just don't want to be late for our reservation. We've been on the waitlist for weeks for this one."

Deciding it's too early in our relationship for our first real argument, I sigh and accept his apology. "Fine." I poke him in the chest. "But if that happens again, I won't hesitate to tie you up and torture you."

He pops those dimples and all is forgotten. "Careful, baby. I might like that."

Three

Harper

"Here we are," Cam chirps proudly as he parks his sporty, red BMW at the curb. "Supposed to be the best French cuisine in the state." He hops out, races to my side of the car and opens the door, offering me his hand.

I step out onto the asphalt and into the heat, the humid air sticking to my skin like syrup. I stumble slightly in my skyscraper heels and Cam reaches out to catch me.

"You alright?" he asks, his edges softening with concern.

Nodding, I reassure him with a smile. "I'm good. Just haven't eaten much today and I'm starving."

Cameron sets a hand on my lower back and leads me inside the restaurant and into a climate-controlled space where I feel like I can finally breathe again. That is, until he takes a seat in front of me, and all the air is squeezed from my lungs.

What in the Alexander Graham Bell is up with me tonight? Did my grandmother slip one of her funky stones in my purse as some sort of sick joke?

"You don't look well, Harper. Are you sure you're okay?"

"Just happy to be here with you," I tell him, sprinkling on a little extra charm for good measure. Cameron doesn't say anything in response. He just nods, opens his menu, and silently peruses.

I open mine as well but can't bring myself to read a single word on the page, let alone think about food. Peeking over the top of the leather binder, I glimpse around the dimly lit restaurant in search of a distraction.

Couples of all ages are seated intimately throughout the main dining area, the small, cozy tables lined with crisp linen cloths and lit with the soft glow of candlelight. Every station is adorned with a single red rose in a tall, slim vase. The crimson flowers would be a nice touch if I didn't absolutely despise the fucking things.

Setting my sights on an elderly couple holding hands across the table, I mindlessly reach for the basket of warm bread the waiter dropped off. But Cameron's fingers lace around my wrist, stopping me in my tracks.

"You'll ruin your appetite, baby." He smiles politely and removes his hand, retreating to his side of the table.

I snort. It's unladylike, but whatever. Cam knows I lack in that department at times and doesn't seem to mind. Another thing I appreciate about him. "I could eat an entire cow right now." I snatch a piece of bread out of the basket and shove it in my mouth, making elaborate sex noises when the bread melts like butter on my tongue. "God, that's good." I lift the basket and gesture for him to try a piece, but he shakes his head and returns his attention to his menu.

I shrug my shoulders, set the basket down directly in front of me, and scarf down two more pieces before busying myself with sipping the glass of Bordeaux Cam ordered for me. Something I've learned about Cameron is that he has excellent taste in wine. A quality I admire because I haven't a clue what I'm looking for when selecting a vino. Gin martinis are my preference. Extra dirty. Extra olives. But right now, the wine is providing me with a very pleasant buzz, and for that, I'm grateful.

The waiter pops out of nowhere, a giant smile stretched across his kind, round face, and I realize I still haven't decided on what to order.

Scanning the menu quickly, I settle on the beef bourguignon and drop the menu on the table, satisfied with my decision. Cam peers at my empty wine glass and gently lays his menu on top of mine.

"I'll have the lamb. She'll have the Parisian salad with the dressing on the side. And we'll take a bottle of the Bordeaux please."

My mouth pops open before my brain has a chance to stop it. "I thought we were in the twenty-first century where women place their own orders," I say boldly, earning me a glower from the soldier sitting across from me. "I mean ..." A nervous cackle comes from somewhere. Me, I think. Jesus. "I was actually hoping to order something else," I add politely, shifting uncomfortably in my seat. The waiter cocks a brow at me, and Cam's jaw slides in irritation. Shit. Fuck. "Could I get the beef bourguignon instead, please and thank you?"

"Of course, madame," the waiter responds gently.

"It's mademoiselle, not madame," I correct. "I'm not married." More nervous laughter erupts from my side of the table.

Someone get the girl a muzzle!

The waiter flashes me an apologetic smile, then bows and scoops our menus off the table, vanishing as quickly as he came. Cam leans forward and props his elbows on the table, his gray eyes darkening to that of angry storm clouds. "I'm a little on the traditional side, Harper, and we're in a high-end establishment. But nonetheless, I apologize for being presumptuous when ordering on your behalf."

My shoulders slump as guilt trickles into my bloodstream. He's right. He shouldn't have assumed. But how I reacted was totally rude and unnecessary. I may have the mouth of a sailor, but I'm not a total cavewoman. "I didn't mean to—"

"It's fine, Harper." He smiles sincerely, and I relax back into my seat.

The waiter returns with the bottle of wine and a pitcher of ice water. I stare at the bobbing cubes, wishing I could somehow magically shrink down and join them, just to cool the embarrassment heating every inch of my skin. But then a sudden shiver rolls down my spine and every cell in my body comes to life, their buzzing vibration drowning out the low chatter of the other dinner guests.

"Harper." Cam's voice snaps me back to reality.

"Hmm. Sorry, what?"

"I was saying—"

"Yes, of course. Stay at my place tonight. Got it." I force a smile, but I'm not interested in conversation at the moment. Because now my scalp is tingling and I'm almost positive I'm being watched.

Careful to not alarm Cameron, I fold my napkin on the table and slowly stand, my chair making an obnoxious scraping sound on the polished hardwood floor. "Excuse me for a moment. Just need to use the ladies' room." Dropping a chaste kiss on Cam's cheek, I saunter off to the restroom and lock myself inside, dropping my forehead to the solid slab of wood and groaning.

I take a few cleansing breaths and calm my frazzled nerves.

It's become clear that I'm terrible at dating long term. And poor Cameron is taking the brunt of the force from the lack of filter between my brain and my mouth. I almost feel sorry for him, except I fucking don't, because he knew what he was getting himself into from the get-go. I held nothing back on our first date, and he seemed to appreciate that about me. So ... whatever.

A sudden knock on the door startles me.

"Just a minute," I holler, then scurry to the sink to wash the sweat from my palms.

I leave the bathroom in a hurry, determined to not allow a little bump in the road to completely derail my evening with Cameron. But just as I round the corner toward the dining lounge, I slam into a massive wall of muscle and am sent careening backward.

"Shit. Fuck. I'm so sorr—" Stepping back, I lose my balance in these awful fucking heels that I've crammed my poor little toes into. But before I tumble to the floor, a pair of big, rough, tattooed hands grip my forearms, keeping me upright. The contact causes every single hair on the back of my neck to rise. Not out of fear, but out of … something else.

I suck in a sharp breath, inhaling an intoxicating cocktail of sandalwood and something else I can't quite peg down. The scent sends me soaring high, and I instantly decide it should be illegal to smell that good.

But when my eyes take in a crisp, black dress shirt stretched deliciously across a broad chest, then roam up over short, dark facial hair and a strong, chiseled jaw, landing on a pair of warm, coffee-colored eyes, I yank my arms free and take one giant step back.

Zak Shephard.

"What are you doing here?" I snap out, sounding far bitchier than I intended but not giving two flying fucks because Zak's an asshat who doesn't deserve my respect. The man is a pig and should be treated as such.

He angles his head at me, his eyes raking over my body as if he has X-ray vision and can see straight through the thin fabric of my satin dress. I hate when he does that.

A deep, gravelly voice scratches along my nerves when he responds plainly, "It's a restaurant, Harper. What do you think I'm doing here?"

A date. Of course he's on a date, dumbass. It's Zak Shephard. King of Fuck and Chuck. Lord of all the ladies' men. Ruler of all the douchebags in the land.

Normally, I wouldn't judge a person for their dating preferences. After all, it's not like I have the best track record. But Zak ... he ruins relationships. *Friendships.*

Smoothing out the front of my dress and fixing my hair, I snip out, "Right. Well, enjoy." Stepping to the side, I go to shuffle past him, but come teetering back when his hand wraps around my wrist, halting me.

I hiss and jerk my hand away as Zak's eyes flick down my body. Crossing my arms, I ask bluntly, "Can I help you?"

His intense gaze pins me in my place, his overwhelming presence sucking all the oxygen out of the air around us like an all-consuming vortex. This is what happens every time I'm alone with Zak. He suffocates me with his judgy eyes and disgusted sneers.

The dude fucking hates me. But the feeling is mutual. Our dislike for each other stems all the way back to the time Zak held me captive in my own apartment while Stella's stalker was on the loose four years ago. It's not that I'm still bitter about that. In fact, I'm actually totally over that. Now ... I hate Zak Shephard for an entirely different reason. He cost me a solid friendship when he fucked Amelia, the bartender at Stella and Joel's wedding, who also happened to be a dear friend of mine. I had warned her to stay away from him and his wandering cock, but she didn't listen. And for whatever reason, she decided to take her heartbreak out on me. As if I had anything to do with his failure at being a decent human being.

When Zak doesn't respond, I say, "Okay. Good talk." Our arms brush when I move past him, and I swear I feel his fingertips skim over the palm of my hand but chalk it up to me losing my damn mind. I'm being super extra weird tonight, and I haven't a clue why.

I plop back down into my seat and frown at Cameron. He makes no move to glance up from his phone, so I pull my own out and check to see if it's a full moon so I can blame the lunar cycle on my insanity.

Nope. Just me being a crazy person.

When I clear my throat, Cam tucks his phone away and rakes his eyes over me, then he smiles a devastating smile and pops his dimples. But my nerves are fried like bacon and I can't seem to match his level of calm.

The waiter appears with a rolling cart and sets our plates in front of us. I stare down at the bowl of beef bourguignon, my appetite having vanished into thin air. Unfortunately, so has my wine buzz and now I'm stone-cold sober.

Thanking the waiter, I take a microscopic bite of my dinner as Cam watches me over the top of his wine glass. A dribble of sauce slips down my chin, and I snatch my napkin off my lap and carefully swipe it away.

But the side of my face is blazing hot and I can't ignore it any longer. I glance over at the hallway by the restrooms to meet Zak's heated gaze. As much as I loathe the man, I have to admit, his sex appeal ranks off the charts. All sharp lines, hard planes, and ink that peeks out of his shirt collar, creeps down his hands, and dusts over his knuckles. He's the definition of a bad boy. I understand why women drop to their knees in front of him, I really do. But if you were to scroll through the dictionary to the word *asshole*, you'd find his name listed right there beneath it. Capitalized. In bold.

And right now, that asshole is standing on the other side of the restaurant, out of Cameron's view, shooting me a death glare like I just slipped his ditzy date a note informing her he's riddled with sexually transmitted diseases. I peel my eyes from Zak and slug back a glass of cold water, but it does nothing to douse the fiery ball in the pit of my stomach.

The heat on the side of my face intensifies with every gulp I take. When I glance over at the hallway again, I see that Zak's still watching me. We lock eyes briefly before he turns and saunters off down the hall with his hands stuffed in his pockets.

Good riddance.

Cameron and I finish dinner and leave the restaurant, Cam helping me back into the passenger seat of his car and laying the single red rose from our table across my lap. We barely make it through my apartment door before our lips are crashing together. There's a fire inside me right now, and I feel like I'm slowly crumbling beneath the weight of the pressure I'm putting on myself. It takes all of three seconds for greedy hands to roam beneath my dress, and I lean into his touch, desperately seeking more from him.

He mutters against my lips, "I never had a chance to tell you how beautiful you look tonight."

"Thank you," I whisper, a cheesy grin plastered on my face.

Dropping his forehead to mine, he slips his hands beneath the lace of my panties and gives my bottom a firm squeeze. "Harper ..."

he grates out, his eyes hooded and nose brushing with mine. "Is it too soon to tell you that I'm in love with you?"

A heavy sadness weighs on me. I want to return the words, but it feels … rushed. Is two months too soon to say the three big words? I don't think so. Stella and Joel fell head over heels in love within a few months. But I'm not Stella. I'm not a swoony, mushy, ooey gooey bitch. Yet again, neither was she. Actually, now that I think of it, she was cold and hard and bitter as fuck before she met Joel.

Instead of lying and returning Cam's admission, I seal my lips over his and lead him to my bedroom. But he pulls away and steps back, raising a palm in the space between us.

"I'm going to take a shower. I'll see you in bed." He stalks off down the hallway and disappears into the bathroom, the door quietly clicking shut behind him.

I slip out of my dress and into a pair of sleep shorts and a tank top and flop down in bed. I must pass out immediately because I wake in the middle of the night, curled up against Cameron as he sleeps peacefully beside me.

Rolling onto my back, I thumb my right palm, the ghost of Zak Shephard's touch still lingering.

Fuck him.

Four

Zak

I'M THE FIRST TO throw my hand up for a small mission in South Africa. Liam throws his up next, then finally Brooks. Glaring at Joel, I mouth *fuck you* from across the war room table. Stella's seven months pregnant now and in nesting mode, so he's been ducking out of jobs when he can. Which means I've been shackled to Liam, who's growing more terrifying by the day. I've been meaning to talk to him about that but afraid it might push him over the edge. And Brooks—Harper's boy toy.

God help the idiot who fell straight into her trap. Except maybe this one is different, because his heart is still intact and they're still together, which is entirely unusual for Harper.

We go wheels up to South Africa and I sleep most of the plane ride there. Liam catches a couple hours of rack time too, but mostly he can be found glaring at walls and fiddling with his switchblade.

We drop into a jungle outside a small African village where we've been informed an organized crime group is holding a government official hostage. Normally, this is something the military would handle, except this time, our extraction isn't an innocent civilian. He's a traitor. A member of the White House who's been selling off classified information in exchange for paydays. It's a matter of national security. If word gets out that there's been a leak, shit will hit the proverbial fan. So we've been called in to extract the hostage and leave things nice and tidy.

And by *nice and tidy*, I mean blow the place to smithereens so there's no evidence of us ever stepping foot there.

We move boots through the sweltering African heat, successfully acquiring the asset and coming out with nothing more than a few bumps and bruises. It takes all of five hours and we're back on the plane, doing the same things but in reverse.

We land on US soil, haul ass to headquarters, and begin our special flavor of interrogation.

"Jesus," Sloane, our huntress, hisses. "What the hell did you boys do to him?"

I smile down at the White House official who's been putting our entire country at risk for a petty thirty million dollars. He's wound up in thick, rough rope that's designed to leave painful ligature marks. One eye is swollen shut—courtesy of Liam—and his jaw is busted, his dry, cracked lips wrapped snuggly around a grenade.

Leaning down, I tauntingly flick the pin of the explosive with my index finger. "I could paint the sky red with you with just the tug of this pin." I won't, of course, considering our location. But the threat has old Joe shaking in his Italian leather shoes.

Poor Joseph's eyes blow wide as tears leak down his busted-up face. He's well into his sixties, would have retired with a big, fat government pension. Could have bought a cozy little cottage somewhere, taken his grandkids fishing on weekends, kept his wife and twenty-five-year-old mistress both content. But instead, he chose *this*. Soon enough, his body will turn up on the west coast of the US after a very tragic boating accident.

"You're all the same," I sneer in his face. "Greedy, filthy fucks who don't give a flying rat's ass what happens to the world once you're gone. But unfortunately for you, people like us exist." I stand to my full height and raise my arms at my sides. "And the thrill we get from making the last hours of your life a living hell ... Well, let's just say that's the type of happiness money can't buy."

Joseph lets out a garbled whimper and fresh tears begin pouring from the corners of his comically wide eyes.

Circling him slowly, I continue, "I guess we're greedy fucks too, when you think about it. But instead of cold, hard cash, we prefer blood as payment." Tapping him on the temple with the butt of my gun, I snarl into his ear, "And there's nothing more beautiful than the crimson splatter of pieces of shit like you."

The sharp stench of urine permeates the air.

"I ain't cleaning that up," Sloane mutters, then blows a bubble with her gum and pops it between her teeth.

Liam steps out of the darkest corner of the room and flips his switchblade open. Then the sobbing really begins, and I sit back and watch as Liam does what he does best. I enjoy the chase, getting a few good hits in. But I'm a medic by trade. A soldier built to put people back together—not rip them apart. I don't really have the stomach for that. I'd rather simply put a bullet in his head and call it a day. But we have a laundry list of information we've been tasked to obtain.

Joseph doesn't hesitate to spill the beans. He's not military and has never undergone any sort of torture training like the majority of the sick fucks we take down. But that doesn't stop Liam from making him pay for all the innocent lives Joseph has put at risk.

I glance over at Brooks, who's been suspiciously quiet ever since we landed. He has the same waxy sheen that a body has after it's been drained of all its blood. He's a SEAL. He's seen some shit. But I can tell by the way he's flinching with every pained cry that erupts from the other side of the room that this is something he hasn't yet grown accustomed to.

Slapping Liam on the back, I excuse myself from the room before the real sick shit begins and wait in the hall as another bloodcurdling scream filters through the walls. The door flies open and Sloane books it out of the room and down the hall toward the bathroom, her hand clasped over her mouth. Next comes Brooks, a blank expression on his face as he saunters off in the same direction, shaking his head in disbelief.

"Holy hell. What the fuck is he doing in there?" I murmur to myself, then stride back into the room, nearly gagging when my eyes land on Joseph's. Only they aren't in his head anymore.

Grimacing, I shuffle past the pair of peepers laying on the floor, their lifeless gaze staring back at the body they once survived in.

"Davis," I growl, snagging Liam's attention. "Did you get what we needed?"

He nods once, and that's all the permission I need to pull my gun from my waistband and end Joseph's suffering.

"Nighty night," I chirp before putting a bullet between his hollow eye sockets.

Liam glares at me, rage palpitating off him in thick, riveting waves as he swipes his bloody blade on Joseph's shirt then folds it and tucks it back into his jeans.

"I wasn't done with him," he snarls. "He deserved more. He helped kidnap a governor's thirteen-year-old daughter."

I rake my hand through my hair and blow out a breath. "I know, man. But fuck." I shake my head. "You need some help, brother. You're in too deep with this shit."

Liam's lips curl into a snarl and he storms out of the room, slamming the door behind him. I glance down at Joseph and swallow the bile rising in my throat. His eyes have been spooned out of his skull. His bottom lip has been ripped down, a shredded flap of meat dangling from the exposed bone of his chin. His ears have been sliced clean off and lay haphazardly on the floor next to him. I don't dare inspect the rest of his body.

"Jesus Christ," I murmur, dialing Mac to let him know we have what we need.

"Uncle Zakky," Lainey squeals and runs toward me, her tiny fingers reaching for me. She lets out a giggle when I toss her in the air and swiftly catch her.

"Hey, little monster. Where's your dad?"

"Outside."

Setting her on my shoulders, I zigzag through the house, dipping and swerving like an airplane. But I soon come to a standstill in the doorway of the kitchen. Wetting my lips, my eyes roam over the curve of a tight ass in ripped jeans as a woman bends over the bottom drawer of the freezer and rifles through it. Long, lean legs. A thick head of blonde hair. Stark white toenail polish on pretty, tanned feet.

A sweet floral scent that makes my blood boil.

She stands and spins around. "I can't find the—"

Our eyes clash and a sardonic smirk toys with my lips as Harper quirks a perfectly groomed brow and pops a hip. She glances up at Lainey, then back to me, her expression softening for all of a millisecond before she rearranges her face back into a glare.

"Auntie Harper," Lainey screeches and bounces on my shoulders. I roll Lainey off and set her on her feet, and the little tornado takes off toward Harper. "Can I have a fwweeezie?"

"Sure, honey. What color do you want?"

"Pink!" the tiny monster exclaims.

Harper pulls a small, pink Freezie from the bottom drawer, snips the top off, wraps it up in a paper towel, and hands it to Lainey. Lainey says a quick thanks then disappears out the patio door and into the backyard where I spot Joel, a garden hose in hand as he fills a small kiddie pool with water.

Harper returns her attention to me, her eyes narrowing as I flash her a thousand-watt smile. It drives her nuts when I'm polite, so naturally, I make extra efforts when she's around.

"I heard you landed a hotel deal. Sounds like a big move for your travel blog. Congratulations," I manage to offer with sincerity.

But as always, I extend an olive branch and Harper snips it off with a scoff and an eyeroll.

"Like you care."

"You're right. I don't care. Just trying to be polite."

She mutters something under her breath that I can't quite make out, although I'm certain it was an insult. Angling my head, I take a step forward, that floral perfume sucking me in like some sort of invisible undertow, dragging me deeper and deeper into the tide.

"If you could see past that bitchy attitude of yours, you'd realize I'm actually a nice guy, Harper."

"Nice guy," she deadpans. "I didn't realize shaggy dogs like you could possess such a quality."

I shrug and saunter over to the fridge, our arms brushing on my way past her. The contact sends a wave of heat rippling through my body, like the aftershock of a bomb detonating. I ignore the sensation and grab two beers from inside the door, pausing shoulder to shoulder with Harper and leaning in, my lips almost grazing the shell of her ear. "Maybe you're right, Harper. I'm not a nice guy. Because shaggy dogs like me eat innocent creatures like you for breakfast, *kitten*. And although I enjoy the chase, enjoy watching you squirm, I'll enjoy the capture and punishment more." Harper's lips part briefly before her mouth clicks shut. "You'd be wise to remember that the next time you decide to talk back."

Five

Harper

THAT ASSHOLE IS FUCKING infuriating. How dare he call me "kitten." I'm no kitten. I'm a freaking lioness. I will rip his entire giant, stupid, muscular body to shreds if he so much as breathes in my general direction again.

Pissed at myself for allowing Zak to get under my skin, I jam my key into my apartment door and fling it open with so much force that it bounces off the wall and comes back to smack me. Gah! Sucking in a deep breath before I lose my shit and stomp back to Stella and Joel's to give Zak a piece of my mind, I shut the door behind me and take a few calming breaths, spotting Cam's keys on the table.

Weird. I didn't see his car in the parking lot. I must have been too distracted plotting Zak Shephard's death. Which, by the way, I've settled on poisoning him. Slowly.

"Cameron?" I call out. Silence. Dropping my keys next to his, along with the thousand travel magazines I picked up at a stand on the street, I stroll into the kitchen. "Hey. How come you didn't answer when I called you?"

Stormy, gray eyes meet mine from across the island. Resting his palms flat on the chipped laminate countertop, Cam pins me with an accusatory look. "Where have you been?"

"Stella's," I respond honestly. "She's hoping to put in a vegetable garden at Casa del Sol for the residents there. So I was helping her plan it out." When Cam's eyes narrow to slits, I decide to elaborate. "Stella's going to be taking some time off when the baby arrives, so she wants the trauma victims she houses at her mother's estate to have something to nurture and grow while she's away."

"Seems like something she could have planned out on her own, no?"

I shrug. "Pregnancy brain has her in a chokehold."

"Hmm," he hums thoughtfully. "Why'd your phone go straight to voicemail?"

Why the fucking interrogation?

"Because it died and I forgot my charger at home." I pull my phone from my purse and slide it across the island to him. "See for yourself if you don't believe me."

Cam snatches my phone up and presses the power button. As I knew it would, the screen remains black.

"It's dead, honey. I'm sorry if I worried you."

Cam circles the island and I back myself into the counter. He cages me in with strong arms and leans forward, sliding the tip of his nose down the bridge of mine. "I don't mean to be an asshole, Harper. I've just seen too much shit in this job, and I need to know you're safe at all times."

Sighing, I rest a palm on his racing heart. The tempo feels ... angry.

I lift up on my toes and kiss him gently on the lips. Then I sprinkle on all the charm and say, "I know. I'll grab another charger and keep it in my purse for emergencies. Fair?"

He nods. "Fair."

"So anyways ..." I drag a finger down his shirt, doodling on his chest. "I was thinking ... there's this new art exhibit in town that I want to check out ..." I bat my eyelashes and smile shyly up at him.

"And you'd like if I took you ..." he finishes for me.

"Actually, I was hoping you could just drop me off and I'd go alone." Sarcasm. It runs thick in the Hilton gene pool.

"Hmm." A playful glint sparks in his eyes. "And what would I get in return?"

I shrug my shoulders and glance up and to the right, tapping a finger on my chin as I feign consideration of what I have to offer him. "How about ... road head?"

Warm, wet lips crush over mine as Cam presses his hips into my pelvis, grinding his erection between us. Groaning into my mouth, he takes the kiss deeper as his hands roam my body with restrained desire. He ends the kiss and drops his forehead to mine, his chest rising and falling with labored breaths as he closes his eyes.

"I'll have to take a rain check, baby. We're wheels up in a few hours."

Sadness sweeps in, flushing out every ounce of arousal and excitement. Cam's been home for all of one week and he's already being called back to duty. His job is unpredictable. I knew that when I met him. But that doesn't mean I can't still be disappointed when he has to leave.

Pinching my chin, he lifts my face to his. "Why don't you come see me off this time?"

Without another word, I'm grabbing my bag, slipping back into my flip-flops, and riding with him to Sweetwater's private jet. This is the first time he's invited me to be there when he boards the plane. We're over three months into our relationship and reaching yet another milestone. With each day that passes, I can see everything I desired finally coming within reach. The only hurdle remaining is meeting his parents, which he's promised we'll do as soon as he's back from this mission.

Sitting anxiously in the passenger seat, I rake my eyes over his camo-clad body and fight back the urge to nibble on him.

"You look hot in your uniform."

Cam flashes me his dimples and adjusts in his seat, stretching his legs out and widening his knees.

"How about that road head you promised?"

Sucking my bottom lip between my teeth, I unlock my seat belt and perch on my knees on the seat. I reach for his belt buckle, unzipping his fatigues and freeing his already-hard cock. I wet my lips and lean in, blowing hot breath on the tip before slipping it past my lips and taking him into my mouth, my body swaying when the car takes a sharp left turn.

Cam steers the vehicle with one hand and grips the back of my head with the other as I slide my hand into his briefs and fondle his balls. He groans when I wrap my free hand around the base of his cock and slide it up and down with my mouth. I eagerly hollow out my cheeks, sucking him hard and fast and drooling all over him the way he loves. It doesn't take long before warm jets of cum shoot to the back of my throat, and I swallow every drop of it.

When I'm finished, I zip him up and plop back down into the passenger seat, grinning at him like we just committed some sort of heinous crime that nobody can ever know about.

A large, warm hand slips to my thigh and gives me a gentle squeeze. "When I get back, we'll check out that new art exhibit in town."

Beaming with pride for making my man so happy, I say, "I'd like that."

A little while later, a large, steel building comes into view and a tiny piece of my heart breaks off as we roll across the asphalt to the waiting plane. Heat ripples from the jet engines as the pilot sits perched high up in the cockpit, waiting patiently to cart my boyfriend off to some dangerous destination and drop him like a hot potato.

Cam grabs a duffel bag from his trunk, then takes my hand and leads me toward the building. Stella and Joel are already here with Lainey, and I spot Liam inside the building loading what looks like cases of weapons onto a dolly. He catches me watching, nods once, then tosses a black bag large enough to fit a body inside on top of the pile.

Mac and Sloane exit out a side door, dressed head to toe in camo. Sloane offers me a little wave, and the two disappear into the back of the plane.

Cam stiffens beside me, his grip on my hand tightening, and I peek up to see his face harden into a glare so intense I'm certain he could light the entire building on fire with his retinas. A bead of sweat forms on my lower back and trickles between my ass cheeks as the core temperature of the earth rises by a million degrees.

I follow Cam's line of sight to another door at the side of the building and locate the source of my discomfort.

Camo clad, just like the rest of them, but looking entirely too relaxed to be getting on a plane to some foreign country to go save the fucking world, is Zak Shephard. His brown eyes meet mine for all of a millisecond, then slam to the man at my side. Long, intentional strides carry him to the waiting plane, and he disappears inside of it with Sloane and Mac.

Cam's voice snatches me from my thoughts. "Looks like we're taking off any minute. Are you going to be okay for a few days while I'm gone?"

Sighing dramatically, I reassure him, "I'll be fine, Cameron. I already told you, I'm a big girl and can take care of myself." Opening my palm, I chirp, "Keys, please."

Cam reluctantly fishes a fob out of his pocket and drops the single car key into my hand. "Park it at your place and don't move it until I'm back."

I expected that, considering that stupid car is practically his child. Shooting him a mischievous smirk, I promise, "Don't worry. She'll be just fine."

He leans forward and plants a kiss on my forehead. "I'll be back within a week. Love you."

I want to wrap my arms around him and tell him I love him too. I want to kiss him and smell him and make him promise he'll come home to me in one piece. But I don't have a chance to open my mouth before he's bolting across the asphalt toward the waiting plane.

I glance over at Stella, Joel, and Lainey. Joel has Stella wrapped up in his arms, her pregnant belly squashed between the two of them and her face buried in his chest. Lainey's wrapped around his tree trunk of a leg, clutching his fatigues with her tiny fingers.

Watching the scene feels too … intimate. I peel my eyes away and turn toward the car, pausing when I spot Zak standing at the back of the plane. There's at least a hundred feet between us, but I can feel the heat of his gaze as if he were pressed right against me. Shaking it off, I bolt for Cam's car and hide behind the safety of the tinted windows and blast the air-conditioning. No doubt I'll be leaving a sweat stain in the shape of my ass on the driver's seat of Cameron's precious little BMW.

I know he specifically instructed me to take his car back to my place and park it, but I have one quick stop to make before I put his baby to bed for the next week.

Pulling into my grandmother's driveway, there's a hint of nostalgia that wafts around me, wrapping me up in its warm, buttery-soft embrace. Nan's house has always been my favorite place on earth. There isn't a corner of the world that compares to the comfort of her home.

"Hello, deary," Nan greets me at the front door like she always does. I swear she sits in her chair all day long and stares out the front window of the house, waiting patiently for me to pull up. Her house has turned into a fish bowl. Unless it's with me and absolutely necessary, she doesn't leave the property. It took me nearly a year to convince her to sell the house in Michigan and move across the country to California so I could be near Stella, who's practically a lifeline for me at this point, so I know this will likely be the last house she ever lives in. It breaks my heart that she's made it into a prison.

I wrap my arms around my grandmother's meek frame, careful not to squeeze too tight. Although she claims age is nothing more than a number, I know she's losing weight and growing frail.

"Hi, Nan. Smells amazing in here. Whatcha making?"

She roams into the kitchen and I follow closely behind, watching her fumble with her baking utensils.

"Made you a batch of those pear muffins you love so much." She slips on a pair of mittens and reaches into the oven to pull out a pan of freshly baked muffins.

Sniffing the warm, cinnamon-scented air, I say, "Mm. They look delicious."

She plops the pan on the stovetop and returns her mittens to their respective home in the rickety drawer with all her hand-knitted dishcloths. She turns and forces a weak smile, one that doesn't reach her eyes.

"What's wrong, Nan?"

She clucks, then waddles off to the living room, and I peer at the dial on the front of the stove. This is the second time I've caught her forgetting to shut it off. Sighing, I switch the oven off and go in search of my grandmother. I find her in her chair, staring at the blank television screen. Unease creeps into my chest like the roots of a bad weed, wrapping its long fingers around my heart and squeezing.

"Nan. Is everything alright?"

She reaches over and pats the couch. I take a seat and stare unblinking at her. Her face is shrouded with concern, her lips pursed tight, her brows furrowed.

She takes a deep breath, then tells me, "I'm worried about you, dear."

"You don't need—"

She shuts me up with a hand in the air. "I wasn't finished."

I slump back into the couch, wishing it would open up and swallow me whole.

"I married your grandfather because I couldn't bear the thought of living without him."

"Nan, I know—"

"Shh. Still not finished, deary. The way that man used to look at me ..." She clutches a rose quartz stone to her chest and swipes away a tear before it falls. "I was his entire world. All it took was a simple glance in my direction and I was knocked swiftly on my arse." I stifle a giggle because Nan never curses. No clue who I inherited my potty mouth from. "I married your grandfather because there wasn't a doubt in my mind that he was designed specifically for me. We fit together like two puzzle pieces. Now, don't get me wrong, we had our fair share of tiffs." She pauses, her eyes flashing with a memory. "But they never mattered. He was my everything, deary. And I only hope that you someday marry a man who makes you feel as safe and as loved as your grandfather made me feel." She lifts the stone to her mouth and kisses it, then brings it back to her chest.

Swallowing the lump in my throat, I force a smile and say, "You have nothing to worry about, Nan. I'm the happiest I've ever been."

Tick. Tick. Tick.

Six

Zak

"W E'VE GOT INTEL ON Ortiz's whereabouts," Mac tells the team, pausing briefly when the plane hits turbulence. Ortiz—the name Diego Perez gave us before I sent him to meet his maker. "He's hiding out in a bunker in the middle of the jungle we're dropping into. Surrounded by a shitload of guerrillas strapped with AKs. Guess he caught wind that we managed to snatch Perez and is taking some precautions."

I glance at Joel and Liam. Both of them are standing stalk still, their muscles tense and gears turning in their heads. Liam's eyes dart to mine then back to boss man.

"Now …" Mac puffs his chest out and adjusts his posture, steeling himself for breaking news I have a sneaking suspicion we're not going to be impressed with. "I have a contact within the Federov Bratva. It appears we have something in common." *The fucking*

Russians? "The Colombians have been invading their turf and causing problems. He wants the cartel dismantled just as much as we do. Figured we could use this to build an alliance of convenience."

"The Russians are trading in skin?" Joel asks from across the plane.

"Negative. The Federov Bratva is under new leadership and they've decided to forego human trafficking and focus on other *endeavors.*"

"Drugs," I deadpan. Mac nods once. "And you think it's wise to get in bed with them." It's more of a statement than a question.

"Yes and no. But we need their assistance. Ortiz is ours. We'll do this job alone. But by the looks of things, we're going to need some assistance the higher up the cartel chain we move. Their military reach is extensive, and we don't have the resources to do it alone. And the US government has decided to step back from this one for fear of starting a war. So we're on our own if we still intend on bringing the cartel down. Consider it a voluntary contribution to our country."

Jesus fuck. I shove a hand through my hair and blow out a breath. This is dangerous shit we're playing in, but if this is the only option we have to finish what we started, then that settles it.

"You all know the drill. We have four hours until we drop in. Everyone rest up and get some food into you. No telling how long we'll be there, but we'll have limited supplies, so get it while you can."

I obey like a good little soldier, catching a couple hours of rack time and stuffing myself full of food and water. Our bodies are conditioned for this kind of shit—deprivation. We're used to it. But that doesn't mean we don't miss a good meal, clean water, and a warm, wet pussy when we're out on a mission.

Some time later, we parachute into a thick jungle. The stifling humidity sits like lead in my lungs as we move boots through the overgrown vegetation and wade through waist-deep swamp water. Something large swims past my legs. I pause and wait until the ripples on the surface of the water dissipate. Then I continue on, keeping Davis and Stone at my three and nine. Somewhere behind us is Mac and Brooks, and Sloane's located a few clicks out, running surveillance.

We continue on like this until darkness creeps in and we're forced to post up for the night. We find an undisturbed spot in the thickest part of the jungle, hook our hammocks, and take shifts on watch. Just before daylight strikes, we pack up and move on.

By the third day, the jungle has slid comfortably to the top of the list of places I fucking despise.

When we finally approach what looks to be an old bunker, we call in a helo on standby in case we need to make a quick exit.

Liam comes through my comm. "Tango at ten o'clock." His silenced rifle makes a subtle whizzing sound and the guerrilla hits the ground.

Signaling for everyone to spread out, Joel disappears off to my left, Liam to my right, and I drop to a knee with my weapon aimed. Peering through my scope, I spot another tango.

"One o'clock." I shoot. "Tango down."

Approaching the concrete block building that looks like it was dropped here from another world, we move boots and surround the perimeter, quietly taking down tangos one at a time. Sloane's in our ears, utilizing a drone to cover what we can't see. She tells us the place is swarming with guards, reminding us to move slow and steady and to not raise any alarms.

I spot Liam off in the distance with Linda, his favorite sniper rifle, all set up and ready to watch our six as we move in. Mac signals for the rest of us to push forward.

Adrenaline moves through my veins like a dangerous riptide as my fingers tingle in anticipation of what's to come. Ideally, we'd like to bring Ortiz in alive, but that doesn't mean I wouldn't rather pop a cap in his skull and get the fuck out of here.

"Infrared shows a tango in a south room on the top floor. My guess is it's Ortiz," Sloane informs us. Checking my compass, I move toward the south side of the building. "Two guards stationed outside the nearest entry point."

"I'm on them," I bite out.

"I'm behind you," Brooks comes in. I feel him at my back, but I can't see him. Moving toward the south entrance, I pop the two guards off and slip inside the building, dragging the bodies against a wall and out of view from other guards. Brooks filters in behind me, and we make our way up the stairs to the top floor.

It was only a matter of time before someone realized we're here. Today, it took less than three minutes between the time Brooks and

I entered the building to the time gunfire erupts outside and the others engage.

Keeping one ear open for any signs of life around me, I listen carefully to Sloane's instructions in my other as she guides us down the hall and to the door Ortiz is cowering behind.

Brooks and I bust into the room just in time to catch Ortiz attempting to squeeze his gut out of a tiny window. I grab him by the scruff of the neck, thump him in the head with the butt of my rifle, and drag him out the door with Brooks following closely behind.

Just as we round a corner, Sloane warns, "Two ahead."

Brooks slides in front of me and squeezes the trigger twice, and I hear the dull thud of bodies hitting the floor. Nodding once to him, we make our way out a different door than we came in.

It isn't until we exit the building that I realize we're surrounded. Dropping Ortiz's limp body to the ground, I take aim and start firing. Brooks takes off around the side of the building to clear an exit, the whiz of his rifle hissing in the nearby background.

Liam comes in. "Get out of there, Shephard." Several guerrillas drop dead about seventy feet from me, and I know Liam's covering me until I can make a clean getaway.

But when I reach down for Ortiz, he's gone. "Fuck." I bolt the same direction Brooks went and keep my eyes peeled for the dirtbag who somehow managed to slip away from me.

I spot him off in the distance, his filthy, white shirt sticking out like a sore thumb against the green and brown of the muddy hill he's climbing on all fours. Steadying my rifle, I peer through the scope and peg Ortiz in the shoulder—the same spot one of his lackeys nailed me last time we were here. *That's karma, baby.*

But Ortiz manages to push on and disappears out of sight into the thick of the jungle.

Fucking idiot. He'll be lucky if he survives a day out here alone. Judging by his round belly and three chins, something will be eating well tonight if I don't hunt him down first.

Ignoring Mac's orders to not go after him, I take off up the hill and follow the path of stomped-down ferns.

Where'd you go fucker?

I catch movement out of the corner of my eye and swing my rifle, finding myself staring into the yellow eyes of a snake dangling too close for comfort in a nearby tree. I'm not sure if it's deadly, and I don't care to find out. So I blow its head off, its long, thick body falling limp in front of me.

Mac's in my ear again, but this time he's trying to reach Brooks. Radio silence is his only response.

"Find him," Mac snarls.

Slowing my breathing, I drop to one knee in hopes that my silence will lure Ortiz out of hiding. I spot movement to the right and watch as Ortiz hobbles from one shrub to the next, a large patch of red soaking through his white shirt. But then Brooks slides out of nowhere and taps Ortiz on the back of the skull with the barrel of his gun. Ortiz stumbles to his hands and knees, pleading something in Spanish that I can't quite make out from where I'm sitting.

Brooks keeps his gun aimed as Ortiz lifts his palms in the air, and they appear to have some sort of heated discussion. But I still can't hear a fucking word of it because Brooks has shut his goddamn comm off. A major violation of how this team operates.

I watch and listen for another moment until Brooks's voice finally comes in. "I've got Ortiz. Bringing him down now."

I lift my rifle and shoot. Brooks startles, swinging his gun at me, then lowers it. Glancing over his shoulder, he spots the guerrilla I took out before he had a chance to sneak up and slit his throat.

Nodding a thanks, Brooks grabs Ortiz by the scruff and shoves him forward. We trudge back down the slippery hill, just as the whir of a chopper comes into earshot. It picks us up less than a mile out and lifts us to safety.

Ripping my helmet and earpiece off, I tower over Brooks and snarl, "What the hell did he say to you?"

Brooks glares up at me from his seat on the bench, his pretty, blond hair soaked with sweat and slightly darker than usual. We're all fucking filthy and in need of a hot shower and three days rest. And Jesus Christ, I need to get fucking laid. I'm coiled tighter than a two-dollar watch.

Shrugging his shoulders, Brooks tells me, "I don't speak Spanish."

I narrow my eyes at him because it sure as hell looked like they were having a conversation back there. Cranking my head toward Ortiz, who's slumped down in a corner of the chopper, his arms and legs bound with ties, I repeat my question in Spanish. His wide eyes dart to Brooks then back to me.

I lunge for Ortiz, wrapping my hands around his fat throat, and I *squeeze,* watching the life slowly fade from his black eyes. Opening and closing his mouth like a fish out of water, Ortiz garbles out a slew of words. Lessening my grip, I allow him enough oxygen to speak.

"He told me to stay calm and that it would be less painful that way."

The sound of Santiago Ortiz's skull cracking sends a sickening thrill through me. This bastard's been running free for too long. And now, I'm sitting back and watching as Liam does what he does best.

We managed to get two more names out of him—Antonio Sanchez and Manuel Garcia—but I know he's packing much more valuable information than he's letting on.

"Ah fuck. He shit himself," Liam snarls, pressing his forearm to his nose.

Laughter rumbles from my chest. Even Liam, the man who takes great pleasure in torturing fucks like Ortiz, has some limits. Human feces is apparently one of them.

Sighing, I stand and stalk toward Santiago. "We want a list of locations. Every place you useless flaps of meat hold your victims captive. Once we have that, maybe we'll be able to come to a more ...*pleasant* ... agreement."

"I can't give that to you because *I don't know.*"

"Ah, come on. Surely you don't expect me to believe that, do you?" I glance over at Liam rustling through a black duffel bag. Nodding in Liam's direction, I drop my tone so only Ortiz can hear me. "See that scary fucker right there? He's unhinged. Completely lost the plot. If I were you, I'd take my chances and start spilling the beans."

Santiago's eyes blow comically wide and a string of bloody drool dangles from his busted bottom lip. Fuck, he's an ugly bastard. The sound of a power drill whirring interrupts Santiago's panting, and I turn to face Liam.

"Are those screws?" I ask, eyeing the studded clusterfuck attached to the end of the drill and swallowing the vomit rising in my throat.

A sadistic smile spreads across Liam's face as his eyes light with a bone-chilling, psychotic look. The answer is *yes*, they're screws. A shit ton of them.

"Jesus, Davis." I shake my head in disapproval. "Put that fucking thing away."

Liam grumbles something under his breath, then returns the drill to the bag, replacing it with a dull scalpel instead. "Better?" he asks, glaring at me like he just walked in on me in bed with his mother.

"Much." I flash him a sardonic smile. "Well, Santiago," I chirp, slapping the poor fucker on the back. "It's been a real slice. I'll catch you on the other side."

Then I turn and leave the room, booking it down the hall and out of earshot of Santiago's garbled screams.

I find myself staring at the flickering neon sign hanging crooked in the window of my favorite bar downtown. Traitor's. It's the kind of place lonely hitchhikers go to drown their sorrows in cheap whiskey and stale beer. Where hookers frequent in anticipation of scamming some miserable, married family man who'd rather sit at a seedy pub than be home with his wife and kids.

It's the same bar my old man dragged me to for my first legal beer when I turned of age. My dad's never been a fan of my life choices, but booze and football are two things we have in common, and we cling to that since we really have nothing else to talk about.

Dropping into a stool at the bar, I order a beer and stare at the mirrored wall behind the line of bottles. The bartender slides a brown bottle in front of me and I take a long pull. But the crisp bubbles do nothing to fill the hollow void in my gut. I can't get the image of Brooks and Ortiz out of my head. I must be losing my damn mind, because I've also conjured up an image of Brooks between Harper's legs, fucking her hard and rough, the way I imagine she likes it.

A flash of blonde catches my eye in the bar mirror, and I'm slammed back into reality. Groaning, I spin in my seat, locking eyes with the last person on earth I'd ever expect to see here.

What the hell is a hoity-toity princess like Harper doing in a shithole like this?

I take a moment to drink her in. Long, lean, and tanned, all neatly packaged up in a tight black dress that she has no business wearing in a den of pussy-deprived convicts. She's asking for trouble.

Not my problem.

I peel my eyes off her and spin back around. But avoiding her proves difficult when she appears beside me, her soft, floral scent infecting my system like a steady drip of poison.

"What do you want?" I snarl, not bothering to look over at her.

She slides into the seat beside me, her dress inching up her thighs. I peer down and steal a glance at her bare knee brushing against my jeans. She avoids my question, orders a gin martini—extra dirty, extra olives—then folds her hands neatly on the bar top in front of her.

"Going to answer my question, kitten? Or just sit there and piss me off?"

Straightening her spine so the fleshy swell of her tits heaves over the low neckline of her dress, she takes a slow, deep breath in, then exhales shakily. It's as if her entire body is rejecting the words she's about to say. "I wanted to thank you for making sure Cameron made it home safe."

I all but scoff. "He's a grown-ass man, Harper. He can take care of himself."

"I know that." Her eyes bore into the side of my face. "But he told me you saved him."

I finish off my beer and stare at her in the mirror. She's like Medusa. Look directly at her and your dick will turn to stone.

"If you're so grateful to have him home, why aren't you with him right now?"

She glances over her shoulder and sucks her bottom lip between her pretty, white teeth. I take the opportunity to glance in her direction. If she weren't irritating as all hell, I'd be inclined to say she's the most beautiful woman to walk the earth. But her beauty is nothing more than a distraction. A tool in her arsenal kit of manipulation and man-eating tactics.

"He's having dinner with his parents," she murmurs, a sadness sweeping across her face.

"And you're not there, why?"

"Because I had to run Nan to an appointment."

"I see," I deadpan, dipping my gaze to her cleavage. "Not sure if you're brave or stupid wearing a skimpy dress to a bar filled with truckers, hitchhikers, and felons."

"And mercenaries," she adds with a smirk.

Is she flirting with me?

The bartender slides a glass in front of Harper, and she flashes him a charming smile and thanks him. When she takes a sip, I have to force myself to look away from her pretty, pink mouth.

"So, why are you here, Zak?"

I hate how she says my name, all breathy and soft and fucking sweet. "Drowning my sorrows like the rest of them."

"No hot date tonight?"

"Look around. Does this seem like the kind of place I'd bring a date?"

"I mean, you don't peg me as the romantic type to wine and dine a woman before ..." She flips her hair over her shoulder, exposing soft, supple skin. "You know."

I turn in my chair, my thighs caging hers in. She pinches her knees together when our legs brush, obviously uncomfortable with our close proximity. The contact sends a sharp crackle through my body, like static electricity. Placing one hand on the back of her stool and the other on the bar top, I lean into her. I should get up and walk away, but her scent is an anchor weighing me down.

"I'm a gentleman, Harper. Any woman I fuck is treated like a queen before I take her to bed."

Her blue eyes flare wildly, as if what I said affects her on some deeper level. But I know it has nothing to do with my statement and everything to do with my vulgarity. She insists I'm an asshole, yet she's shocked when I behave like one.

"But I'm sure your boyfriend does that for you, doesn't he?" There's a bitterness to my tone, and I have no idea where it came from.

"Fuck you, Zak," she sneers, then goes to stand, awkwardly attempting to escape the cage of my thighs and arms.

"Why are you here, Harper?" I ask, stopping her in her tracks.

The pulse in her throat picks up speed, and I find myself wondering what it would feel like under my tongue.

She crosses her arms and scowls at me. "Saw your vehicle in the parking lot on my way home and thought I'd stop in to thank you in person. But clearly, that was a mistake."

Narrowing my gaze and pinching her chin between my fingers, I force her eyes to mine. "You seem to make a lot of mistakes for such a smart girl."

Her eyes round at the edges and she gnaws on her lip. But then she slips her snarky mask of confidence back on and swats my hand away from her face. "Touch me again and I'll remove your balls from your body."

My lip twitches in amusement and I release her chin and stand, dropping a wad of cash on the bar to cover both of our tabs.

"Be careful, kitten. I don't take too kindly to threats." Leaning in so my lips brush the shell of her ear, I add, "I'd hate to see you bite off more than you can chew. Although I'd enjoy watching you choke."

Seven

Harper

"Y OU READY, BABY?" CAMERON calls down the hall.

"Five minutes," I holler back, inspecting myself in the mirror above my bathroom sink.

Today's the day I meet his family, and I'm a nervous fucking train wreck. My hands are clammy, my legs feel like overcooked spaghetti noodles, and I've had to pee at least a million times in the last hour. I know I'll have no issues winning Cam's father over, because he's a man and men are easy. All I have to do is bat my eyelashes and laugh at his jokes, and he'll be wrapped around my pretty little finger in no time. It's his mother I'm concerned about. Mrs. Brooks is a well-known cardiologist and famous in this dumpy little town. Despite Cameron's incessant reassurance that his parents will love me, I'm not entirely convinced. Normally I'm a confident person, but there's something about meeting future in-laws that has parts of my body sweating that I didn't realize possible.

Adjusting my hair for the final time and smoothing my hands over my flowy, pink dress that reaches all the way down to my knees—much longer than I'm used to—I take a deep, cleansing breath and remind myself who I am.

You've got this, girl.

When I go in search of Cameron, I find him dressed in a pair of pale gray slacks and a crisp, white dress shirt with the top button popped open.

"Hi, beautiful," he greets me with a pop of his dimples and a chaste kiss on the cheek. "You look great."

"Thank you. You clean up alright yourself, champ."

Cam escorts me out to his car, opening and closing the door for me. The drive to his parents is filled with small talk about his family and what I should expect. He gives me the lowdown on his brother, Daniel, who according to Cameron will likely put the moves on me tonight.

Yay for me. Not only will I have to behave like a lady, but I'll have to beat his brother off with a stick while simultaneously not ruining my hair or breaking a nail in the process.

We pull up to a large, iron gate, the hinges creaking as the doors part way. My nose remains firmly pressed against the car window as I take in the grandiose estate. I knew his family was wealthy, but Jesus. Cam parks the car at the front of the house, which is approximately the same size as my entire apartment complex, and helps me out of the vehicle and up to the front door.

And now my ass is sweating.

We're greeted by Cameron's mother, a classy woman in her sixties with the most beautiful shade of silver hair pulled back into a tight chignon. Her pale blue pantsuit is perfectly creased and fitted to her thin frame. Her twinkling gray eyes rival the clear diamonds adorning her ears and wrists. She's incredibly poised and put together, and it does nothing to calm my frazzled nerves.

"Cameron," she coos, pulling her son in for a hug.

"Hi, Mom," he responds sweetly, pulling away from her and returning to my side. He nudges me forward, and I have to refrain from turning and glaring at him. "This is Harper. Harper, this is my mother, Carmella."

"Harper. So beautiful. It's lovely to meet you." She snatches my hand and yanks me forward into an awkward embrace, patting my back like she's burping a baby.

"You too, Mrs. Brooks," I squeak out.

"Oh, please. Call me Carmella."

Cam smiles approvingly as Carmella ushers us inside, offering me a glass of wine in which I immediately accept. My nerves are rattled and I'm about two degrees from becoming a human volcano and spewing gibberish. So the alcohol is appreciated.

I meet Mr. Brooks shortly after. It turns out he's a total hard-ass and completely squashes my theory about men being simpletons. And then I meet Daniel, Cameron's younger brother, who oddly enough looks nothing like the rest of the family.

I make it through dinner unscathed, despite Daniel's passive aggressive comments that I should find myself "a real man" and his subtle attempts at touching my leg beneath the dinner table while his older brother sits next to me.

We pull up to my building and Cam helps me out of the car. We walk arm in arm to my apartment and lock ourselves inside. "So your brother is a fun guy," I quip, my sarcasm thick as molasses on a cold winter day. I kick my shoes off at the door and saunter over to Cameron, who's already in the kitchen typing away on his phone. "Everything alright?"

Stormy eyes meet mine, and I can feel the irritation rolling off him in waves.

"Everything's fine," he says plainly, locking his phone and setting it screen down on the counter.

Long strides bring him in front of me, and he snakes an arm around my waist, dragging me into him.

He smirks down at me, dragging the tip of his nose up and down the bridge of mine. "You want to talk about my brother some more? Or are you going to shut up and let me make love to you?"

Make love. It sounds so ... civilized. Boring even. But that doesn't stop the wet heat from instantly pooling in my panties.

Slinging my arms around Cameron's neck, I bring my mouth to his and gently nip at his bottom lip. "I've been meaning to tell you something."

Cam pulls his face back and peers down at me through hooded eyes, the warmth of his body melting my resolve.

"I love you too," I whisper, but the second the words roll off my tongue, an image flashes behind my eyes and I blink it away, sudden shock reverberating through me.

Thankfully, Cam doesn't seem to notice. "Mmm," he hums against my lips, his tongue delving into my mouth and tangling with mine.

He pushes the kiss deeper until I'm panting and his hands are roaming up my dress and squeezing my ass. He lifts me into his arms and carries me to the bedroom, dropping me on the bed. I bounce up onto my knees, the roof of my mouth suddenly desert dry and a bitter taste lingering on the back of my tongue.

"Cam. Wait," I rush out, panic creeping into my chest like a bad weed.

But Cameron ignores my hesitation and begins undressing in record speed, ripping his belt off and kicking out of his slacks.

"Cam," I repeat louder. And off come the socks. Fuck. "Cameron!" I finally screech, my breathing erratic and blood crashing through my head like dangerous, white water.

Cam pauses and stares at me unblinking, his head angled and brows pinched tight in confusion. "What's wrong, baby?" he asks, concern softening his edges, his erection pressing against his briefs and begging to be freed.

Jesus, Mary, and Joseph.

"I ..." I swallow around the boulder in my throat. "I'm totally exhausted and ... can we just postpone this for another night? Pretty please?"

Cam's jaw slides in the dim lighting of the bedroom, his gray eyes darkening just a fraction. But then he blows out a bated breath and nods. "Sure, Harper. Another night. You sure that's all that's wrong, though? You look ... distressed."

"Yes," I breathe out, my shoulders relaxing a hair. "Just had one too many glasses of wine at dinner, I think."

Liar, liar, pants on fire.

Guilt slithers into my veins, embedding itself so deep in my soul that I don't think I'll ever rid myself of the feeling.

The second I lay my head down and Cameron's arms and legs coil around me, holding me close, another image flashes behind my eyelids. This one of coffee-colored eyes, dark facial hair, and a Colgate smile that could melt an Arctic glacier.

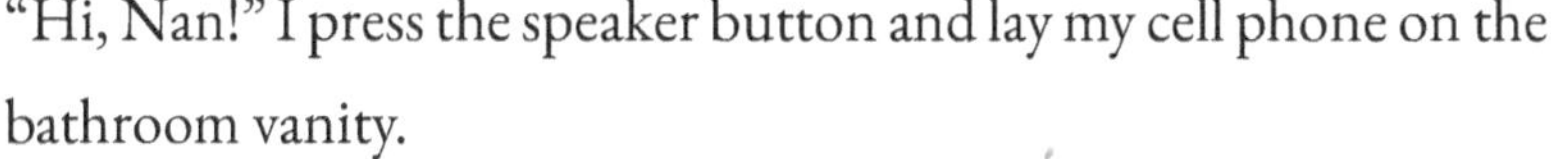

"Hi, Nan!" I press the speaker button and lay my cell phone on the bathroom vanity.

"Hello, deary. How are you?" My grandmother's soft, sweet voice filters into the room, wrapping around me like a warm, fuzzy blanket. My mood brightens instantly.

"I'm good," I chirp, rummaging around in my cosmetic bag for my mascara. "Just doing my makeup right now. Cam's taking me out tonight."

Nan's silence stretches on before she sighs and responds gently, "That's lovely, Harper."

"How are you doing, though? Anything exciting going on over there?"

"I have a new neighbor," she tells me. "A handsome, young man who has offered to help me weed my gardens."

I pause mid-mascara, a grin stretching across my face. "And by *weed your gardens* you mean …"

A clucking sound pops through the phone. "He's young enough to be my grandson, Harper."

"Uh huh."

She tsks, then begins chuckling. Her happiness has always felt like sunshine to me. But I'm worried she's lonely living by herself. She insists she's fine, but I'd feel much better if she would accept my offer to move her into a retirement community where she can still be independent but help will be nearby at all times. I promised we'd find one close enough to my apartment that I can still visit at least a couple times a week. But naturally, like all Hilton women, she's as stubborn as an old mule and refuses.

"How are things going with Cameron, dear?"

Slicking on a layer of ruby lipstick, I tell her, "Things are great. It's only been five months but I think he might be the one."

Another long silence stretches on, and with each passing second, the rope around my heart cinches tighter.

"That's wonderful, dear. Which reminds me. I—"

A soft knock on the bathroom door cuts my grandmother off. "Hey, Nan. I have to get going. But I'll call you later and we'll chat, okay?"

We say our goodbyes and I swallow the rock in my throat that forms every time I have to let her go, then open the door to find Cam dressed smartly in a navy-blue suit and white dress shirt. His shoes are as polished as the rest of him, and his short, blond hair is slicked back with not a single strand out of place.

"Wow. You look hot," I chirp, drinking him in like the fine specimen that he is.

His eyes dart down the length of my body and his expression sours disapprovingly. "How come you're not dressed yet?"

I peek down at my shorts and tee. Lifting my lids, I smirk up at him with a mischievous quirk of my brow.

"You don't like it? I was going to pair it with my favorite Crocs and a burlap bag."

Cam steps back and frowns. "Get dressed, Harper. We're going to be late."

"Okay, cranky pants," I mutter as he walks away.

The moment we pull up to the art exhibit, something feels ... off. My nan always told me I had the *Hilton Sense*. That I just hadn't tapped into it yet. I don't necessarily believe in her proclaimed abilities. But I don't *not* believe in them, either. It's like refusing to believe in monsters. We insist they're fictional, but when something goes bump in the night, we're freaking the fuck out and hiding beneath the covers.

Excusing myself from Cam's side, I slip into the restroom and use the toilet, then wash my hands, running my wrists beneath cold water in an attempt to lower my core temperature. But my heart is still jackhammering against my ribs, refusing to submit, and I'm about ready to reach inside my chest and bitch-slap her. And then there's the chest pain ... Fuck. Is this what a panic attack feels like?

Inhaling a lungful of oxygen, I straighten my spine, smooth my dress down my body, and make my way back to Cameron. I slide in beside him and he hands me a fresh glass of champagne. I sink it in one shot, my eyes tearing up as the bubbles sting my nostrils.

Leaning in, Cam whispers, "What took you so long?"

I'm quick on my feet and lying has always come naturally to me, so I tell him without hesitation, "I bumped into a girl I went to school with. She's still as chatty as I remember." Flashing him a big, fake, cheesy smile, I pray to the baby Jesus that Cameron buys my little fib.

He does, nodding and returning his attention to the painting that looks like a giant, hairy nipple. I suppose the saying is true: *art is subjective.*

My purse begins vibrating and I mutter out a quick apology before I pull my phone from my bag and stare at the blinking screen.

High Park Hospital.

"Excuse me for a moment," I say quietly, then scurry away from Cam's side and book it to the front doors of the museum. Before I even step foot out of the air-conditioning and into the sweltering California heat, I answer the call.

"May I speak with Harper Hilton, please?"

I rush out, "This is she. What's going on?"

"Miss Hilton, this is Francesca from High Park Hospital. I'm calling about your grandmother, Phyllis Hilton."

Eight

Harper

I'M NOT A RELIGIOUS woman. I don't believe there's some big, beautiful extraterrestrial being with a grand plan hanging out somewhere above the clouds and watching us mortal humans struggle through life. I don't believe in heaven or hell or angels.

But in the off chance God does exist, I decide to pray like hell the entire five minutes it takes me to drive Cameron's car from the museum to High Park Hospital. I skid to a stop outside the emergency entrance, parking haphazardly at the curb and darting through the hospital doors. The stench of sterilizer and death are the first thing I smell, and it only amplifies my body's desire to empty itself every time I breathe.

Slamming my palms on the nurse's station, I spit my grandmother's name out at the woman on the other side. The nurse leads me down a long, dingy corridor. We pass through the radiology department, a small waiting room with old, worn-out plastic chairs, and cross into a tiny room with faded pink walls.

And there lays my unconscious grandmother, tubes running from her nose and arms and connecting to a thousand beeping machines. Hot tears track down my cheeks as my heart shatters into a million jagged pieces.

Francesca, the nurse who called me, speaks softly. "She needs to rest. But you can stay with her as long as you'd like. A doctor will be in shortly to brief you."

She disappears, the door clicking shut behind her as I take a few unsteady steps toward my grandmother. Her complexion is paler than usual, every muscle in her face slack. If it weren't for all the wires and hoses, she'd look like she's resting peacefully. I reach for her hand and lace my fingers with her frail, bony ones. She's lost too much weight over the last few months, slowly wasting away before my eyes.

"Oh, Nan. I'm so sorry. I should have been there with you."

Her eyelids twitch, and I wonder if she can hear me. But she doesn't wake up. She just lays there, still and silent. I sweep her white hair off her forehead and kiss her soft cheek, my tears plopping onto her pale blue hospital gown and absorbing into the thin, starchy fabric.

My phone buzzes. And buzzes. And buzzes.

Finally, I take the call.

"Where the fuck are you?" Cam snaps out.

"I'm—"

"No, Harper. You took off without telling me where you went. What the hell is wrong with you? I had to make an ass out of myself by asking museum security to pull up the feed so I could find you. And what do I see? You taking off out the front doors and stealing my fucking car."

"Cam, please just—"

"Shut up and listen to me. I swear to fucking god, Harper—"

"My grandmother had a heart attack," I blurt out, my voice cracking from emotion. "That's what the call was—the hospital. That's where I am right now."

Heavy, angry breathing is all I hear before the line goes dead. I blow out a shaky breath and stare down at my nan. I'll deal with Cam later. For now, my grandmother is all that matters.

There's a soft knock on the door a moment later. I glance over my shoulder at a middle-aged man in a white lab coat, a stethoscope slung around his long, weathered neck. His eyes are a similar gray as Cameron's, but softer in color and rimmed by dark bags like he hasn't slept in years.

"Miss Hilton?" He extends a hand.

I accept it numbly and choke out, "Is she going to be okay?"

The doctor's thin lips pinch tight. "We're not entirely sure of the extent of the damage to her heart tissue yet, but we're hopeful. It's really up to your grandmother, I'm afraid." The doctor drags a chair from the corner and places it beside my grandmother. "Have a seat, Miss Hilton. We're going to run a few more tests, and as soon as we have results, you'll be the first to know."

He leaves without another word and I collapse into the chair and grip Nan's hand like it's my lifeline. Dropping my forehead to our clasped fingers, I sob until I fall asleep, waking to the sound of footsteps approaching.

"I brought you something to eat," a wispy female voice says.

I whip my head to the side and peer up at a face I haven't seen since Joel and Stella's wedding two years ago. Long, fiery-red locks. Pretty, sage-green eyes. And a killer body that makes me look like a drowned rat.

Amelia. My friend that Zak slept with and never called. The one who blamed me for her heartbreak, although I have no fucking clue why. I had warned her to stay away from him, but she was thinking with her vagina and not her head.

She sets a tray of food down on the table beside the bed.

"Didn't realize you worked here," I murmur.

Amelia's lips lift into a small, gentle smile. "Finally graduated nursing school." She takes a few cautious steps toward me, her fingers knotted in a ball in front of her. "Look, Harper. I want to apologize for how things went between us." Her head moves side to side. "It ... it wasn't your fault. Zak. He—"

Another knock on the door interrupts her apology, and Francesca reappears. "Amelia ... you're needed in Mr. Robertson's room."

Amelia nods to the nurse, then returns her attention to me. "If you need anything at all, Harper, please don't hesitate. Your grandmother is a sweet woman. I hope she makes a full recovery."

Amelia's sneakers make an annoying squelching noise on the tile floor, the sound of her footsteps fading as she disappears down the hall. When a male nurse comes in and quietly sets a cot up in the corner of the room, I curl up on the lumpy slab of foam and listen obsessively to the steady beep of Nan's machines. A few times throughout the night, I hear someone sneak in and fiddle with something, then leave quietly.

I spend the entire night staring up at the tile ceiling, it's dull, yellowish hue not so different from the lackluster emotions that have swallowed me whole. Cameron was pissed when he called. I can't say I blame him. I should have run back into the museum and told him what was happening. He would have driven me to the hospital and stayed by my side, being the sweet, supportive boyfriend he is. Or at the very least, I should have called him after I left the exhibit. But I wasn't thinking straight, the horrifying thoughts of my nan laying alone in a hospital bed blurring my better sense of judgement.

Sighing, I roll onto my side and stare at my nan's profile, her features softly illuminated by the tiny bedside lamp, remembering all the times she talked about my grandpop. How passionate they were about each other. The unmeasurable amount of love and devotion they poured into each other.

Sorry, Grandpoppy. I'm not ready to let her go yet.

The next morning, the sun is shining, the birds are chirping, and the sky is the perfect shade of blue with fluffy, white, picturesque clouds dotting the horizon.

And my nan is still sound asleep.

"It's not a bad thing, dear," the doctor tells me, and I have to choke back a fresh sob from his use of my nan's nickname for me.

Dear. Deary. Sweet little dear.

"It may take another day or two before she's alert. But for now, we have some test results to discuss."

I listen carefully as the doctor spews a bunch of medical jargon at me like I have even a teensy-weensy idea what any of it means.

"Basically, she's going to be alright for the time being. But her chances of another heart attack are significant. However," he adds, a swell of hope rising in my chest, "with a change of diet, some light exercise, and the right combination of medication, we can reduce that risk significantly."

I thank the doctor, take a quick bird bath in the adjoining bathroom off my nan's room, then swiftly return to her side. I call Stella to fill her in on what happened and assure her I'm fine and that Nan will be as well, but she insists on putting Joel on daddy duty and racing over to the hospital immediately.

She's followed closely by Liam, whose doom and gloom presence is oddly reassuring, then Zak, who hovers quietly around the door, stealing the odd empathetic glance at my nan.

"Oh, sweetie," Stella coos, rushing to my side and pulling me in for a hug, smashing my face into her giant boobs and stroking my back as I suck back the tears that threaten to fall.

"I'm okay," I tell her, peeling my sweaty cheek off her chest and taking a step back, swiping away the smudged mascara beneath my eyes. I must resemble a feral raccoon because when I glance over at Zak again, his jaw is set tight and brows furrowed low as he glares at my puffy eyes and ruddy cheeks like he's contemplating putting me out of my misery.

Nine

Zak

THERE ARE A THOUSAND pros of residing in a small town. But there's one very large con that outweighs all of them. You can't fucking go anywhere without bumping into someone you hope to never see again.

"You," the redheaded nurse seethes, pointing a long, scarlet fingernail at me.

Fuck my life.

I swipe a hand through my hair and glance around the room. There are four sets of eyes nailing me to the wall right now, but the only ones I see—the only ones I *feel*—are Harper's. Because those bright blue orbs of hers are searing a gaping hole right through my face.

Returning my attention to Amelia, I say, "Let's chat, shall we?" I gently wrap my hand around her bicep and lead her out into the hall, ensuring the door clicks shut behind us.

She folds her arms across her chest and scowls up at me, her face the same shade of red as her hair and her entire body vibrating in anger. I'm also certain she's thought of at least forty creative ways to unalive me.

Blowing out a ragged breath, I prop my hands on my hips and stare down at her, bracing myself for impact. "Alright, Amelia. Let's hear it."

"So *now* you remember my name?" she snips out, her statement thick with accusation. When I don't respond, she continues on, her pitch lowering a fraction. "You never called and I want to know why."

I quirk a brow at her. "You would have wanted me to after what happened?"

Her expression sobers and a sharp breath exits through her nostrils. "Well ... no. But still ... your little slipup was—"

"A dick move, I know. But it was an accident. And I'm sorry for that. But it happened and I can't take it back." Her lips turn down into a pout, and I hook her chin with my forefinger. "You're a beautiful woman. And very sweet. But—"

"But I'm not what you want. I get it." She takes a step back and her eyes dart toward Harper's grandmother's room. After how that evening went, I'm incredibly surprised she's even standing here talking to me.

An awkward silence stretches on before I slice through it. "You deserve someone who can give you the world, Amelia. I'm not it."

Sighing, she finally accepts the situation for what it is—a clusterfuck—and saunters off down the hall, her full hips swaying in her skin-tight uniform.

"Jesus bloody Christ," I murmur to myself, dropping my head back and staring at the ceiling.

"Such a gentleman," a familiar female voice says. "Letting her down so easy. It's almost as if you've done this a thousand times."

I groan and drop my gaze to Harper. She's standing outside her grandmother's room, her tired eyes lifted by the smug grin on her face as she folds her arms across her chest and leans against the door jam.

"Speaking of gentleman ... where's your *dreamy* boyfriend? Seems this is something he should be here for."

Harper adjusts her posture, lifting her nose in the air confidently. "I left him at the museum when the hospital called yesterday. He'll be here soon, I'm sure." Closing the space between us, I crowd her against the wall and stare down at her until she finally breaks and admits the truth. I don't typically enjoy making women nervous, but with Harper, I find it ... satisfying. The way she squirms beneath the heat of my gaze. The small bead of sweat that forms on her upper lip. The way her pulse jumps beneath her jaw. "Fine. He's not coming," she squeaks out. "I pissed him off and I think he's punishing me or something."

"Harper Hilton pissed a man off," I retort dryly, dishing the same sarcastic attitude onto Harper's plate as she serves me on the regular. "No way. How could that be possible? You're such a fucking delight to be around."

"Guess we have that in common," she snaps back, a small flame of defiance dancing in her eyes.

I lean in and press a palm to the wall beside her head. The air thickens to mud as the irritatingly pleasant smell of peonies and lilacs assault my senses. My dick twitches in my jeans, and I bite back a groan.

God, this woman is frustrating. Gorgeous as fuck. But frustrating.

As if my body has a mind of its own, I lift my hand, pausing midair in hesitation before allowing myself this one small moment of weakness. My knuckles skim across her smooth forehead as I brush a loose strand of hair off her face, tucking it behind her ear. Her mouth parts slightly, and it takes every ounce of restraint to not sweep my thumb across her plump bottom lip just to see if it's as soft as it looks.

I release a long sigh and sink my hand into my pocket, thumbing my coin to keep from touching more of her. "We have nothing in common, Harper. Polar opposites, actually."

She blinks slowly, small puffs of warm air skittering across my throat as she struggles to get her erratic breathing under control. We're so close, our breaths are mingling as we exchange the air from our lungs. Fuck. I can practically taste how delectable her mouth must be. How sweet and salty and addictive she is.

Her eyes flutter shut briefly, her long lashes fanning across her high cheekbones.

"Harper." A male voice booms down the hall, ripping me free from the filthy thoughts churning in my head.

Brooks. What perfect fucking timing.

I stand to my full height and turn to face him. His stance is wide, his fists are balled, and he looks like he's ready for a fight. Harper bristles past me and runs into his arms.

"Cam! Thank god you're here," she rushes out, curling herself around his waist and burying her face in his shoulder.

His beady eyes never leave mine.

I lean against the wall and shove my hands in my pockets in the least threatening way possible, rolling my coin between my fingers. No need to ruffle any feathers. "Nice to see you, Brooks. What took you so long?"

Peeling Harper off like an old Band-Aid, he storms over to me and gets in my face. "You making a move on my girl?" he asks, his jaw ticking and eyes thinning into slits.

I've got a good four inches on him, and at least forty pounds of lean muscle. But this isn't a dick-measuring contest. And right now, my teammate thinks I'm interested in his woman. It's almost laughable.

Chuckling dryly, I say, "The love of your life's grandmother was just hospitalized, and you're going to pick a petty fight *here*? *Now*?"

His lips curl into a vicious snarl, baring his teeth. The beady-eyed bastard almost looks scary. *Almost*. To the average person, he'd look pretty fucking mean right now. But to me ... he's just a puppy dog. And he's pissing all over his territory.

Harper slides up to Brooks's side and sets a hand on his arm. "Come on, sweetie. Nan could wake up any minute now and I want to be there with her."

Shooting me one final glare, Cam reluctantly disappears into the room with Harper, closing the door behind them.

Victim extraction.

It's what we do best. That, and blowing shit up, of course.

"Looks like an easy job today, boys," Mac says from across the plane. "Less than twenty tangos on site. Not sure how many civilians there are, but we're not leaving without every last one of them."

I glance at Liam, who's fiddling with his switchblade, rolling it between his knuckles as he glowers at the floor. Victim extraction always makes him a little extra antsy, as if pulling civilians out of chaos scratches an itch that nothing else can quite reach.

"We'll take prisoners if we can, but it's not a priority. From what Sloane dug up, the guards here are kept in the dark. They have one job, and one job only: guarding the merchandise."

"Thought we were bringing the Russians in on this," Liam says plainly, staring up at Mac.

"We are. But this extraction should be quick and clean. No need to use up resources when it's not necessary. Now ... are we all on the same page?"

We all nod, then begin strapping up and preparing for the drop in. My eyes slide to Brooks, but he keeps his focus trained on the mission and pays me no mind. I was surprised when he agreed to come along on this mission rather than hanging back with Harper and her grandmother, who's now conscious and raising all sorts of hell for the hospital staff. I imagine between the stubborn, old woman and her irritating granddaughter that Brooks used this mission as an excuse to get some space.

His focus ultimately works to our advantage. Because when he manages to locate a hidden entrance a hundred feet from the underground bunker, we make a clean extraction. And once again, he proves himself an asset to the team.

Fourteen women and children ranging from ages seven to forty-one litter the plane floor, all bundled up in thermal blankets and trembling in fear. They're malnourished, dehydrated, and beaten and bruised, and there's not a doubt in my mind they've been sexually assaulted. This particular cartel have a knack for testing the product before shipping it out to buyers.

But all victims are alive, and as far as we're concerned, that's a fucking win.

They'll land on US soil with us to be properly treated by the team of doctors and nurses on our payroll, identified, and sent home, wherever home is for them, with whatever support they need.

When we get back to headquarters, Brooks takes off to the hospital again and Mac drops into the chair at the head of the war table. "We're meeting with the Russians in four days." Mac slides a file across the table and we take turns flipping through it. "Mikhail Osmanov is the second in command of the Federov Bratva, soon to be head of the organization. He's ruthless, a certified genius, and has more blood on his hands than all of us combined, but I haven't a doubt in my mind he'll be useful."

I glance over at Liam, who's wearing his usual look of constipation. I'd be lying if I said I'm not worried about his mental state. Whatever it is that's haunting him has slowly been eating him alive from the inside out. One of these days, I'm afraid he's going to snap. But I'd prefer if my balls remained firmly attached to my body, so I don't say a word to him about it.

"Will Brooks be joining us for this meeting?" Joel asks.

"Negative. He's staying with Harper until her grandmother is home and settled."

Liam leans forward, propping his elbows on the table and cracking his knuckles in his fist. "Well then. Let's meet this Russian prick and cut ourselves a deal."

Ten

Harper

I T'S BEEN FOUR LONG, sleepless days since I got the call that nearly killed me, but the doctors have finally cleared my grandmother to go home. I tried to wear her down, to convince her to let me stay with her for a while, but she's as stubborn as a ketchup stain and refused. So she'll have to settle on me showing up every day at the ass crack of dawn and not leaving until bedtime.

I slide the cab van door open and help my nan into the back seat. Cam offered to drive us but getting Nan in and out of his BMW would be a task, so I sent him on his way, reassuring him that I've got this and that it's best if I handle this on my own. Nan's as cranky as the day is long right now, and I don't want him in the line of fire.

We pull up to her house and I help her out of the vehicle, pay the driver, then walk her up the stairs and get her settled in. An hour later, I'm sitting at the kitchen table scribbling out a grocery list of all the healthy foods the doctor recommended my nan keep in stock when the doorbell chimes.

"Are you expecting company, Nan?" I holler down the hall toward her bedroom.

"Unless it's the handsome neighbor, tell them to buzz off."

Rolling my eyes, I swing the door open and come face to face with a short, plump woman in her fifties with bright, cheery eyes and rosy cheeks. She's wearing a gray nurse's uniform that does nothing for her fair complexion, and there's a large, black duffel bag sitting at her feet.

"May I help you?"

She smiles sweetly and extends a hand. "My name's Joanie. I'm the nurse."

Confusion and uncertainty swirl in my stomach as I replay my conversations with the doctor. He never mentioned sending a nurse, and even if he had, I can't afford private home care.

Shaking my head, I say, "I'm sorry. There must be some sort of confusion. I didn't hire—"

She swats the air and clucks her tongue. "Those boys don't mess around. We supply only the best of the best, and they pay us handsomely to do so. Now, where's the lovely patient?" Her eyes dart around the house behind me. "I hear she's quite the firecracker."

I hold a palm in the air. "Hang on. What boys?"

"Sweetwater Security, honey. I received a phone call from a very handsome soldier the other day. He advised that a family member needed some assistance and that he'd pay for your grandmother's care for as long as you need it."

Tears spring to my eyes and warmth spreads in my chest as I put two and two together. Cam hired my grandmother a private nurse.

Stepping to the side, I welcome the nurse in and lead her to the bedroom and introduce her to my grandmother, who's less than enthused about the situation. But once I tell her Cameron was the one to hire Joanie, her mouth snaps shut and she doesn't say another word.

The nurse flutters in and out of the house, lugging medical devices in and setting them up with a competency that tells me she's done this a thousand times. When she offers to run errands, I politely decline. It's been four days of bird baths in a smelly hospital bathroom. I reek of sweat and that generic antibacterial hand soap they use in public washrooms, and my hair looks like a family of rats has taken up residence in the back. Cam was considerate enough to bring me a change of clothes, but I'm craving a hot shower and a greasy cheeseburger from the little drive-in joint around the corner. And as much as I love my grandmother, I'm in dire need of a mental break.

I kiss my grandmother on the cheek, promising I'll be back in a few hours, then take a cab back to my apartment, spotting Cam's flashy red BMW parked haphazardly between two reserved parking spots. We all have quirks. Parking like a douchebag is one of Cameron's.

I slip inside my apartment, drop my purse on the console table, and kick off my shoes, my feet aching from wandering the hospital halls for four days. But the second I turn around, I come face to chest with a wall of pissed-off Navy SEAL.

"Jesus," I hiss, backing away from Cameron. "Ever hear of personal space?"

Stormy clouds of accusation close in over his eyes as his lips press into a firm line. "Are you sleeping with him?"

"What?" I shake my head in confusion. "Who?"

Cam takes a step forward, puffing his chest out and balling his fists. His nose grazes mine but I don't recoil or back down.

"Shephard. I saw you two in the hallway at the hospital looking pretty cozy. Are you sleeping with him, Harper?"

I press a hand to Cameron's chest, his heart pounding against my palm as he glowers down at me. Chuckling softly in disbelief, I say, "No, Cam. I'm not fucking Zak Shephard."

Cam's sharp jaw slides in irritation, but as he searches my face, his rage seems to simmer and his gray eyes droop at the edges, regret seeping into his sobering expression.

He blows out a ragged breath and cups my jaw in his hands, dropping his forehead to mine and peering into my eyes. His tone drops an octave. "I'm so sorry, Harper. I just ... I know how he is with women. It's disgusting."

Makes me wonder what Cameron would think of me if he knew all the dirty little details of my track record.

"It's fine. Really. But I would never cheat on you, Cam. You have to believe that."

He peels his clammy forehead from mine and peers down at me in anguish. "Why was he at the hospital?"

"The whole crew showed up, sweetie. Not just him. That's what these guys do. It's kind of one big family. And you're part of it now too," I remind him gently, eager to lift his mood and move on from our spat.

"I don't trust Shephard. Don't want you spending too much time with him."

I snort. "Fine by me." In another attempt at brightening the mood, I tell him, "I appreciate you hiring a nurse. That was very generous of you."

"What nurse?"

"A nurse showed up at Nan's today. She said Sweetwater sent her. I assumed ... She said ..." I shake my head to clear the confusion clouding my brain. "It must have been Joel. Stella must have twisted his arm into hiring her."

"Awfully nice of them," he responds plainly.

I glance at the clock. "Shit. I need to grab Nan's groceries and pick up her prescription at the drugstore before they close. And I told Joanie I'd be back before dinnertime."

A warm hand sweeps a strand of hair off my forehead. "I'll take care of it."

"That's a super sweet offer, Cam. But seriously. If you show up there without me, Nan will probably bite your head clean off."

Cam's mouth tilts into a crooked grin. "Is that what I have to look forward to when we're old and gray?"

That earns him a swift swat across the chest. But I don't respond, because the depressing thought of being old and gray and not young, healthy, and hot is something I'm not yet prepared to process.

Cam and I say our goodbyes and I have a quick shower, washing my hair at lightning speed and slipping into a pair of leggings and a tank top. I take a cab to Spanky's Grill and order the greasiest, nastiest cheeseburger piled high with zesty dill pickles and extra fried onions. I slide back into the cab, dropping the grease-soaked take-out bag on the seat beside me and reaching for my cell phone. I contemplate calling Stella to tell her Cameron thought I was sleeping with Zak Shephard. She'd probably think it's as hilarious as I did.

But as we drive to the pharmacy, my finger hovers over Stella's name. I sit like this for what feels like hours, my mind ping-ponging back and forth.

Call her. Don't call her. Call her.

I don't call her.

Eleven

Zak

THERE'S A STEADY DRIP that echoes throughout the warehouse, slicing through the silence surrounding us. Mac, Joel, Liam, and I stand in line, side by side, dressed in our Sunday best and weighed down with weapons. Sloane, as always, is sitting a click out in a surveillance van, watching the perimeter with a drone.

"If this goes sideways, we bail out. Don't bother trying to take prisoners. This man is a fucking ghost. If he gets his hands on one of you, I'm not sure we'll get you back," Mac warns just as the oversized garage door slides open and two armored vehicles roll in, parking side by side, their headlights aimed directly at us.

The drivers cut the engines but remain positioned behind the steering wheels. Four armed guards filter out of the trucks, two from each vehicle, then a large Russian in a black Armani suit slides out of the back seat. His polished black dress shoes glint with each step he takes, his footfalls echoing off the walls of the empty building.

My eyes shift from him to his guards, then back to him as he stops ten feet in front of us.

"Gentlemen, it's a pleasure to meet you," he drawls, his voice gravelly and his Russian accent thick.

His fingers are decorated with tattoos and silver rings. I recognize the black ink on one knuckle as the trademark symbol for the Federov Bratva. A small diamond nose stud that adds to his contradictory appearance winks at me.

"Please excuse my guards, but I'm sure you understand that I can't take any chances."

Mac steps forward and I slide my finger over the trigger just in case.

"Of course," Mac acquiesces. "However, I expect this meeting to go smoothly. We're here to do fair business, not ruffle any feathers or cause any heat."

Osmanov smiles and nods, his white teeth straight and as polished as the rest of him. But his calm demeanor is merely a fortified veneer of what lies beneath the surface. This man's a certified genius. *Literally.* He's known as one of the most intelligent mobsters to ever exist. So why would he do business with a company who takes organized crime groups like his down?

He scans each of us, then asks, "There are two of you missing. Where are they?"

"Brooks is tending to a family matter. And our huntress is running surveillance on the building. Same as you ... we're taking precautions," Mac responds coolly.

Dragging a tattooed knuckle over his beard, Osmanov hums thoughtfully, the gears in his head turning over.

Mac forges on. "Well, then. Let's get on with this, shall we? It's our understanding that we're trying to bring down the same cartel that's stomping all over your territory." Osmanov nods once, urging Mac to continue. "We're willing to make a deal—a fair one. Within certain limitations, of course. We join forces, take out the Colombians together, then go our separate ways and never speak again. We have the resources and skillset, but we're lacking in manpower, so the slimy bastards keep slipping away. And obviously, we have nothing to offer them as bait."

"So, you'd like some assistance. Set a trap, perhaps?" the Russian finishes for Mac.

"Affirmative."

The Russian sighs. "I have plenty of men who would gladly put a bullet in any one of those fucker's heads."

Mac blows out a held breath and drags a hand through his salt-and-pepper hair. "Alright, then. In the meantime, we've taken out Diego Perez and Santiago Ortiz. Do either of those names mean anything to you?"

Osmanov narrows his eyes, scans each of us, then nods once. "Ortiz was a waste of skin. Don't know the other."

Clearing his throat, Mac tells the Russian, "Ortiz gave us a location and two more names—Antonio Sanchez and Manuel Garcia.

We extracted fourteen civilians but there was nothing there you'd be interested in. However," Mac pauses briefly, "you should know we prioritize human trafficking over ... other endeavors."

Osmanov strokes his thumb over his bottom lip, then begins slowly pacing in front of us like a large, pissed-off cat. "Is there a point you're trying to make here?"

Mac lifts his chin and folds his arms. "If it comes down to choosing between your product and innocent lives, we will choose lives."

Osmanov's mouth curves into a crooked grin. "I have no issues with that. I'm not after the product anyway. And we don't deal in the skin trade. I want this cartel brought down entirely. Reclaiming product would be a petty move. And I assure you, gentlemen, I am not a petty man. The Colombians have been an irritant for far too long and it's beginning to wreak havoc on the family business." Osmanov pauses and stands directly in front of Mac. "You have yourselves a deal. But don't mistake my humanity for weakness. I have a tendency to lose my temper when someone strays from the path."

It's not a threat. It's a promise.

Mac extends his hand and Osmanov's eyes slide to each of us before he slips his palm into Mac's. And just like that, we're in bed with the Federov Bratva.

———◆O◆———

It's been three short weeks since we met with Osmanov, but he's already proven he's a major asset to have on our side because after two more quick extractions from Colombian hell, there are another forty women and children who get to go home. What started as a contract from the government to bring the Colombian cartel down—a contract they broke and backed out of—has morphed into a voluntary mission fueled by the passion to put an end to human trafficking. Although it would be incredibly naive of us to believe we could ever accomplish such a thing.

So for now, we move forward one mission after the other, the cartel none the wiser that it's us who's been stealing their product and slowly dismantling their hierarchy piece by piece. We leave no trace of who we are or why we're involved. It would take a major leak of intel for the Colombians to locate us or catch wind of when we're coming.

"Anyways, enough about me. What about you, Zak?"

I drag myself out of my thoughts, realizing I haven't heard a single word the sexy brunette across the table from me has said since I picked her up this evening for our date. Laura? Lisa? Doesn't matter. After tonight, she'll never see me again. In the meantime, I'll act the perfect gentleman, fuck her to within an inch of her life, then send her on her merry way.

Flashing her an easy smile, I prop my elbows on the table and lean in. "I could listen to you all night, sweetheart. Besides, my life is pretty boring. Nothing much to talk about."

She giggles like a school girl, a blush creeping from her ample tits all the way up to her overdone, fake lashes. She begins droning on again about something I can't give two fucks about. Her cats, I think.

Within seconds, my brain has strayed from the path and I've started thinking about the leggy blonde that finds great enjoyment out of making my life miserable, dancing through my nightmares like the little terrorist that she is. Come to think of it, I haven't seen her in person since her grandmother was admitted to the hospital five weeks ago.

But then she's not just drifting through my mind, she's sitting right there, across the bar with her thick, golden mane in one of those wide, loose French braids that would look fucking phenomenal wrapped around my fist. Her hard, toned body is clad in a deep red dress that makes the blue in her eyes pop. She peeks up from her glass and our eyes lock.

Jesus Christ. She's a total knockout. But that mouth of hers ...

Harper scowls, then returns her attention to the dark-haired beauty in front of her. Stella.

I set my whiskey on the table with a thud and smile politely at my date, cutting her off mid-sentence. Rising to my feet, I plant a small kiss on the top of her head and mumble into her hair, "Order yourself another drink, sweetheart. I'll be back in a few minutes."

She giggles, then waves down the waiter to order another one of her fruity, pink umbrella drinks.

My cock twitches with every step I take toward Harper, as if my dick is a compass and Harper's due north.

"Ladies. Pleasure seeing you here." I sprinkle on the charm and stand between Harper and Stella, bracing my hand on the back of Harper's chair. My knuckles graze the soft skin of her bare shoulder and she shifts in her seat, recoiling from the contact. She averts her eyes, allowing me the opportunity to check her out without having to look into her deep, oceanic pools.

Stella cranes her neck and glances around the dimly lit bar. It's a classy place—the kind you take a high-maintenance date when you hope to get laid. Stella locates the table with the busty brunette then smiles and twiddles her fingers at her while Harper busies herself by fiddling with her napkin and looking everywhere but at me.

That's when I see it—the ring. Every muscle in my body galvanizes as I stare down at the simple, solitaire diamond on Harper's left hand. Anybody with eyes could tell it's high quality and probably cost a small fortune, but it's too ... simple. And not at all Harper's style.

Not my problem.

"Cute date, Zak. Where'd you find her?" Stella chirps, peeking up at me with a smirk.

But I can't peel my eyes off Harper. The intensity of my stare is obviously causing her some discomfort because her arms are now folded across her chest, which only causes the swell of her perky tits to heave over the daringly low neckline of her dress. And her pulse is jumping erratically in her throat.

Dragging my gaze off the twitchy blonde, I smile at Stella. "Went puppy shopping at a dog shelter with Liam. Found her there."

That catches Harper's attention and her eyes slam to mine. "Careful, Zak. She might have fleas."

"Harper!" Stella squawks, glowering at her best friend.

I smile and return my attention to Harper. "When did that happen?" I ask, tipping my chin to her left hand.

Harper scoffs and rolls her eyes so dramatically, I'm surprised they don't fall out of their sockets and tumble across the floor. "None of your business," she snips out.

"Well," Stella drawls, dropping her napkin to the table and standing, her hand smoothing over her growing baby bump. "I have to pee again. I trust you two won't kill each other while I'm gone? I really don't have the stomach to be cleaning up blood right now."

I kiss Stella on the cheek and wait until she's out of earshot before I slide into her chair and stare Harper down.

She glares back at me. If looks could kill ...

"Can I help you?" she asks sardonically.

Leaning forward, I repeat gentler, "When did he propose?"

She gnaws on the inside of her cheek, then stares down at her drink. "Last weekend at his family's cottage."

"Hmm," I hum. "How adorable. Let me guess ... he took you out on a paddle boat and popped the question while a hundred white swans float gracefully on top of the smooth, glassy surface."

Her expression sobers and she glances around the bar, seemingly in search of someone. "No, actually. Not that it's any of your business, but he took me out for dinner and slipped it into my drink. Now you should probably get back to your date. Looks like she's getting antsy." Harper lifts her glass to her mouth and I watch as the clear liquid slips past her lips, disappearing down her throat as she swallows a large gulp of her martini. How a woman can make such a simple act look pornographic is beyond me.

"How many of those have you had?" I nod toward her now empty glass.

She pops the last olive into her mouth and chews, leaning back in her chair and narrowing her eyes at me. "Not nearly enough to survive this conversation," she responds dryly.

That tongue...

"Do you have a ride home?"

Her pupils dilate. "Sure do."

"No you don't. I'll take you home."

She all but scoffs. "And abandon your sure thing over there? Doubtful." She peers over at the table across the room. I don't bother looking. I already know my date is sitting there anxiously awaiting my return.

"My date's not your problem. Unless of course, you're jealous I'm here with her ..." I quirk a brow, my lips lifting into a grin. A sick satisfaction tickles the back of my skull as I watch her eyes light with determination. But the pink hue dusting her cheeks betrays her confidence.

"Jealous? Of a woman who clearly doesn't have two brain cells to rub together? No, Zak, I'm not jealous. What I am, though, is done with this little chitchat. Now, shoo big-bad-dog-at-the-top-of-the-food-chain, before I sink my kitty cat claws into your smug, arrogant face."

I sit there a moment longer, watching as Harper moves through a series of emotions. When Stella returns, I stand and pull her chair out for her, offering her a hand as she takes a seat and scoots forward. Naturally, Harper rolls her eyes at the gesture.

Stella glances at Harper, then to me, then shakes her head and snorts. "Jesus, you two. It's like someone cranked the heat up in here by a million degrees."

"It's probably all the pregnancy hormones," Harper quips back, pinning Stella with a glare. "I heard they can cause hot flashes and your best friend stabbing you with a fork."

Stella surrenders with both palms in the air. "Just making an observation."

Deciding now's a good time to dip out, I plant another kiss on Stella's cheek, flash Harper a thousand-watt smile, and saunter back to my table. My date instantly starts babbling on about something else and I find myself slinking down into my chair and watching Harper order two more rounds of martinis. When I finally get sick of the sound of Laura, Lisa, Lindsay, whatever's incessant desire to kill me with words, I offer to call her a cab. She's disappointed of course, as am I. She had a smoking hot body and very little self-esteem, which also meant *no* wasn't likely in her bedroom vocabulary.

I take a seat at the bar, out of Harper's view but where I can still see her. And hear her, that sultry voice drifting over the low, ambient music and causing my dick to lengthen. I switch to water and wait idly for them to finish. When Stella offers to give her a lift home, Harper declines and tells her she'll order a cab instead.

"You'd rather take a ride in a smelly cab than call Cam?" Stella asks curiously.

I'm wondering the same thing.

"I don't want to bug him tonight. He's stressed out about work and has some family stuff going on that he doesn't really like talking about. So, yeah, I'll just grab a cab and head home. Maybe pop some corn and work on my blog." Her words are slightly slurred, but not terrible. Still, it's obvious she's had too much to drink.

"Are you sure, sweetie? I really don't mind giving you a ride."

"It's out of the way for you, Stell. And it's late. I'm sure Joel will be waiting up for you."

When Stella says her goodbyes and strolls out of the restaurant, I watch Harper closely, examining her as she anxiously fiddles with her engagement ring. Her cheeks expand as she blows out a shaky breath and glances around the bar again, sweeping a strand of hair behind her ear and returning her attention to her lap. She's texting someone. And judging by her body language, she's frustrated with the conversation.

Polishing off the remaining liquid in her glass, she stands and moseys off toward the restroom, her heels clicking quietly on the hardwood floor. I slip down the hallway behind her, mesmerized by her long legs and the sway of her narrow hips. When she disappears into the women's washroom, I loiter outside the door and shoot Liam a text.

Me: Any idea where Brooks is right now?

Davis: Nope. Why?

Me: No reason.

Raking a hand through my hair, I pace the hall and wait for Harper to reemerge. I hear the water running, the hand dryer, then the door whips open and out she comes, startling when she sees me.

Her brows plummet and she scowls at me. "Did you follow me back here?"

"Yeah, I did." Closing the space between us, I crowd her against the wall until she's forced to angle her head to look up at me. Then I inhale that fucking scent and every muscle in my body tenses. Pressing both palms flat to the wall on either side of her head, I dip my gaze to hers and say, "You two moved pretty quick. How long has it been?"

Her lips part and she stares up at me with giant doe eyes. She looks ... uneasy. But then her mask of confidence slides right back into place, and I find myself wondering why the hell she's so anxious all of a sudden.

"Six months," she tells me. "But when you know, you know."

Her knee bumps my leg as she wobbles on her feet, and I slip my hand around her throat to track her pulse beneath my thumb, ignoring the way her smooth skin contrasts with my rough, tattooed paw. A flash of anger crosses her face and she sucks in a sharp breath.

I bring my lips to within an inch of hers and growl, "I can see right through you, Harper. And I'm ninety-nine percent sure that you're lying to yourself about something. Perhaps not about your feelings for Brooks, but ... *something*."

"And I'm ninety-nine percent sure that I'm about to thrust my knee into your dick if you don't release me right now," she sneers, her tongue darting out to wet her lips.

Smirking, I release her throat and sink my hand into my pocket, thumbing my coin. Harper's back remains sealed to the wall as she idly watches me pace before her.

"What the hell do you want, Zak?"

Deciding I need out of this small space, I snatch Harper's hand, ignoring the zap of static shock that snaps through me every time we touch, and drag her out the side door, the cool evening air slapping harshly against my heated skin. Harper yelps and stumbles in her heels, and I spin and scoop her up, throwing her over my shoulder and pinning the backs of her toned thighs with my forearm. She's a tiny thing, but not as delicate as she looks.

"Oh my god! Zak," she screeches, her fists pummeling my back as I make my way across the dark parking lot. "Put me the fuck down right this second!" I swat her ass and she releases a shocked gasp. "You asshole," she hisses.

I stop at my blacked-out Grand Cherokee Trackhawk and set her gently on her feet. Her fingers find purchase in my dress shirt and she glares up at me, steam practically billowing from her nose.

"I told you I'm taking you home. Now get in." I swing the passenger door open and wait for her to clamber inside. She shoots me one final warning glare then does as she's instructed. I reach across and buckle her in, my hand brushing over her hip in the process. When she reaches up and swipes her hair out of her face, that too-simple rock on her hand winks at me, and I'm reminded that she's officially off-limits.

My dick doesn't get the memo, but I'll deal with him later.

I slam the door and hop into the driver's seat, pressing the start button and peeling out of the parking lot. I need to get her home. Fast. Then I need to disappear for a while until my head's straight and I'm not tempted to fuck an engaged woman.

Harper sits quietly, her cheek pressed to the passenger window and her eyes closed. Her fingers are fidgeting in her lap though, so I know she's not sleeping. Because I'm an idiot, I set a palm on her bare thigh and squeeze. She swats my hand away, and I can't help but chuckle at our frustrating routine.

I retreat to my half of the vehicle and try for some small talk. "How's your nan doing?"

"Fine," she mumbles, a tightness in her tone as if someone has a noose snaked around her throat.

"Good. I'm glad to hear," I respond truthfully.

Seconds tick on and the side of my face sizzles from Harper's gaze.

"It was you," she sneers, but her statement lacks accusation. It's more like it just dawned on her that I did something out of character. "You hired the nurse."

I glimpse her in my peripherals because I know that if I look over at her, I'll want to touch her again. To feel her soft skin pepper with bumps beneath my fingertips.

"I trust Joanie's been taking good care of her," I say blandly, avoiding admission that I covered the cost of home care for her grandmother.

A palpable tension so thick it's difficult to breathe solidifies between us. When Harper doesn't respond, I chance a peek at her. Big mistake. Because now she's sucking on her bottom lip, and I want nothing more than to pull it from between her teeth and watch those pretty, plump lips stretch around my cock instead.

"Why'd you do it?"

I snort. "It wasn't for you, kitten. It was for your grandma. Saw her lying in that hospital bed and felt bad for the old lady. I know she's stubborn and would refuse to spend a dime on home care, and you can't afford—"

"How do you know all this?" she asks with narrowed eyes.

"You do a lot of talking and I have ears."

Pointing her gaze back out her window, she mutters under her breath, "You're still an asshole ... but thank you."

Moments later, she's back to resting her head. But now there's a calm, comfortable silence humming in the cab of my SUV. It's unnerving. And highly worrisome. The moment I let Harper Hilton under my skin, I know she'll wreck me. Just like she wrecks every other man that crosses her path.

It's only a matter of time before she does the same to Brooks.

Twelve

Harper

I FUMBLE WITH MY keys until Zak finally gets frustrated and snatches them from my hand. He sinks the key into the hole with ease and ushers me inside my apartment, closing the door behind us. I step out of my heels, my feet aching from the abuse they've weathered, and slump down onto the couch. Zak disappears into the kitchen, returning with a glass of water in which he impolitely demands I drink all of, only to leave and return with another glass. This time I sip it.

"Eat anything tonight?" he asks gruffly.

I smile against the rim of the glass. "Why? Worried I'll waste away to nothing?"

He drops into the chair in the corner and drags his eyes down my body as if mentally calculating the pounds I've dropped in the last few weeks. I've been so busy with Nan that food hasn't been a priority for me. "Yes, actually. If you disappear, who'd be left to grate on my last nerve?"

I snort. "I'm sure you have plenty of willing prospects to fill the position." It sounds like an insinuation, but it's not. It's just a simple fact. Women drop like flies around him.

"None quite like you, kitten." He flashes me a wide, dazzling smile. It's the same Colgate, panty-melting smile he flashes all women.

"Are you saying I'm *special*, Zak the-big-bad-dog Shephard?"

Leaning forward, he rests his elbows on his thighs and clasps his giant, tattooed hands between his knees. I've never really noticed before, but he has really beautiful hands. Can a man's hands be beautiful?

Okay, Hilton. That's enough of the martinis for a while.

Zak angles his head at me, a smug grin tugging at his lips. He has a nice mouth too. It's firm, but looks soft. I bet he's a great kisser.

I'm snatched away from my thoughts when Zak murmurs, "Special doesn't begin to describe you, Harper Hilton."

Did ... did he just *compliment* me?!

Suddenly, my cozy little living room feels entirely too small for the two of us and the wet spot in my panties will soon be large enough to put out a California wildfire. I need Zak gone. Like yesterday. Because if I'm being completely honest, I don't trust myself to make smart decisions in my inebriated state.

"You should go."

Zak's warm brown eyes flare, something hot and fierce pulsing behind them. He stands, and I'm once again reminded of the sheer size of him. Tall and muscular but in a purely athletic type of way. Agile and fast. *Dangerous.*

The coffee table is the only piece of furniture separating us, and he looks like he's about ready to hurl it across the room and tackle me.

Instead, he reaches across the table and demands, "Give me your phone."

Eyeing him suspiciously, I ask, "Why?"

He drags his other hand through his hair, messing it up in all the right ways. "Just give me your fucking phone, Harper."

"What's the magic word?"

"*Now,*" he snarls.

Rolling my eyes, I snip out, "Since you asked so nicely …" I pull my phone from my purse, unlock it with my thumb, then drop it into his palm. He clicks away on it, then hands it back to me a moment later.

"Eat something before bed," he orders, then marches to the door. With his hand on the knob, he pauses and glances over his shoulder. "And lock the door behind me."

I do as I'm told, locking the deadbolt immediately after Zak leaves. Then I saunter to the kitchen and rummage around for something to eat. I don't have much in the way of groceries right now since I've pretty much cleaned myself out of house and home the last few weeks, not really having time to do my own shopping since I've been so distracted with Nan. So I settle on a microwave dinner and crawl into bed.

Only I can't sleep because my brain is working overtime and there's an annoying little voice in my head that keeps reminding me how fucking reckless I can be. If Cameron finds out Zak brought me home, he'll no doubt think the worst considering he's already unjustifiably suspicious. The thought plays on a loop as I toss and turn, kicking the blankets off, then tugging them back up my body. Decision making has never been something I excel in.

Sighing in defeat, I roll onto my back and stare at the ceiling. My good hand drifts to my throat, and I brush my fingertips over the tender flesh of where Zak wrapped his hand. He hadn't hurt me. Quite the opposite actually. I didn't flinch in fear or pain. I flinched because his touch ignites something wild inside of me. Something I've never felt before. And it's fucking terrifying.

And then when I realized it was him who hired Joanie for my nan, I nearly melted into a puddle of human goo in the passenger seat of his vehicle. Sure, he said he didn't do it for me. I'd be a stupid, stupid woman to believe Zak Shephard would ever do anything nice for me. In fact, I'm certain that if he could, he'd use me to scrape the dog shit off the bottom of his shoe. But it was still an incredibly kind thing for him to do. And the more I think about it, the more I struggle to see what Zak could possibly gain from helping my grandmother.

But if there's one thing I know about Zak, it's that he doesn't do anything that won't somehow benefit him in the long run.

So ... what is it that he wants?

Nan stares at me with a concerned look marring her gentle features. It's as if she doesn't recognize the granddaughter sitting before her. The truth is, I'm changing—growing—at a pace much quicker than I thought possible. In six short months, I've gone from being a flirtatious singleton without a care in the world to a happily engaged woman with everything I want laid out in front of me.

"You look different, deary. Like someone has put a cap on your light. Is everything alright?"

I force a weak smile and sigh. "I'm fine, Nan. Just been super busy." That's not entirely true. Actually, that's not at all true. Even though Nan's recovering well and I have Joanie's help, I've put my own life on the back burner. Cam's been gone on missions a lot lately and Stella has highjacked my wedding plans, which I'm grateful for because it's been the last thing on my mind. So that means my days have been filled with scrubbing my apartment top to bottom, reorganizing my collection of travel magazines, and binge watching every nineties horror film that ever aired.

I glance over at the grotesque bouquet of roses on my nan's bedside table. "Who sent those?"

"I'm not sure. They were delivered to my doorstep this morning. No note. Just the flowers. Pretty, aren't they?"

A warmth spreads in my chest at the size of the smile on my grandmother's face. But that warmth is quickly swallowed whole by an image of two mahogany caskets—one for each of my parents—surrounded by a lavish display of crimson roses, all wrapped in silk ribbons and adorned with tiny, insincere notes of condolences.

I shake the thought from my head and suggest playfully, "Maybe it was the handsome neighbor."

She swats the air and tsks. But then she brings up a topic that lassos a chain around my heart and squeezes until it bursts.

"I have an appointment with a lawyer tomorrow to review my will and power of attorney. I'd like for you to join me." She continues on, detailing her wishes to me verbally so I understand the reason for certain requests. By the time she finishes, I want to curl up in her lap and cry. "There's only one condition, deary. Everything is to remain in your name for as long as you shall live. And once you pass on, my assets will be transferred to your children. And if you should not have any children, then there's a list of charities I'd like it to be divided amongst instead."

I know what she's saying ... that she doesn't want Cameron to take anything if we divorce or if I predecease him. Sweet Nan—forever protecting me even when it's not necessary. Regardless, I dutifully accept and move on from the topic as quickly as possible.

The next day, I'm getting ready to pick my grandmother up when Cam shows up at my door. Drunk as a skunk. At two o'clock in the afternoon.

He shoulders past me into my apartment, slurring and stumbling. My blood rolls through my veins like liquid lava when I spot the car keys in his hand.

"You drove like this?" I screech, slamming the door and pinning him with a fierce glare.

He shucks his jacket off and smiles crookedly at me, the smell of bourbon wafting off him. He stalks over to me, his eyes red and glassy, his breath hot and acidic. He slips one hand around the back of my neck and drags me into him and kisses me. I press my palms to his chest and shove, but he doesn't budge.

"Cam, stop," I mutter against his lips, but he doesn't let up. I know fighting him off will only anger him in his inebriated state, so I let him slip his tongue into my mouth and take what he needs. He pulls back, his lips glistening from the sloppiness of his drunken kiss.

Gross.

"I've fucking missed you," he slurs, then shoves me roughly against the wall. My shoulder blades meet the drywall with a thud and he kisses me again, but this time there's a different type of hunger bleeding through. It's not sweet or loving or anything I want from him.

And that becomes clear when his hand dips into the front of my leggings and I slap him across the face. Hard.

His head whips to the side and my hands immediately fly to my mouth as I gasp at the pure horror of what I just did. Cam licks his lips, then slowly turns his face back to mine and sneers. But he doesn't retaliate.

"Oh my god," I blurt. "Cam, I'm so sor—"

Large hands cup my jaw as Cameron crushes his mouth to mine again, kissing me and grinding his hips into mine. "I want you, Harper. Right now."

Searching his face, I see nothing but desire and anguish. He's fighting an internal war right now, and he's desperately clinging to my affection in an attempt to soothe his battle wounds. His family is in total chaos, his father having somehow discovered that Carmella cheated on him and that Daniel isn't biologically his. And I know Sweetwater is balls deep in some Colombian cartel problem that they're working tirelessly to bring to an end.

I'm not typically a people pleaser, but this is my fiancé and he needs me right now. He needs release. And I can give that to him.

Nodding, I lift onto my toes and kiss him, wrapping my arms around his neck and allowing him to take whatever it is he needs from me. He carries me to the bedroom and lays me down on my back. My leggings and tank top are soon peeled from my body and Cam's cock makes its grand appearance, thrusting inside of me and fucking me slow and soft as he whispers words of adoration in my ear.

"I love you, Harper. I can't wait to marry you, baby."

Nodding, I swallow the mountain of rocks in my throat and wrap my legs around Cam's hips. His thrusts lose their rhythm as he buries himself deep inside of me, his cum filling my womb as he showers me in kisses everywhere. My nose. My ears. My eyes and forehead.

"I love you too, Cameron."

Thirteen

Zak

"**A**LRIGHT, BOYS. LISTEN UP.**"** The room goes quiet as all eyes slide to Mac. "Thanks to Sloane and Osmanov's team, we've located Sanchez and Garcia. This mission's a little heavier than the last few, so Osmanov will be sending in a team of soldiers with us. Once we acquire the targets, we'll hand them off to the Russians and we'll focus on extracting the victims. Do we have an understanding?"

We all nod in agreement and listen attentively as Mac details the extraction plans. That night, we drop into Colombia and move boots, closing in on the little red dot on our GPS that tells us where these two fucks are hiding out. Mac was right. This job's a hell of a lot bigger than the last few, but the Russians have provided a decent assist so far, so I have no reason to doubt that this will go as planned.

But when we finally locate the civilians, I have to tamp down a swell of rage heaving violently in my chest.

"Jesus fucking Christ," Liam snarls into my comm as he covers his nose with his sleeve.

I do the same and glance around the dark belly of the shipping container, the only light spilling in from the door we just busted through, and the only sounds the terrified whimpers coming from the remaining survivors of this hell.

My eyes land on a young girl with sandy-brown hair and wide, brown eyes. Her terrified gaze darts from me to Liam, and she releases a sob, curling her knees into her chest and making herself as small as humanly possible. The rest of the team work on checking bodies for signs of life. There isn't much, judging by the stillness and stench of death permeating the air. Slinging my rifle over my shoulder, I drop to my haunches in front of the girl and flick my eyes over her sickly little body in search of any major injuries. From what I can see, she's still whole, albeit malnourished and trembling in fear.

"Do you speak English?" I ask lowly.

She sniffles, her upper lip crusted in dirty and dried snot. She nods slowly.

Forcing my lips to lift into a nonthreatening smile, I say, "My name's Zak. What's yours, sweetheart?"

"T-Taylor," she rasps out, her bottom lip wobbling.

"Taylor. That's a very pretty name." Tears track down her cherub cheeks, leaving streaks all over her angelic little face. "I know we look like a bunch of scary guys with all these weapons and face paint and stuff, but I promise we're not going to hurt you. Nobody here will. We're going to get you out of here and get you home, okay?" I nod encouragingly, praying to God this girl will go willingly.

"O-okay."

"Good. Now I'm going to pick you up, alright? And we're going to go for a ride in a helicopter. Have you ever flown before, Taylor?"

Another sob wracks her body and she squeezes her eyes shut, her tiny fingers clutching something near her hip. When I realize what it is, my heart splits in two. I eye the limp hand she's holding onto and pray to God there's still a heartbeat, but judging by the grayish hue of the flesh, it's unlikely.

"My ... my ..." She breaks out in tears.

I move carefully around to her side and confirm what I feared most. The body belongs to a woman who looks an awful lot like an older version of Taylor. Choking back my own tears, I glance around and motion for Liam to join me. If there's anything I know about Liam, it's that he'll make sure the body makes it back to her family.

He crouches beside me, his frame slightly beefier than mine and his face a fuck of a lot scarier. But Taylor doesn't seem to fear him.

"This is Liam. He's a good friend of mine. And he's going to make sure your mom gets home too, okay?" Fuck, I can barely get the words out.

Taylor's eyes bounce all over the dark space, then finally land on mine, and she nods. I carefully lift her into my arms and she releases her mother's cold, lifeless hand. Liam doesn't utter a word. He just lifts the dead woman into his arms, sweeps his hand over her eyes, then stomps out into the scorching Colombian heat.

Just as we step out of the container, gunfire erupts all around us. Mac's in our ears, barking out orders. Joel's right there too, counting off tangos. The whir of a helo comes near, but it's still too far out to get the civilians to safety while so many bullets are whizzing by.

Liam and I duck back inside the shipping container and set Taylor and her mother back down. The girl is panicking, her cries desperate as she claws at my arms, begging me to not leave her behind.

"I promise I'll be right back for you, sweetheart. I promise," I tell her over and over, but she doesn't believe me. Her little fingers find purchase in my Kevlar vest as she clings to the only hope she has of making it out of here alive. I pry her hands off me and shout over the piercing sound of nearby shots, "Taylor. I promise you. We will be back for you and your mom, okay? You have to trust us. Please, sweetheart."

She licks at her chapped lips and crawls backward into the container, hiding in the same corner I found her in. It's dark in here. Nobody will bother with her. To the cartel, she's worth nothing right now. They'll be more concerned for their own lives than the life of a single innocent child.

Davis and I slide out of the container, rifles aimed and pegging off tangos one at a time. There are more than we initially thought, but that happens sometimes. Sneaky fuckers. A bullet pings off the steel wall behind me and I duck, firing back, praying Taylor stays put. Kids have a dangerous way of not listening to simple instructions.

I spot a Russian off in the distance—a huge bastard who's marching through the jungle like he owns the fucking place. He takes down two Colombians with his gun and two more with a knife.

"Brooks? You close by?" Joel comes in.

"Negative. I have two civilians and we're nearing the chopper." His breaths are labored, so I know he's on the move.

Mac comes in next. "The Russians have Garcia and Sanchez, and they're itching to get out of here. We need to get the civilians to the helo. *Now,*" he orders.

"Fuck," I shout, then check in on Liam.

He nods at me from the other corner of the container, then ducks again, dodging a stray bullet.

"There's too many of them. We need more assistance down here, boss," I bark into the comm at Mac.

"Sending two in right now."

Less than thirty seconds later, I've got two huge Russian soldiers flanking my side, popping off shots left, right, and center. I spot Brooks off to the side, no civilians in tow and too far from the chopper to have been on his way there just a minute ago.

Coordinating with the Russians, Liam and I duck back into the container to recover Taylor and her mother.

"You need to hang on tight so I can protect us, okay?" Taylor wraps her limbs around my torso, clinging onto me for dear life and hiding her face in my chest.

The Russians cover us while Liam and I haul ass toward the chopper. Just as we reach the flattened ground where the bird sits idling, another gunshot rings out.

This one strikes true.

"Fuck!" I shout, catching Taylor before she slips off me. I leap into the helo and lay the little girl down. Her screams are deafening and her brown eyes are wild and overflowing with paralyzing pain. Liam pops in beside me and sets her mother down, then covers her corpse with a blanket before coming to my side with our emergency medical kit.

"Ah, fuck, Shephard," he murmurs, eyeing the growing patch of blood on Taylor's abdomen. He gets to work opening the kit and unpacking sterilized tools while I remove Taylor's shirt and inspect the bullet hole.

"She's losing a lot of blood, but I think the bullet missed any vital organs. Bite down on this, sweetheart," I instruct as I slide a tongue depressor between her teeth. She'll be unconscious shortly and free of agony.

She cries out, but does as she's told. *Tough fucking kid*. Liam hands me a syringe, and I clean a spot on her forearm and inject her with a sedative. She's out within seconds, and I get to work fishing the bullet out before it settles in too deep. Her body is weak and infection will set in fast if I don't treat this immediately.

I retrieve the bullet, discarding it onto the floor of the helicopter, clean the wound, dump cauterizing salts into it, and give her a shot of antibiotics.

Behind me, the guys are helping civilians to safety while the Russians hold the Colombians off long enough for us to get everyone inside. Once Taylor's situated and stable, I join the guys on the ground and start lifting bodies into the chopper. There's no time for pleasantries or respect. This is life and death and these people need to get the hell out of here.

Finally, it comes to an end and we're lifted out of the danger zone. But it's not without casualty. Liam's been shot in the leg. The big bastard hadn't even noticed until he sat down and the blood started pooling on the floor at his feet. I convince him to let me treat it while we fly out, then we all sit quietly, our eyes darting from dead bodies to living human beings to each other.

I glance at Brooks, but I don't have the energy to question him right now, nor do I need to cause a scene in front of the civilians. I'll deal with him later. But there's an obvious nervous energy wafting off him, and I don't fucking like it.

He wasn't where he said he was.

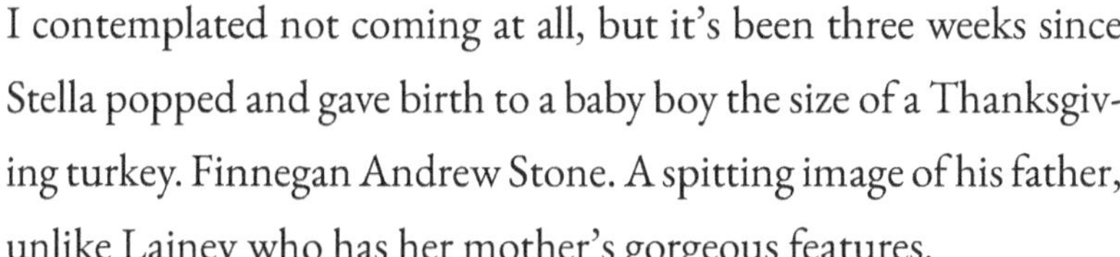

I contemplated not coming at all, but it's been three weeks since Stella popped and gave birth to a baby boy the size of a Thanksgiving turkey. Finnegan Andrew Stone. A spitting image of his father, unlike Lainey who has her mother's gorgeous features.

"Oh my god," Harper swoons, her blue eyes twinkling in delight and Brooks glued to her side as she stares down at the baby sleeping peacefully in her arms. "He's so perfect. I could just eat him."

"Please don't," Stella chirps.

I watch quietly as Stella peeks over at Joel, whose piercing blue eyes are fixated on his wife, a goofy grin plastered on his face. These two are still madly in love and it's enough to make me want to toss my lunch.

Everyone takes turns holding the new baby. Even Liam manages to grow the balls to hold the little bundle of joy in his giant, trembling hands. I can't help the smirk that spreads across my face. Liam harbors some demons, but if there's one thing we all know for certain, it's that he'd give his life for any woman or child. But fear flashes in his eyes when Finnegan begins fussing, and he makes quick work of unloading the baby back into Stella's arms.

Then he disappears out the patio doors and lights a cigarette, streams of smoke leaving his nostrils as he stares out at the tree line at the back of the property. I watch in awe as Harper stomps off after him, snatching the cigarette right out of his hand and stomping it into the ground beneath her foot. She points a pink-painted fingernail at him and begins rambling off lung cancer statistics and how his teeth are going to fall out of his head. Liam's lip twitches in amusement. He reaches into his pocket and slides out another cigarette, lighting it up and blowing a ring of smoke up and away from Harper's scowling face. Harper's eyes narrow to slits and she scoffs, then spins and storms off, flipping him the middle finger on her way back inside.

Brave little kitten.

Feeling the uncomfortable heat of a gaze boring into the side of my face, I glance over at Brooks, whose eyes are thinned, a glower pinching his brows tight as he watches me closely. When our eyes clash, he lifts his glass of bourbon to his lips and downs the remaining liquid. Setting his empty tumbler on the table with a thud, he rises and gestures for Harper to relocate herself to his side. When she creeps in beside him, he wraps an arm around her waist and welds her body to his.

Shifting my focus to the wall behind Stella, I watch in my peripherals as Brooks nuzzles his nose into Harper's hair, whispering something in her ear. Moments later, they're saying their goodbyes and leaving.

Not my fucking problem.

Fourteen

Zak

"CAN I GET YOU anything else?" the bartender from Traitor's asks from the other side of the corner booth I'm stuffed into.

"Just the bill, thanks."

The bartender scurries off, returning a few moments later with a small leather binder, my bill tucked inside. I slide my card out and slip it into the pocket of the binder and hand it back to her. She flashes me a smile then disappears again, and I take another swig of my whiskey just as a gust of cool evening air sweeps into the bar.

Every nerve ending in my body sparks to life as my eyes fixate on Harper's lithe body as she moves through the front doors of Traitor's. Wetting my lips, I drink her in. A pair of long, tanned legs. A set of toned thighs barely concealed by a short, black dress that hugs a set of narrow hips and a tight ass. A thick mane of wavy, blonde hair that falls just above the curve of her spine.

Why the fuck is she here again?

She heads straight for the bar, perches her ass on a stool, and orders a gin martini. Extra dirty. Extra olives. Then she pulls her cell phone out, types away on it, and sets it down in front of her. She stares down at the tiny device as if willing the screen to light up with a message or call, her thumb spinning her engagement ring around and around as she fidgets anxiously.

I slip my phone out and fire off a text message.

Big Bad Dog: Hi, kitten.

I sit back in the dark corner booth, sipping my whiskey as I watch Harper fight some internal battle that I know nothing about. She picks up her phone and glares at the screen before responding.

Kitten: Clever dog slipping your number into my phone.

Big Bad Dog: Want to play a game?

Kitten: Nope.

I go to type out a message but pause when I see her typing again.

Kitten: Fine. What's the game?

Big Bad Dog: Truth or dare.

Kitten: What are we? Twelve?

Kitten: (Eye roll emoji) Truth.

Big Bad Dog: What are you doing right now?

She takes a sip of her martini.

Kitten: Watching a movie. Your turn.

Big Bad Dog: I'll follow your lead. Truth.

Three little bubbles pop up on my phone, then disappear. Then pop up again. She's typing, deleting, then retyping.

Kitten: Have you been following me?

Interesting question.

Big Bad Dog: No.

She shifts in her seat, crossing her legs and tugging the hem of her dress down. It's a pointless feat, because not even ten seconds later, it's ridden back up her thighs, exposing smooth, tanned skin that would look fucking beautiful painted with the faint bruising of my fingertips from gripping her flesh while she rides my cock.

Kitten: Dare.

Big Bad Dog: I dare you to tell me why you'd ask such a strange question.

Kitten: You can't dare someone to tell a truth. That's cheating.

Big Bad Dog: So is lying about watching a movie.

She slams her drink back. Tapping my finger on my whiskey glass, I wait patiently for her text.

Kitten: (Yawning emoji) You're boring me. Don't big, bad dogs like you have other innocent creatures to prey on? I'm busy.

Big Bad Dog: Doing what? Watching the ice in your drink melt?

Kitten: Actually, watching paint dry. It's much more interesting than talking to you.

I can't hide the smile that splits across my face. She's an irritant, but she's entertaining. And fucking gorgeous. And I still don't know why she's here.

Big Bad Dog: Dare.

Kitten: Hmm. That's easy. Find the nearest cliff and hurl your body over it.

Big Bad Dog: I've done that a thousand times. It's lost its thrill. Since you dodged my last dare, you owe me one.

I adjust my dick in my jeans, watching as she straightens her spine and stares at her phone, her thumb still fiddling with her ring. Then she flags down the bartender and orders another drink.

Kitten: Fine.

Big Bad Dog: I dare you to turn around.

Her muscles tense as she reads my message. She spins slowly in her chair, our eyes locking immediately and her ocean blues flaring wildly. The air in the dingy dive bar hums with energy as static electricity charges the space between her and me. It's magnetic. It always is. But that pull has grown too strong, and I'm no longer in control of my own body. I lift my hand and curl my finger, summoning her over to my booth.

With her head on a swivel, she glances around the bar. She's nervous. Why that annoys me is something I don't care to unpack. Finally, when she's satisfied that there's nobody in here she knows, she stands, plucks her martini glass off the bar, and saunters over to me, stopping on the other side of the table. It's smart to keep some distance between us, but I'd be lying if I said I'm not tempted to drag her into this booth, slip her panties to the side, and ...

Fuck.

"What do you want?" she snips out.

"Have a seat, Harper. Let's finish our game."

The booth is a semicircle, only large enough for three or four people. Harper scoots in behind the table, sitting as close to the edge of the leather bench as possible, maintaining that distance we'd be wise to keep.

Staring at me unblinking, she says, "I believe it was your turn."

"Truth."

She sucks on her bottom lip for a moment before lifting her chin and asking, "Why'd you put your number in my phone?"

"Because you didn't have it," I respond honestly, although it's not the whole truth. "Your turn."

Inhaling deeply, she says, "I'm not sure this game is fun anymore."

"Choose, Harper," I snarl.

"What's the magic word?"

Frustrated, I reach across the length of the bench and grab her by the hips, dragging her across the leather so she's sitting right next to me, her bare thigh flush with my jeaned one. The little yelp she lets out snags the attention of a few random drunks, but they quickly avert their eyes when they realize she's glued to my side. I'm a regular at this shithole, and people know better than to fuck with me. Harper splays both palms on the table in front of her as she desperately tries to maintain a semblance of composure.

I intend on shredding that composure to bits.

Leaning into her, I whisper, "The magic word, kitten, is *now*."

She inhales a shaky breath and her eyes flutter shut for a moment before exhaling slowly. "Dare."

Brushing the back of my knuckles over her leg, I dare, "Call your fiancé and ask him where he is right now."

Despite the hot, humid air being exchanged between us, goosebumps pepper the soft skin beneath my touch as I skim my fingers up and down her exposed thigh. There's a stickiness to the heat cloaking us, like I'm right back in the jungle, wading through the murky swamp. But I can no longer navigate these waters. My next steps are unclear, and there's no telling where this might take me.

"No," she breathes out, refusing to meet my eyes. But I know it's only because she doesn't trust herself in this moment. Fuck, I don't trust myself either.

"Why not?"

A shiver rolls down her spine. "Because he's at his parents," she tells me plainly, then sinks the rest of her martini.

A small dribble of liquid trickles down her chin and I can't stop myself. I reach up and slowly swipe the drop away, dragging the pad of my thumb across her smooth bottom lip. Her mouth parts as she exhales a small puff of warm air. I meet her gaze, her pupils blowing wide as she stares back at me. Time suspends itself, the hum of the bar fading into the background as our bodies react to the unexpected contact.

When I finally peel myself away, I retreat to my side of the booth, raking a hand through my hair and blowing out a ragged breath. Being in Harper's presence is like tightrope walking over a deep canyon—dangerous, thrilling, and a stupid fucking idea. But that doesn't seem to stop me from toeing the line.

Harper reluctantly accepts my offer to give her a lift home, asking me to drop her off at her grandmother's house instead of her apartment. It's further out of my way, but I don't protest. Spending time with her isn't smart, but it's addictive and I can't bring myself to say no. She doesn't speak a word the entire ride. Neither do I.

I pull into the driveway, groaning when I realize the house is shrouded in darkness, not a single exterior light on. I walk her to the door and lean against the brick wall, watching in amusement as she fiddles with her keys in the pitch black.

Studying her profile, I realize that even in the dark, she's a total knockout. Sharp, angular features emphasized by big, blue eyes and a soft mouth with a sharp cupid's bow. But then that gaudy diamond on her left hand glitters, and I shove all my burning desires back down where they belong.

When she finds the right key, she pauses and peeks up at me. I can tell she wants to say something, but she's hesitating. When her mouth clicks shut, I take it upon myself to break the silence.

Standing to my full height, I tell her, "You have my number if you need anything."

She cranes her neck, white puffs of air leaving her parted lips as the moisture of her breath is greeted by the plummeting evening temperature. That goddamn mouth of hers. I can't take my eyes off it.

Her eyes dart to the space over my shoulder, and I angle my head to see what's caught her attention.

Movement. Peering into the bush at the side of the house, I reach back and grip the handle of my gun in the waistband of my jeans, ready to pull and fire. Harper's fingers find purchase in my shirt as I sweep my free arm back and push her behind me.

Taking a slow, quiet step forward, I cock the hammer and exhale. But soft laughter slams into the back of my head, and Harper takes a step back as a pair of round, green eyes emerge from the bottom of the bush. I release the grip of my gun and the stale air from my lungs.

Fucking stray cats. This town is littered with them.

"Jesus," she hisses. "Paranoid much?"

Spinning to face her, I press her into the wall and sneer down at her. "There's a fine line between paranoid and prepared, Harper."

Her face goes slack and she opens her mouth to speak. But I clamp my hand over her lips and lean in, my breath grazing the shell of her ear. "I'm not in the mood for whatever it is you were about to say."

Wild, blue eyes flare with defiance, and I feel her tongue dart out against my palm. And she fucking *licks*.

An irritated growl vibrates from my chest as I release her mouth, then drag my slick hand down the side of her neck—*hard*—smearing her saliva across her flesh. I step back and stuff my hands in my pockets, thumbing my coin in an attempt to ease the rush of adrenaline pumping through my veins.

"Get your ass inside the house, Harper. And lock the fucking door."

She glowers at me for another beat before disappearing behind the door. I hear the lock click and blow out a bated breath. But there's a nagging sensation in the pit of my stomach, and I can't bring myself to leave. So I park my SUV at the curb and watch the house, settling in for a sleepless night.

Just as I'm getting comfortable, a light blinks on in one of the rooms at the side of the house, and I squint my eyes to bring the shadow behind the curtain into focus.

Palming my dick over my jeans, I watch as Harper walks past the window several times. She's pacing. I can't see her face. I can't see anything but the silhouette of her body roaming about. But it feels like I'm right there in that room with her, sweeping her long hair over her shoulder, my fingers grazing her back as I slowly unzip her dress from behind. What kind of panties does she wear? Does she opt for comfort or is she the frilly, lacy type? It wouldn't matter. She could be wearing a diaper and still make it look sexy as hell.

Harper pauses, standing still in front of the window. She turns her head, sensing something. Like she knows she's being watched.

I sit still as a statue in the driver's seat, my heart beating steady in my chest and forcing all the blood in my body to my dick. A hand slips between the curtains as Harper peeks through the parted fabric, her eyes locking on my vehicle immediately, the dark tint on my windows blocking me from her view.

Sorry, kitten. I'm staying put.

Instead of closing the curtains like a normal woman would, she shoves them all the way open and turns her back to me. Then she does the exact thing I was imagining myself doing. She flips her long hair over her shoulder and reaches behind her. I can practically hear every tooth of her zipper parting way as she slowly unzips her dress. She angles her head, peering at my vehicle over her shoulder as the black fabric of her dress splits open exposing soft, smooth flesh and the lengthy curve of her spine.

Rubbing my swollen cock through my jeans, I let out an agonized groan. She's fucking with me right now. Teasing me. This is how she hooks her claws into idiots who can't control their urges. This is how she hooked Brooks.

Naughty little bitch.

Unbuckling my belt and jeans, I free my rock-hard dick and wrap my hand around the base, tugging once. She wants to put on a little show for me, then I'll shamelessly take what she's offering and fuck my fist right here. It's late enough that none of her neighbors are awake. It's just me and her with nothing but two thin layers of glass separating us while the rest of the world sleeps.

I begin pumping my hand, sweeping my thumb over the bead of cum leaking from my tip as Harper makes a show of slipping her dress off her creamy shoulders and down the length of her arms, the fabric pooling around her hips. Her bare back is completely exposed, her velvety smooth flesh illuminated by the warm glow of the single lamp beside the bed. I lay my head back and peer at her through hooded eyes, imagining sinking my teeth into her neck and then licking the sting away.

The sounds I imagine she makes ... Fuck.

She spins around, one arm across her chest, barely covering her perky tits as her gaze somehow finds mine in the pitch black. Her eyes twinkle with mischief as she shimmies her dress the rest of the way down her body, showcasing her tiny pink thong. Of course it's pink. It's also pathetically small and I want to shred it with my teeth.

My movements are erratic now and I can feel my balls tensing as I near coming. As if she can hear my thoughts, she smiles sweetly, her face lifting into an all-knowing smirk that tells me she knows exactly what she's doing to me right now.

She drags one manicured fingernail down the length of her torso, circling her belly button twice before sliding her hand into the front of her panties and teasing her clit. Her head falls back and her mouth parts on an exhale.

"Jesus," I grate out, my dry tongue sticking to the roof of my mouth.

The thought of barging in and fucking her against the wall enters my mind, those long legs of hers wrapping snuggly around my waist as I plow into her, fucking her until she forgets her own name. Forgets her fiancé's name.

She drops her chin back down, her hand retreating and her face splitting into a smile. With a waggle of her fingers, she slides the curtains shut, blocking her body from my view.

"Fuck, Harper," I hiss, blowing my load into my hand and slapping the steering wheel with my other as I come hard at the thought of invading her pussy and painting her inside walls with my cum, claiming her as my own.

When my breathing returns to normal, I clean myself up with the paper towels I keep in my vehicle, stuffing my dick back into my jeans and dropping my head back against the cool leather seat. The light in her room blinks off and my phone chimes from beside me.

Kitten: Get lost big, bad dog. You're being creepy.

I don't respond, but I do stay awake the entire night, my eyes never straying from the house. Not until daylight creeps in and the inky black sky fades to a hazy gray as the sun peeks over the foggy horizon.

Fifteen

Harper

I KNEW I'D FIND some fucked-up feeling of security at Traitor's. But when I rolled up in the cab, I hadn't seen Zak's vehicle in the parking lot and considered changing my mind and going home. But I didn't, because for some stupid reason, I had the feeling it was exactly where I needed to be. And as much as it pains me to admit it, when Zak remained parked at the curb outside my grandmother's house, a rush of relief flooded my system and I got the first full night's rest that I've had in weeks.

Because right now, I'm keeping a secret that not even my fiancé knows about. I've considered going to the police, but what would I tell them? That I have a feeling someone has been following me? Pfft. Big fucking whoop. There's no evidence. I haven't seen or heard anything or anyone suspicious. It's just ... intuition, I suppose.

"What's going on with you, deary?" Nan asks from her chair, another one of her stones clutched in her fist.

I drop my head into my hands and groan. Putting on my big-girl panties, I reassure her, "I'm fine, Nan. I should probably get going though."

Nan nods, but deep down, I think she's hoping I'll stay here a little while longer. My gut tells me to stay, but when have I ever been one to listen to her?

By the end of the day, I've dragged my pathetic, moping ass home and have settled back into my apartment. My phone buzzes and I pull it from my purse, reading the text.

Cameron: I'm coming over. Been missing you like crazy.

Me: Miss you too. See you soon.

I slip into the shower and allow the warm water to soothe my aching muscles. Good grief, I'm tense.

I change into a pair of cotton shorts and a tank top and apply a fresh dab of makeup, making sure to use a little extra concealer around my eyes to camouflage the dark circles hanging low beneath them.

Cam shows up an hour later, drunk again.

"Harper. Baby."

I take a step back and raise a palm in the air, warning him to not come any closer. But fear has leeched into my veins, seeping into every organ and muscle in my body as my natural instinct to run takes hold. But this is Cameron—my sweet, loving man. He's never made me feel unsafe. He's never physically hurt me.

"Cam. You're scaring me," I caution him.

He closes the space between us, shoving my hand down to my side and cupping my jaw. I squeeze my eyes shut as an eerie feeling crashes over me like a torrential downpour, washing away every ounce of security I've ever felt within his embrace.

"Fuck, Harper. I've been thinking about you so much," he slurs, his words sloppy as he plants wet kisses all over my face.

"I've been thinking about you too." *Liar.*

"Then fuck me, Harper. Show me you still love me."

Still? Since when did I ever make him believe I didn't?

I carefully wrap my fingers around his wrists and pull down, prying his hands from my face. My cheeks are on fire, every muscle in my body is tense, and my heart is beating wildly in my chest. My fight and flight responses are kicking in, but I'm not yet sure which one will triumph.

"Not like this, Cam. Please. Can we talk when you're sober?"

He sweeps a free strand of hair from my face, tracking his finger with his eyes as if he's admiring the way his touch makes me shiver. When his gaze fixates on my mouth, I shift my eyes to my cell phone charging on the counter. But even in his inebriated state, Cam catches the movement and his lip curls in disgust at my betrayal.

Before I have a chance to retreat, the back of his hand cracks against my face and I cry out, my body hitting the floor with a sickening thud. My wrist buckles beneath my weight when I throw my hands out to catch myself, and a searing pain shoots up my arm.

"Cam!" I screech, frantically sweeping my hair from my eyes and peering up at him through blurred vision, my cheek burning as if someone has taken a blowtorch to it.

"I knew I couldn't trust you," he snarls.

Stormy eyes glare down at me and I immediately begin crab walking backward to my living room. His heavy boots hit the floor with several long strides as he closes the space and lunges at me.

"No!" I scream and roll onto my stomach, reaching for the blue porcelain lamp my grandmother gave me when I moved into my apartment and had no money to buy decor. I miss the lamp by an inch, but manage to grab its cord just as Cam's hands lock around my ankles and drag me toward him. The lamp clatters to the floor beside me, and I grip the cord like it's my lifeline.

Kicking and screaming, I tap into the adrenaline coursing through my veins and allow it to take hold, my feet connecting with his chest and jaw several times before he rolls me over, climbs on top of me and straddles me, pinning my wrists above my head. I still have the cord in my fist, but my arms are rendered useless.

"Cam! Get off me!" I scream, bucking my hips wildly in a pathetic attempt at derailing him.

"I know you've been sleeping around, you little slut. And my fucking teammate of all people. You just can't keep your legs closed, can you?"

"What? Cam! No. I don't know what you're—"

His arm rears back, then barrels toward me in a closed-fist punch. My head lulls to the side and I fade in and out of consciousness, disco lights framing my peripherals as my vision blurs with blinding white spots. I feel a trickle of something warm trailing from my nose to my mouth. I lick my lips and copper floods my mouth.

I hear Cam grunting on top of me, a string of profanities spewing from his mouth as he rips and claws at my clothing. Coming to, I tighten my grip on the cord and blink away the stars behind my eyes. When I hear the zipper of Cam's jeans, I scream as loud as my burning lungs will allow.

"No! Help! Someone—" My cries for help are cut short when Cameron seals his hand over my mouth and nose, depriving me of air.

He leans in, his hot breath crawling across my face, a million tiny bugs scattering beneath my flesh. "I've been watching you, Harper. Following you. I know he drove you home from La Castille." The restaurant Stella and I met for drinks at and I bumped into Zak. Shit. "And last night. When you waltzed into that bar alone and came out with him. When you undressed for him. You're a whore. Just like my fucking mother."

He releases my mouth and busted nose and I gasp, my lungs expanding painfully as I suck in as much oxygen as my body will allow.

"Cam. It's not what it looks like. I swear." I force my hips upward until I'm sure my spine is going to snap against the sheer force of it repeatedly hitting the hardwood floor.

But Cameron adjusts himself on top of me, pressing his hips into mine and flattening me to the floor. His grip on my wrists relents just enough for me to break free of his rough embrace, and I take what might be my only opportunity to retaliate, tugging the cord until I feel the cold porcelain base at my fingertips. Wrapping my hand around the narrow neck of the lamp, I raise it high and smash it down over Cameron's head. A rain of porcelain shards fall around me, and I squeeze my eyes shut against the assault.

When I open them, I watch in terror as a trickle of blood trails down his forehead and cheek, slipping down the sharp line of his jaw and plopping onto my face.

"Stupid bitch," he bellows, his rage thickening before my eyes.

"No. Please!"

I drop what's left of the lamp and scream at the top of my lungs, but my voice cracks until all that comes out is panicked wheezing.

Someone has to hear me. *God, please. Someone find me.*

Rough fingers shred the remainder of my shirt and shorts, my flesh searing from the fabric being ripped from my body. He stuffs a balled up piece of cotton into my mouth, muffling my cries. Hot tears slip down my cheeks, pooling on the floor on either side of my head as I plead for mercy with my eyes.

My body grows tired and my thrashing is reduced to mere twitches and tugs against Cameron's hold. But then he pulls a knife out from somewhere behind him, and a renewed sense of fear slams into me.

I shake my head frantically, desperate for Cameron to release me. But Cam's not here. I don't even recognize this hideous monster looming over me. This man is evil and vile, and he's going to fucking kill me. I can feel it in my bones.

Nan. My poor, sweet nan. *God, if you're listening, please protect her. If you can't protect me, please, please protect my grandmother.*

Cam presses the cold metal blade against my throat, tipping my chin higher than naturally comfortable. I suck in a sharp, short breath through my bleeding nose and freeze, fear paralyzing me completely.

"Listen to me, bitch. Here's how this is going to work. I'm going to fuck you. And I'm going to make it hurt. And if you fight it, I'll end your pathetic, useless little life." Dragging the sharp tip of the blade down my throat and over my collarbone, Cam leans forward and snarls in my ear. "And then ... you're all his. Because I don't want your used-up pussy after he's been inside of it. We could have had a beautiful life, Harper. Could have made lots of pretty little babies and been happy. But you just couldn't resist, could you?"

My chest heaves violently despite my best efforts to remain still. Squeezing my eyes shut, I feel the blade glide lower, over the swell of my breast and to the top of my bra. Then it travels inward, carving a path down my sternum. A quick flick of his wrist and my bra pops free on either side of me. Cold air assaults my nipples and they pucker against my will, capturing Cameron's attention.

"I'm going to miss these sweet little tits," he growls, his tone thick with lust and his eyes crazed.

The cold steel drags across my pointed nipples and I release a sob. Cam's wide eyes follow the path as the blade travels further south, down the center of my stomach and circling my belly button twice. Just like I had done with my finger last night while I undressed for Zak. I fight against my body's natural desire to struggle, desperate to remain perfectly still in case he slips up and flays me wide open. But it doesn't matter because a moment later, he angles the blade and cuts into my flesh, dragging it down my side in one slow, agonizing movement. A bloodcurdling scream rips from my throat as white-hot pain shoots through my torso and into my back. I feel the blade exit my body and I fade in and out of consciousness.

Please don't let me die like this.

Warm liquid spills from the wound, trickling over my hip and seeping between my body and the hardwood floor. Before I have a chance to fight it, exhaustion comes for me and everything goes black.

Sixteen

Zak

WHOMP. *WHOMP. WHOMP.*

My fists connect with the leather punching bag at the boxing gym I frequent, my body humming with angst and adrenaline. The owner is a retired SEAL and has offered around-the-clock access to the team to use at no cost. So I'm here at two o'clock in the morning, not a single soul in sight, taking my frustrations out on an inanimate object.

Whomp. Whomp. Whomp.

Despite my stint as a medic, I'm not particularly fond of the guts and gore that come along with my job. I never really have been. But I've been feeling a little twitchy lately, and right now, there's nothing I'd enjoy more than bathing in the blood of the sick fucks who think they have the rights to women's and children's bodies. Since I can't do that, I'm settling for the next best thing.

But this isn't cutting it, and I have a sneaking suspicion the only way I'll ever find true relief is by feeling the crunch of human bones beneath my fist and the spatter of blood on my skin.

My phone chimes from my gym bag, and I slip my gloves off and glare at the screen.

Davis: We need to talk.

"What?" I growl into the phone the second Liam answers my call, then press speaker and set my phone on the bench while I towel the sweat from my body.

"Brooks shot the kid."

I pause. "What are you getting at, brother?"

"Taylor—the girl we pulled out of the container in Colombia. It was Brooks who shot her."

Every muscle in my body galvanizes as I take in what my team-mate's telling me. "How do you know this?"

"The bullet you extracted from her ... I pocketed it and sent it for testing. I had a hunch and followed it. Turns out the striations match his rifle."

"Jesus fucking Christ," I blurt. "You mean to tell me that one of our own shot at a goddamn kid?"

"Or he was shooting at you and missed," he suggests plainly.

I give my head a shake and begin pacing. Releasing a ragged breath, I ask, "The girl ... how's she doing?" I haven't had a chance to go see her since we landed back on American soil, but Liam's been checking in on her often, maintaining some distance but ensuring she's well and safe.

"She's fine. Home and recovering. Her father asked about you though. Think you should pay them a visit."

Swiping my hand through my sweat-soaked hair, I nod in agreement. It was purely coincidence that Taylor's father lives in a small town on the border between California and Nevada, only two hours from my place.

"We need to tell Mac."

"Already did," Liam clips out. "He's called a team meeting first thing in the morning."

"Where's Brooks now?"

"Not sure. Mac decided to not raise any suspicions so he fired off a text telling him we're going wheels up tomorrow. Brooks should be showing up the same time as the rest of us and we'll get our answers then."

"Fuck," I snarl, my fists clenched at my sides and ready to unleash on Brooks's ugly fucking mug. The bastard shot at me and hit a kid instead. What the fuck was he thinking?

"Get some sleep, brother. Looks like it's going to be a rough day."

We end the call and I pack up my bag and lock the door behind me, sliding into the driver's seat of my SUV. My fists connect with the leather of the steering wheel several times, my heart hammering in my chest and adrenaline coursing through my veins like dangerous white water.

Peeling out of the parking lot, I drive like a bat out of hell down the highway. I'll catch a few hours of rack time and then haul ass to headquarters and we'll settle whatever the fuck this is once and for all. Brooks's career is as good as over, and depending on how tomorrow goes, his life potentially as well.

Rolling into my driveway, my headlights sweep over the front of my house and I catch a glimpse of something at my door.

I cut the engine and hop out, a sudden shiver rolling down my spine and settling deep in my lower back. Reaching behind me, I remove my gun from my waistband, disengage the safety, and stalk around the front of my house, my view of the front step obstructed from the tall shrubs around the side of the porch.

When the concrete step finally comes into view, what I see causes flames of fury to lick at my insides with a forked tongue and a block of ice to form inside my chest.

A heap of naked flesh. Long, tattered, blonde hair. And blood. A fucking ton of it.

"Harper." I race toward her and drop to my haunches, taking in her unconscious state, my fingers flying over her body and inspecting her for fatal injuries. There's a lengthy gash from her ribs to her hip. It's not deep enough to have damaged any organs, but it's bleeding badly.

"Zak." It's barely a whisper, but it slams into me like a freight train. My eyes dart to her face as her lids crack open and her head lulls to the side to peer at me. She's not with it.

"Fuck." I carefully lift her naked body into my arms, her limbs and head bobbing limply as I make haste of rounding my vehicle. "I've got you, kitten," I murmur into the top of her head, placing her gently in the passenger seat and gunning it to the nearest hospital.

I dial Joel and let him know that he needs to call in a surgeon for Sweetwater and to call Mac and let him know I won't be there in the morning.

"Harper. Stay with me. We're almost there," I promise, my free hand gently shaking her bare thigh, keeping her awake.

"Zak," she rasps out, her tearstained face slack and painted black and blue. "You found me."

"Of course I found you. I'll always find you. Stay with me."

Skidding to a stop at the front of the emergency entrance, I scoop Harper into my arms and book it through the hospital doors, immediately greeted by a team of nurses and a doctor I know and trust with my own life. I lay Harper down on the bed they've wheeled out and what I see causes every hair on my body to stand on end.

I didn't notice it before because it was dark and I was too distracted making sure she's not injured in any fatal way, but now, beneath the bright, fluorescent lights, I fucking see it. The message is loud and fucking clear.

Scrawled on her naked torso in blood—her fucking blood—is all capitalized letters.

ALL YOURS.

Rage and guilt swirl violently in my stomach as the surgeon's wide eyes dart from Harper to me, his lips parting as he stares at me with a deeply concerned look etched on his face.

Brooks. He fucking did this.

Harper's completely unconscious now, so I'm robbed of the chance to tell her I'll be right here when she wakes up.

Swallowing the deep-seated urge to stay by her side, I watch the professionals cart her away.

"Fuck," I roar, sending my fist through the drywall in the corridor. My outburst earns me some looks. People scurry away from me as I anxiously pace the halls, my boots pounding on the tile floor as I work to get my rage under control.

"Zak," a familiar voice says cautiously. "Take a breath, honey."

I lift my gaze to find Amelia staring at me, empathy softening her features as she rakes her eyes over me. She takes a step forward, setting a hand on my arm. I hiss and glare down at where she's touching me and she jerks away as if I've burned her. She turns and disappears down the hall and behind a set of steel doors.

I storm up and down the hall, refusing to relax until I know Harper's alright. Until her giant, blue orbs are staring mischievously back at me, testing my willpower as she spews smart-ass remarks that should earn her a spanking.

Amelia returns with a cup of coffee to which I impolitely decline. As if hearing my thoughts, she says, "I'll go check in if you want. See what's going on."

Dropping into a seat in the waiting room, I glance up at her and nod. She scurries off again and I sit there anxiously awaiting her return. Never thought I'd want to see her again, but right now ... Fuck.

The emergency doors slide open and more familiar voices fill the empty silence. In filters Liam, then Joel and Stella, Finnegan sleeping peacefully in his stroller and Lainey in Joel's arms.

Stella spots me first, gasping as her hand slams over her chest. Her eyes dart over my bloody clothing, and all the color drains from her face as tears stream from the corners of her hazel eyes.

She rushes over to me and drops to her knees in front of me, gripping my thighs. "Where is she? Where's Harper?"

I seek out Joel's approval. He nods and I rip the Band-Aid off.

"She's in surgery."

Stella's hand flies to her mouth and a violent sob wracks her body. Joel sets Lainey on her feet and drags Stella into his arms, cradling the back of her head as she buries her face in his chest and cries.

I turn my attention to Liam. "Where the fuck is Brooks?"

He shakes his head, his wolf eyes piercing and rage flickering behind his amber irises. "Mac and Sloane are on it."

My fists ball on my thighs, my jaw clenched so tight I think my molars might crack. This is a rage I'm unfamiliar with. This is a rage that's fucking dangerous.

Lainey appears before me in fuzzy, pink pajamas and purple slippers with unicorns on them.

"Uncle Zakky," she says quietly, completely accustomed to seeing the grown men in her life looking like they just rolled out of a war film. My shoulders drop and I stare back at the tiny human before me. "Umm," she hums and haws. "You have something on your face." She reaches up and touches my cheek, her little hand so fucking warm and soft. A contrast to the ice in my veins right now.

I swallow around the boulder in my throat and nod.

"I know, sweetheart."

Fuck, kitten. You better make it out of this alive.

Seventeen

Harper

THERE'S A STEADY BEEP of a machine coming from somewhere nearby and I desperately want it to cease. It's high pitched, incessant, and unforgiving, and with every piercing note that punctures my eardrums, the fuzzy ball in my head stirs.

Peeling my tongue from the gritty desert of the roof of my mouth, I rasp out, "Nan." But it's nothing more than a wheeze.

Beep. Beep. Beep.

I wet my dry, cracked lips and try again. "Nan." This time something comes out, but it's barely a whisper that's quickly wisped away by the quiet, stagnant silence.

When I inhale, I catch a whiff of a familiar scent. Sandalwood and something else. Something comforting. But I can't pry my eyelids open because they feel like cheese graters against my eyeballs. And for as long as they're closed, I can pretend I'm not really alive. I don't want to be alive right now. Paralyzing pain has denied my body's natural instinct to fight back. Everything hurts, every bone and muscle in my body rejecting every breath I take. My face, my back. The space between my legs.

Cameron. The lamp. A knife. Screaming.

I've been watching you, Harper. Following you.

I try to raise my arm, my body wailing in protest as a sharp, stabbing sensation shoots from my ribs and into my spine, settling into the base of my neck.

I'm going to fuck you. And I'm going to make it hurt.

"No, please." The words fall from my lips, but I don't understand why.

The comforting scent grows stronger and something warm and rough touches my forehead, sweeping my hair off my face. Panic continues to build like an undertow, picking up strength and speed as I struggle to clear the hazy fog in my brain and organize my thoughts and memories.

"I've got you, kitten." A voice. It's deep and gravelly.

Zak.

Nausea rolls through me hot and heavy as a blinding light penetrates the thin flesh of my eyelids. There's movement. A rustling sound. Something tugging on the inside of my elbow. Within three beeps of the machine, all the pain fades and darkness takes hold.

Eighteen

Zak

I SCOWL AT THE doctor we've put on Sweetwater's payroll and listen with bated breath as he recounts Harper's injuries.

"She's suffered a pretty nasty concussion, but her scan came back clean, so from what we can see there's no brain damage or major memory loss. The gash down her side wasn't deep enough to cause any permanent damage. We've stitched her up, so she'll be a little uncomfortable, but mostly it's superficial." The doctor pauses, his brows pinching tight as he adjusts his posture. He inhales deeply, then continues on. "It's obvious that she was sexually assaulted." Every vertebrae in my spine clicks into place as I refrain from sending my fist flying through the wall again. I already knew Brooks raped her. I saw the evidence seeping from between her legs when I scooped her off my front step. But that doesn't make it any easier to hear. "There are several internal tears, but no medical intervention was necessary. She'll be sore for a week or so, but overall, she's going to be just fine."

I blow out a held breath as the desire for revenge simmers on low deep inside my chest. Brooks signed his own death warrant the second he laid hands on Harper. And now, I'll be the judge, the jury, and the fucking executioner. I'll decide the price he pays, and I'll be the one to collect on his debt.

There's only one issue. We can't fucking find him.

"The stitches can be removed in ten to fourteen days depending on how she heals. It's my understanding you have a medical background, Mr. Shephard?" I nod once. "Then you know what to look for in regards to infection." I nod again. "Very well, then. You call me directly if you have questions or need anything. I have some paperwork to finish up, and a few other tests to run, but she should be free to go home later today."

I mutter a quick thanks then go in search of my teammates, finding them loitering outside Harper's room.

Sloane's been searching for Brooks for two days straight but has come up empty. We've set surveillance up on his house as well as his parent's property, although I doubt he's stupid enough to return to either of those locations. But we'll leave no stone unturned.

"The doctor's releasing Harper shortly," Mac reminds me, as if I didn't already know. Of course I knew. I've been wandering these halls like a fucking apparition, terrifying the medical staff and barking orders like a caveman. Mac crosses his arms over his burly chest and angles his head. His question hangs in the air between us, the words never spoken, but just as loud as if he'd screamed them.

I drag a hand through my hair. "You already know she's coming home with me."

Joel slides into the conversation. "You might need to fight my wife on that one, Shep."

I glare at the steel door that Harper's been locked behind for two days. I haven't been able to cross that threshold since she came out of surgery and woke briefly in a panic before a nurse sent her back into a morphine-induced slumber. It's not that I don't want to be in there with her. I fucking want to in the most primal way. But I can't, because I'm afraid that if I do, I'll be drawn to her like a moth to a flame, and this time I won't be able to peel myself away before I go up in smoke. I'll be tethered to Harper, anchored down by her irritating beauty and sharp tongue, and that's where I'll stay until the moment I take my last breath.

"Stella can argue with me until she's blue in the face, but you and I both know there's no safer place for Harper than my house. Brooks could come looking for her. Could want to finish the job."

I hope he fucking tries.

Joel's brows shoot sky high as amusement flashes in his eyes. "Finally admitting it, huh?"

My face whips to his. "There's nothing to admit, brother. It's just a fact. She needs protection and you're tied up with two kids and an irate wife. And Liam's on grandma duty. So that leaves me."

Mac chuckles, his head whipping side to side before he slaps a hand down on my shoulder. "Best of luck to you, son. You're going to need it."

Joel, Mac, and Sloane leave a moment later, and I hover around the only barrier between me and the little blonde that I'm sure is going to give me an aneurism. Finally, I grow a pair and slide into the room, shutting the door carefully behind me.

Harper's asleep again. It's completely normal considering what her body has been through. I'm mildly grateful for it, because the second she opens those baby blues of hers, I know I'm going to face a battle with myself all over again. I'll be forced to confront the hurt and betrayal behind her eyes and want to rip my hair from its roots just so I have something to do with my hands other than touch her.

I stuff myself into a chair in the corner of the room, maintaining as much space between myself and her as possible, and wait patiently for her to wake. In the meantime, I swing through a wide array of emotions. Anger, frustration, empathy. But the one that sits heavy in my gut, never relenting, is guilt.

I prop my elbows on my thighs and drop my head in my hands, groaning in frustration at my sudden inability to keep my shit in check. This isn't me. I'm not a man with a short fuse. I don't allow my nerves to get the best of me. But that's just what Harper does to me. And that's exactly why I shouldn't be here. But I can't stay away, either.

Against my will, my eyes drift shut. Fuck, I'm tired.

I must have dozed off, for how long, I'm not sure, because I wake to the sound of sheets rustling and a soft whimper.

I pop an eyelid, remaining perfectly still as I watch Harper carefully swing one leg over the side of the bed, wincing briefly before swinging the other over. She takes several deep breaths and wiggles her toes, her face pinched tight and hands balled into fists and pressing into the mattress. She's in pain, no doubt, and pushing herself when she shouldn't be.

"Going somewhere, kitten?"

She lifts her eyes to mine and her teeth begin chattering audibly. "Where's my grandmother?"

"She's fine. Liam's keeping her company."

Harper's eyes well with tears, her throat bobbing as she swallows. "She ... she didn't see me like this, did she?"

I shake my head and her shoulders relax a fraction. "No, she didn't. But she's not happy about it."

"And Cameron?"

Hearing his name spill from her lips causes hot irritation to scratch beneath my collar. "Sloane's on it."

Releasing a shaky breath, she nods in understanding and shifts uncomfortably on her bottom.

"I need to pee," she rasps, her cheeks deepening to a bright shade of pink.

Scrubbing my hands over my face, I rise from the chair and go to her. She hisses, but doesn't protest when I slip my arm around her waist and hold her upright as we shuffle across the floor toward the bathroom. It'd be a fuck of a lot easier to just carry her, but she needs to move around to keep the blood flowing. We stop at the toilet, and I release her and back away as she stares at me expectantly, her hand wrapped tightly around the handrail at her side.

"I can't go with you in here, Zak."

Groaning, I cross my arms and turn around to face the wall.

"Can you just leave? Please?" she whines.

I know I'm invading her privacy, but fuck her privacy. Her safety is what matters. Can't have her stumbling around and ripping her stitches open.

Finally, she heaves out a dramatic sigh and relieves herself. When I know she's finished, I turn around and return to her, helping her to a standing position and to the sink. I hold her gown closed at the back as she washes her hands. She's been poked, prodded, and stitched up. She's laid in a hospital bed for two full days, unable to bathe properly or function without the support of a nurse or a friend. Amelia even came in and sponge bathed her, cleansing her body of the dried blood from Brooks's little art project.

But for reasons unknown, I feel the need to keep her body covered despite all of that. A last ditch effort at preserving her dignity, I suppose.

Until I spot her engagement ring twinkling back at me, and irritation crawls beneath my skin. Why the fuck hasn't she removed it?

Not my problem.

I help her back to her bed, folding her sheets back until she's laying comfortably, then tug them back up over her body. She avoids eye contact, as do I. Naturally, if we're not bickering, we're not speaking at all. And since I don't think she has the energy to spit those fiery flames she seems to reserve specifically for me, I keep my mouth shut and simply let her do her thing.

The doctor enters the room, his eyes darting from Harper to me then back to her, silently questioning whether I should remain present for this or not. I stiffen, waiting for her response. Harper gnaws on the inside of her cheek, then nods for the doctor to proceed. I understand why he was seeking her approval. It's because he knows the next part is going to be hard for her to hear. Although she's already aware of the extent of Brooks's assault.

It's my turn to feel the sharp stab of a knife to my gut. So I relax into the chair and listen.

"We've completed a rape kit and have submitted it to the police for their records."

And the knife twists.

"You're still within the grace period of taking an emergency contraceptive if you wish to do so. There would be some side effects that aren't terribly pleasant, but—"

Harper cuts him off. "Yes. I'd like a contraceptive, please. I know what the side effects are."

I stare at Harper, waiting for any telltale sign of what she's thinking but right now, she's as blank as the day is long and I can't get a read on her. When she peeks over at me, I loosen my grip on the chair arms and feign indifference.

After a long stretch of awkward silence, Harper's big, blue eyes fill with water and her bottom lip wobbles as suppressed emotions rise to the surface. She's going to cry, and I don't know how the hell to deal with it. She's staring at me, waiting for me to come to her, to hold her and tell her whatever it is she needs to hear right now, but I'm not going to do that. If it were any other woman, I'd be by their side in a heartbeat. But not with Harper. Never with Harper. Because if I go to her, if I feel her in my arms, I'll never want to let her go. And that just can't happen. I won't be just another man she catches in her web, chews up, and spits out.

So, I sit stalk still and wait for the doctor to clue in. He does eventually, sliding in beside Harper and holding her while she sobs into his lab coat, her fists balling the starchy fabric in a death grip.

Her sobs eventually fade to sniffles and hiccups, and I just sit there like a selfish prick, watching her thank the good doctor for his kindness.

When the hug that lasts a million years finally ends, I'm about ready to grab the doctor by the collar and introduce his face to my fist.

He clears his throat and stands, backing away from Harper.

Smart move, doc.

"I'll send a nurse in with the medication shortly. Then you're free to go home. You call me directly if you have questions or need anything."

Nineteen

Harper

I SLUG DOWN THE emergency contraceptive in front of Zak, watching his jaw slide as the water slips down my throat, dousing the fiery ball in the pit of my gut.

"You look like shit, Zak. You should go home."

Irritation flickers in his eyes as he stands and stalks toward the bed, gripping the handrail on either side of my body as he leans in close. I snap my mouth shut, my self-consciousness rearing its ugly head. I'm positive my breath could knock out an entire army. Or at the very least, the brooding mercenary hovering dangerously close to my face right now.

I narrow my eyes at him and do the only thing I know how to do when it comes to Zak. I say something snarky to piss him off. "Unless you'd like to have your eyeballs clawed to shreds, I suggest you back the fuck off." I tuck a stray strand of greasy hair behind my ear and force myself to maintain eye contact as his masculine scent overwhelms my system, kicking my body back into high gear.

His warm breath fans over my neck as he brings his lips to my ear and whispers, "You're coming home with me, Harper. So get used to me hovering over you like this. Because until your fiancé's bloodied corpse is laying at my feet, you're under my protection."

The beep of the machine at my side reaches a new tempo as my heart takes off into a gallop. I shift uncomfortably beneath the sheets, Zak's raw intensity grinding my resolve into a pulp.

He backs away just in time to see the heat creeping into my face.

Wry laughter erupts from my chest, then quickly fades to a pained groan because *Jesus fuck that hurts*. "Absolutely not," I tell him, but the look I get in return ... Shit. "You're nuttier than a squirrel's nest if you think I'm going home with you."

Zak's brows shoot to his hairline. "A squirrel's nest? Really?"

I close my eyes, summoning the strength to not locate the nearest heavy object and hurl it at Zak's head. "Never mind," I grit out. "Not the point. The point is that it's not happening. Unless you want to wake in the middle of the night to your fingernails being removed with pliers and your eyebrows singed off ..."

But my threats lead me nowhere, and before I know it, Zak's wheeling his SUV around to the front entrance of the hospital and hoisting me into it like I weigh nothing at all. He tucks my little white paper bag filled with pills behind my seat, then slides into the driver's side and navigates us out of the hospital parking lot. I try to beat my heart into submission, but it's too busy attempting it's grand escape to pay any mind to my brain's instructions. And my lungs have completely checked out, obviously high as kites from sucking in too many of Zak's pheromones, which are becoming increasingly difficult to avoid when I'm confined to such a small space with the asshole himself.

Forcing myself to relax and not think about how his tattooed knuckles are about ready to burst from gripping the wheel so tight, I lay my head back and close my eyes, allowing the deep hum of the engine to lull me to sleep. Some time later, I wake in an unfamiliar room, on an unfamiliar bed, with an unfortunately *very* familiar presence surrounding me.

As if he hears my eyelids open, Zak appears at my side, his brows pinched tight as he stares down at me with a tormented expression on his face.

"You shouldn't stare. It's rude," I rasp out, pressing my knuckles into the bed and dragging myself into a sitting position.

Mother fucking Theresa it hurts.

My body is so slick with sweat that I feel like a freshly peeled avocado. And every inch of my skin hurts. Even the roots of my teeth ache. The morphine is wearing off and I'm beginning to realize the extent of Cameron's assault in a more vivid state of mind.

"You've been bedridden for nearly three days. It's normal to feel this way," Zak tells me as if he's inside my brain. "We'll keep you moving and you'll loosen back up over the next day or so."

I release a frustrated groan, irritated at the thought of being imprisoned in Zak's house for the foreseeable future.

But when I glance over at the nightstand and spot a bowl of steaming soup and a grilled cheese sandwich, I can't help the smile that creeps across my face. The bed dips with Zak's weight as he takes a seat beside me and sets a tray over my lap. He places the food on top and hands me a spoon.

"You need to eat," he tells me.

"Zak, the big, bad dog, made me soup and a sandwich. How domestic," I say teasingly.

"I did. But sadly," he sighs, "I'm all out of arsenic." Then he smiles. I hate when he does that. It's … unsettling.

His smile fades as he stares back at me. There's this strange magnetic pull between us that never really relents. It's always there, sometimes stronger than others, and right now, it's sucking me in. An unrelenting force. Like gravity—always present, always grounding me.

But then he stands and that magnetic pull releases like a rubber band giving way, and I'm left floating off into outer space until it recharges and drags me back down to earth. Zak turns to leave, but I reach up and grab his wrist. His eyes move to where our bodies connect, and I know he feels it too.

But then his gaze darts to my engagement ring and his coffee eyes darken to obsidian. He gently peels my fingers from his wrist with his free hand.

"Eat your food, Harper."

Then he storms out, slamming the door behind him.

"Zak didn't really give me much of a say in the matter, Stell."

"Oh, puhleasseee," she draws the two syllables out. "You had a choice, Harper. You always have a choice."

She's right. I had a choice. But I didn't have the energy to fight him on it. Instead of admitting it, I steer her in another direction. "I didn't want to be a burden to you guys with Lainey and Finn. Besides, you're insanely crazy after you give birth. All those post-partum hormones have you in a chokehold."

There's a sharp intake of breath before she rushes out, *"I am not insanely crazy!"*

"You're right. Only a little crazy. You're a busy mom, Stell. And that's totally fine. But I'd be left laying there like a vegetable, stinking up your guest room like a rotting potato."

She sighs dramatically. "You're right. You do smell oddly like a rotting potato. And I have a bionic nose. So it's probably best that you smell up Zak's house instead. Besides, I hear Zak Shephard quite likes the stench of rotting vegetables."

I smile, then hiss because holy raging balls of fury my face *hurts*!

"First of all, potatoes aren't technically vegetables—they're roots. Second of all, Zak ... He ..." What is he? My friend? Fuck no. That's not it. My protector? "He's just ..." There are no words for what Zak is.

"He's taking care of you, Harper. In case you aren't already aware of this, that's kind of what these guys do. They take care of their women."

I snort, then whimper. *Ouch.*

"Their women," I deadpan. "Sure. Except I'm fairly certain the idea of being in the same time zone as me has Zak fantasizing of someday standing over my casket, tossing a clump of dirt on top, then sauntering off whistling a happy tune while he goes in search of the next bimbo that bats her lashes at him."

"First of all, Zak doesn't sleep with every bimbo that bats her lashes at him."

"You're right. Only every second one," I volley.

"Second of all, the only funeral Zak's interested in attending is Cameron's. If he's even fortunate enough to get one."

Annnnd there it is. The big bucket of ice water waiting to douse the only pleasant conversation I've had in days has finally tipped over, washing away the remnants of my dwindling happiness. My mood sours once again and regret takes the wheel as I go barreling back toward reality.

Zak's going to kill Cameron. I'm not sad about it. He raped and beat me to a pulp, so technically he started it. If there's one thing I know for certain, it's that my fiancé is a dead man walking. Every breath he takes is a gift from the universe.

Knock. Knock.

Zak looms in the bedroom doorway, his giant frame eclipsing the hall light as his eyes remain glued to mine.

"Mind if I get a few minutes with the patient?" he asks Stella.

Stella narrows her gaze, but only briefly before leaving the room with a promise to return whenever Zak's done doing whatever it is he needs to do.

The man is an energy vampire, and right now, he's sucking everything out of me and this room with his broodiness. I'm not sure what his problem is, but he looks like he's about ready to flip this entire bedroom upside down.

His gaze slides to the diamond ring on my left hand that I haven't been able to bring myself to remove yet. I've been counting the times he's done that and we're at precisely seven since he first saw me in the hospital bed. Every time he glances at it, there's a strange fizzing sensation in my chest, like when you drop a Mentos into a Coke. I know it's ridiculous that I'm still wearing it. But removing it feels ... Well, I'm not entirely sure yet.

"I need to change your bandage," he tells me.

I roll my eyes. "That can wait."

"No, Harper. It can't."

"Stella can—"

Zak raises his voice, his tone demanding and sharp. "Fuck, Harper. For once, just stop talking."

"I'm not sure what crawled up your ass and died, but if you're going to be a dick, I'll gladly relocate to Stella and Joel's."

He ignores my statement and comes around to the side of the bed, his hands flexing as he stares down at the blankets covering my body. He's seen me naked and bloody. He's been in the room while I peed, pinched the back of my hospital gown to keep my bare ass covered. So why the hesitation to lift a damn blanket and take a peek at my injury?

"Gonna need you to lift your shirt, kitten," he instructs gently.

"And I'm going to need you to choose one of your fifteen personalities and stick with it for more than five minutes," I retort dryly.

When he doesn't respond, I simply roll my eyes and do as I'm told, despite my desire to irritate him further. His eyes don't wander away from the task at hand. In fact, he makes a conscious point of keeping all of me covered except for the space he needs to peel back my bandage and inspect my stitches.

"They look good," he tells me. "No infection. How do you feel?"

"I feel fine. Just sore and tired."

The back of his hand presses to my forehead to check my temperature. The contact sends a shiver rolling down my spine and my arms erupt in goosebumps. Luckily, the sleep shirt Stella helped me into earlier has long sleeves and hides any evidence of my body's reaction to his touch.

"No fever," he murmurs, then slips into the ensuite, returning a minute later with a fancy first aid kit. When he opens it, I eye the surgical utensils suspiciously.

"Why do you have that?" I ask curiously as he proceeds to rummage through the kit until he finds what he's looking for.

"I was a medic in the Navy for a while," he responds gingerly, as if it's not at all impressive. It totally is. Medics see some of the worst shit. The blood and guts and gore. *The death*. "Just a habit to keep this kind of stuff around the house. But it's come in handy more than a handful of times." He peeks up at me again, his coffee eyes dark but soft and inviting.

"I didn't know you were a medic."

"Most people don't. It was short lived. The government wanted me doing something else. Didn't have much of a say in the matter."

There's a tenderness to him as he gets to work, and it's completely unnerving. I much prefer when he's being an asshole so I can hate him. But this part of Zak—the calm, collected man whose large fingers are working skillfully, caring for my wound like I'm someone important ...

"What did they want you to do?"

Zak peeks up at me through dark lashes, then returns his attention to changing out my bandage. Every brush of his fingers, every skim of his big, rough hand is gentler than I thought possible from a man of his size and profession.

"They recruited me for Delta Force," he responds humbly.

"Isn't that like ... capturing terrorists and stuff?"

"Some of it. I was on a team more geared toward covert operations with the CIA."

The CIA. Woah. Big stuff. "I thought you, Joel, and Liam all met in the Navy and retired as SEALs?"

He nods thoughtfully. "We met as SEALs. Did missions together for a few years. Kept in touch after we all went separate directions and looped back around to join Sweetwater when our contracts were up."

"Your parents must be proud."

"My mom is. Dad … not so much." There's a hint of remorse in his tone now, as if speaking of his father is something he doesn't often do.

"Does he not know what you guys do? That you risk your lives to save others?" I feel defensive on Zak's behalf for some unknown reason, like I want to put in a call to his father and give him a piece of my mind.

"He knows."

Curiosity clouds my better judgement and before I know it, I'm pressing on for more information.

"How could he not be proud of the man you are?" That came out wrong. It sounds entirely too much like I think Zak's a good guy. Sure, he saves lives and all that crap, but he also takes them without remorse. "I mean—"

He chuckles softly to himself. "It's fine, kitten. You don't need to backpedal."

My breath hitches when something cold touches my side. Glancing down, I watch as Zak dabs an alcohol-soaked cotton ball around the long, jagged gash that runs lengthwise down the side of my rib cage.

"I had an older brother who joined the Navy before me," he tells me, catching me off guard. "Being a soldier was in his blood, the same as it's in mine. We both looked up to our old man. Both wanted to walk in his footsteps and someday retire as veterans who can say they made a difference in the world." Something in my chest cracks as I listen to Zak's story. I didn't know any of this about him because he never really talks about himself—a quality I suppose I've overlooked. "Brandon was gunned down in Afghanistan two years after he signed his life away. I was seventeen when I came home from school and found my mom on the kitchen floor, huddled up against the cupboards, crying and clutching his tag and shirt." I swallow the lump in my throat and hold my breath to stop the tears from falling. I don't have siblings and both of my parents are gone, but I have Stella and Nan. The thought of losing them so tragically ...

"So when you decided to join the Navy, your dad didn't like it," I guess, hitting the nail on the head.

Zak nods solemnly. If I thought he looked exhausted before, I was dead wrong. Because now he looks utterly drained.

"What does your mom do?"

"She's an OR nurse." He shakes his head and I swear I see his lip twitch in amusement. "Refuses to retire. She says she likes helping people, but I think she just continues to work so she doesn't have to listen to my dad yelling at the television during football season."

My lips curl into a smile despite how much my face hurts. Does Zak like football? Is he a sports fan? I can totally picture him slugging back beer and devouring a heaping plateful of chicken wings.

"All done," he says, then closes up the kit and stares at me. "You're going to need a shower soon."

Disappointment takes hold as he ends the conversation there. A thousand burning questions sear the back of my brain, but I don't think he has the energy to answer them. And the thought of hot water and soap ... Hell yes. I haven't bathed properly in ... Christ ... I must smell like roadkill.

"Tomorrow," he adds with finality, then leaves the room after helping me get comfortable again.

Stella returns a moment later, taking her seat beside me and rambling on about how fat her ass got during her pregnancy with Finn. But I don't hear any of it because now my mind is wandering aimlessly, searching for answers I hadn't known I desired.

Twenty

Harper

I STUMBLE TO THE sink and wash my hands, eyeing Zak in the mirror as he turns away from the wall and faces me. He was right when he told me I'd loosen up in a day or two. If it weren't for my bruised and swollen face, the general ache throughout my entire body, and the sharp pain when I raise my arms higher than my shoulders, I'd actually feel pretty normal.

"You know I can make it to the bathroom and back by myself, right?"

Zak's scowl intensifies as he stares at my reflection in the mirror. He's in a strange mood again today, and I'm not sure if it's because I'm an inconvenience to have around, or if it's something else. After our little chat yesterday where he gave me a glimpse into what his life has been like, he's pretty much been MIA except for when I need his help, distracted by the constant barrage of mercenaries filtering in and out of the house as they search high and low for Cameron.

Shutting the tap off, I dry my hands on a towel and shuffle back to bed, Zak crowding me from behind in case I fall. I crawl carefully beneath the covers and wait for him to say something. Anything. The intense silence is killing me. But he gives me the same amount of relief as a wire sponge would being rubbed repeatedly over bare skin and says nothing at all. He drops into the chair in the corner of the room and frowns.

When I get tired of the silence, I ask blatantly, "What's your problem, Zak?"

He finally opens his gob and speaks. "Stella came by again. Dropped something off for you from your grandma. Said she wanted you to have it." He reaches into his pocket and pulls out a stone, then tosses it onto the mattress beside me. I pick up the turquoise crystal and rub it between my fingers, its smooth surface warm from Zak's body heat. "And this." He slips an envelope off the dresser that I hadn't noticed was sitting there and lays it beside me.

I open the envelope and unfold a small piece of paper, recognizing the floral border from the little notepad Nan keeps on her kitchen table to scribble reminders and grocery lists on.

Hi Deary,

This stone is a very special stone. It's meant to bring you luck, help you heal old wounds, and provide you with protection. I know you're struggling, Harper. I can feel it in my heart that there's something more going on deep down inside of you than what has happened with Cameron. And although I can't say for certain what it is, I can say for certain that you are not a lost cause. You are not hopeless. You are not weak. You are beautiful and strong and resilient, and when you forget who you are, this stone will serve as a reminder and give you the strength you need to forge on through whatever fire you're facing. I believe in you, deary. You must believe in yourself too.

I love you, Harper.

Be seeing you soon.

Nan

Hot tears prick at the edges of my eyes. Nan has always known when I'm fighting an internal battle. But this, right now ... The floodgates open and here come the waterworks. I'm not a pretty crier. I'm an ugly, snotty, gross crier who makes weird noises and gets all drooly and sweaty. So naturally, I avoid doing it completely. Ever. But right now, I'm a sopping mess. So I can understand why Zak just sits there and watches me while I drown in a pool of salty sadness.

When I'm done bawling, I swipe my tears and snot away with the sleeve of my nightshirt and glance over at Zak. His hands are gripping the arms of the chair so tight that his knuckles have bleached white.

"Sorry," I sniffle. "I know me being laid up in your guest room is a major cockblock for you. I'm sure you're already regretting dragging me here."

The outsides of his eyes round briefly as a flicker of something resembling guilt enters his expression. If I had blinked, I'd have missed it. Part of me wishes I had.

"You have no idea what I'm thinking, Harper," he says lowly. His unexpected statement surprises me, because I'm fairly certain I know exactly what he's thinking. "No, you don't."

"I'm sorry." I shake my head. "Am I speaking my thoughts out loud or something? Or are you just reading my mind?"

"I don't need to read your mind, kitten. Your eyes tell me everything I need to know. Like right now, you're considering whether you should stay with Stella and Joel instead." I scowl at him. "And now you're plotting my death."

"Wow. You really *can* tell what I'm thinking."

His lip twitches in amusement. And now I'm thinking about how to get rid of his body. A wood chipper, perhaps. Or maybe a gas leak causes a tragic explosion.

I decide on the wood chipper.

"Think you can handle a shower?" he asks, interrupting my murderous thoughts.

"God, yes."

"With my help," he adds with the quirk of a brow.

"Oh for crying out loud." I pound my fists on the bed. "I'm perfectly capable, you know."

Zak's eyes narrow to slits. "Then get out of bed and undress for me."

"Excuse me?"

"You heard me. Show me you can undress yourself, and I'll let you shower without help."

"Fine," I snip. "But like hell am I going to let you watch."

"I've seen your body, kitten. Scraped you up off my front step, completely naked." He stands and crosses the room, every step closer causing a shock wave of anxiety to jolt through me. "Saw you bleeding out, your fiancé's cum dripping down your thighs." He looms over me like an apparition. "I saw everything, Harper. And you're worried about this? About me catching a glimpse of something when you and I both know you're not going to be able to lift your own shirt over your head and stand upright long enough to bathe properly?"

It hurts a little, hearing the state in which Zak found me. The state in which my fiancé dumped me. Actually, it makes me fucking furious, but my anger is misplaced, and as much as I want to take it out on Zak, it would be pointless. This isn't his fault, as much as I enjoy pretending it is.

"You don't need to remind me, you know."

He angles his head at me in question. "Don't I? Because I'm fairly certain you don't remember a fucking thing from that night."

My shoulders sag and I feel myself slipping beneath the surface, being sucked back into that night. I've done a damn good job of forging on, of being strong. But right now, with Zak telling me these things and staring at me like I'm some pathetic, weak woman ... it feels like I'm right back in my apartment, falling in and out of consciousness while Cameron fucks me raw and calls me every name in the book while I lay helpless and bloody beneath him.

"You're right," I agree bitterly. "I don't remember *a thing*. I remember *everything*."

Zak's jaw slides, his sharp edges curling in on themselves. He sweeps a hand through his hair. "Let's go," he says, skipping right past my admission. "Show me you can undress, and I'll leave you be."

Throwing invisible daggers at him for his sudden mood shift, I set my stone and note on the bedside table and climb out of bed, shuffling back toward the bathroom that I just came from moments ago. Zak flips on the light and turns the shower on, checking the temperature before returning his attention to me. I catch a glimpse of myself in the mirror and cringe. I've seen myself more than a few times already, but it doesn't get any easier.

My long hair once tied up in a messy bun no longer requires an elastic to stay put. My face is littered with bruises and cuts, mostly around my jaw, one large gash in particular slashing through both of my lips on one side of my mouth. The rest of my body is bruised as well, but it's all manageable with the cocktail of painkillers I've been prescribed. I suppose in the grand scheme of this shitstorm, I'm lucky I'm not in worse condition.

Swallowing the lump in my throat, I rasp out, "Can you at least turn around?"

Reluctantly, he does, but I catch him peeking in the reflection of the glass shower door.

"This is a new level of humiliating, you know."

A frustrated groan comes from Zak's side of the bathroom. I decide there's no sense in dragging this out. Gripping the hem of my nightshirt, I lift it up to my breasts before a sharp pain radiates throughout my rib cage and into my back. I let out a soft whimper and drop my shirt back down, trying again and failing.

"You naked yet, kitten?" Zak asks, his tone all-knowing and arrogant.

"No," I state miserably.

He turns around and a smug grin splits across his stupid, handsome face.

"I've been stabbed and shot more times than I can count, Harper. It's okay to need a little help."

"Thank you for putting the visual of you laying helpless in a bed in my brain. I'll cherish it forever."

He chuckles, then closes the space between us and stares down at me. It's obvious he's enjoying this. But then his expression sobers and he seems to come to some sort of realization.

"I promise I won't touch you anywhere unnecessary. I'll help you when needed, but you have my word that I won't make this any more uncomfortable for you than it already is."

I roll my eyes and scoff.

"Harper," he says with warning. Rough fingers pinch my chin and lift my face as his eyes meet mine. "You're pretending to be tough when you don't need to be. It's okay to be vulnerable sometimes. But you need to trust me. Got it?"

Sucking my busted bottom lip between my teeth, I nod in understanding. I also know I have nobody else to help me right now, so this is it for me.

Thanks, universe, for being a total asshole.

"Good girl," he says, then steps to the side and drops his hands to the hem of my shirt. "Tuck your chin to your chest and lift your arms straight out in front of you, but only as high as is comfortable."

I do as he instructs and my nightshirt is lifted up my body and swiftly pulled over my head and arms. My hands instinctively fly to my chest and I cover my bare breasts while I stand awkwardly in the middle of Zak's bathroom wearing nothing but a pair of cotton undies, a waterproof bandage sealed around my stitches, and a look of shame all over my battered face.

I avert my eyes from Zak's, but I can feel his gaze on my face—not my body—and for that, I'm grateful.

He leads me to the shower and swings the door open, cupping my elbow as I step beneath the spray. Then he retreats and begins undressing.

"Woah. Hold on, cowboy. What are you doing?" I ask, panic suddenly rising like a riptide.

He doesn't answer. Just continues tearing his shirt off, exposing a whole chaotic canvas of colorful tattoos, all of which are skillfully done. Whoever his artist is has made a killing off him.

And the muscles. Christ on a salted cracker. I've seen Zak shirtless before, working out or swimming at Joel and Stella's, but never like this. Never up close. And certainly never while practically naked in his shower. Next to go are his jeans, and before I know it, he's standing in nothing but a pair of black boxers barely concealing a bulge that makes me feel supremely sorry for the women he's railed.

Those poor vaginas never stood a chance.

He slips in behind me and having him this close, with his chest brushing up against my back and the hot water streaming over our bodies, feels some fucked-up shade of comfortable.

Closing my eyes but never removing my arms from my chest, I spin around and tip my head beneath the spray. I can hear Zak shuffling around me, then he's at my back again, squirting something out of a bottle and into his hand.

Strong fingers find my scalp and oh, dear heavenly father, it feels *good*.

The scent of sandalwood wraps around me like a cozy blanket, filling my nose and lungs as Zak washes my hair with his shampoo and nearly brings me to spontaneous orgasm through an unsolicited scalp massage.

"Anyone ever tell you that you should moonlight as a hair washer at a salon? Women would go nuts." Not that they don't already.

His chest rumbles with laughter, and the vibration travels all the way down my spine and straight to my clit. It's oddly relieving to know that Cameron's assault hasn't stripped me of my ability to feel. But it's highly unnerving to know it's Zak Shephard who's making my body come to life.

Clenching my thighs, I ward off the dull ache settling in my core. Nothing can happen between us.

Zak instructs me to tip my head back again as he rinses my hair. Then he lathers up a cloth with soap and begins massaging my shoulders and back. Normally, I wouldn't let a man care for me like this, but I'm out of options and I happen to be enjoying the way his strong hands knead at my aching muscles.

I angle my head and pop an eyelid, peeking at Zak over my shoulder. His brows are pinched tight, his mouth is in a firm line, and he looks like he's about to blow a gasket.

"You don't need to do this. I can wash my body," I inform him.

He scowls at me, then steps closer and slides the cloth around the side of my torso that isn't bandaged, working gentle, calculated circles over my ribs and hip. He moves lower, kneading my trembling thighs. Then he kneels in front of me, lifts my foot, and washes it too. My hands instinctively fly to his shoulders for balance, and I realize the mistake I've made when he glances up at me, his eyes swiftly darting to my bare breasts.

His mouth parts and he blows out a puff of air before dragging his gaze back up to mine.

I must have a mortified look on my face because he says, "It's fine, kitten. Remember?"

I cup my breasts as a monsoon of embarrassment swallows me whole.

When he finishes washing every nonsexual inch of my body, although I'm not going to lie, it felt phenomenal when he touched my feet—new kink unlocked—he rises to his feet and stands behind me again, reaching around and offering me the cloth.

He clears his throat, and I know exactly what he's implying. I need to wash my lady bits.

God, why me? Can't you just smite me instead? Maybe send a swarm of angry wasps my direction? A flesh-eating disease, perhaps? Anything but this.

Unfortunately, God takes no mercy on me.

Zak's hands find my hips, steadying me on my shaky legs. I slide the cloth beneath the soaked fabric of my panties and wash myself, shame taking root so deep inside of me that I'm certain it's going to become a fiber of my very being.

But I can't ignore the way Zak's fingers dig into my flesh. Or the way his breathing has grown ragged. Or the way his big, hard body is now flush with mine, and I'm positive I can feel his cock pressing against my backside.

"He's an idiot, Harper," he murmurs into the back of my head, causing me pause. "They're all fucking idiots."

All? Who the hell is all? I stomp down the heat rising in my core and click my mouth shut, not wanting to provoke any sort of reaction from him. Not here. Not now. Not ever.

When I'm finished cleansing myself, Zak takes the cloth from me, discards it, and helps me out of the shower. He bundles me up in an oversized towel that feels like a plush cloud against my heated skin, then slips a towel around his waist before tossing his wet boxers into a laundry basket along with my nightshirt.

I make my way back to the bed, feeling an awful lot like I'm doing some PG version of a walk of shame, and slide beneath the cool sheets.

Zak slips out of the bathroom and halts, his eyes nearing black as tiny droplets of water cling to his rippling body. My tongue darts out, wetting my too-dry lips as we stare unblinking at each other.

Then in a flash, he's gone, slamming the door on his way out.

I wake sometime later to find a stack of men's crisp, clean dress shirts folded neatly on the bedside table, a small scrap of paper laying on top. I pluck the note off the pile and read it.

Button-down shirts so you can dress and undress yourself.

Twenty-One

Zak

I RESUME MY NEW favorite form of exercise—pacing—while the rest of the team stands around my living room, staring at me like I've grown a second head. It's been four long, miserable days since Harper came home from the hospital. And three fucking days since Sloane first located Brooks in Panama. But he's gone MIA again, and I'm itching to get my hands on him like a junkie itches for their next hit.

"So, Shep," Sloane says, popping her gum between her teeth. "How's your girl doing? Healing up nicely?"

I swipe a hand through my hair and pin her with a glare. "Not my girl," I snarl.

She flashes me a blinding smile, her unusually long incisor teeth glinting at me. "Jeez. Who shit in your cereal this morning?"

I release a miserable groan and continue wearing a hole in the floor.

"We need to let Osmanov know," Mac tells me, as if I didn't already know that's what he was about to say.

I skid to a stop and face my boss.

"No," I refuse bluntly, my fists now balled so tight that my arms are aching with the need to put a hole in something. Gone are the days where I was the cool, collected one on the team.

"He's an ally right now, and not telling him would be compromising the partnership."

"Because the Federov Bratva are so fucking honest," I retort sarcastically.

Mac drops his hands to his hips and shoots me an apologetic look. "Unless you have another suggestion, son, our hands are tied. We need Osmanov on our side. As much as I want Brooks back in our custody, he's not worth the lives of the civilians we risk losing if we don't have the Bratva behind us."

"Fuck," I snap out, then begin pacing again. "Brooks has classified information on all of us and Osmanov. You realize the Russian's going to go hunt him down himself, right? And you said so yourself... once he gets his hands on someone, we'll never get them back."

"Don't see any other options here, Shephard."

The room falls into deafening silence until all I can hear is Sloane's incessant gum chewing. Someone clears their throat, and we all glance over at the hallway to find Harper's grandmother hovering in the doorway, her vivid blue eyes trained on me. Liam brought the old lady over for a visit while we sort out a plan for Brooks.

Nobody says a word as I stare back at the old widow. She approaches cautiously, then reaches up and pats my cheek with a wrinkly hand. She's a sweet lady, albeit a little on the insane side, but so far her and I get along just fine. Aside from her mental instability, she reminds me a little of my own grandmother when she was alive. Dalia Shephard was a spitfire in her day. Tough, ambitious, and full of piss and vinegar. Mrs. Hilton is the same. I suppose that's where Harper gets it.

"Don't you worry your little heart, soldier. Your opportunity will come. I can feel it in my bones."

She smiles softly, then turns and waddles off down the hall, disappearing into Harper's room again. It was a strange encounter. Completely random. But for some reason, her words provide me with a sliver of relief. She's always spitting strange, delirious shit. She claims she's all-knowing, speaking of various colors she sees surrounding us and feelings she has. Some version of a psychic, which only solidifies her insanity. But that doesn't stop me from clinging to the hope that she's right.

After another hour of tossing ideas around, we collectively come up empty-handed. There's no fucking way around it. We need to inform Osmanov to avoid the risk of losing his alliance.

Mac makes the call as I stand idly by and listen. Osmanov does a whole lot of grunting and groaning, then thanks Mac for his transparency and hangs up. I know what that means: we'll never see Brooks again. And I'll never get to taste the sweet zest of the revenge I so desperately seek.

⬤

Another long, endless day passes. Made even more unbearable when Harper finds me in my home gym, avoiding her like the fucking plague and bench-pressing to work out my frustrations. I side-eye her standing in the doorway. She looks fucking miserable, but healthy and strong. Her body has done a damn good job of repairing itself.

And she's wearing one of my dress shirts, the top two buttons popped open exposing too much of her smooth, tanned flesh, the hem falling mid-thigh of her long, lean legs.

Fuck my life.

I drop the bar on the rack and sit up as she anxiously approaches. "Need something, Harper?" I ask, my tone thick with irritation. I snatch my water bottle off the floor and take a long pull. My body is slick with sweat, but only a fraction of my energy has been depleted.

Harper's eyes flare as she takes a step toward me, her gaze flicking over my bare chest and stomach, down to the crotch of my sweat-pants, then back up. She circles around behind me and stops. I can smell her now. Doesn't she have any other perfume she could wear? Perhaps something that reeks of dirty feet so I don't get a raging hard-on every time I fucking breathe?

Slugging back another gulp of water, I drop my elbows to my knees and stare at the floor in front of me, waiting for Harper to leave so I can finally have some fucking peace again.

Warm hands meet my bare shoulders and every muscle in my back tenses.

Glancing over my shoulder at her as her fingers knead at the ropy tissue, I tell her, "You shouldn't be here." I mean it in more ways than one. She shouldn't be in this room with me. She shouldn't be in this house with me. She shouldn't be anywhere fucking near me right now. Because I'm on edge and not feeling entirely in control of my actions.

She releases a soft sigh and continues to work away the tension in my back and arms. It feels fucking incredible, and I'm finding myself in a bit of a predicament. Because now all my blood has rushed to my dick and it's straining painfully against the inside of my boxers.

"Why so tense?" she asks sweetly, her thumbs working perfectly calculated circles down the muscles lining either side of my spine. Her tone is candy-coated, but if you peel back that sugary layer, you'll find her words laced with ill intentions.

"I'm always tense when you're around, kitten." I can practically feel her smiling in pride at that. It's her goal in life, I think. To drive me mental.

Snatching her wrist in my hand, I drag her around in front of me and grip the backs of her thighs, pulling her to stand between my knees. Her palms lay flat on my shoulders and she stares down at me with a puzzled look on her face.

"If you keep touching me like that ..." My threat trails off.

She leans down, my dress shirt gaping and giving me a generous view of her cleavage, her tits bundled up in a pale pink lace bra. Wisps of her shiny, blonde hair brush my jawline as she whispers in my ear, "You'll *what*, Zak?"

Giving her ass a firm squeeze, I tug her onto my lap, twisting us until I'm laying flat on my back and she's straddling my hips, her feet planted on the floor on either side of the bench. She makes a weak attempt at climbing off, wincing when she twists the wrong way and her stitches remind her that she's still injured.

But I'm not in the mood for her games. She knows exactly what I want because she can feel it pressing into the crack of her ass this very second. But I won't take it, because that would mean admitting something to her that I'm not ready for. And her body is still recovering from another man's assault. But since she's feeling bold enough to taunt me the way she is, even after everything she's been through, I don't see the need to tiptoe around her feelings.

"Zak." She says my name like a warning.

"Harper." I return hers just the same.

She narrows her eyes on me and rolls her hips. It's unintentional, but it causes my balls to draw upward. I lace my fingers through hers, holding our hands palm to palm and tugging her forward so her chest is flush with mine. Her hair spills around us, drawing a curtain as we breathe each other's air. There's a brief moment where our gazes lock and her eyes round at the corners as if she's just realizing something.

"You make me sick to my stomach," she says lowly, her lips barely brushing mine and causing static electricity to crackle through my bloodstream.

"We both know that's not true." I thrust my hips upward and grind my dick into her ass, allowing myself a fraction of the friction I'm craving.

Her mouth falls open, but her shocked expression vanishes in a *poof*, replaced by a veneer of confidence and control. The shift happens as quick as the flip of a switch.

She angles her head and tosses her hair over one shoulder and brings her mouth to my neck, dragging her plump bottom lip up the side of my throat and to the shell of my ear. "You're lucky I'm not vomiting all over you right now."

A low rumble vibrates from my chest and I feel her pert nipples harden against my bare skin through the thin fabric of her bra and my shirt. Goosebumps scatter across her arms, all the tiny hairs on her body standing on end.

Releasing one of her hands, I allow my fingers to drift slowly down her body to the hiked-up hem of my shirt. She sucks in a sharp breath and her eyes flicker with fear. I pause, searching her face for any further hesitation.

"I won't hurt you," I remind her.

When she exhales softly and relaxes back into me, I reach beneath my dress shirt and slide her panties to the side, tracing the seam of her smooth pussy with my middle finger. She whimpers softly when I circle her clit.

"You're soaked, Harper. So don't tell me I make you sick when your pussy is dripping wet for me." I bring my slick fingers to my mouth and sample her sweet nectar, watching as her blue orbs blow wide at my vulgarity. "Now get out of here before I decide I want more than just a taste."

"You're such an ass," she hisses, then pushes off of me and stands.

Before she reaches the staircase to leave, she turns back around and begins fiddling with a button, her busted bottom lip taking a brutal beating between her straight, white teeth.

"Uhm ..." She clears her throat and lifts her chin. "Do you think you could give me a ride to my apartment in the morning?"

I pause and think. Stella went by her place to clean up the blood and broken glass already so Harper doesn't have to see that shit when she goes home. *If* she ever goes home. I get the sense she's going to take off running at her earliest opportunity. Because that's what Harper does every time something in her life goes wrong—she hops on a plane and flits off to some foreign destination. But she's not stupid. She won't leave here until Brooks is declared dead. And I know she won't leave her grandmother behind.

I stand and close the space between us and stare down at her. "For what?"

Her eyes roam all over the span of my gym, from my weights to the treadmill then back to me. "I'd like my laptop and a few other things."

"Fine," I agree reluctantly. Even though I'd rather burn her apartment building to the ground before allowing her to step foot in it again.

Her shoulders sag in relief and she nods. But that plump bottom lip of hers is begging to be touched, and I can't stop myself from reaching out and swiping my thumb over it just to feel the smooth skin beneath my fingertip. Her eyes flutter shut as she breathes shallowly before me. Her face is still badly bruised, her mouth swollen on one side and a shallow gash splicing from her upper lip to her lower one. But she's still beautiful. In a tragic sort of way.

"You're a mess, kitten. But still gorgeous," I murmur, stepping into her. Harper's long and lean, but the top of her head still barely meets my chin. It's as if her body were built to fit seamlessly against mine.

"Zak," she breathes out, pressing her palm flat to my chest, directly over my heart.

I fucking hate when she says my name. It stirs something inside me.

Hooking her chin with my forefinger, I meet her eyes. "And you need therapy."

"What ... No." She shakes her head and huffs out a dry laugh. "No, I don't need therapy. I just need him gone. For good. I need to know he can't hurt anyone else. He will, Zak. He'll hurt others. He ..." She begins to unravel, panic seeping into her cracked foundation. "I couldn't live with myself if he hurt anyone else. I should have fought harder. I should have never let him—"

"Shut up, Harper." Cupping her jaw in both hands, I swipe away her tears as they leak from her eyes. She winces when my thumb rolls over her swollen cheekbone. "None of this is on you." *It's on me*. "And yes, you do need therapy. You're a fucking disaster, woman. Still wearing his ring for Christ's sake." Her mouth hinges open like she wants to say something. As if she has any justifiable reason for that too-simple diamond to still be wrapped around her ring finger. "Just take the help."

She releases a bated breath and a part of me wants to wrap my arms around her and hold her while she cries it out.

But I deny myself the satisfaction. That magnetic force between us is becoming too strong. It's time to put some distance between us.

I step back, dragging myself out of her orbit. Her eyes flutter open and she blinks away the glassiness. She's an emotional wreck, and although I'm not typically a man to shy away from giving a damaged woman a night of hot sex and raw pleasure, I can't bring myself to do that with Harper.

"You should get some sleep," I tell her, avoiding looking directly into her eyes.

Even as I turn away, I can feel her disappointment burn through me like a blowtorch.

Until she's out of my house and out of my life, I'll continue being the asshole I need to be. It's the only way I can be sure she'll never want me. I won't give her the opportunity to sink her claws into me, to turn me into a needy, pathetic excuse of a man, only to stab me in the back the second I decide to walk away.

Harper Hilton will never have a place in my heart. And the only way I can ensure that is by making sure she never wants in to begin with.

Twenty-Two

Harper

"I'LL JUST BE A few minutes," I tell Zak, then carefully slip out of the passenger seat of his vehicle and walk toward the secured entrance at the front of my apartment building. I'm feeling good today, the fresh air and sunshine from the drive here having helped lift my spirits.

I arrive at the front entrance of my building and feel Zak lurking behind me like an overprotective bodyguard. Turning to face him, I tell him, "I can do this on my own."

"Well aware. But you're not going to."

Rolling my eyes at his dramatics, I let us in the front doors and we make our way down the hall to my door.

Sinking my key into the lock, I turn the knob and take a step over the threshold. The first thing I notice is that everything is spotless.

Pretty much exactly the way I left it. But there's the faint stench of bleach lingering in the air.

Zak slinks in behind me, closing the door and turning the lock. I'm entirely safe with him guarding me, but the fear of Cameron coming back to finish the job is still very much real. Still palpable.

I saunter through my apartment into the living room. My eyes scan the space, taking in the bare table beside the couch where the lamp my grandmother gave me used to sit. My gaze settles on the floor where it all happened. Three faint grooves are dug out in the hardwood, and I know they're from me clawing at the floor while Cameron dragged me toward him.

I trace the pad of my thumb over my broken fingernails as a wave of nauseating memories come filtering back.

Swallowing the painful lump in my throat, I lift my chin and muster up the strength to peel myself away from my thoughts. Someday, I'll look back on this and it will all just be a blip on the radar. It will be nothing more than another shitty life event that I powered through.

I snatch my laptop off the coffee table and spin around, spotting Zak leaning against the wall by the hallway. Pushing past him, I move to my bedroom where I scrounge up my collection of stones from my grandmother, dropping them into a fabric bag in my purse. I rummage through my closet until I find a duffel bag, stuffing it with a few other unmentionables and not sparing my bedroom a second glance as I bolt down the hall toward my front door. It no longer feels like home, the very walls and floors of my apartment harboring the ghosts of the horrors I've endured here.

But Zak's on me like white on rice, grabbing my arm and tugging me back toward him. A gust of air escapes my lungs as he spins me and pins me against the wall.

"Let me go, Zak," I rush out, struggling against his hold as fear and anger seep into my veins.

His hands are wrapped snuggly around my wrists, restraining my arms to the wall on either side of my head. He dips his face to within an inch of mine, his warm, minty breath fanning the loose hair around my face.

"*Let. Me. Go,*" I seethe through labored breaths, my face heating with fury as Zak holds me captive.

His brown eyes flare, darting from my face to my left hand as he swiftly adjusts my wrists so they're pinned in one of his giant paws above my head. His other hand slinks around my throat, his thumb pressing upward into my jaw and tracking my pulse.

He won't hurt me. Zak won't hurt me.

"Take it off, Harper."

Panic rises like a simmering volcano, incinerating the remaining composure I had left.

"Your ring, kitten," he clarifies softly, and I let out a whimper of relief, even though I feel anything but relieved. "Take off your ring, or I'll take it off for you." He releases my hands but not my throat.

"Get away from me," I screech, my palms flying to his chest and shoving as hard as I can. My side smarts from the tug of my stitches. And he barely fucking budges.

When I see the look on his face, I let out some sort of pained cry and pound his chest over and over again, unleashing all my pent up rage and frustration, but his hand around my throat never relents. He's not hurting me. He'd never physically hurt me. But don't words cut deeper than knives? I feel him tensing beneath my assault, but he just stands there and takes it, his fingers wrapped firm but gentle beneath my jaw while his other hand roams over my ribs and settles at my hip, pressing me into the unforgiving drywall.

When all my energy is spent and my arms fall limp, I glower at him, panting and exhausted and wishing like hell he could feel the pain I feel right now. "I hate you, Zak. I fucking hate you," I sneer.

He angles my head and brings his lips to my ear, his hot, humid breath fanning my heated flesh. "I know, kitten. Me too."

My adrenaline rush quickly subsides and I'm left feeling weak and drained of all fight. Sagging against the wall, I squeeze my eyes shut and allow the uncontrollable aftermath of coming down from a high to take over. My body trembles. My teeth chatter. My heart is pounding painfully hard in my chest. And my sewn-up rib cage feels as though someone ran a laser beam up my side.

But all I can focus on is Zak's rough hands on my body. One on my throat, gently holding me in place. The other roaming freely over my curves. I should be repulsed by his touch. But I'm not. His touch has never felt dangerous or harmful the way it should.

He lifts my shirt up my side and peeks down at my stitches. I feel the hem fall back into place and he presses further into me, the heat of his big, strong body welding me to the wall as his rough hands cup my jaw and he drops his forehead to mine.

He's too close. He's too warm and big and strong and solid and everything I don't fucking need right now.

"I'm going to ask nicely one more time. Take that awful fucking ring off your finger, Harper. Or I'll take it off for you."

My head whips side to side. As much as I'm desperate to remove the ring and simply move on, I can't. It's as if I have unfinished business—like I'm seeking closure—and removing the ring prematurely would be catastrophic to the process. So until I know Cameron's dead, the ring serves as an accelerant to my rage. I only hope I have the opportunity to face him one final time before he takes his last breath.

I try to turn my face away from Zak's but his hands hold firm. Our noses are touching, our breath mingling. We're inhaling each other's air once again, and for a brief second, I don't hate it.

"No," I respond hoarsely.

"Harper," he warns. "Take off the fucking ring."

Why does this bother him so much?

Finding Zak's eyes, it dawns on me. This is Zak Shephard. A gentleman who won't fuck a committed woman. What lukewarm sentiment. I should have known it would come to this.

So I do what I know how to do best. I hit him where it hurts.

"Why, Zak? So you can fuck me against the wall in the same room Cameron raped me in? So you can slide your cock inside me before my pussy is fully healed? Just so you can scratch my name off your roster and move onto the next?"

He peels his forehead from mine and frowns down at me. Something registers on his face and he backs off like I've burned him. Finally, I have some room to breathe. Bitterness is swirling violently with anger in my gut and I'm absolutely not fucking okay. But the space I begged for comes at a cost, because without Zak's heat, I'm suddenly chilled, my core temperature plummeting to that of a frozen corpse. It's as if I've stripped down to my birthday suit and stepped outside in the middle of a snowstorm.

"Fuck, Harper. I didn't …" He looks sorry. He really does. But I know it's only because he's a master manipulator. "It won't happen again," he promises, his eyes hooded and dark and a sober expression on his face, all that lust-fueled mania wiped clean.

I've bruised his oversized ego. Normally, I might feel a shred of guilt for that, but right now I don't have room for guilt with all the other emotions taking up residence inside me.

"Get the rest of your stuff and let's go," he instructs softly, snatching my duffel bag up off the floor from where I dropped it. He disappears into the kitchen and after several calming breaths, I pry myself from the wall and finish collecting my things, never looking back even as I walk out of my apartment and we drive away.

Twenty-Three

Zak

*W**HY, ZAK? SO YOU can fuck me against the wall in the same room Cameron raped me in? So you can slide your cock inside me before my pussy is fully healed? Just so you can scratch my name off your roster and move onto the next?*

Harper's bitter questions play over and over in my head like some sick record stuck on repeat. It's been three days since I took her to her apartment with the intentions of instilling just enough fear in her that she'd stay away from me. It was a selfish move—one that I wholly regret. Because watching her struggle against me with terror bleeding into her eyes only fanned the flames of possessiveness burning within my veins.

We've avoided each other since then, bumping into each other in the halls of my house before she disappears into the guest room again. But somehow, she's still everywhere. Even when she's not.

And those silly little rocks her and her grandmother obsess over keep popping up in random places. So much so, that I've started to collect them in a dish in my bedroom.

Harper's fully independent now, capable of feeding and bathing herself. Thank fuck, because it's already difficult enough for me to keep my hands to myself. To not lay her on her back and fuck her into oblivion until she forgets every shitty thing Brooks ever did to her.

And that goddamn ring of hers ... She still hasn't taken it off, which only serves as a reminder of how fucked up she really is. And the way it seems to wink at me every time I get close enough to smell her sweet, floral scent. Every time I catch a glimpse of her changing through the cracked bedroom door. Every time she saunters into the room, her long, blonde hair still wet from her shower, her face free of makeup. That ring is testing me. Daring me to break the rules and slide inside her pussy anyway.

I knock twice and wait, listening as Harper's hushed voice filters through the wooden door. I can tell by her tone that she's on the phone with her grandmother. I turn to leave and give her some privacy, but the door swings open. Harper stands on the other side with her phone pressed to her ear. She raises a finger indicating she'll only be a moment.

I wait patiently for her to say her goodbyes to her grandmother, then cross over the threshold into the guest room.

I expected the space to be in chaos, a reflection of Harper's mental state. But instead, it's tidy. Her clothes are all neatly tucked away in the closet. Her little rock collection is laid out on the bedside table. Her laptop is sitting on the desk in the corner, the screensaver of her and her grandmother staring back at me. I glance over at the open ensuite door and see her bath products are all lined up on the vanity.

"Did you need something?" she asks, popping a hip and staring expectantly at me.

I clear my throat, dragging myself from the thoughts of what it might be like to have her belongings in my bedroom instead. "Your stitches can come out now."

"Oh," she breathes out, fiddling with the hem of her shirt. Her bruises have healed enough that she's capable of slipping in and out of her own clothing now. Which is a relief for me, because watching her traipse around my house wearing my shirts like dresses was fucking killing me. "Will it hurt?"

I shake my head. "It'll tickle. Maybe the odd little pinch. But it won't hurt."

"Okay. Just let me grab my purse and we'll—"

"I'll take them out for you." She's so high strung and on edge ever since the assault. She needs an outlet. She needs to take back some control over her life. She needs to feel powerful. And I know exactly how to give that to her.

She pauses, straightening her spine and glancing back over at me. "Shouldn't a doctor do it?"

I shrug and sink my hands into my pockets, thumbing my coin. "If you'd rather make a trip to the hospital ..."

"No." She raises a palm in the air and shakes her head. "No. It's fine. You can do it."

I lead Harper into the ensuite and she climbs up onto the counter, swinging her legs while I rummage around in the medical kit I keep on hand. Finding what I need, I stand a safe distance from her and lift her shirt up her stomach and tuck the hem into the side of her bra so she doesn't need to awkwardly hold it for me.

I get to work, carefully freeing her of her stitches. With every gentle tug, her abdominal muscles tighten.

"I'm sorry for the other day," I offer quietly, discarding a piece of thread into the trash can by my feet. "I shouldn't have touched you."

She sighs and relaxes her shoulders. "It's fine, Zak. Really."

I lift my eyes and find her staring back at me, her lips pressed firm and her breathing calm. She's at ease right now. Except the pulse in her throat is jumping, picking up speed the longer our gazes remain locked.

"I meant what I said, Harper. It won't happen again."

Her mouth opens then clicks shut as if she wants to say something. It's probably best she doesn't, because every time we hold conversation, we fight like cats and dogs. Instead, she nods and focuses on a spot on the wall.

I get back to work, removing her stitches one by one until there's nothing but a pink, jagged scar running down the length of her ribs, stopping just above her hip bone. She inspects the scar herself, tracing her finger over the indent.

"It still has plenty of healing to do, kitten," I reassure her. "It won't look like that forever."

"I know," she says quietly. "I just hate that I'll always have a reminder."

She hops off the counter and stares at her reflection in the mirror as I sanitize the devices I used and return the kit to beneath the sink.

Standing behind her, I rest both hands on her shoulders and give her a gentle squeeze. "It won't just be a reminder of what he did to you, Harper. It'll be a reminder of what you survived. Remember that."

Her glassy eyes meet mine in the mirror. That magnetic pull is back and stronger than ever, and all I fucking want to do is wrap my arms around her waist and bury my nose in her thick hair.

But then it happens again. That goddamn ring winks at me. And I back away.

Harper blinks away her tears and turns around to face me. "Thank you," she says sweetly. "I ..." She swallows, her cheeks heating to a dark shade of pink. "I appreciate everything you've done. Truly."

Quirking a brow at her, I say, "I bet those words tasted like vinegar leaving your mouth."

She smirks, her vivid eyes twinkling. And I clench my molars until I'm sure they crack.

"You're welcome," I murmur, then slip out of the bathroom and make my way across the guest room.

"Zak," Harper rushes out, snagging my wrist then suddenly jerking her hand back. I spin around to peer down at her. "I overheard you talking to Liam the other day. I know about the little girl. Taylor." She waits a beat. Gnaws on the inside of her cheek. I recount the telephone conversations I've had with Liam about Taylor, recalling a particular one I had in my kitchen yesterday afternoon. "I'd like to meet her."

"When I'm back," I promise. Confusion enters her expression and I elaborate. "We're wheels up tomorrow, so you're staying with Joel and Stella."

She almost looks disappointed by that information, but she swiftly rearranges her face and nods.

"Pack what you'll need for a few days. I'll drop you off in the morning."

I leave her alone and go in search of refuge, finding myself once again in my home gym, working my frustrations out.

Twenty-Four

Harper

Stella takes me in with open arms as Lainey latches to my leg and squeals, "Auntie Harper!"

"Hi, honey." I lean down and give her butterfly kisses. "Guess what."

"What?" she says, bouncing on her feet.

"We're going to have a sleepover."

Squeals and giggles follow shortly after and she takes off toward Joel, jumping up and down and informing him of the news. Judging by the sour look on Joel's face, he's not entirely impressed. But he puts up with it because he knows Stella would string him up by the balls if he so much as says a peep. Besides, I know he's extra stressed with everything that's going on with Sweetwater. And Joel's a man who doesn't particularly enjoy relinquishing control. It's one of the few things we have in common, I suppose.

Stella ushers me inside while Zak finishes unloading my bags and dropping them at my feet in the foyer. I hear another vehicle pull into the driveway and I know it's Liam with my grandmother.

The whole exchange happens so fast, I'm left spinning. Before I know it, Zak's leaving again, shooting me a strangled look before shutting the door behind him. I hear his vehicle take off and something coils inside my chest.

"It's so nice to see you, Mrs. Hilton," Stella says sweetly to my grandmother, wrapping her in a hug and patting her back.

Ever since Finnegan was born, Stella's been a little overwhelmed, understandably so. Raising children isn't for the faint of heart. She's also stepped back from work, but I know she's eager to return as soon as possible. What started as a passionate hobby of locating missing persons has quickly evolved into something greater. She now has over thirty people on her payroll, assisting in research and opening cold cases and digging up the dirtiest, darkest secrets in order to bring bodies home to families. She's even repurposed her mother's mansion into a supportive community where trauma victims can go to heal. She's able to live out her passion because of Joel and Sweetwater and their extensive reach into government and police records, offering her information she otherwise wouldn't be privy to.

In other words, my best friend is a total badass and I'm incredibly proud of her.

Settling in, I help Joel move our luggage into the spare rooms, setting my grandmother up in the bedroom directly across from mine.

"How are you holding up?" he asks me out of the blue. He's not typically a touchy-feely kind of guy, but he's softened significantly since Lainey was born. I know beneath his hard, grumpy exterior, there's an exceptionally good man in there.

I shrug. "I'm doing okay."

Joel drops a bag on the bed and clears his throat, peering at the cracked door before returning his attention to me. "Listen, Harper." He rakes a massive grizzly paw through his hair. "I won't pretend to know what you're going through. But I want you to know that Shep ... he's ..." He blows out a frustrated breath, obviously uncomfortable with whatever conversation he's attempting to have with me. "He's all sorts of fucked up right now. What Brooks did to you ..."

"It's fine, Joel. Really. You don't need to say anything." *Seriously. Stop talking, big guy.*

"Yeah, I kind of do. Zak's not what you think he is. He's not a toy you can fuck with then forget about. He's my best friend and as much as you're Stella's, I won't let you hurt him."

I can hear every vertebrae in my spine click into place as I stiffen my posture.

"We'd have to actually *like* each other for me to hurt him."

Joel's piercing blue eyes narrow skeptically on me as he all but scoffs. Stella warned me he's like a human lie detector test. Unfortunately for him, I'm well practiced in the art of manipulation. I can lie like a fucking rug.

Sighing and rolling my eyes, I feign not being even the tiniest bit affected by his accusation. "Alright, Joel. Don't be going all soft on me now."

"Knock knock," Stella's voice drifts around the door, rescuing me from this brutally awkward chitchat. Poking her head around the corner, she says, "Someone wants to know if it would be alright if she slept in here tonight."

On cue, Lainey squeezes past her mother and stands before me, staring up at me with giant, hazel eyes rimmed in thick lashes. Her dark curls are tied up in two pigtails on the top of her head. She's so cute, I could just eat her little face.

"Of course she can," I respond eagerly, warmth spreading in my chest. "We can paint each other's nails and eat candy and watch movies and cuddle."

"Yay!" Lainey bounces and turns to her mom. "See Mommy! I told you she'd want to have a swummber party."

The rest of the day flies by and Joel informs us that Sweetwater has landed successfully in the middle of a Colombian jungle and are moving boots toward the target.

But it does nothing to ease my nerves. These mercenaries put their lives at risk on every job to save people they've never met. To bring down the bad guys so we can sleep peacefully at night, each one of us unbeknownst of the monsters that lurk in the darkest corners of the earth. The irony of it all is that Cameron was one of them. He was supposed to be a good guy. A savior. Instead, he's on the other side, fighting a battle he'll eventually lose.

Lainey is bundled up in her favorite unicorn blankie beside me and the most adorable little snores are coming from somewhere beneath the heap of blankets and pillows. But I can't sleep. Not when there's this dull nagging sensation in the pit of my stomach that tells me my world is about to be flipped upside down and turned inside out. The question is ... when? And will I be fortunate enough to land on my feet like I always do?

Two more days pass of snuggles and cuddles and giggles with Lainey. I sneak candy from Stella's secret stash into my bedroom and Lainey curls up beside me and we veg out on junk food and binge-watch Disney princess movies. It's the ultimate slumber party and a welcome distraction from the reality that's waiting for me outside these four walls.

But it all comes to a screeching halt when Zak returns and picks me up. I glance across the cab of his SUV for the hundredth time, biting my lip and taking him in. He's six-foot-something of pure danger right now. Dark camouflage and war paint, his corded arms flecked in blood and dirt, his tattoos peeking out from beneath all the filth. Even his disheveled hair is sexy. But his eyes are dark and hooded. He looks exhausted, and it makes me second-guess whether picking a fight with him would be a wise decision.

So I keep my mouth shut and stamp down the urge to say something snarky.

Besides, when he showed up at Joel and Stella's early this morning to pick me up after a three-day mission in Colombia, he was so fucking sweet to my grandmother that it gave me a toothache. And this time when he offered her to come stay with me at his place, oddly enough, she actually agreed. Which means even eighty-year-old women with weak hearts aren't immune to his charm. Zak had helped her in and out of the vehicle, carrying her luggage and offering her a hand up the single step into his house. He even went as far as ordering a grocery haul of all the baking ingredients he could get his hands on just so she has something to do in her spare time.

This is the nice guy Zak pretends to be to lure unsuspecting bimbos into his lair. This is the gentleman women drop their panties for. Normally, it would irritate me. But right now, the way he smiles sweetly at my nan and she smiles back, it doesn't just irritate me. It infuriates me. He's leaving an impression on her, and that can't happen because she'll end up forming some silly ideas of her own.

"My my," Nan says, her blue eyes gleaming with mischief as she saunters around Zak's kitchen, making a dramatic show of yawning. "I think it's time for my nap."

Aaaand cue the ideas.

"You haven't even eaten breakfast yet, Nan." *I'm onto you.*

She shoots me a sly grin and waddles over to Zak, offering him a hug and a thanks for welcoming her into his home.

"Sleep tight, Mrs. Hilton," Zak says, then plants a chaste kiss on her cheek. He chuckles softly when he has to swipe a smudge of war paint off her face that transferred from his lips. Good lord. It's like watching the Grim Reaper kiss Princess Peach.

I stick my finger down my throat and fake gag at him behind my nan's back. He winks at me and flashes his stupid, beautiful smile. *Cocky asshole.*

Nan wanders off to her room without so much as shooting me a glance. Guess I'm chopped liver now.

"You don't need to do that, you know," I say to Zak. But he ignores me and swiftly disappears into the laundry room. I'm hot on his heels, following him into the small, boxy room. It's a mistake because when he peels off his shirt and exposes all that ink and landscape of lean muscle, the words dangling on the tip of my tongue suddenly fall to their peril.

"Do what?" he asks coyly, then begins unstrapping his holsters from his thighs and discarding them on a shelf beside the washing machine.

"Uh ..."

He removes the last holster and stands to his full height, gazing down at me with dark, tired eyes.

Okay. Who cranked the heat up in here?

"Spit it out, kitten."

Licking my lips and forcing myself to stop ogling the V of his lower abdomen like a horndog, I slide my gaze to his and lift my chin. "You're being too nice to her."

Zak angles his head at me, an amused expression crossing his face. "You're complaining that I'm being too nice to your frail, old grandmother," he deadpans. It makes me sound like a brat, but I'm not above it.

"It's not that you're being too nice. It's that she'll know you're faking it." That's it. That's what I was trying to say.

"But I'm not faking it," he counters, taking a step forward so I'm forced to inhale his scent. There's still a hint of sandalwood there, but it's mingled with sweat and musk and the overwhelming pheromones that make women crumble like Nature Valley peanut butter bars.

He's absolutely filthy right now. If it weren't for his coffee eyes and that Colgate smile of his, he'd be unrecognizable with all the paint and mud smeared over his face.

He takes another step forward and I match it, taking one back to maintain the space between us. We do that a few more times until my back is against the wall and Zak's hovering over me, one palm pressed flat beside my head while his free thumb traces the bow of my upper lip. His touch sends a shiver rolling down my spine. It starts at the base of my skull and crawls down each of my vertebrae, settling deep into my core.

"This mouth," he says hotly, his eyes tracking the movement of his thumb as it tugs my lower lip down, baring my bottom teeth to him. He releases it with a *pop*. "It's irritating. Keep it shut, Harper. Or I'll find something more productive for you to do with it."

My heart takes off into a gallop and a bead of sweat forms on my lower back. I know he'd make good on the threat, but my brain has gone into hibernation and for some stupid reason, I'm tempted to spit venom and piss him off just to see how far he'd actually take it.

With an arrogant smirk, Zak steps back and begins unbuckling his belt. But I can't peel my sweaty ass off the damn wall or avert my disobedient eyes. Instead, I watch as he slides his belt through the loops, the leather whispering on its way through. He drops it on the shelf with the rest of his gear, and I have to swallow the saliva pooling in my mouth.

His gaze stays steady on mine, assessing how I react. I can feel the thud of my racing heart all through my body, right down to my throbbing clit.

"Finally, you have nothing to say," he says, then unfastens the top button of his fatigues.

Fuck. Fuck. Fuck.

When I realize my jaw is unhinged and I'm mouth breathing, I snap it shut and steel my spine. But that doesn't stop the heat from rising in my chest and face. I'm literally blushing like a goddamn school girl.

"If you plan on sticking around for more, kitten, I suggest you shut the door so your sweet, little grandmother doesn't walk in and get an eyeful. Wouldn't want her to suffer another heart attack."

He's giving me an option. Close the door and watch him undress. Or leave.

Stealing one last glance at his sculpted body, I bolt faster than a bull out the pen, Zak's arrogant chuckle chasing me as I book it down the hall, locking myself in my bedroom. I press my back to the cool wooden surface and take a few calming breaths. But now I'm pent up and frustrated and in desperate need of release.

Rummaging through my luggage, I locate what I'm looking for. Slipping my shorts down my legs and crawling into bed, I hit the power button of my favorite little bullet vibrator and give my traitorous vagina what she's begging for.

Twenty-Five

Harper

ANXIETY ROLLS THROUGH ME like food poisoning, souring my stomach contents until the blueberry muffin my nan baked threatens to make a reappearance. After avoiding Zak for a full two days after our little encounter in the laundry room, he sought me out and informed me he's taking me shooting.

I've never held a gun, much less shot one before. I'm not sure if I'm terrified to my very core or if I'm merely thrilled by the thought of wielding enough power in my hands to end an entire human life.

Naturally, I fought Zak on his wardrobe demands, but when he explained that malfunctions happen and I could be burned, I clammed up immediately. So, doing precisely as he instructed me to, I rush to the closet and rummage through it to find a pair of jeans, a long-sleeved shirt with a high neckline—no cleavage—and a pair of leather boots. I say a quick goodbye to my nan, feeling guilty for leaving her here alone even though she promises she'll be fine. Then I meet Zak in the kitchen where I find him typing away on his phone. He must feel me vibrating all the way from the other side of the room because he stops and glances up at me.

He licks his lips and nods in approval of my clothing, then ushers me out the door and into his vehicle, navigating us down the highway.

"So are we going to a gun range or something?" I ask, fiddling with the hem of my shirt and staring anxiously over at Zak's profile.

"Yes and no," he responds. "Mac has a country property we use for shooting and training."

An image flashes behind my eyes. One of Zak racing toward me when he found me on his front step. It's followed quickly by images of him undressing in his laundry room. All muscles and ink and dark hair and eyes that make women's mouths pool with saliva and panties flood with wet heat.

Zak focuses his attention on driving while I stew uncomfortably in the passenger seat, surrounded by his scent and frigidly cool demeanor. Something's different about him that I can't quite put my finger on. But all is forgotten when we pull down a long, gravel road that leads deep into a heavily wooded area. After a short, bumpy ride, we park at a clearing and hop out. He retrieves a large, black bag from the trunk and leads me down a narrow dirt path. The bugs are thick and I'm instantly grateful for my long pants and sleeves.

The duffel bag makes a *thud* as Zak drops it on the picnic table and I search around the open space. Hay bales are scattered haphazardly around the open grass field, their white wraps splattered with vibrant bursts of paint. There are several wooden structures that mimic deer stands where hunters post up and wait for their prey to cross their path. A couple old, rusted-out antique vehicles litter the field, their flat tires sunken deep into the soil and tall grass sprouting around their frames.

"Do you guys paintball?" I ask, peeking over at Zak and grinning, imagining him peppered in paint splatters while laughing and firing off shots at his friends.

"Occasionally. Mac's grandkids set this up. Couple of teenage boys looking for a place to fuck around."

He unzips the bag and begins laying an assortment of firearms out on the table. When he pulls out a gun as long as my arm, I can't stop myself. "Oooh. I want to shoot that one!"

He chuckles and lays the gun on the table. "Not a fucking chance, kitten. You'll kill us both." He tosses me an army green baseball cap. "For your hair."

"What's wrong with my hair?" I ask, slipping my sleek ponytail through the back and tucking any strays away from my face.

"Nothing right now. But ejected cartridges will change that real fast."

He hands me a pair of safety glasses and earmuffs, sliding his own on as well and resting his muffs around his neck, then does a final inspection to make sure we're both protected and ready to go.

"See those targets out there?" he asks, his voice low as he leans in beside me and points out at the open field. His shoulder brushes mine and a renewed sizzle of excitement crackles through me.

I follow his line of sight and spot three large, white boards with red rings painted on them.

"Those are yours. You're going to shoot a small handgun first, and if you do alright with that, I'll let you shoot something larger. But for now, we start with a gun that will fit in your purse. Got it?"

I nod again, the grin on my face so goofy that I could star in a Saturday morning cartoon.

Zak selects a gun from the picnic table and comes around behind me, his stomach flush with my back. All the oxygen leaves my lungs in a whoosh as he reaches around and hands me the firearm, showing me how the safety switch works and how to properly load and unload the weapon. I pay attention only twenty percent of the time. The other eighty percent of the time my brain cells go on vacation while my ovaries do backflips off my uterus.

He kicks my feet apart with his, showing me the optimal stance for firing, then presses himself into my backside again, his fingers skimming over my hip and up my side, turning my body to just the right angle. But there's a large bulge digging into my lower back that I know for certain is not a gun, and it's distracting as fuck.

"One hand here," he instructs, his tattooed paw guiding my hand around the grip of the gun and my index finger hovering beside the trigger. "And the other for support." He wraps his hands around mine and adjusts my fingers until I'm holding a fucking firearm and feeling like a total badass. "There's going to be a bit of a recoil when you fire. It can hurt if you're not prepared for it."

"Recoil?" I ask, peeking up over my shoulder at him.

"Kickback. Small objects can wield a lot of power," he says hotly in my ear. It sounds like an insinuation, but I shrug it off. "Don't shut your eyes when you fire. It's a rookie mistake. The key is to keep your sight on the target and exhale when you pull the trigger. Don't squeeze fast or hard. This gun is sensitive and the calmer you are, the better your shot will be. Ready?"

"Yes," I squeak out, my heart jackhammering so hard in my chest I'm surprised it's not flying out of my body and leaping across the field.

Zak's hands leave mine, skimming up my arms and to my shoulders where he slides my earmuffs onto my head. He doesn't step back or give me space, and I wonder if it's because he doesn't want me toppling over from the backfire, or if he's struggling to not touch me the way he promised he wouldn't.

I aim, steadying my breathing and recounting everything else he instructed me to do. When I apply a small amount of pressure to the trigger, the gun punches back and a dull ache radiates up my arms and through my shoulders.

"Nice shot, kitten," he says proudly.

I lower the gun and stare out at the target, spotting a fresh hole in the corner of one of the targets.

"I hit it. Oh my god. I shot a freaking gun and actually hit the target," I squeal, then spin around and set the gun on the table, leaping toward Zak. It isn't until I'm smiling into the crook of his neck that I realize my legs are coiled around his hips and his arms are wrapped around my waist.

"You did," he murmurs into my hair, his lips grazing the sensitive flesh beneath my ear.

I freeze, the zaps of electricity from the sudden contact traveling all the way down to my toes. Zak's arms galvanize around me, holding me tight, and I'm not sure how to react. Because somehow, these strong arms that have never held me like this feel so familiar. So safe.

Feeling him inhale deeply through his nose, I lower myself to my feet and clear my throat, averting my eyes. Zak does much of the same, snatching the gun from the table and handing it back to me.

"Again."

Giddy and smiling, I accept the weapon and shoot again. And again. And again. Until I'm hitting near the bullseye of each of the targets every single time. When I've emptied another clip, Zak pulls out one of the long guns.

"Ready for Karen?" he asks, grinning like a schoolboy and caressing the weapon like it's a prospective lover.

"Karen? Really?" He shrugs. "Is Karen going to give me a black eye when I shoot her?" I ask, accepting the gun and nearly dropping it to the ground when I'm unprepared for the weight of it. Hoisting her back up, I stand and face the target while Zak takes his place behind me, once again guiding me into position.

"No black eyes," he says, a soft chuckle vibrating from his chest and humming through my body as he presses into me. Jesus, he's solid. And the heat radiating off him is making me feel feverish.

"She'll give your shoulder a good nudge though. Nothing you can't handle."

This time, instead of removing his hands from mine, he holds the rifle with me, providing me the support I need because, holy nickels, Karen's a heavy bitch.

We go through the motions and fire. I miss the first shot, but the second and third hit the target. I've never felt so powerful in my entire life. So in control.

And in this moment, it occurs to me that this is why he brought me here. This is why Zak wanted to take me shooting. To give me back some semblance of power over my life. Over my fucked-up situation.

I lower the gun, my arms aching and tired from holding it's weight, and turn around to face Zak again. But he doesn't move away like I expect him to. He just stands there, his hard body a wall in front of me, his brown eyes taking on an inky darkness, something ominous and longing lurking behind them.

He reaches for Karen and engages the safety, then lays her onto the table. My body sways, giving in to the magnetic pull between us as my hips drift forward until I'm leaning into him. He still smells like himself, but there's a hint of gunpowder and the woods blending with his masculine scent.

"Harper," he says softly, slipping my earmuffs off and lifting my hat, turning it backward on my head. "You're—"

"I'm what, Zak?"

He doesn't make a move to touch me, but I can see the war waging inside him.

"You brought me out here to give me a sense of security. So I can feel powerful again. So why are you looking at me like I'm a weak, defenseless woman?"

A breeze kicks up and Zak tucks a loose strand of hair behind my ear, tracking the movement with his eyes. "You're neither of those things, kitten. You have claws sharper than any wildcat I've known. But you're—"

"Fucked up." I take a step back from him. "I know."

"Yeah," he says lowly, swiping a hand through his hair. "But that doesn't seem to stop you from getting under my skin, does it?"

I lift my chin in defiance and scowl at him. "You just can't handle being around a woman who sees through you and your phony little gentleman act."

He angles his head. "Why are you so determined that I'm not a nice guy, Harper?"

I snort. "Because if Hugh Hefner and you tallied up the women you've screwed, you'd put him to shame."

"Says the brat who can't keep her legs closed."

"Keep my legs ..." I shake my head, my brows pinching tight. "What are you talking about?"

He scoffs, and I'm tempted to reach up and gouge his eyeballs out with my thumbs.

"I'm talking about you always finding some shiny, new toy to play with. Some idiot to get wrapped around your finger, only to rip his heart out and crush it in your pretty little hands. You're a fucking black hole, Harper. You suck everyone and everything into your orbit, use what you need, then spit them out."

Okay. So, this escalated fast.

"Fuck you," I screech, my elevated tone causing a flock of birds to flea their nests. "I may date a lot but at least I don't have some fucked-up belief about women being a set of orifices to stick your dick in." I'm pacing now, and there's a maniacal laugh coming from somewhere. Me, I think. But I can't be sure because I'm fairly certain I've finally dropped off my hinges. Somehow, this conversation has taken a nosedive and left my sanity somewhere in the dust.

I skid to a halt and stare back at the man whose number one mission in life is to make me want to hook his balls up to a live car battery. "You've literally fucked your way through every vagina within a hundred-mile radius. So who are you to judge?"

His eyes sweep pointedly over my body, a smug grin on his stupid face. "Well ... not *every* vagina."

Disgust makes its grand entrance and my mouth decides to go on strike, audibly clicking shut at his revolting insinuation.

"You'd spread your legs for me in a heartbeat, Harper. Just like you've spread them for every other man you've spent more than five minutes with."

Oh, he did not just say that!

Closing the space between us, I go face to chest with a six-foot-too-many-inches mercenary, my fists balled and ready to defend myself as his accusation brings the blood in my veins to near boiling. Against my own volition, I draw my hand back and my palm connects with his cheek with a searing crack. His head twists to the side, and just when I think he's going to retaliate—because why the fuck wouldn't he when I just up and slapped him—he turns his face back to mine, and he fucking smiles.

Okay … why the hell does it feel like the Hoover Dam just exploded in my panties?

"I wouldn't fuck you if you and Cameron were the last two men on earth," I sneer.

Zak's smile vanishes into thin air, his jaw clenched tight and eyes darker than obsidian. His reaction lights something inside me. I'm on a roll, and ripping his ego to shreds feels fucking phenomenal. I've got some pent-up anger to dispose of and Zak's just the guy to take it out on.

"You're no better than I am, Zak. You're a player, a phony, and a hypocrite. Yet here you are, calling yourself a nice guy while slut-shaming me when you know nothing about me. As far as I'm concerned, you're no better than Cameron."

Twenty-Six

Zak

Harper takes off down the path toward the vehicle and I hang back, packing up the guns. She's not wrong. I'm a fucking hypocrite. But to compare me to Brooks? Fuck no. It took every ounce of restraint for me to not bend her over one of those antique cars and spank her ass for even mentioning Brooks and I in the same goddamn sentence. If she never wants to see me again after this, then so be it. I'll gladly take her back to my house, pack her shit, and send her on her way.

Except I fucking can't. Because Brooks is still on the loose. So for now, I'm bound by a moral obligation to protect her while she traipses through my house and my fucking mind, leaving her annoying little rocks and the ghost of her scent everywhere she goes.

Slinging the bag over my shoulder, I peer up at the sky just as a raindrop hits my face. The sun is gone, a shroud of storm clouds closing in and blocking it from view. I need to get the hell out of here before the rain turns the road into a mosh pit and we get stuck down this godforsaken back road together.

Loading the guns into the trunk of my vehicle and sliding into the driver's seat, I slam the SUV into drive and pretend Harper's not sitting next to me. It would be a fuck of a lot easier if the diamond on her left hand wasn't winking at me as she incessantly spins it around her finger with her thumb.

Fuck that ring and everything it stands for. And fuck this two-hour drive that feels like a lifetime in hell.

The tension in the air is so thick I can taste it, and the rain is coming hard and heavy now, the wipers barely keeping up with the downpour as I drive like a bat out of hell down the open highway. The quicker I can get home, the quicker I can escape Harper's infuriating presence.

"I know I slept around a lot," she murmurs softly.

Gritting my teeth, I bite my tongue and don't respond. But I can feel her eyes boring a hole straight through the side of my face.

"But I wanted more. I wanted to settle down. And Cameron ... He made me feel loved."

"Just stop, Harper. I don't want to hear it."

Silence stretches on and I make the mistake of glancing over at her. She's got that fucking bottom lip sucked between her teeth again and she's staring at me with those giant, blue eyes of hers.

She's right. I'm an asshole.

Inhaling a deep breath, I grip the steering wheel until my knuckles bleach white and listen to what she has to say, despite the fact I already know it's going to flay me wide open.

She blows out a breath and shakes her head. "I've never been loved by a man before because I've never allowed them to get close enough to do that." She turns her gaze to the window, seemingly lost in her thoughts. "Being vulnerable sucks." The last part is barely a whisper, her words muffled by the slap of rain pelting the windshield.

I mull her admission over in my head for a while, allowing the truth to burn my chest as punishment to myself for being a fucking dick. When I realize that there's no form of self-inflicted pain that could take away the guilt I feel for allowing Brooks to nearly kill her, I pull off onto a no-maintenance road and cut the engine and hop out, ignoring Harper's questions about where we are and why we're stopping.

Pacing in front of my Trackhawk, I let the rain soak through me. But no amount of rainfall could wash away the cocktail of emotions inside me right now. Rage, fury, guilt, shame. The desire for revenge. The violent concoction rivals the storm rolling in around us.

I pause and stare past the glaring headlights to find Harper's face through the windshield, her features blurred and distorted by the rivulets of water streaming down the glass.

She climbs out of the vehicle and takes cautious steps toward me, meeting me in front of the vehicle and staring at my heaving chest. A warm hand presses over my throbbing heart.

"I'm sorry," she rasps out. "I didn't mean to—"

"Look at me, Harper," I say gently, lifting her chin with my finger. "You're a fucking mess."

I step into her, allowing the warmth of my body to penetrate her chilled exterior. Except it's me who begins to thaw, my insides heating to a balmy degree and melting the block of ice in my chest.

This fucking woman ...

"And you're giving off all sorts of signals that make absolutely no sense. One second you're slicing me wide open with your sharp tongue and snide comments. The next you're beaming at me, smiling like ... Fuck. I don't know." I swipe a hand through my hair, the wet strands clinging to my forehead. My eyes track a water droplet as it cascades down the bridge of her nose, dangling on the tip before dropping between us.

A shiver wracks her body, and fuck if I don't want to wrap my arms around her just to stop her from shaking.

Lifting her eyes to mine, she says, "None of it makes sense to me either."

She drops her empty gaze to my chest again and holds her breath. I expect her to retreat the way she always does. But her feet stay firmly planted in the soil. She has no idea what she needs right now. Even if she did, she wouldn't know how to ask for it. Because Harper never asks for anything. She just takes what she requires to survive, never seeking more than the bare minimum to get through another day. Materialistically, she only ever accepts gifts from the wealthy. It's a quality I've admired about her since the day we met. Something I'm not afraid to admit I find exceptionally attractive. Emotionally, she's really no different, because whatever Brooks gave her … it wasn't enough. And still, she accepted it from him, despite the fact that she deserves more. More laughing. More passion. More everything.

But I'm calling a spade a spade. Harper is fucked up in more ways than one. She just has no goddamn idea how beautiful all those flaws of hers are. She's perfect in her own tormented fashion. And for some reason, I find myself wanting to damage her in a way she's never been before. I want to invade her body, mind, and soul, just to give her a taste of her own sick medicine she's poisoned me with for the last four and a half years. I want to infect her with something she's never felt before. The same as she's done to me.

She peeks up at me again through thick, wet lashes, pain and confusion evident in her oceanic pools. It's the moment I finally cave to my own selfish desires.

"Fuck, Harper," I growl, slipping an arm around her narrow waist and dragging her into me while my other hand cups the back of her neck and pulls her in for a long, deep kiss. Just as I suspected, she tastes incredible. Sweet, salty, and too fucking good.

Harper is everything. And there isn't a doubt in my mind she's going to rip me to shreds and leave me to bleed. Just like Brooks did to her.

Twenty-Seven

Harper

I'VE NEVER BEEN KISSED like this. Not by Tommy Hugo in college when we played spin the bottle and found ourselves locked in a closet together for seven minutes of heaven. Not by the countless men I've dated, only to break up with them weeks later because I was afraid they'd eventually grow tired of me and break my heart like Trent did in high school. And I've certainly never been kissed like this by Cameron.

It takes all of five seconds and I'm weak in the knees while Zak explores my mouth with his skilled tongue. My fingers find purchase in his soaked shirt, the fabric clinging to every rippling muscle of his solid frame.

He breaks the kiss and I come up for air, staring up at him in search of some sort of resolution to the conflicting emotions running rampant through me. Just the headlights illuminate the space around us, casting long shadows on the tree line and highlighting Zak's anguish.

"What do you want from me, Harper? Tell me point blank so I know what the fuck to do right now. Because I can't read you anymore."

"I ... I don't know," I admit truthfully. "I feel like I'm spiraling. Like there's no rock bottom for me to ever hit and rebound from. I keep reaching out in hopes of clinging to something, in hopes of tethering myself to someone, but there's just nothing there for me to grab onto." Tears are leaking from my eyes. Big fucking shocker. I'm a train wreck and there's no saving face anymore. And Zak, who's staring at me with this pitiful look on his face, like he's mourning the loss of something he never knew existed, is only making me feel worse.

I'm so fucking sick of crying.

"Tell me you trust me," he demands gently, catching me off guard.

"Why?" I breathe out, pointlessly swiping the tears from my cheeks as we continue to be pelted by the rain.

"Because I can be that tether for you, kitten. I can hold you down until you're back on your feet." His arms around me cinch tighter, pulling me into him again. His lips brush softly over mine as thousands of tiny lightning bolts strike down everywhere our bodies connect.

Pressing his forehead to mine, he repeats, "Tell me you trust me, Harper. Then cling to me like your fucking life depends on it. I can handle the aftermath when you finally let go."

Nodding against his lips, I whisper, "I trust you." The truth is, every broken, fucked-up piece of me trusts this man. It makes no sense at all, but I do.

His mouth is on mine again, kissing me with a tenderness I don't deserve after the shitty things I said to him earlier. But that tenderness quickly evolves, snowballing and picking up surface space as our passion escalates into a frenzy of teeth and tongues and fingers flying over each other. Greedy hands roam freely over my curves. Rough fingertips dig into my ass, pulling my hips into his.

"Fuck, you taste like bad decisions," he growls, guiding me to the hood of his SUV and pressing my back against the still-warm metal grill.

Heat radiates from the engine and I'm cocooned in warmth from both Zak's body and vehicle. His hands explore every inch of my lithe frame, his deft fingers grazing every hill and valley as his mouth plunders mine, drinking from me like a thirsty man lost at sea. He spins me around, melding his body into my backside and grinding the bulge in his jeans into my ass.

"Zak," his name slips from my lips.

Cold raindrops pelt my face and body as I splay my palms on the warm metal in front of me. His hot mouth feels feverish as he kisses and sucks beneath my ear and rocks into me.

He groans into my flesh, his breath fogging the air between us as he whispers in my ear, "I'm going to fuck you like this, Harper. Right here, just like this. I won't be gentle, but I'll take care of you. I won't hurt you. You hear me?"

I nod and suck my trembling bottom lip between my teeth. My legs quiver, threatening to give out on me, but Zak's solid frame keeps me pinned in place.

"Good girl," he murmurs against my throat, then angles my head and takes my mouth again. "Fuck. You're going to be the death of me."

His lips never leave mine as he snatches my left hand in his and carefully slides my engagement ring off. I don't protest, but it feels strange not wearing it. Like I'm lighter somehow. Like it's been weighing me down and trapping me beneath its heavy, hollow sentiment. Zak doesn't say a word as my ring vanishes before my eyes.

"Zak," I pant as his hands skate beneath my shirt to cup my breasts. "I ..." He tugs my bra down and rolls my hard nipples beneath his thumbs. "Oh god."

He retreats, his hand roaming down the length of my torso, over every rise and fall of my ribs, gently drifting over my scar and to the front of my jeans. His other hand comes around my throat, his long fingers wrapping snuggly around my windpipe as he makes quick work of undoing my pants and sliding his hand down the front of my panties.

"Holy shit," I breathe out when he finds my clit, circling it with his middle finger. He traces my seam, gathering my juices and smearing them over the throbbing bundle of nerves. "Fuck, Zak." My head slams back to his chest, resting against his strong, steady heartbeat as he brings me near orgasm with just his hand.

I feel him smile against my jaw. I bet he looks absolutely devastating right now, soaking wet and flashing that panty-melting smile and those warm coffee eyes glinting in the pouring rain. I want to see his face when he slides his cock inside me. I want to be his undoing and I want to witness him fall apart between my legs.

He pushes a finger inside of me and I gasp, the intrusion sudden but completely welcome as he crooks his finger and presses into that deliciously sensitive spot within my core. He massages my aching clit with his thumb as he works a second finger inside, stretching me out and making my knees buckle.

"Fuck, you're wet. You feel so good, Harper. So tight," he growls, his hot breath in my ear and sending a fresh wave of goosebumps scattering over my entire body as he thrusts in and out of me.

He works me over, slowly increasing the pressure and speed until I'm curling my fingers inward, not caring that my nails are scratching the paint on his hood.

"Not yet," he snaps, then withdraws his hand, leaving me empty and aching for release.

I hear his belt buckle and zipper come down. His hand returns to my throat, squeezing just hard enough to threaten, but not hard enough to hurt me. His mouth finds the juncture between my shoulder and neck and he bites down, his teeth sinking into my flesh. I cry out from the sudden shock of pain, bucking against him. He tips my head to the side and runs the flat of his tongue over the welt, licking away the sting.

"I've wanted to do that since the moment I laid eyes on you," he tells me, his lips trailing up the length of my neck and to the shell of my ear. "I'm going to push your limits, drag you out of your comfort zone, and you won't fight me on it, because the kind of pleasure I'm going to bring you ..." He slides the tip of his cock through my wetness, and I feel something cold and metallic circle my clit.

"Oh god," I moan. *He's fucking pierced?*

"God can't save you from me, kitten." His cock nudges my entrance, applying just the slightest amount of pressure where I need it most. In one heady thrust, he pushes inside, his cock long and thick and so much more than I can handle. I cry out, but my moans are drowned by the rain and absorbed by the lush forest walls surrounding us.

"That's right. It fucking hurts, doesn't it? To be invaded by something you never knew you wanted. Welcome to my fucking world."

I suck in a sharp breath and try to relax, but I'm tense and Zak knows it. He stills inside me, his grip on my throat tightening as he continues his ministrations with his other hand, his fingers massaging my clit until the ache dulls and my muscles relax around him.

"You good?" he asks lowly, as if he gives a shit about my comfort right now. I knew he'd do this to me. I knew he'd make me confess that I trust him, only to screw with my mind and make me feel things I've never felt. Fuck him.

I nod eagerly, my bottom lip trembling as sheets of rain slam down over us. Zak slides out of me, hissing when he pushes all the way back in at an agonizingly slow pace. The steel balls of his piercing hit just the right spot deep inside of me.

"Fuck, kitten. Your pussy takes every inch of me so well. You're so fucking perfect, Harper. You have no goddamn idea what you've done to me."

I probably look like a feral raccoon with my mascara pouring down my cheeks and my pants around my thighs as Zak rails me from behind against the hood of his vehicle. And his filthy mouth is only making the scene worse, because with every dirty word he whispers in my ear, I can feel my inner thighs grow slicker with my juices.

"I fucking hate you, Harper Hilton. But this cunt …" He thrusts all the way in again, giving my cervix a nudge. It's uncomfortable feeling him that deep inside, but it doesn't hurt. "I'd happily die buried inside of it."

"You don't hate me," I rush out, wincing when he slams into me hard.

"No?" He begins thrusting faster, deeper. The pressure is building low in my core, and I know I'm going to tumble over the edge soon.

"No," I shake my head. "You just hate that you wanted me and couldn't have me."

His chest hums against my back, a deep chuckle rumbling from his chest. "You're right. But now I have you, kitten. And I'm going to make you regret every time you've opened your pretty little mouth and spit those fiery flames at me. You're going to regret teasing me."

"You don't have me, Zak," I bite back. "I'm not yours. I'll never be yours."

His hand abandons my clit, and I let out a whimper from the loss of stimulation. "I'll have your pussy whenever I want it from now on, Harper. So yeah, that makes you mine."

I spot his hand rising in my peripheral. It comes down with a sharp *crack* on my ass cheek. I buck and cry out, the searing pain amplified by the fact my skin is soaked from the rain.

"Tell me you're not mine. *I dare you*," he snarls, nibbling on the shell of my ear and tugging it roughly between his teeth.

I don't typically conform to a man's expectations, especially ones who piss me off. But something about Zak's words, his tone weaved with threat, makes me clam up. When he's satisfied that I'm not going to talk back again, he rewards me with a few strums of my clit. It isn't long before my muscles contract and I feel my orgasm barreling toward me full tilt, this time unstoppable. Zak fucks me hard and fast, just the way he said he would, but there's a tenderness to his kisses and the way he's holding me close. My body is pinned between him and the vehicle, and I'm not entirely sure I'm going to walk away from this without any damage.

"Zak. Fuck, Zak," I cry his name over and over as I reach the peak of my high, then go barreling over the side, spiraling out of control just like my fucked-up mental state.

Zak groans and fucks me through my orgasm, my walls contracting around him until he's tensing behind me and grunting out his release.

"Harper. My fucking Medusa." I feel him throbbing inside of me as his erratic movements slow, warm spurts of his cum filling my womb as we both come down from our highs.

He trails gentle kisses up and down the side of my face, my jaw, my neck. I let out a soft whimper, realizing now that I'm crying again. Because it's practically a full-time job for me these days.

"Harper?" He pauses, gripping my jaw in his large hand and angling my face up to his. "Hey, kitten." His hooded eyes meet mine. "Jesus. Come here."

He slips out of me and I wince. *Yep. That's going to hurt tomorrow.* He spins me around, pulling my head to his chest so I can hide my sobs in his shirt. He holds me tight, squeezing me reassuringly and telling me everything is fine even though I know it's not. It'll never be fine again.

But it's not because of Cameron or Nan or my fragile mental state. It's because I've never felt so at ease with a man before. I've never felt safe enough to be vulnerable like this. Zak brings that out of me and it's fucking terrifying because I've spent my entire adult life pushing men away. And here he is, trickling steadily into my bloodstream and plaguing me like some incurable disease.

My fingers find purchase in his back and I release a wailing cry and scream into his embrace, the sound muffled by his solid wall of muscle. It's painful and freeing and exhausting, and by the time I'm done, I'm completely drained. We just had unprotected sex and I don't even have the energy to worry about the repercussions of such a stupid decision. And if I'm being totally honest with myself, I'm feeling a little reckless and the skin-to-skin contact felt … right.

The energy surrounding us shifts and I peel my ruddy cheek from Zak's chest to stare up at him. We're both soaking wet, cold, and I'm fairly certain I just scared off all the wildlife. Glancing up at the night sky, I see the clouds parting way, the full moon casting a dim glow on the shadowy darkness as the rain eases to nothing more than a light mist.

"Shh," he shushes me, sweeping his thumbs over my cheeks to catch my tears. He presses a soft kiss to my forehead and my teeth begin to chatter.

I force a weak smile, still sniffling as Zak tugs my jeans back up over my hips. I hadn't even realized they were still down and that his cock is still out. And still hard. Holy Helen in a handbasket. This is the first time I'm seeing the monstrosity attached to his body that he calls a dick. And the piercing … Fuck.

He stuffs himself back into his jeans and says, "Let's get you warm." Then leads me around the side of the vehicle and opens the back passenger door. Not the front. I peek up at him in question. "Get in, Harper," he says more seriously.

I climb into the back seat and slump down into the cold, stiff leather, wrapping my arms around myself to trap the little body heat I have left. Zak hops in the driver's seat to turn the vehicle on and crank the furnace, switching the heated seats on in the back. Then he slides in beside me and peels his shirt off, discarding it behind the seat and coming back with a thermal blanket. I eye it suspiciously.

How many women has he fucked on that blanket?

He sets the blanket on the console between the two front seats and reaches for the hem of my shirt, lifting it over my head and tossing it with his. We sit there in the dark with nothing more than the light of the dash illuminating our soaking wet bodies and the whir of the heaters drowning out the subtle patter of the final rain drops after the storm.

Twenty-Eight

Zak

I KNEW ONCE I had a taste of Harper, that would be it for me. I've known it since the moment I first laid eyes on her over four years ago at Stella's mother's funeral. Perhaps that's why I've made it my life's mission to push her away. To maintain enough space between us that she couldn't reach into my chest and wrap her pretty little fist around my heart and squeeze until I'm begging for her to take mercy on me.

But it's too late for me now. I realized that the second she cried into my chest and I had this deep-seated urge to absorb every last ounce of her pain and accept it as my own. I had held her for the first time in my arms while she unraveled like a tattered ball of yarn. And I didn't hesitate to throw myself right back into that same situation, locking us in the back of my SUV and mentally preparing myself for the day she decides she's had enough of me.

Grabbing her by the backs of the knees, I swiftly slide her across the seat and onto her back, her long, blonde mane dripping wet and fanning out around her like a goddamn halo. It's funny how the devil herself can look like an angel. Her oceanic pools are wide and staring back at me in the dim lighting of the vehicle. The clouds are clearing now, and within the next ten minutes, she'll be staring past me and through the moonroof at a million twinkling stars.

I force my hips between her gorgeous thighs and lean down to kiss her.

"Zak," she moans into my mouth, and I nearly blow my load again.

I lift my face away from hers and stare down at her. Her hands are ice cold as they cup my cheeks, her thumbs gently stroking the scruff along my jaw.

"Are you sore?" She nods, her fingers sliding north and delving into my wet hair. "Hmm," I hum, nuzzling into the crook of her neck, sliding the tip of my nose up her throat and nipping at her jaw. "That's too bad. Because I'm not finished with you yet."

Pulling away from her, I peel her jeans over the curve of her hips and down her legs as moonlight pours through the windows, illuminating her soft, subtle curves. Hooking my fingers into the sides of her panties, I take my time sliding the flimsy lace down her thighs, relishing the way her skin peppers with tiny bumps beneath my fingers. I toss the pathetic scrap of fabric and remove my jeans and boxers next, dropping them to the floor with the rest of our clothing.

Wetting my lips, I glance down at Harper's pretty, pink pussy, my cum seeping from her entrance. It sends a twisted satisfaction roaring through me. She stares back up at me unblinking, the heat of my gaze warming her trembling body as I sweep my eyes over every inch of her exposed flesh, my heart cracking wide open when I reach the jagged scar marring her rib cage.

She must sense the shift in mood, because she props herself up on her elbows and frowns. My eyes slam to hers and I shake my head. "You're beautiful, Harper. Every fucked-up piece of you." I nudge her thighs apart and nip at her quivering bottom lip, laying her back down and kissing her. "This fucking mouth though ... It's addictive. Toxic. Perfect." I slide my tongue over her sharp cupid's bow, dropping kisses across her jaw and down the side of her throat to her collarbone.

Her hands find my hair again and she tugs hard. My cock throbs painfully between us, desperate to be inside her again.

"Zak," she breathes out. And it's fucking game on.

Sliding my hand beneath her back, I skillfully unclasp her bra and help her out of it. My mouth waters at the sight of her laying naked and vulnerable beneath me. I suck a hard nipple into my mouth, nibbling gently and eliciting a throaty moan from her as my other hand trails gently down the front of her torso, circling her belly button twice the way she did when she teased me in the window.

She freezes, releasing a soft whimper. I peer up at her in question.

She swallows, hesitation sweeping over her expression. "He ..."

"He what?" I snarl, anger injecting itself into my bloodstream at the mention of *him*.

"He followed us that night. From Traitor's. He watched me when I ..." When she stripped for me. "And then he mimicked it with his knife before he ..." She squeezes her eyes shut, willing away whatever emotions are bubbling to the surface.

Keeping my eyes fixed on her face, I retrace the path of my fingers with my lips, planting gentle kisses down the center of her stomach, then circling her belly button twice with the tip of my tongue.

"He'll never touch you again. Do you hear me?"

Her lids crack open and she peeks down at me through thick lashes, her lips parting as small puffs of air fog up the space in front of her mouth. "Yes."

"Good. Now mention him again while I'm between your legs and I'll spank that pretty little ass of yours until you're screaming."

I drag my tongue across her hip bone and inhale deeply, filling my lungs with her natural scent as my fingers lightly graze over her scar.

"Mmm. I can smell your arousal, kitten. And it's blending beautifully with the scent of my cum dripping out of you."

Her breath hitches when I slip my hand between us and scoop my leaking cum from her thighs, shoveling it back inside her with two fingers.

"What ... what are you doing?" She rushes out, panic seeping into her tone.

"For as long as you're in my home and under my protection, this pussy is mine, Harper. You relinquished control the moment you said you trust me." I punctuate my next question with a strum of her clit with my thumb as I bury my fingers deep inside her tight cunt and crook my fingers. "Do we have an understanding?"

"Ah," she moans, wide, blue eyes staring back at me as she sucks that bottom lip between her teeth and considers her response. "I'm not on the pill, Zak. And you—"

"I'm snipped. You have nothing to worry about."

She releases a held breath and her mortified expression softens, but there's something else dancing behind her pretty blue eyes now, and I'm not quite sure what it is. Disappointment? Impossible.

Hiking her legs over my shoulders and snatching her tiny wrists in my hands, I pin her fists at her sides, her thighs squeezing my head as I lean in and blow warm air across her engorged clit.

"Jesus," she hisses, her head dropping back to the seat and her jaw hinging open.

My tongue darts out and I circle her bundle of nerves, tasting her like this for the first time. "Christ, I hate you. But fuck if this isn't the sweetest pussy I've ever had," I tell her as I continue teasing.

She struggles against my restraint, but I don't relent. "Zak, please."

I nip at her clit with my teeth, gently tugging it between my teeth. She gasps, her gaze slamming to mine as she watches me through hooded eyes. "Careful, Harper. Beg like that and you might discover the hard way that I love the sounds you make when you're pleading for mercy."

Adjusting her wrists so they're wrapped in one of my hands on her stomach, I suck her clit into my mouth and insert a finger into her tight pussy, making a come-hither motion against her front wall. When I add a second, she moans and a satisfied rumble comes from deep within my chest, relishing the way her pussy feels stuffed full of my cum and fingers.

When a dribble of our juices seep from her entrance, I lap it up, the salty tang of our cocktail stinging the tip of my tongue. I hover over her, bringing my face within inches of hers.

"Open that sharp little mouth of yours and stick your tongue out for me, kitten."

Her eyes blow wide and she snips out, "Fuck you."

Chuckling, I withdraw my fingers from her cunt and slide the head of my cock up and down her seam, the steel balls of my piercing teasing her clit. Lining my tip up with her entrance, I ease inside of her, my balls tensing as she takes every fucking inch of me. She winces, her face pinching tight as she stretches to accommodate my size.

Rolling the wad of salty sweetness around in my mouth, I grip her jaw and force her mouth open, our toxic serum glistening on my fingertips digging into her cheeks. "Don't make me ask twice." She sticks her pretty pink tongue out and I spit into her mouth. "Good girl. Now swallow it."

An arrogant smirk splits across my face as she glares up at me, her blue eyes flaring with defiance as she does exactly as I instructed.

Repositioning her wrists above her head, I lean down and sweep my tongue over her lips, slowly sliding my cock out of her, then slamming all the way back in. Her tits bounce beneath me as I fuck her slow and hard, our tongues tangling as she whimpers into my mouth. Every thrust into her causes a swell of something maddening to heave in my chest as some sick, primal obsession takes root.

"Fuck, Harper. You're killing me."

"You promise?" she asks sardonically.

Releasing her wrists, I wrap a hand snuggly around her throat, tracking her quickening pulse beneath my thumb while my other hand slips between our connected bodies to circle her clit, eliciting a small mewl from her.

"Yeah, I promise. Because you're the only woman in the entire fucking world who can bring me to the brink of insanity, then drag me back away from the edge with just a glance."

Her eyes flutter shut, a single tear slipping free, the tiny water droplet like a crystal-clear diamond adorning her cheek. I lap it up, tasting her salty sadness on my tongue.

"No more tears, Harper. I'm sick of them."

Bright, blue orbs stare back up at me as I plow into her, her fingernails biting into my bare back and dragging outward across my ribs. I've no doubt my body will look like a Jackson Pollock painting by the time she's done with me.

"My broken, fucked-up little wildcat."

Her breathing grows ragged, her labored breaths short and choppy as her greedy pussy sucks me in further, her tight walls clamping down around me as I squeeze my hand around her throat to prevent her head from knocking against the door.

"Zak," she cries out, my name echoing off the walls of my SUV, her long legs trembling as she convulses around me.

I fuck her straight through her orgasm, my balls tightening painfully as my cock hardens to steel inside of her. I find my own release, warm jets of my cum filling her up as I claim her for the second time tonight.

"Fuck, Harper," I hiss, my jaw clenched tight and teeth threatening to crack as I thrust into her one final time, seating myself deep inside of her and crushing my lips to hers.

Hot, humid air sticks to our skin like honey, our bodies welded together as we remain connected as one, our hearts hammering wildly against one another as I drink thirstily from her.

When our breathing returns to normal, I swallow the mountain of rocks in my throat and slip out of her, my cock twitching at the loss of her warmth. She winces and a small trickle of guilt works its way into my chest, seeping into my cracks and cementing itself there.

I reach between the front seats and shut the vehicle off, the air in the cab thick and hot from our writhing bodies. I snatch the blanket I keep in my vehicle in case of an emergency and unfold it, wrapping it around my back and shoulders. Then I grab Harper and roll us, flipping us so I'm on my back and she's sprawled out on top of me. She's cocooned in the blanket, my arms wrapped around her as I hold her close. My legs are bent and my head is propped up on the door because I'm too fucking tall to be laying on the back seat. But Harper's limbs are intertwined with mine, her cheek pressed to my chest and her hands in my hair, and I've never been more comfortable in my entire life.

"I have a question," she murmurs, my scalp tingling as her fingers gently wind through my hair.

"Mm," is the only sound I can make because damn this is doing something to my insides right now. I'm walking on thin ice.

"What the hell are we doing?"

"Cuddling."

She lifts her head. "I know that. But ... why aren't we just going home?"

Home. My home. With her and her crazy, old grandmother. Why does her saying it like it's *ours* make me feel some type of way?

"Just shut up and relax. For once, Harper, just enjoy something without questioning it."

She searches my face for a moment before laying back down and melting like butter into my body.

She's right. What the fuck are we doing? What's this game we keep playing? Why am I laying here with her in my arms when ninety percent of the time I'd rather ...

Fuck. I've lost the will to conjure up ways to make her life a living hell. Instead those thoughts are replaced by ways I could make her moan my name. Ways I could make her eyes light with determination and excitement. Ways I can make her forget all the fucked-up shit Brooks ever did or said to her.

Ways I can make her fucking smile.

⚫

I wake in a startle, sitting bolt upright and blinking away my sleepy haze. Glancing at my watch, I realize it's six o'clock in the morning. The sun is just barely rising and Harper's fucking missing. Grabbing my jeans and boots and tugging them on, I notice her clothes are gone too, which gives me only a sliver of hope that she left willingly.

We're in the middle of nowhere. Where the fuck did she go?

Just as I hop out of my SUV, Harper comes sauntering out of the tree line with a satisfied smile plastered on her face.

I rip into her immediately. "What the fuck, Harper. You can't just take off like that without telling me."

Her smile fades and she frowns at me. "You're not the boss of me."

I swipe a hand through my hair. "Why'd you leave like that? You had me—"

"I had you *what*, Zak? Worried?" She huffs out a sarcastic laugh and rolls her eyes, then saunters right past me toward the passenger door. "Doubtful. But if you must know ..." She turns around and opens a tiny fabric bag that she keeps buried somewhere in the depths of her purse and flips it upside down, dumping its contents into her hand. "I was picking berries." She pops a handful of wild raspberries into her mouth.

I watch as she chews and moans, the sweet sounds reminding me of being buried balls deep inside her last night. My dick twitches and Harper's blue eyes dart to the front of my jeans then back up.

An all-knowing smirk splits her face. "Sleep well?" she asks coyly.

Closing the space between us, I snatch the bag out of her hand and dump the rest of the berries into my palm, tossing them into my mouth before she has a chance to protest. She glowers at me, her lips turning down at the corners.

"Slept great. Now get in the vehicle." I hand her back the empty bag. "Your grandmother will be getting worried."

She swats the air. "Already called her."

"And?"

She quirks a brow. "You getting soft on me, big, bad dog?"

"Keep it up, Harper. I dare you."

I retrieve my shirt from the back and slide into the driver's seat, seeing that Harper's already eagerly sitting in the passenger seat, buckled in and ready to go. She seems different today. Like someone dumped kerosene on the dying embers of her spirit and lit that shit ablaze once again.

That fiery spark is back, and for some fucked-up reason, I hope to hell I'm to blame for it.

Twenty-Nine

Harper

"Hey, Nan." I knock gently on her bedroom door.

"Come in, deary."

Cracking the door ajar, I peek around the corner to find her sitting up in her bed with her nose stuffed in the same historic romance novel she's read a million times, one of her crystals clutched tightly in her hand. A rose quartz, I believe.

"I was wondering if you'd maybe want to come out to the kitchen and help me bake something sweet and fattening. You know ... a moment on your lips, forever on your hips type of thing."

She arches a brow at me and grins. "I think you've had plenty of sugar in the last twenty-four hours, don't you?"

My face goes slack. "What are you talking about, Nan?"

She tsks and rolls her eyes dramatically. "I may be old and my ticker may be weak, but these peepers still work just fine. And when you called this morning all high pitched and giddy ..."

Fuck. Fuckity. Fuck.

She knows. My sweet, old, frail grandmother knows that a giant, tattooed mercenary who takes lives and saves others for a living railed her beloved granddaughter against the hood of his vehicle in the pouring rain. And then again in the back of his SUV. That he murmured filthy words in my ear while fucking me hard and spitting in my mouth ...

Err ... she doesn't know all of that. But she knows enough to be embarrassing the hell out of me right now and that alone is horrifying. I officially want to die.

As if she can read minds, which I'm beginning to wonder if she can, she adds, "Don't be embarrassed, deary. I was young once too."

I press my fingers into my eyes and scrunch up my face. "Nan. I'm sorry."

"Oh, pishposh." She swats the air then climbs off the bed and saunters over to me, her expression softening around the edges. "Please just tell me he treated you with respect."

Pfft. Respect? Uhm ... suuuure.

Groaning and tapping my forehead repeatedly against the wooden door, I murmur, "Yes, Nan. He was a perfect gentleman."

She watches me for a beat, waiting for me to falter or say something I'll regret. But I choose to keep my mouth shut and avoid eye contact instead. Just to be safe.

Finally, after what feels like an eternity, she clicks her tongue and strolls past me, her slippers shuffling on the hardwood floor as she strolls down the hall toward the kitchen. I peel my forehead off the wooden surface and watch her walk away.

"I'm not getting any younger, dear," she calls back at me.

As if I needed to be reminded.

Nan and I busy ourselves in the kitchen, whisking and folding and baking up a storm. We make snickerdoodles, peanut butter cookies, a cherry pie made from scratch, and two batches of pear muffins.

Zak appears while we're tidying up, dressed in a pair of low-slung jeans and a white tee that stretches deliciously across his broad chest and shoulders, his dark hair still damp from a shower and clinging to his forehead. He looks like a fucking snack and I hate him for it.

He makes his way around the island toward my grandmother and plants a kiss on her cheek as if it's the most natural thing in the world. When he peeks over at me, I roll my eyes and take my frustrations out on a burnt cookie sheet.

"You ladies have been busy," Zak says with that stupid Colgate smile of his. Little does he know that I'm currently fantasizing about how satisfying it would be to insert acupuncture needles into his eyeballs.

He grabs for a pear muffin and I instantly reach out and smack the top of his hand. "Those are mine. Hands off."

He grins and peers down at my grandmother, who's smirking up at him with love in her eyes and shit in her pants. I can tell she's up to no good, as always. Nan grabs a muffin and hands it to him. Traitor.

Zak thanks her, peels the wrapper back, and takes a greedy bite right in front of me, his eyes never leaving mine. I lift a soapy hand to my face and scratch the tip of my nose with my middle finger, discretely flipping him off behind my nan's back.

He grins, then shoots me a wink and vanishes. All the oxygen in the room returns in a whoosh and I can finally breathe again.

"I like him," Nan chirps as she closes up a plastic container filled with cupcake liners and returns it to its place in a drawer.

"Of course you do," I mutter beneath my breath.

Rolling my eyes, I get back to cleaning the kitchen, placing the baked goods in brand new Tupperware I found in the cupboard and storing the extras in the freezer. I take a look around the large span of the kitchen and huff out a sigh of relief. Baking is fun and all, but cleaning up afterwards ... Fuck that. I'm over it.

Nan shuffles off to her room again, leaving me alone with my thoughts. I'm growing bored of sitting around. I'm used to a life of spontaneity. One filled with travel and adventure. But there's another hobby I've grown quite fond of since being cooped up here.

Deciding on yet another round of self-love, I lock myself in my bedroom and fish out my favorite bullet vibrator. I run myself a bath, selecting a sexy playlist on my phone and setting it on the ledge beside the tub. I sink down beneath the bubbles, allowing the warmth of the water to relax my muscles. Laying my head back and closing my eyes, I slide my vibrator between my legs. I eagerly click the power button, expecting a sudden vibration to steal me from my never-ending train of thoughts. But nothing happens.

Frustrated, I raise the toy in front of my face and try again. Still nothing.

"Stupid, battery-powered boyfriend," I murmur to myself, angrily twisting the end of the toy off and staring down into an empty battery compartment.

Now I know those batteries didn't just grow legs and walk off, so where the fuck are they?

My phone pings with a text and I groan audibly.

Big Bad Dog: Looking for something, kitten?

I open the picture he sent of two batteries in the palm of his hand and feel a pang of annoyance hit me dead center in my throbbing vagina. Asshole.

Typing like a mad woman, I respond boldly.

Kitten: That's okay. My hand will work just fine.

Satisfied with my response, I do exactly that, slipping my fingers between my folds and circling my clit in a failed attempt at drowning out the hum of the adrenaline coursing through me. Eventually, I give up trying and exit the bathtub, my lady balls blazing blue and frustration ripping through me.

Fuck you, Zak Shephard. You want to play dirty? Then let's play dirty.

Thirty

Zak

LOCKING MYSELF IN MY office, I pour a glass of whiskey and take a seat in front of my computer. Two monitors blink to life before my eyes and I tap through the keys until I find the room I'm searching for. Taking a swig of my drink and setting the glass down on the desk, I crack my neck side to side and stare at Harper's sleeping form. I'm invading her privacy, but so fucking what. There's a pair of batteries in my desk drawer that are evidence this isn't the first time I've done it. Why stop there?

Harper's out cold. I can tell by the way she's sprawled haphazardly across the mattress, one leg kicked over top of the covers, showing off her long, lean body as she sleeps peacefully behind closed doors. Her thick, blonde hair is fanned out around her, looking all sorts of angelic even though I know there's a little hellion beneath the mask of innocence she wears so well.

It's confusing hating Harper and everything she makes me feel but simultaneously being unable to let her go.

My eyes slide to the second screen and my palms immediately begin to itch with irritation. An empty room with a steel chair I bolted to the cement floor of the concrete cellar.

Flipping the speaker on in the chamber, I hit the play button and set the song on repeat. Nobody outside of that cellar will hear a thing because the concrete walls are a solid two feet thick and soundproof. A nursery rhyme sung by a young child blares through the speaker hanging high over the empty chair. I watch in fascination, a sick smile on my face as I imagine the overwhelming satisfaction I'll feel when Brooks is strapped to that chair.

This is what we refer to as *sound torture*. And it's highly effective when used correctly and in combination with other forms of torture. In this case, I'll pair it with sleep deprivation. Brooks will never rest peacefully again. Not even when he's six feet under.

I haven't decided how I'll do it yet, but I know one thing for certain. I'm going to make it long and fucking painful. I've never been a fan of the guts and gore, but I'll make an exception for him.

If we're lucky enough to find him before the Russian does.

⚫━◆O◆━⚫

"Is that her?" Harper asks, squinting out at a little girl swinging on a playset with a tall, slim man behind her, pushing her gently as her shiny, brown hair cascades behind her.

"That's her." I put the vehicle in Park. We both file out and walk across the freshly cut grass toward Taylor and her father.

Taylor plants her feet on the sand beneath the swing and stares at us, her big, brown eyes darting from me to Harper then back again. She peeks up at her father who nods reassuringly at her. His gaze swings to me as he watches his baby girl approach me.

"Hi, Zak," she murmurs shyly.

"Hi, sweetheart." I drop to my haunches in front of the girl and smile at her. She looks good. Healthy. Recovered and back to a normal life. As normal as it could get without her mother. "I brought someone who wants to meet you."

Taylor's eyes move back to Harper. I can feel Harper's heartbeat in my own chest as it pounds against her ribs. Standing, I gesture to Harper and introduce the girls to each other.

The kid beams at Harper and stretches her arm out, offering a handshake.

Her father chuckles and shakes his head. "She sees me doing that with clients and picked it up, I guess," he says, then offers me his hand. "I'm glad you could make it. Wanted to thank you in person for bringing my Tay back to me. My wife, too." He swallows and averts his eyes.

I nod rather than speak.

"Dad?" Taylor tugs on her father's sleeve. "Can I show Harper the ducks?"

Taylor's dad looks to Harper for approval before granting permission. The girl's tiny hand slides into Harper's and she hauls her across the grass to a small pond where they feed the ducks birdseed from a little vending machine near a bench.

Her father and I take a seat nearby and watch, shooting the shit about things that don't matter. I get the sense he doesn't want to talk about what the kid and her mother went through. Can't say I blame him. Some things are better left unsaid.

I watch as Taylor turns to Harper and lifts her shirt a few inches up her side, showing Harper the scar from where she was shot.

"She likes showing off her battle wound," her father tells me.

I offer him a polite smile, but return my attention to Harper. I watch her hesitate for a beat before lifting her shirt and showing the kid her own battle wound. They're bonding in the most unfortunate kind of way—through trauma.

Harper's eyes find mine again. This irritating woman is fucking with my head. She's invading my mind like some annoying pest that I can't seem to exterminate. Being inside of her was a mistake. It was a moment of weakness that should never have happened. But I'd be lying if I said I don't desperately want to do it again.

We spend another hour at the park before Harper and Taylor say their goodbyes, promising they'll stay friends and keep in touch. I have no doubt she'll carry through on that promise.

On the drive back, Harper rests her head on the passenger window, doodling on the steamed up glass in front of her face, fat water droplets splatting the windshield as we make our way back to my place.

"Do you know how to boil a frog, Zak?" Her question blindsides me and I glance over at her. She looks exhausted all of a sudden, and I have to refrain from reaching over and touching her.

"No. But I get the sense you're about to enlighten me."

She adjusts in her seat to face me. "If you drop a frog into boiling water, it'll immediately sense danger and jump out. It's a natural response. But if you put the frog into the pot of water *before* boiling, then slowly increase the heat, the frog will complacently allow itself to be boiled alive."

"Where'd you learn that?"

She stares down at her fingers knotted in her lap. "I've been doing some research about trauma and domestic abuse." She shrugs her shoulders as if her taking the first step to healing and accepting what happened isn't a big deal. *It fucking is.* "I was Cameron's frog. Except ... he didn't turn the heat up slowly." She peers over at me. "He dropped me into that boiling water and walked away. But ..." She swallows hard, and I have a renewed desire to hunt Brooks down and rip him limb from limb. "I survived. Somehow."

I don't respond, because there are no words.

◆◇◆

I flop down on the couch and kick my feet up on the coffee table. I haven't relaxed in weeks. Always on edge. Always on alert. And sleep has completely evaded me. Knowing *he's* out there, living his fucking life. Sloane still hasn't located him, and it's beginning to look like we never fucking will. But Brooks's whereabouts hasn't been the only thing weighing on me. *It's her.* The little she-devil that's been traipsing around my house in skimpy pajamas with her face free of makeup. Her and her sweet little grandmother baking up a storm in my kitchen and making my house smell fucking phenomenal. The sounds of her pretty little bare feet tiptoeing back and forth between her room and her nan's.

She's comfortable here, and that's more concerning for me than whether I'll ever have the revenge I seek on her abuser.

Clicking the power button on the remote control, I stare at the black screen of the television hung above the fireplace in my living room. I point and click again but the screen remains black.

Smacking the remote against my palm, I mutter out a string of profanities. Technology ... it's great when it works. Pain in the ass when it doesn't. Popping open the back of the remote, I stare down at the empty battery compartment of the remote and a sadistic grin splits across my face.

Naughty little kitten.

Snatching the other remotes up for the surround sound system, the lights, and the fireplace, I check the back of all of them, finding they've all been raided.

Swiping my smirk away with the back of my hand, I march down the hall to Harper's room, pressing my ear to the door and listening carefully. A faint buzzing noise comes from deep within the room and my dick instantly hardens in my jeans. She's playing a dangerous game. This dog is hungry, and there's a kitten on the other side of the door that's just begging to be eaten.

Twisting the knob, I slip inside the room and shut the door behind me, pressing my back against the cold wooden surface.

My eyes dart from the buzzing toy laying on the table beside the bed to the bathroom door that's been left intentionally ajar, steam billowing from around it.

I snatch the vibrator off the table and click it off, then creep toward the bathroom, swinging the door open but finding the room empty. Glaring at the mirror above the sink, I read the words scribbled in steam.

Hello, big, bad dog. Want to play a game?

It's the same message I sent her the night she walked into the bar and I decided to play a game of truth or dare. This naive little kitten is fucking with me. Teasing me.

Shutting the running water off and stuffing the vibrator into my back pocket, I check each room, avoiding her grandmother's room knowing the old lady is resting right now while her innocent little granddaughter leaves vibrating toys and provocative messages around my house.

I find Harper in the backyard, perched on the ledge of the in-ground pool with her legs dangling in the water. She's wearing nothing more than a skimpy, pink bikini. I peer up at the pink-and-orange sky, the sun setting just beyond the tree line of my property. Pretty soon the stars will be out.

Harper peeks over at me, a playful glimmer in her eyes. She's trying to hide her amusement and failing miserably. I take a step toward her and she slips into the water, dunking her head beneath the surface and popping back up in the deep end of the pool. Her hair is plastered to her back and shoulders, her mascara smudged slightly beneath her eyes, her lips pink and parted while she stares back at me.

"Enjoying yourself?" I ask snidely.

"Very much so." She lays on her back and floats lazily, her arms sweeping back and forth as she drifts to the center of the pool.

I slip my shirt over my head and my jeans down my legs, snatching the vibrator out of my pocket and tucking it into my palm. I stand at the edge of the pool and stare down at her. Wetting my lips, I allow my gaze to roam freely over her lean curves as they sink just beneath the rippling surface. My eyes find the scar running down the length of her side and I grit my teeth and ball my fists.

"You're testing my patience, Harper."

She bats her eyelashes, feigning innocence as her blonde hair fans out like a halo around her head. There are two little horns beneath that thick mane. I'm certain of it.

"What *ever* are you talking about, Zak?"

I slip into the pool and stalk toward her, swimming slowly and intentionally and circling her like prey. Her body reacts, her nipples poking through the thin fabric of her bikini as tiny bumps erupt all over her toned stomach and arms. I want to feel every single one of those bumps beneath my tongue.

"I'm talking about you being a battery thief."

"You started it," she retorts. "I just finished it."

"This is not even close to being finished, kitten." I swim closer and she takes a long stroke away from me. "Do you think it's wise of you to tease and run?"

Her pouty bottom lip disappears between her teeth as she continues to back away from me. She slowly shakes her head back and forth, but her eyes give her away. She loves this twisted little game we're playing.

"Then why do it?"

Her gaze darts over my bare chest, studying the ink painting most of my upper body before returning to my face. She doesn't respond, so I take her silence as consent to make good on my threats. Closing in on her, I press her back into the cold tile of the side of the pool, my hand wrapping snuggly around her throat and angling her head so she's staring up at the sky. Her legs come around my waist as she uses my shoulders to balance herself.

Of course she fits perfectly around me.

"Is this what you wanted, Harper?" I click the vibrator on and slip it beneath the front of her bikini bottoms, pressing it against her clit.

"Ah," she gasps, her eyes blowing wide as her pulse jumps beneath her jaw. "Fuck you, Zak."

"Mmm," I hum against her neck, withdrawing the vibrator and molding my body to hers. "That sharp tongue of yours is going to get you into trouble." I feel her swallow against my palm and I tighten my grip. "You didn't answer my question, kitten. Is this what you want?" Slipping the vibrator beneath the string of her bikini top, I slowly drag the toy across her ribs, inward to her heaving tits, watching in awe as her nipples harden further and the most beautiful shade of pink creeps up her chest and into her cheeks. Her body trembles when I drag the vibrating bullet over one of her nipples, circling it slowly and eliciting a soft moan from deep within her throat.

"Answer me," I snarl.

"Yes. Yes, that's what I want."

Studying her pulse and the way her pupils dilate, I tell her, "Then beg for it."

"Never," she snips.

My lip twitches in amusement. "Such a determined little thing. But you know what?" I move the vibrator to her other breast, teasing her equally on both sides. "I have all night. And there's nothing I'd love more than to deprive you of sleep, only to hear you beg me to fuck you in the early hours of the morning."

I return the vibrator to her lower half, sinking it inside of her tight pussy and pressing it against her front wall. The toy is small and discrete—about the size of my thumb—but it packs a punch.

She lets out a garbled string of curse words and bucks her hips into mine as I keep her face pointed to the sky and the vibrator pressed against the spot I know will drive her fucking wild.

But she doesn't give up, and I have to admire her tenacity.

"We're going to play by *my* rules now," I snarl. "This is *my* game. *My* house. You want to come, you find me first. And this vibrator ..." I slip it out of her and press it to her clit again, drawing another sultry moan from her. "Belongs to me now."

"No ... Oh god," she cries out when I thrust two fingers inside of her, crooking them into her G-spot while holding the vibrator against her sensitive bundle of nerves with the heel of my palm.

I place a soft kiss on the sensitive flesh beneath her ear and glance up at the sky, our cheeks pressed against each other. "Do you see any stars yet, kitten?"

Her gaze flicks across the sky, the pinks and oranges of the setting sun fading to a hazy purple. She shakes her head.

"Me neither. They'll be a little while yet. But if I don't hear you beg before the first one comes out, then you're not going to come at all. And I'm going to take this adorable little toy of yours and lock it up with my guns."

She scrunches her face and blows out a ragged breath through her lips. "I have others, you know."

A sadistic laugh bubbles from my chest. "Oh I'm sure you do. But not in my house, you don't."

Peering at me through thick, wet lashes, determination flickering behind her irises, she hisses, "I have a big, fat dildo that makes your dick look like my baby toe."

Angling my head, I ask sardonically, "Is that so?"

"Yes."

I withdraw my fingers and the vibrator, sweeping my hand around her hip and pressing the toy against the tight knot of her ass. Every muscle in her body tenses and her expression sobers completely.

"Keep lying to me and I'll fuck this hole too. And I'll make sure it hurts, just to prove a point."

Her bottom lip trembles and she sucks in a few sharp breaths. "Fine," she rushes out. "Fine. You win. I don't have one." She pauses and smirks. "I have *several*."

She's testing me, determined to see how far I'll take my threats. I won't fuck her ass without priming her first, but she's more naive than I thought if she thinks she can push limits and not pay the price.

Baring my teeth, I snarl in her ear, "Then be prepared for pain, kitten. Because if I find out that's true, that you have a bunch of sex toys hidden in my house, I'm going to stuff every single one of your holes so full with them that you'll be begging me to take mercy on you."

Her eyes flare wildly and her pink tongue darts out to wet her lips. "That's a risk I'm willing to take."

Nodding slowly, I accept her response for what it is—a bold-faced lie. I won't call her out on her bluff though. Not unless I discover a collection of silicone dicks tucked away somewhere in my home. I'm a man of action. *Words mean nothing.*

Pressing the vibrator back to her clit, I give her just enough stimulation to have her back arching and her nails biting into my flesh. My cock is painfully hard, testing the thread count of my boxers. And it's taking all my willpower to not fuck her right now and give her everything she needs but won't ask for.

"Make no qualms about it, Harper. Just because you refuse to beg, doesn't mean I won't still take what I need. It'll be *you* who goes without. Not me."

Her lids pop open and her jaw goes slack as I pump my fingers back inside of her, applying pressure to her clit with the toy.

"I'm ... I'm ..." She's unable to form words. But I know exactly what she's about to say. *I'm going to come.*

"No, you're not."

She's trying so hard. She really is. I feel her walls clamp down around my fingers and I withdraw them, not allowing myself the pleasure of feeling her pussy contract around me. Not yet anyway. She blows out a frustrated breath as her body shudders at the loss of her orgasm. It's too bad, really. It would have been earth shattering.

"Nice try," I tell her, dropping the vibrator on the edge of the pool and freeing myself from my boxers.

Tightening my grip on her throat, I whisper in her ear, "You're going to take my cock slow and deep while you gaze at the stars. You're going to feel every inch of me deep inside you. And I'm going to fucking enjoy every last second of it. Because it'll be the last time I allow myself inside of you." I wet my lips. "You're bad for me, Harper. Toxic as fuck. You make me twitchy and irritated, and I don't like it. But I own your orgasms for the time you're traipsing around in my home looking like goddamn Medusa, making me hard every time you fucking breathe."

She releases a strangled whimper and peers at me through hooded lids. She opens her mouth to speak, but I press a finger to her lips, shushing her. Then I trace the bow of her upper lip with the pad of my thumb. Her mouth is fucking beautiful, but all it does is spew shit I don't want to hear.

Something passes over her before she exhales a soft puff of air.

"Now beg for it. Tell me you want me to fuck you like this."

Sliding her bikini bottoms to the side, I rub the tip of my cock along the seam of her pussy, the steel balls of my piercing massaging her clit. Then I line the head up with her opening and nudge her gently. Her bottom lip trembles and she finally nods.

"Use your words, Harper. Tell me you need my cock."

Wild eyes peer back at me as she pants, the pressure against her pussy coaxing the words out of her. "I need your cock, Zak. Please."

"Good girl." I slowly sink inside, releasing a muffled "fuck" when I feel how tight and wet she is, how good it feels to be inside of her again. Her pussy feels like home after a long stint in the jungle, and that's a fucking problem.

She sucks in a sharp breath as she stretches to accommodate me. "I hate you," she seethes, spitting venom and glaring at me as I take my sweet time savoring every slow thrust into her.

"I know, kitten. I fucking know." I gently drag my knuckles over the scar on her side, feeling the rise and fall of where Brooks's blade sliced through her. She stares up at the sky with my hand around her throat as I nibble along the length of her jaw, my thumb stroking her pulse, tracking her heartbeat.

Long, lean legs tighten around me and her breathing grows ragged. Her walls begin to contract as she carves half-moons into my shoulders with her fingernails.

The sun is gone and the sky is quickly nearing black. I gaze up and find one lone star hanging high above us.

"Do you see that?"

She nods and curls her fingers into my biceps. "Yes."

I pick up the pace, sliding in and out of her, almost fully removing myself before plunging back in all the way, filling her completely.

Her lids flutter shut and she intentionally contracts her pussy. I can see the effort painted on her face. She's purposely squeezing my dick, egging me on.

"Oh, sweet, innocent little kitten," I taunt, licking along her bottom lip. "You shouldn't have done that." I slip my free hand beneath the back of her bikini and tease the sensitive flesh around her puckered hole. She tenses again. "Has anyone ever fucked you here before?" I ask, applying pressure to the spot that has her entire body galvanizing.

"N-no."

A sick thrill moves through me. Maybe I could allow myself inside her just once more. It would be a victory to steal this from her. It's not something I typically bother with. Anal isn't really my thing. But with Harper ... it would be a first of hers that I have the satisfying privilege of claiming. And I want it. *It's mine.*

"Good. That's good," I grunt, gently sinking my finger to my first knuckle.

She bucks from the intrusion and releases a raspy moan. Her fingernails drag down my arms, leaving scratches in their wake as I fuck her slow, the pool water lapping at the walls at her back.

"He left me a message, Harper." Her eyes widen as she struggles against me. But I don't relent. "And he used your blood to fucking do it. He thinks you're mine."

She swallows hard against my palm and rasps, "What message?"

"*All yours,*" I grate out through clenched teeth, my chest constricting at the memory of her laying broken and bleeding on my front doorstep. "Painted it on your perfect little body as if you were some fucking art project." Her bottom lip wobbles and I snag it between my teeth. "Is it true, kitten? Are you mine?"

Panicked breaths leave her nostrils as she peers back at me through hooded eyes. She shakes her head, and I bite back the urge to punish her for denying a truth we've both been dancing around for years. I know she's not giving this up. *Not yet.*

"Count the stars for me. How many do you see?"

Her eyes roll back and she blinks her vision into focus, counting out the stars. "F-four."

"Four. How fitting. The same number of years you've been haunting me for. But I own you now. And I own this sweet little cunt."

She inhales sharply as I crush my mouth to hers, our tongues tangling and bodies connected in more ways than one.

She breaks the kiss and sneers, "You'll never own me, Zak."

Shaking my head, I respond, "I already do. You just haven't accepted it yet." She glowers at me, angry at herself for conforming. "God, I can't stand you. But fuck, Harper. You feel so fucking good. Too good. *Too fucking right.*"

Rolling my hips, I continue to fuck her into oblivion, taking my time and relishing in the way her body responds so naturally to my touch. Her back arches as her cries echo through the open air of my backyard and my name spills from her lips. Sealing my mouth over hers, I swallow her sweet sounds of pleasure as my thrusts become unhinged. My balls tighten and I seat myself deep inside her tight pussy, painting her inside walls with my cum.

When we've come down from the high, our eyes clash and our mouths connect in a panicked fervor. I cup her jaw in my hands and kiss her like this is the last time I'll fucking taste her.

More. I need more of her. Hating her but needing her on a primal level has become somewhat of a problem for me. One that I don't have a fucking solution to.

It's then I decide that until I can rid my life of her entirely, nobody else will touch her. She's mine to play with until I've flushed her from my system. Until I can finally get back to my normal life. *Without Harper.*

The only issue is ... I'm not so sure I want to.

Thirty-One

Harper

Z AK PULLS AWAY FROM me, the ripples of the pool water casting a kaleidoscope of colors over his muscular frame. I haven't a clue what he's thinking, but it feels ... final. As if he just came to some sort of conclusion.

He slips out of me and I whimper at the loss of connection. I peek down at his cock and begin salivating all over again. He's long and thick, and the tip is decorated with two silver balls that seem to hit the exact perfect spot inside me. He pulls his boxers back into place, concealing his still-hard cock from view, then turns and plants his palms on the edge of the pool, effortlessly lifting his huge body out of the water and climbing to his feet. He scowls down at me for another beat, then snatches his clothing off the ground and storms into the house.

I drop my head back and peer up at the navy sky, my heart beating so hard I can feel it throbbing behind my eyeballs and my lungs threatening to explode from my labored breathing.

So many stars. I couldn't count them if my life depended on it. What I wouldn't give to zoom off the face of the earth and land somewhere up there with them. And what Zak told me—the message Cameron left on my body—makes the thought of fleeing all that more desirable.

Adjusting my bathing suit, I make my way out of the pool, grabbing my vibrator and a fresh towel off the rack and wrapping it around my body. I can feel Zak's cum seeping out of me and pooling in my soaked bikini bottoms as I drag my pathetic—albeit sexually satisfied—ass back to my room to change, bumping into my grandmother on my way. She looks me up and down, almost as if assessing me for damage, then clucks her tongue and shuffles away.

Fuck my life.

I tie my hair up into a messy bun and take a quick rinse in the shower, cleansing my body of the pool chemicals and slipping into a pair of satin sleep shorts and a tank top.

I slide beneath the covers and grab one of my stones off the nightstand, holding it in front of my face and reveling in how the moonlight filtering through the windows bounces off the pale pink surface. It's a rose quartz. The same type of stone my nan holds close when thinking of my grandpop. It's not smooth like the other stones. It's rough and jaded. A metaphor, I suppose, for how I feel lately.

There's a soft knock on my door a while later.

Assuming it's my grandmother, I spring from bed and swing the door open, surprised when I come face to face with Zak. He's normally so cool, calm, and collected. He's usually highly calculated and in control of himself. He's the level-headed one at Sweetwater. But right now, he's anything but all of that. He looks ... unhinged.

"What—"

He cuts me off with his hands in my hair and his lips on mine, groaning into me, taking what he needs and leaving my head spinning.

"Zak." I plant my palms to his chest and shove him away. He takes a step back and swipes a hand through his freshly showered hair.

"Fuck," he snarls. It's abrasive and angry sounding. And I don't fucking like it because it's not *him*.

"What's your probl—"

"Just shut up for a second and fucking kiss me, Harper."

He lunges forward and pulls me into his arms again. His kiss is needy and desperate and entirely confusing because it was mere hours ago that he told me he hated me, then fucked me and walked away like I was yesterday's trash.

"I can't do this," he murmurs against my lips.

"Jesus, Zak. Do what?"

He drops his forehead to mine, his arms locked tightly around my waist as he holds me close.

"All of this. You're fucking wrecking me, Harper. I don't even know who the hell I am right now."

"Well for starters, you're scaring the shit out of me."

His eyes flutter shut and he lets out an agonized groan. "I'm sorry."

"Apology accepted. Now, please. Let me go."

He gives me a gentle squeeze, then reluctantly releases me. I realize after losing his warmth that I didn't really want him to let me go. But his eyes are dark and haunted, and it's obvious he's barely keeping it together.

On cue, his phone vibrates in his pocket. He makes no move to answer it, just stares at me with a pained expression marring his ruggedly handsome face.

"Zak."

He shakes his head. "No."

"Yes. You need to answer it. It could be about …" I can't even say it anymore. I can't even think it. I'm done thinking about *him*. If I never have to hear Cameron's name again, it would be too soon.

Zak slides a hand through his hair and pulls his phone out of his pocket and glares at the screen. I take a seat on the edge of the bed and watch as he anxiously paces the room while whoever's on the other end rambles on. He ends the call a moment later and shoots me an empathetic look.

"Was it about him?" He shakes his head and I swallow the lump in my throat. "Wheels up?" I ask, familiar with the term used by the military that means they're going to be flying out.

He nods, and for some reason the thought of him leaving again causes my chest to tighten with anxiety and my stomach to sink like a rock in a lake.

"When?" I ask quietly, my fingers knotted in my lap.

"Tomorrow morning," he grates out. "Back to Colombia again."

"Oh." It's barely a whisper. Several tense seconds tick by. "You should get some sleep."

Coffee eyes meet mine from across the room. "Harper ..."

"No, Zak. Whatever you're going to say, I don't want to hear it right now."

He stares at me with a pained expression. Time suspends itself as his eyes rake slowly over every inch of my body as if committing it to memory. Then he leaves.

⸻⬦⬥◦⬦⬥⸻

I watch as Lainey peeks at her baby brother sleeping peacefully in Stella's arms. She giggles and smiles sweetly up at her mother, and I avert my eyes in an attempt to suppress the tears that threaten to fall.

"Did you hear that, Mommy?" Lainey asks hopefully. "He wants me to sing to him."

My heart crawls into my throat, lodging itself there and blocking my airways. Jesus, I'm emotional.

I glance over at my nan sitting across the room, her little satchel of stones in her lap as she rummages through it, searching for one in particular just as Lainey begins singing *Twinkle, Twinkle, Little Star*. I don't remember much of my parents. But that song ... My mother used to sing it to me every night before bed, her soft hands gently stroking my back until I'd drift off into a dream-filled sleep.

"You okay, sweetie?" Stella's warm hand finds mine.

"I'm fine. It's just sweet watching you two is all." *Lying.* I'm so good at it these days. Watching them isn't sweet. It's painful as hell. But as I've grown accustomed to doing, I stuff that pain deep down in the depths of my bitter soul and bury it beneath a fortified layer of optimism and charm.

Nan's bright blue eyes soften as she peeks up from her lap and pins me with an empathetic look. I hate that she sees me so well.

"Have you heard from Mac at all?" I redirect the conversation toward Joel, who's sitting in his favorite chair beside the fireplace, watching over his family.

He scratches his short beard with his knuckles and shakes his head. "Not yet. But I'm sure they're fine." He glances at me, his piercing eyes glued to mine.

What is it with everyone and the pitiful looks they keep shooting me today? Am I really so obvious? Do I have *Zak and I fucked and now I'm worried about him* scribbled across my forehead?

The doorbell chimes and I jump out of my skin. I'm on edge after Zak's kiss in the bedroom last night. The strangled look on his face when he walked out the door to go on another mission ... He wanted to tell me something. And I refused to listen out of fear of it being something that might wreck me.

Joel stands to answer the door but I cut him off. "I'll get it. I need a minute anyway."

He hesitates for a moment, then sinks back down into his chair. But I can feel his gaze burning into the back of my head as I walk away.

I take a peek at the small monitor on the wall beside the door, spotting a young man standing patiently on the front step. He's wearing a lavender-colored golf shirt with *The Flower Shoppe* sewn into the sleeve.

I swing the door open and he flashes me a wide smile and chirps, "A delivery for Hilton."

My heart starts jackhammering against my ribs as all the blood in my body freezes to ice. Nan and I are at Joel and Stella's. Nobody knows we're here but Sweetwater.

I remind myself that Joel's house is locked down like Fort Knox.

"Uhm." I clear my throat. "Which Hilton?"

"Order says Miss Hilton. That's all I know." He pulls out a clipboard and hands me a pen. I sign at the bottom and hand it back. He scuttles off to the white van parked at the curb, retrieving a large bouquet of roses and making his way back to me. He holds them out expectantly, but I'm completely frozen in place.

The flower boy shuffles from side to side, looking all sorts of anxious as I stare at the crimson petals before me.

"Uhm. I'll just leave them here." He sets them down at my feet and offers me an apologetic smile, then disappears down the street in his van.

I stare down at the flowers, my stomach churning violently. *Something isn't right.* There's a small card attached by a plastic stick poking out of the bouquet, but I can't bring myself to reach down and pluck it out.

"Who was it?" Stella asks from behind me and I startle. "Jeez, Harper. You're jumpy today." Her eyes follow my line of sight to the disturbing gift at my feet. "Who are they from?"

"I … I don't know."

"Well, are you going to bring them inside or just stare at them all day?"

Dragging myself from my daze, I lean down and scoop the flower arrangement up off the step and haul it inside, finally finding the courage to open the card and read it.

My deepest condolences.

That's all it says, written in plain capital letters with bold, red ink.

"That's so strange," Stella says beside me, snatching the card out of my hand and reading it aloud. "It must be a mistake."

"He knows I'm here." The words coat the inside of my mouth like tar. "He …"

Stella grabs my hand and guides me to a seat at the island. "Who, sweetie? Cameron?"

I nod slowly and blink away the burning sensation behind my eyelids. *More tears. Fucking great.*

Stella calls for Joel, who appears in the kitchen within a heartbeat. His eyes dart to the roses, then between Stella and I, and he vanishes, a door slamming shortly after. I hear his deep voice echoing down the hall as he speaks to someone on the phone in Stella's office.

I break down and begin sobbing, unraveling at the seams like a ball of tattered yarn, all my frayed edges raw and exposed. Stella pulls me into her chest and buries my face in her giant boobs, shushing me and stroking my hair.

"There's no way he knows, sweetie. The guys covered everything up. Technically, Cameron doesn't even know if you're alive or not."

I feel my nan's hand on my back. "Harper. Deary. Everything is going to be just fine."

"No. No, it's not. He's going to do something bad. I just know it. I can feel it."

"Perhaps," Nan hums. "But it's going to be alright."

I peel my sticky, snotty face off my best friend and find comfort in my grandmother's embrace next.

My deepest condolences.

Zak. It's Zak. He's going to go after him. Not me. Not my grandmother. I wiggle free from my nan and suck back my tears and stiffen my lip. I bolt down the hallway in search of Joel, finding him sitting in Stella's office with his head in his hands and a tormented expression on his face.

"Joel," I say cautiously, that ominous feeling growing stronger with every silent second that ticks by. "Who was that?"

He glances up at me looking all sorts of anguished. And I know. I just know.

Something happened to Zak.

Thirty-Two

Zak

I DROP HARPER AND her grandmother off at Joel and Stella's once again, every cell in my body screaming at me to not leave things the way I did with her. Walking away after confessing that she's got me completely twisted up inside was the hardest fucking thing I've ever done. But Sweetwater was going wheels up and duty calls. When I return home, I'm tying up some loose ends, finishing a job I should have finished weeks ago so I can finally get Harper out of my home and my mind. Sloane's been searching high and low for Brooks, but there's been absolutely no fucking trace of him anywhere. It's as if he just … vanished. There's a chance Osmanov has already gotten his hands on him, but I'm confident the cocky Russian prick would have gloated that he located him first. So it's unlikely.

We land in the last fucking place on earth that I ever want to see again. But this is it. This will be the final trip to take down the Colombian cartel.

But with every passing moment of being here in this hellhole, I realize something's not right. Alvarez is looking entirely too comfortable in the plastic ties we have him laced up in. I sweep my gaze around the room, eyeing each of Osmanov's soldiers individually, assessing them for any signs of nervousness. Any clues that might indicate that they know something we don't.

But I find nothing out of the ordinary. They're all focused and waiting for their orders to trickle down the chain of command.

An unexpected explosion rings through and shots are fired.

"Fuck, Shephard. We've got company. Move out. Now." Liam's words are drowned by the sharp, steady ringing in my ears from the blast as I glance around and realize we're being ambushed by guerrillas. A fucking ton of them.

"Not without Alvarez," I shout, slinging my rifle over my back and swiftly cutting his ties and hauling his ass out of the chair. I leave his arms bound behind his back and drag him toward one of the blast holes in the side of the building. This is all too familiar. This entire situation. The day I dragged Ortiz out of the burning building and was shot in the shoulder. It's like that day is on replay but with a different cast and crew.

Just as I'm about to shove Alvarez in front of me and step outside into the Colombian heat, I feel the cold nudge of metal against the side of my neck and stop dead in my tracks.

Alvarez topples forward with a grunt and I angle my head, eyeing the man at my side who has the barrel of his AK aimed directly at my throat.

Sneaky Colombian bastards.

◆─◇─◆

Sweet, plump lips meet mine as a soft floral scent drifts into my nose, sending me soaring high like the most intoxicating drug. Gentle fingers caress every inch of my tense body, drifting lazily over the ridges of my abdomen, counting the valleys of muscle as warm breath skitters across my neck and goosebumps rise all over my body.

Harper. My bold little kitten with sharp claws, a forked tongue, and a lithe body designed specifically for me.

"Wake up," she says, an urgency in her tone, her hands gripping my arm and shaking me. "Hey. Wake up," she says again, but this time in Spanish. And her voice is distorted. It's raspy and rough. Not soft and sweet.

It's not her.

Lifting my head and prying my eyelids open, I bring my vision into focus against the pounding in my skull. Blinking to adjust to the dark, I roll my head from side to side to take in my surroundings. It's pitch black and I can't see a goddamn thing. The smell of rotting flesh, human feces, and something else vile permeates the air, burning my nostrils and lungs as I inhale the putrid stench.

My first instinct is to reach for my weapon, but my arms are restrained, stretched out at my sides and secured tightly to something solid.

Sniffles and whimpers surround me, the pained sounds coming from near and far. Tugging on my restraints, I hear the clank of chains. *Heavy* chains.

Where the fuck am I?

Tugging again, it all comes full circle. I've been captured by the Colombians.

My guts roil and I lean to my side, emptying my stomach contents onto the floor beside me. The acidic bile in my nose and throat do nothing to abate the foul stench wafting around me.

I wiggle my fingers and toes, focusing on slowly regaining feeling in my limbs as my body comes alive with adrenaline. I know I've been relieved of all my weapons. I can feel it in the way my fatigues fit looser than usual around my thighs, my straps and holsters all having been removed.

My pupils adjust further, just enough for me to catch glimpses of movement as a woman clambers away from me and huddles in the corner. She sniffles, the sound echoing and reverberating off the walls. Wherever I am is constructed of steel. A shipping container by the sounds of it.

"Do you speak English?" I ask as unthreateningly as possible.

There's a stretch of deafening silence where I can hear the maggots picking at rotting bodies. The odd pained cry slices through the silence, until a female voice disturbs the eerie stillness again.

She speaks in Spanish, obviously not understanding my question. "Who are you?" she rushes out in her native tongue.

Male voices filter through the steel and I hear the woman release a terrified whimper. The end of the black tunnel parts way, and I wince at the bright sunlight that blasts me. My eyes adjust once again, and the sound of horrified hostages levitates into panicked cries and desperate pleas as three masked men come forward.

Fucking cowards. Too afraid to show their ugly mugs. Just their eyes and mouths are visible through the holes cut out of their black ski masks.

I scan the exposed skin of their arms, searching for any distinguishable scars or tattoos, spotting one that has an AK tattooed on his forearm, a Spanish quote running parallel to the length of the gun. *The Colombian cartel.*

I gather bits and pieces of their conversation and put it together. We're being sold to the Russians—the Petrovs. The sick fucks running the trafficking ring Sweetwater's been working on taking down behind the scenes. The little hope I had of remaining in Colombia dwindles before my eyes. The transaction will be clean and quick with little to no opportunity for escape. I know this because the Petrovs are the best in the business. They're the sick bastards who took Liam's baby sister, Rachel, and fucked her up ten ways to Sunday before we finally found her and brought her home.

I glance around the space, taking inventory of the civilians. There are seven women and children still alive. And two dead bodies, their stomachs bloated and their flesh a waxy gray.

How long have these people been in here?

My head is knocked sideways by the butt of a gun, and I lift my gaze to peer into the eyes of one of the masked men.

"You," he sneers in Spanish, his dialect somewhat unusual. *Spanish isn't his first language.* "I've been waiting for this moment for too long."

I lick my chapped lips and grin arrogantly at him. "I'm flattered you have a hard-on for me but you're not really my type."

His lips press into a firm line and he takes a step forward as his booted foot finds my ribs. Twice. I crumple over, my arms still strung out at my sides, sputtering as the wind is knocked from my lungs. I manage to curl my legs under me so I'm on my knees. The man drops to his haunches in front of me, bringing his masked face inches from mine, his rancid breath tinged with alcohol mingling with the other vile stenches of this godforsaken shithole.

He pulls a knife from his belt and flips the blade open, dragging the steel tip over his index finger and watching in awe as blood bubbles from the gash. His psychotic eyes meet mine as he angles his head at me. I bite down on my tongue until the taste of copper floods my mouth.

His mouth hooks into a cynical smile, and he stands and begins barking orders in Spanish, instructing one of the other men to select a *sample* from the inventory.

A fucking human being. Not product, you sick fuck.

I watch as the woman who woke me is dragged by the hair to the wall directly across from me. The man snaps his chops and marches toward the sobbing woman, pulling her to her feet and slamming her face against the steel wall and molding his chest to her back.

Every muscle in my body hardens to granite, molten lava flowing through my veins as I thrash and fight against my restraints. "Let her fucking go you piece of shit. I'll fucking kill you. I'll fucking kill you."

The man glances over his shoulder at me and sweeps his tongue over his teeth, flicking his wrist for the two other men to secure me against the wall. I struggle against their restraint, thrashing like a fish out of water as the sick fuck frees his embarrassingly small, flaccid dick and rubs it all over the woman's trembling behind, his unimpressive cock lengthening with every terrified scream she releases. My heart splits in two when he impales her from behind, not bothering to prepare her for his sickening intrusion. She bucks against his hold and screams in pain while I watch helplessly from only a few feet away from her.

I can't fucking get to her. I can't save her.

Tears spill down my face as every nerve in my body lights with a renewed flame of revenge. I don't allow my eyes to close, forcing myself to watch, allowing every sick, twisted word he says to her, every disgusting, uninvited touch to fuel my rage.

He finally grunts out his release, his assault ending soon after it began, and the woman falls to her knees, curling in on herself and making herself as small as humanly possible as she presses her meek frame into the wall. Violent sobs wrack her body and every fiber of my being aches to go to her. To fucking scoop her up and get her the hell out of here.

I keep my eyes glued to her face, desperately pleading for her to seek me out from across the container. Her gaze finally lifts to mine. She's a beautiful girl. Maybe twenty years of age. I tell myself she'll survive this and go on to have a good life. She'll get through this. I'll make sure of it.

Just as her cries begin to fade and she comes down from the assault, a shot sounds off, its piercing resonance reverberating off the steel walls as a warm spatter reaches my face. I squeeze my eyes shut as the terrified screams from the other civilians in the container escalate into a horrifying crescendo of wails and outcries.

My chest caves in on itself as I pry my lids open and stare at the fragments of bone and blood splattered across the wall in front of me. A pool of crimson stretches from what's left of the woman's skull, slowly seeping toward the center of the floor as if reaching out to me.

The man appears before me again, tiny droplets of the essence of life speckling his mask and body.

"Say something, soldier. *I fucking dare you*. There's plenty more pussy in here for me to make another point."

My nostrils flare, air blowing from my nose like a raging bull, my body slick with sweat and itching to wrap my hands around his throat and squeeze until my fingers puncture his jugular and his blood sprays the walls. But this animal before me is un-hinged—merciless—and I won't give him reason to take another innocent life.

Gritting my teeth and fighting against every instinctual urge in my body, I lower my face to the floor in submission. But I will not submit. I will forge the strength from the depths of my blackened soul before I let him win this war.

I'm coming home, kitten. Hang tight.

Thirty-Three

Harper

THREE DAYS HAVE PASSED since Joel took the call from Sloane informing us that Zak had been captured by the Colombian cartel. Three long, painful, agonizing days of not sleeping, not eating, and wanting to hurl my body off a bridge just to end my own miserable suffering.

But that won't solve a thing. Because even when I'm dead, my soul will still wander the earth in search of him. In search of one last reluctant kiss. One last lust-soaked touch. One last stupid, pointless fucking argument.

I've realized something in Zak's absence. It's that Joel was right. Zak's not the man I thought he was. I've been replaying everything in my head, over and over again until it's become this blurry canvas of colors smeared together. Raw emotions have blended until they're no longer independent of each other anymore.

The conclusion I've come to: I don't hate Zak Shephard. I hate that I *don't* hate him. I hate that I'm falling for a man who makes me vulnerable in ways I never thought possible. Because falling for him means guaranteed heartbreak, and that's the very reason I've pushed men away my entire adult life.

The bed dips with the weight of a small body beside me. Soft, warm hands find my back and draw soothing circles.

"Have faith, deary. He'll come home to you when the universe says it's time."

"The universe can eat a bag of dicks," I murmur into my pillow.

Nan lets out a long, slow sigh. "You're so much like your mother, Harper."

I like when she talks about my parents, but I hate that she's doing it right now.

Why not just kick me in the vagina while you're at it?

I don't want to think about the people I've lost. I don't want to think about how life has handed me a giant stack of shit-coated cards and told me to lick them clean. I don't want to think about how there's a very real chance I'll never see Zak again.

"She had a smile that lit up every room she walked into. And the courage she possessed ... unshakable. She was strong and resilient. She was everything I hoped my son would find some day." I bury my face further into my pillow and groan. "She was also irritating and stubborn and enjoyed ruffling your father's feathers. Oh, my poor boy." Nan chuckles softly. "He had it bad for her. He'd dish what he could back, but at the end of the day, her defiance was what kept him going. It's what gave him the gumption to be the man he was. The man I was so very proud of."

"Nan," I let out a soft sob and choke back the tears I was sure I had already depleted.

"Just be quiet for a moment and listen to me, Harper. I know you and that charming young man have some differences." *Pfft. Charming, my ass.* "I know he gets under your skin just as I'm sure you get under his. But being buried deep within someone like that, clawing your way into their warmth and settling in like a tick on a dog is the best feeling you'll ever experience. Knowing you're affected just as much as he is ... that's something to hold onto until he returns."

If he returns.

Sniffling, I roll onto my back and stare up at my nan. Her mouth is hooked into a subtle smirk and there's a twinkle in her eye like she's keeping a dirty little secret. How is she so at ease right now?

"He's coming back, deary. In the meantime, you do what you need to do. You cry and mope and be sad. But then you dust yourself off and get back to who you are. Because he's coming home. You'll see."

Swiping my nose with my sleeve, I garble out, "How are you so sure of this?"

She smiles and pats my hand. "He's carrying a lucky charm," she tells me with a wink. Zak's coin. The one I catch him rolling between his knuckles when he thinks nobody's watching. "Now how about some tea?"

Nan shuffles over to the closed curtains, tugging them back and allowing the sun to stream in. It's harsh rays are blinding and I hiss like a vampire. I'm miserable and really just want to lay in the dark and sulk like the pathetic lump of skin that I am. But she gives me no choice and leaves, returning with a cup of tea and sitting with me for a little while longer.

She tells me stories of when my grandpop went to war. He was a sailor and apparently filled out his uniform very well. Every time he came home, she'd leap into his arms and kiss him all over, showering him in affection and love and never letting go.

When she finally leaves me to rest, I sink down into the mattress and let sleep take hold, dreaming of coffee-colored eyes, a smile that could move mountains, and steady hands that somehow calm me and infuriate me at the same time.

I spend the entire next day doing research on crap that makes no sense at all.

I search for coins that resemble Zak's. I research what color aura reflects his personality. I download recipes for a gazillion different types of muffins. I read about how to successfully plant, grow, and harvest raspberries. And I research astronomy, particularly the stars.

There have been no more surprise flower deliveries since the one with the note. And Joel had it tracked, but it turns out it was ordered anonymously and paid for with a preloaded credit card that ultimately lead him nowhere. There's been no indication that Cameron may be lurking around outside or watching us from afar. It's been totally and completely quiet. The kind of eerie silence that makes a person go batshit crazy.

Joel keeps me updated, informing me that they have some leads on where the cartel could have taken Zak. He reassures me they'll want to keep him alive, although I'm convinced he's only saying that to preserve what little sanity I have left. If he is still alive, I can only imagine what they're doing to him.

I spoke with Sloane on the phone as well. She was quieter than usual, obviously plagued by the loss of one of her teammates. I asked to speak with Mac and Liam, but they're consumed with their search for Zak and Cameron and declined my request. It's as if the body of Sweetwater Security is missing an entire limb and they're struggling to pivot and adjust. I understand the feeling.

In a last ditch effort to distract myself, I decide to bake.

Sprinkling a fine layer of brown sugar on top of the batter, I slide the muffin tin into the oven and set the timer. This is my eighth batch in less than three hours. Pretty soon, the deep freezer in the garage is going to be overflowing. Not that Stella will complain. She's been consuming everything in her path with all the nutrients in her body being redirected to breastfeeding Finnegan. How she manages to keep such a great figure after two babies is beyond me.

"You're going to have to roll me to bed if you keep baking like this," she mumbles from the other side of the island, her mouth crammed full of a pear muffin.

"I need more flour," I tell her, opening and closing every cupboard in the kitchen before starting from one side and doing it all over again. "I ran out of flour. I can't bake without fucking flour."

Is that my voice? God, I sound shrill.

"Harper," Stella says my name calmly, as if approaching a wild horse from behind. "We'll get more flour, okay?"

She appears in front of me, snatching the spoon I hadn't realized I was waving around like a crazy person and setting it on the counter.

"Why don't you go have a bath? They always help me relax."

My eyes dart to the oven with the unbaked muffins inside, and I chew on the inside of my cheek. "But—"

"I'll take them out when they're done. Go. You need to relax."

Accepting defeat, I wander numbly down the hall toward the guest room I've taken over and into the bathroom, scooping up a fresh pair of pajamas along the way. I crank the faucet the hottest it will go and dump a cup of bath salts into the tub, watching uninterestedly as they dissolve beneath the running water. I strip down and sink into the warm water, dragging my finger over the scar up my side, imagining Zak's hands gently caressing it instead of my own. It still hurts sometimes, but not in the typical physical sense. It hurts because it reminds me of the life I somehow managed to escape by the skin of my teeth.

It won't just be a reminder of what he did to you, Harper. It will be a reminder of what you survived. Remember that.

I can still hear Zak's deep voice in my ear as I stare at myself in the mirror, disgusted by the thought of being marked by Cameron forever. Closing my eyes and allowing myself to slump further beneath the surface, I take a few deep breaths and calm my racing thoughts.

It all seems so small now. So insignificant. The feelings I had for Cameron were nothing compared to the hollowness I feel without Zak. He drives me up the fucking wall. There's no doubt that we're oil and vinegar. But even when I'm at my wits end with him, he somehow reaches up and drags me back down, grounding me in some unexpected way. It's unhealthy and toxic. But that's the thing about toxicity. You know it's bad for you, but you can't get enough of it.

I sink further into the porcelain tub, barely registering the sting of the hot water rising over my chin and past my lips, flooding my mouth and nose. It's scalding hot, but nothing really hurts any-more. I don't feel anything. It's as if the part of me that's supposed to send signals between my brain and body has withered away like the petals of the roses rotting on the kitchen table.

For some fucked-up reason, I can't bring myself to throw them away. Because even though they're symbolic of death—Zak's death—disposing of them would feel too final.

And I refuse to accept that any of this is final.

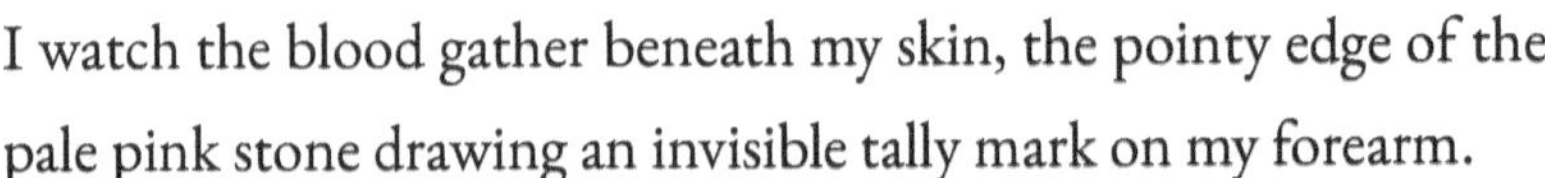

I watch the blood gather beneath my skin, the pointy edge of the pale pink stone drawing an invisible tally mark on my forearm.

Four.

Four days I've sat in this house waiting, watching Joel's every move, praying to high hell that he receives a call from Sweetwater with news of Zak's whereabouts.

But that hasn't happened. And I'm beginning to think it never will.

It's funny how fast a person's flame can be snuffed out. I feel like that's exactly what has happened to me.

I need out of here. I need away from Stella and her insane postpartum hormones. I need away from Joel and his broodiness and lack of telltale expression. And as much as it pains me to admit, I need away from my grandmother. Just for a night. Just one night where I can be alone and not feel like someone is breathing down my neck, checking on me and treating me like I'm some broken little shell of a woman.

Glancing at the clock, I realize it's nearly three in the morning. I've been laying here, wide awake, for over five long, miserable hours. But every minute feels like a decade, and sleep has evaded me completely.

Sifting through my belongings, I gather what I need and sneak down the hall, tiptoeing carefully to ensure I don't wake anyone. They don't need to know I'm leaving or where I'm going. I just need to get there and get some peace. I'll call them later. Or send a text to Stella once I'm there.

I stand in the dark foyer, typing away on my phone and ordering an Uber. When the car rolls into the driveway, I check that the license plate on the vehicle matches my order, then punch in the security code of the alarm system and let myself out, locking the front door behind me before padding down the concrete sidewalk and into the back seat of the car.

The driver makes small talk, but I don't have the energy to respond. So I simply offer him the odd forced smile and head nod until he wheels into the dark, empty driveway.

I knew Zak's SUV wouldn't be here, but that didn't stop the trickle of hope from carving a path through the otherwise desolate space where my heart should be.

I hop out and walk toward the side entrance Zak typically uses, mindlessly punching in the security code to unlock the deadbolt and let myself inside his home. The instant I step over the threshold, his scent envelops me and another crevice forms in my chest cavity like the bottomless gorge of Hells Canyon.

I rearm the system and wander through his house. It feels empty and cold and offers none of the comfort I had hoped for.

Wandering down the hall, I slip into the guest room I've been staying in. But it doesn't feel right. So just like Goldilocks, I try each room until I find one that feels just right.

Standing in the doorway of Zak's bedroom, I stare at the king-sized bed, its charcoal satin sheets strewn about haphazardly from the last night he slept in it. Dropping my purse onto his dresser, I glance around the dark room. The walls are all painted a matte black, a far wall the main focal point of the room—floor-to-ceiling windows with natural wood frames outlining the large panes of glass. The furniture is all solid wood, but sleek and modern. The only color is the rare pop of vibrant blue in the decorative pillows and the tasteful artwork on the walls. It's a blue that rivals that of the touristy beaches of the Caribbean.

I've never stepped foot in Zak's room before now. It's a strange revelation since I've been staying with him for weeks. The large, open space suits him perfectly. All hard lines and clean, crisp accents. And his scent is everywhere.

Selecting a T-shirt from his closet, I bring it to my nose and inhale. Creepy, I know. But there's no one around to judge me. Even if there were, I don't think I could bring myself to care.

Slipping out of my leggings and hoodie, I tug the shirt over my head and tuck my nose into the collar, filling my lungs once more with Zak's authentic scent. Then I wander toward his ensuite bathroom to brush my teeth, pausing when I spot a small glass dish on one of the nightstands that looks oddly out of place. Walking over to it, I lift the lid and peer down at a small collection of familiar stones. *My stones.*

Why does he have these?

Deciding to not disrupt a single part of his bedroom, I return the lid to the dish and glance around the large space, my eyes drawn to a door I hadn't noticed before. Pivoting, I tread toward it, the slab of wood calling to me like a siren in the night.

I twist the knob, scrunching my face when I realize it's locked.

What the hell could be behind it that's worth locking the door?

Curiosity gets the best of me and I rummage around in my purse for a bobby pin, holding my tongue just right as I work at picking the stubborn lock. When I hear a small click, I back away abruptly as if the door has caught fire.

Every nerve ending in my body comes to life, urging me forward to open the door and satisfy my sense of curiosity.

Silly kitten.

I twist the knob and the door cracks open, the hinges whining as the slab parts way and I step into a small office. There are no windows in here for the moon or stars to cast light through, so I flip the switch and swallow my nerves when I spot several computer monitors lining the wall over a large, wooden desk.

My bare feet carry me to the desk, and without thinking, I tap one of the keys on the keyboard and watch as every screen flickers to life. A bubble of anxiety rises inside me, reaching for the surface and rupturing as I take in the sight before me.

It's video footage—all of it live based on the fact I can see myself on the screen. The images blink and different rooms appear before me.

When the guest room I've been staying in pops up, a shiver rolls down my spine. *Has Zak been watching me in my most private moments?* Common sense tells me yes, it's very likely. But for some reason, it doesn't bother me in the least.

But when the guest room is swapped out for another, all the blood drains from my face and pools in my lower half, anchoring my feet to the floor like heavy water balloons. Squinting, I stare at the screen, several of my worst nightmares all coming to life at once.

A small, concrete room with nothing but a steel chair perched in the center, its legs bolted to the floor.

What in the fuck kind of Ted Bundy Freddy Krueger bullshit is this?

I stumble back, losing my footing and knocking into a nearby bookshelf, several items toppling over and falling to the hardwood floor by my feet. Grinding the heels of my palms into my eyeballs until they feel like they're being squashed into my brain, I blink and look again. The room is gone, replaced by Zak's dark, empty kitchen.

Okay. So Zak has a torture chamber, or whatever that room is. No biggie. It's all fine. Everything's fine.

Once the initial shock wears off, I realize I shouldn't really be surprised at all. It's in Zak's nature to be a protector, and I've known of Sweetwater's ... *tactics* ... for several years. And things get messy from time to time. Sometimes bad people need to be tied up and tortured, right?! Sure.

Dry swallowing my nerves like an oversized pill, I leave the office and crawl beneath the cool comfort of Zak's sheets, the smooth satin gliding over my skin as I bury my face in his pillow and inhale. Then, as I knew I would, I drift off into a deep, dream-filled sleep.

Thirty-Four

Zak

It's day four of being shackled to the inside wall of this hellish shipping container. The stench of death and sounds of horror suffocate me as I sit helpless, unable to save a single one of the civilians trapped in this nightmare with me.

The end of the black tunnel parts way, and in filter the same three masked men that have visited twice a day for the last three days, their footfalls echoing off the steel walls as they approach. The leader lays out his demands in Spanish, his eyes darting between civilians as he points and directs the other two stooges into action.

Lolita, a sweet little thirteen-year-old girl that was snatched up while purchasing milk from a corner store tucks her meek body into mine beneath my outstretched arm. It's just as I've instructed her to do, not only because she's safest with me, but because the second one of those fuckers gets close enough, I'm going to make my move.

As I hoped, the leader sets his sights on Lolita and selects her. A sadistic smile splits across his face as one of his men marches toward me and the cowering girl. Her terror-filled eyes meet mine, and my heart cracks in two as he grabs her by the arm and attempts to drag her away from me. He's not carrying a gun, which was a very stupid fucking move on his part.

The leader and his second lackey disappear out the door while the third struggles with Lolita, and I take my shot.

"Zak," she cries out, tiny fingers gripping my shirt as she clings to me with all her might.

I roundhouse kick my leg up, wrapping both of my thighs around his neck and squeezing so tight his eyes begin to bulge.

"The keys, sweetheart," I rush out, struggling against the Colombian's attempt to break free. "I need you to grab the keys from his belt."

Lolita sobs as she climbs out from under my arm and scurries around to the side of the Colombian, his hands grappling at my legs as he attempts to pry me away. It's not like in the movies. This shit can take some time, but I'm not giving in. Not when there are innocent lives at stake and I'm their only hope for survival.

Bearing down and pulling his weight to the ground with me, I wrangle with the Colombian as Lolita reaches for a set of keys dangling off his belt loop and begins fumbling with them.

"Which one?" she asks, panic ripping at her throat as tears track down her dirty cheeks.

The grunting and struggling slows, my eyes continuously darting to the open doorway to ensure the other two haven't heard the commotion.

"It'll be a large key. Keep trying," I urge as trembling hands bring another key to one of the locks securing the chains around my wrists.

"Got it," she chirps, just as the Colombian between my thighs falls still.

"Good job, sweetheart. Give me the keys and hide in the corner, okay? And don't say a word."

She does exactly as instructed, the brave little soldier she is, and hides in a corner. I glance around the open space, making eye contact with each and every person in here, bringing a finger to my lips to remind them to remain quiet. I make quick work of the second lock and free myself, my arms falling limply at my sides and aching like I was just trampled by a stampede of horses. Being strung up like fucking Jesus is no goddamn joke.

Searching the choked-out prick sprawled on the floor, I locate a knife and press my back into the steel wall, stepping over another dead body on my way to the still-open doors. Peering around the corner of the container, I spot the other two men standing near an old rusted-out Jeep. Gripping the handle of the knife tight, I sneak around the back of the vehicle, my feet light and adrenaline giving me the strength to forge on and put an end to these fuckers.

Without hesitation, I come up behind the second lackey, slitting his throat with one foul swoop and snatching his rifle and aiming at the leader before he even has a chance to fucking blink.

Pathetic.

He raises his palms in the air in surrender, cautioning me to not make any stupid decisions along with a bunch of garbled bullshit I don't really care to hear.

"Don't do this, soldier. The rest of them will come for you if you kill me."

I angle my head at him, swiping the sweat from my brow and huffing out a dry laugh.

"Will they though? Or is that just a weak attempt at saving your own sorry ass?" Dark eyes narrow on me, his balaclava still concealing the rest of his features. "Even if I let you live …" I take a step forward, my trigger finger itching. "Which—let's be real—that's not fucking happening, you're as good as dead. You see … you put an expiration date on yourself the second you laid your hands on that woman you raped and killed. And I've been counting down the minutes before I could finally send you to meet your maker. And unfortunately for you, my team's not the only ones looking for you. You and your little friends have made some real fucking enemies of the Russians."

His sarcastic laugh has my finger twitching, ready to blow his head to bits the way he did that innocent woman. But I won't make his death quick. I won't gift him a sweet, painless release.

"If they were coming for me, don't you think they would have found me by now?"

"Hmm," I hum thoughtfully, my ears straining against the sounds of the jungle, a smirk tugging at my lips. "Listen for a moment."

His beady eyes round at the edges as the whir of a large chopper comes near, its *thwap thwap thwap* like music to my fucking ears.

"Sounds like an Mi-38 to me. Mikhail Osmanov's helo of choice if my memory serves correct."

I hear the bird lower and within seconds, the man's gaze roams to the tree line. I don't need to turn around to know there are several Russian soldiers making their way toward us this very moment.

"And their timing couldn't have been better."

Less than fifteen minutes later, I'm accompanied by six huge Russian soldiers. When I finally have the satisfaction of peeling my captor's mask off his face, I realize it's Romero, the shithead we had targeted alongside Alvarez.

I haul Romero to the Russian bird and secure him with ties, then assist Osmanov's men with lifting civilians into the helo. We land in Panama where we're transported by armored truck to an empty warehouse. The steel garage door slides open as gravel crunches beneath the tires. I can feel eyes on us from every direction, so I know Osmanov has taken precautions. As he should.

Four armed guards flank his side as he approaches from a dark corner wearing a perfectly tailored Armani suit and black, polished shoes, his nose stud glinting in the dim lighting of the warehouse. His tattoos are a stark contrast to the rest of him, but I guess that's part of the appeal. I'm not afraid to admit he's a good looking man, but I also know he's not to be fucked with and has no problem getting his hands dirty.

A door slides open at the side of the building and in stroll the last two people on earth I expect to see here—Liam and Sloane.

My shoulders sag with relief for the first time in what feels like decades. But my relief is short lived when I realize what it means that Osmanov found me first and has called upon my teammates to collect me.

He'll require payment. I'm just not entirely sure what that will consist of.

"Hey, Shep," Sloane chirps, approaching me and punching me playfully in the shoulder as if this meeting is totally fucking normal. Her purple-tinted contacts glow in the dim lighting of the warehouse as she winks at me. "You look like shit, loser." She waves her hand in front of her nose. "And you fucking reek."

Liam's wolf eyes dart over me in search of injuries. When he's satisfied I'm unharmed, he nods and takes his place at my side, and the three of us turn our attention to the approaching Russian.

A low whistle comes from the woman at my side. "Jesus," Sloane whispers to me. "I didn't realize the dude was a panty dropper."

"Just keep your mouth shut, Sloane," I mutter to her, keeping my eyes trained on Osmanov as he approaches calmly.

"It's a pleasure to see you again, soldier. I trust my men treated you well," he says coolly, his long legs eating up the space between us until he's standing only a few feet out of my reach.

Sloane pops her gum and smiles sweetly at him. I swear I see his lip twitch in amusement as he scans her fit, camo-clad physique, licking his lips and seemingly appraising her value.

"What do you want?" I ask, cutting straight to the chase. I'm itching to haul ass home, but I know I'm not leaving here without cutting a deal. I'd be stupid to believe he'd ever do something out of the kindness of his cold, black heart.

The Russian scratches his beard with his knuckles as his eyes dart from me to Sloane. "I'd like to make a trade. You see ... I have something I believe is of very high value to you."

"Brooks," I sneer, taking a step forward and flexing my hands at my sides, every aching muscle in my body tightening painfully. The Russian's lips twitch and he nods. "Where the hell is he and how the fuck did you find him?"

"How I found him isn't relevant, soldier. But you should know that when he bailed on your team, he reached out to the Colombians and divulged some classified information that puts my family and Sweetwater at risk. That's how the cartel knew to expect you in Colombia and were able to catch you off guard. And since I've decided that your team may be of use to me in the future, it was my pleasure encouraging him to cooperate." My eyes dart to his fingers brushing over his bruised knuckles as a memory sweeps across his face. "Your boss has been looped in, and that's why your colleagues are here now. To collect you."

He turns and whistles at a guard, who disappears at the back of one of the armored trucks, returning moments later with an unconscious sack of skin that I can't wait to fucking destroy. Osmanov steps back while the guard drops Brooks at our feet. Every nerve in my body buzzes to life as I stare down at his naked form, his face already busted up and body littered with cuts and bruises.

"I'm willing to part with him, but at a cost. You see ... I've found myself in somewhat of a predicament. And if things play out the way I predict they will, I'm going to require a favor. But not from you." He turns his attention to Sloane. I side-eye my teammate standing confidently beside me, her arms crossed and head angled at him as she makes zero effort to be discrete about undressing him with her eyes. "From you."

She adjusts her posture and sniffles, then pops her gum and smirks.

I take a step forward and his guards flinch, but Osmanov quickly raises a hand in the air, halting them. "This isn't her deal to make. This is mine. You take a favor from me. Not her."

His mouth curls into a vicious smile. He's a fucking snake and not to be trusted, but there's a pang in my gut that tells me all hell will break loose if he doesn't get what he wants.

"What is it that you want from me?" Sloane chimes in.

The Russian directs his gaze back to her. "You already know I'm a fair man. But for the time being, I can't say exactly what it is that I'll need. But I do know you have some ... skills ... that could prove useful to me in the future."

Skills. Meaning Sloane's ability to tap into anything and hunt anyone. She's the best in the business and highly desirable. In more ways than one.

"Hmm," she hums thoughtfully, taking a step forward and going toe to toe with the big Russian bastard. She's five foot four on a good day, but she's staring up at him as if he's no threat at all to her. "It seems your skills are far superior to mine. You know," she pops her gum, "since you managed to locate our boy before we could. You put my tech game to shame, gangster."

Osmanov's eyes flare wildly as he stares back down at Sloane. "Who said I was referring to your tech skills, malen'kiy psikh?"

Sloane's eyes narrow on the Russian before she extends a steady hand and chirps, "You have yourself a deal."

The Russian slides his hand into Sloane's and they shake on it, his face lighting with excitement and his diamond nose stud glinting as he holds onto her for a few seconds too long. He rakes his eyes over Sloane one final time. "We'll be in touch soon," he says before spinning on a heel and disappearing into the dark.

"Well, that was fun," Sloane chirps, rolling an unconscious Brooks onto his back with her booted foot. "Let's get him home so you can go get your girl, shall we?"

Thirty-Five

Harper

BRIGHT LIGHT STREAMS THROUGH the large bay windows that serve as a the focal point in Zak's bedroom, the sun's harsh rays painfully blinding and burning my retinas. I tug the sheets over my head to avoid another wave of nausea from rolling through me while my phone buzzes on the nightstand beside me. It's been doing that nonstop for the last several hours. It's Stella. After the twentieth call, I fire a text message back to her informing her I'm fine and that I'm at Zak's. I type out a quick message asking if Nan's alright. When she responds with *yes, but you need to call me back*, I flip my phone over and ignore her some more. For now, I'll remain buried beneath the comfort of Zak's bedding and surrounded by his scent.

Just as I'm drifting back off to sleep, a loud crashing sound comes from somewhere in the house and I bolt upright as all the blood in my body freezes to ice. I hold my breath and strain my ears against the deafening silence, my heart beating wildly in its cagey confinement.

Someone's in the house. I set the alarm when I came in. I know I did. Is it Cameron? Did he follow me here from Stella and Joel's? Has he been watching me all this time?

Jesus, Hilton. You're one dumb bitch.

It's at that moment that I remember one tiny detail that could save my life: I now own a small handgun and I know how to fucking use it.

My eyes dart to the closed bedroom door and I creep out of bed and grab my purse off the dresser, then tiptoe into the office and quietly lock the door behind me. The live monitors cast an ominous blue light throughout the room, and I tap furiously on the keys in an attempt to locate the intruder on the screen. But I don't know what the fuck I'm doing or how to get the damn thing to swap the images out.

I catch a flicker of movement in Zak's home gym in the basement before the screen switches to the empty living room.

They're downstairs. Could I make a run for it and get out of the house before they know I'm here? Maybe. But I have to pass the hall that leads down to the basement to get to the door. They might spot me.

Seconds tick on as I consider my options. There are no windows in here for me to escape through. Maybe I could climb out of the ones in Zak's bedroom. But his house is a back split and it would be too far for me to jump. I'd break my legs. Or my neck.

Loud, heavy footsteps filter through the door and I know who-ever's in the house is back on the main level and roaming around. But they're moving swiftly and the cameras are choosing all the wrong rooms to display on the monitors.

Shit fuck!

I make a split decision to huddle in the dark cavern beneath the desk, folding my body in half to fit comfortably into the tight space. With shaking hands, I dig the gun out from the depths of my purse and disengage the safety and cock the hammer, ready to pull the trigger and blow a hole through any threatening person who walks through that door.

More intentional footfalls shake my very being, violently jerking me toward panic with every step closer.

I'm going to kill someone tonight. I can feel it in my bones.

Several calming breaths later and too many bullshit internal pep talks about how everything will work itself out, I sit vibrating, regretting every decision I made to get me to this place. My index finger trembles violently, hovering over the tiny switch that could end a life. The sound of a key sliding into a lock snatches the remaining oxygen from my lungs.

The doorknob twists and I squeeze my eyes shut and hold my breath, mentally unprepared for whatever events are about to un-fold. With a soft exhale, I pop my eyes open and stare at the dark figure eclipsing the doorway.

Every inch of my skin crawls as two large, heavy boots tread toward me, every slow step feeling perilous as the intruder ap-proaches. Does he see me? I'm not sure.

I cower into the darkness, my entire body paralyzed in fear as light spills in around him, his intimidating silhouette illuminated with a pale halo.

When he glances down at me, my entire world implodes in on itself as a six-foot-too-many-inches mercenary with coffee-colored eyes and dark facial hair comes into view.

"Hi, kitten."

Thirty-Six

Zak

A VIOLENT SOB RIPS from Harper's throat as she stares up at me through thick, wet lashes. I don't think she even realized she was crying while gripping that gun, prepared to shoot the intruder she thought was coming for her.

My brave little wildcat.

The handgun I gave her clatters to the floor and I reach down and snatch her wrist, dragging her out of the dark hollow beneath my desk and tugging her toward me.

"Zak," she rushes out, leaping into my arms and instinctively wrapping her legs around my waist. "You're here," she cries out. "You're fucking here."

"Yeah. I'm here." I bury my nose in her hair, inhaling the floral scent I never imagined myself missing so goddamn much, and tighten my hold, my arms coiled around her tiny waist and squeezing all the oxygen from her lungs.

She hides her face in the crook of my neck as tears flood her cheeks, tumbling off the edge of her angular jaw and absorbing into the collar of my shirt. My hand finds the back of her head, gripping her hair and pulling her face to mine. Our lips meet in a fury, our tongues clashing as we devour each other, desperate to get closer.

But it's not enough. With Harper, nothing is ever enough.

"Fuck, I missed you," I murmur into our kiss, sucking her bottom lip between my teeth and giving it a gentle tug.

Her tiny hands tremble as they roam freely over my back, up to my face and then down my arms as she inspects me for injuries. She won't find anything beyond superficial wounds, but I'll let her do her thing if it helps puts her mind at ease.

Glassy eyes dart over my face, inspecting my busted lip, black eye, and numerous bumps and bruises.

"I'm fine, Harper. Just a little banged up."

She sucks her lip between her teeth and nods. I loosen my grip to lower her to her feet but she tightens her legs. "No. I'm not ready for you to let me go yet. Please."

Dropping my forehead to hers, I blow out a ragged breath and smile. But the subtle shift in the room's lighting has me pulling my face away from hers and turning my attention to the screens.

Harper glances over at the monitors and I study her profile in the blue light, my dick already coming to life despite the fucked-up depravity I just witnessed.

Fucking Medusa.

"Wha ..." She shakes her head and blinks a few times, obviously shocked by what she's seeing on the monitor. "What are you going to do with him?" she asks softly, her face shrouded with concern and eyes wide as she stares at an unconscious Brooks on the screen, his naked and beaten body chained securely to the chair in my makeshift torture chamber.

Tracing her bottom lip with my thumb and tugging it from between her teeth, I hit her with the truth. "I have some things in mind. But first, I need to be inside you."

Smashing my lips to hers, I take a long, satisfying drink of the lean, leggy blonde that I can't stand but somehow also can't stand to be without.

She smiles against my mouth and it's game fucking on. Dropping her ass onto the desk, I allow my hands to roam freely over her lithe body, relishing in the fact that she's here. In my house. Wearing nothing but panties and a shirt she stole from my closet.

"Truth or dare," I growl into her ear.

She hisses when my teeth scrape against her neck as her trembling fingers find my belt, unbuckling it and opening my fatigues in lightning speed.

"Dare," she rushes out as her hand slips into my boxers and wraps around my hard cock. An all-knowing smirk lifts her face and my entire world rights itself.

I groan and rock into her touch. "I dare you to let me make you come while he listens."

She pauses, her body rigid as shock registers on her face. She peeks up at the monitors, her eyes meeting Brooks's on the screen as he lifts his head and peers up at the tiny black orb on the ceiling above him. He doesn't know we're watching him right now, but it feels as if we're right there in that room with him.

I watch in fascination as a million burning questions flip through her mind like a rolodex. When she wets her lips and sweeps her eyes back to mine, I continue my escapade of nibbling and sucking, marking every inch of her exposed skin. Grabbing her by the backs of the knees and yanking her ass to the edge of the desk, I slip her panties to the side and run my middle finger up her slick seam. A soft moan drifts through the silent air, her head slamming back and legs parting further to allow me better access as I tease her clit.

"Did he ever eat your pussy, Harper? Has he ever had his mouth on your sweet cunt?"

"N-no," she pants, her eyes drifting shut as she clings to my shoulders. "Zak. Please just …"

Reaching over to the keyboard, I hit the audio button and whisper lowly in her ear, "You're all I thought about, Harper. When I was in that …" I swallow hard, Harper's gaze fixating on my bobbing Adam's apple. "When I was gone, you're all I fucking thought about. This wicked mouth." I nip at her bottom lip. "This mind." I brush my fingers over her temple. "This fucking gorgeous body." I grip her hip with my free hand and tug her into me. "You're all I wanted. Every goddamn second. You're the reason I made it out alive, Harper."

She shakes her head, her eyes welling with tears. "Zak ..."

"Don't deny me, Harper. Not right now when I need you most."

Her chin wobbles, one silent tear breaking free from the corner of her eye. I swipe it away with my thumb and finish. "Now ... are you going to let me make you come all over my face like a good girl while he listens from my basement, or are you going to tap out?"

Deciding she needs a nudge in the right direction, I gently push one finger inside her tight pussy and crook it, making a come-hither motion and circling her clit with my thumb.

"Jesus," she breathes out, a blush of pink dusting her cheeks. "Okay. Yes. Yes, make me come while he listens." She says the words loud and clear, and I can't help but seek out Brooks's reaction on the screen. I know he recognizes that sweet, sultry voice, because the way he's glowering at the camera, his naked body caked in filth and chest heaving in anger ...

He had this. He had her and he gave her up. But Harper's mine now, and since I haven't had a chance to torture him the way I so desire, I'm going to cling to this opportunity to rub it in his ugly fucking mug.

Reaching up, I adjust the monitor on the wall, the arms of the mount stretching and offering Harper a view of the screen. A sadistic little smile splits across her angelic face, and I can't help the swell of pride rising in my chest.

My psychotic little kitten.

I quirk a brow. "Not as innocent as you lead everyone to believe, are you?"

She hums into my mouth, shaking her head and digging her nails into my back. I abandon her pussy and help her out of my shirt, her tits bouncing freely before my eyes and her golden mane falling in loose waves down her back.

"Fuck, you're beautiful," I murmur, pulling one of her pretty, pink nipples into my mouth. Frantic hands grip my hair, tugging against my scalp as I circle her rosy bud, switching sides and leaving her pussy aching with need.

Her breathing grows erratic as pleasure mixes with the adrenaline of Brooks listening to every sound she makes. Every mewl and moan and sloppy sound of my mouth exploring her gorgeous body.

Hooking my finger into the lace of her panties, I shred them from her body and drop to my knees, guiding her bare feet to my shoulders. "Lay back," I instruct, pressing my palm to her chest and shoving her down. She complies, propping herself up on her elbows and staring down at me with lust-filled eyes. My tongue flicks out, lapping at her wet cunt. Her body trembles from the minimal contact, the anticipation of what's to come causing her nerves to twitch uncontrollably.

I eye her glistening center and begin to salivate at the thought of devouring her. "Your pussy is weeping for me, kitten. Like honey dripping from the walls of your core." I lick the entire length of her seam, my dick rock hard and begging to be freed. "And just as fucking sweet. It's a pity he never got a taste of this."

Wild, blue eyes dart between the monitor and the starving man between her thighs. She's watching his reaction, just as I hoped she would. With my eyes on hers, I circle her clit with my tongue, the tiny bundle of nerves engorged and swollen with blood. The sweetest of sounds, like a melodic symphony of moans and whimpers fills the silence as I slowly increase the pressure and speed, licking and sucking at her pussy.

"Zak." She bucks against my face, her thighs squeezing my head as I insert one finger and crook it at the perfect angle. "Oh god. Fuck."

"That's right. Make him listen while you scream my name, kitten. Show him who you belong to now."

I insert a second finger, applying more pressure to her front wall. Her slick juices coat my fingers, seeping from her opening and pooling in the palm of my hand.

Her grip on my hair tightens as she holds on for dear life, riding the waves of pleasure as I finger fuck her and eat her out like the famished man that I am. She reaches the peak of her orgasm and I withdraw my fingers at just the right moment, her body emptying itself and soaking my face and beard as she squirts all over me.

"No. Fuck. Zak. What—"

"Shut up, Harper," I snap out, standing and freeing my cock.

Her mouth drops open and she stares down at my hand wrapped around my cock, using the juices I collected in my palm to lubricate myself. I drag the tip up and down her soaking pussy, the steel balls of my piercing teasing her clit and eliciting a sharp gasp from her. Coiling an arm around her waist so her back is arched beautifully and her tits are in my face, I push inside her in one heady thrust, groaning as her pussy clamps down around me.

She cries out, her body tense as she works to accommodate my size. I settle inside her, allowing her to adjust to the intrusion. "You soaked my face, kitten. Now clean it up."

She stares up at me through thick lashes, a protest hanging on the tip of her tongue.

"Did I stutter? I said *clean it up.*"

Swallowing hard, she drags the flat of her tongue up the length of my throat and across my jaw, lapping her own juices from my face and neck, her giant oceanic pools wide and doe eyed like some innocent little kitten licking milk from a bowl.

"Good girl," I praise as I begin rocking into her, ravaging her mouth and tasting her sweet nectar on her lips as I slam into her forcefully, taking what's mine.

"Tell me this pussy is mine, Harper. Admit that every time he touched you, every time his lips were on yours, that you thought of me instead. Because nothing compares to this. Nobody has ever twisted me up the way you do. Sinking your sharp little claws into me and dragging me into the depths of hell. You're everything, kitten. You're sweet and vile and irritating and addictive. You're fucking *it* for me, Harper. And I want you to admit that you feel it too." Plowing into her hard, I fuck her deep and rougher than she probably deserves, my balls slapping against her ass as the desk bumps the wall behind it. She exhales sharp puffs of air as I knock the wind from her lungs. "Tell me you're mine," I snarl, my tone leaving no room for protest.

Her eyes dart from me to the screen again, and I see it all over her pretty face. *She's mine.*

"Yes, I feel it too. I'm yours, Zak. But please—"

"Please what? Tell me what you need from me."

Her breath hitches with each thrust, her gaze glued to mine as she contemplates whether what she's about to say is wise or not. I slow the pace and roll my hips, my pubic bone grinding against her clit and giving her the stimulation her body craves.

"Tell me what you need, Harper. And I'll give it to you. No questions asked."

She arches into me, her nipples grazing my shirt and nails biting into my back as I hold her close and nuzzle into her hair. "Please. Just ..." She whimpers, her hesitation thick and frustrating the hell out of me. "Please don't break me," she murmurs softly.

Shaking my head and drawing slow circles with my hips, I whisper in her ear, "You're already broken, kitten. But I'll happily collect your shattered pieces and keep them for myself."

Her soft moans escalate, reaching a piercing crescendo as I keep the pace agonizingly slow. I'll fuck her hard again later. For now, this is hers. This is so she can finally accept that there's some external force binding us against our own volition. Every fiber of my being wants to fuck her until I split her in two, but I just can't bring myself to do it after she begged me not to break her.

Her pussy clamps down around my cock, her throaty cries echoing off the bare walls of my office. She comes hard, her legs trembling and muscles contracting tightly around my dick, sucking me in so deep that I can feel that I'm reaching all the way inside her. White teeth sink into my neck, sucking and licking away the sting as I thrust into her, hot spurts of cum filling her pussy, overflowing and seeping down her ass and onto the desk.

"Fuck, Harper. So good. So goddamn good."

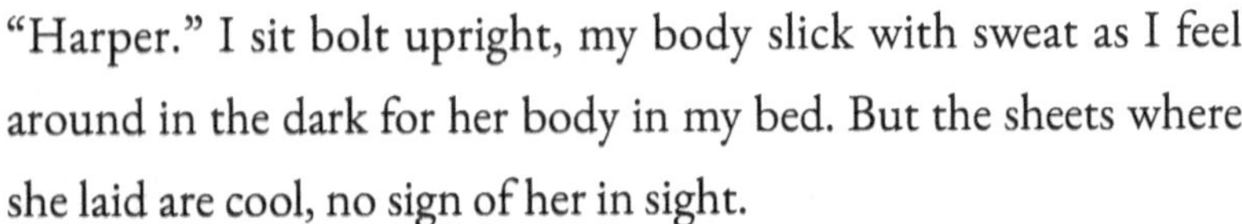

"Harper." I sit bolt upright, my body slick with sweat as I feel around in the dark for her body in my bed. But the sheets where she laid are cool, no sign of her in sight.

Scrambling to my feet, I tug on a pair of sweatpants and slide into my office, searching the screens for the sneaky little kitten who slipped away from me. What I see causes my heart to lodge itself into my throat.

"Fuck," I mutter under my breath, watching in astonishment as Harper wanders through my home gym, my shirt falling mid-thigh and her bare feet padding on the concrete. Her gaze is fixed on the double steel doors at the back of my basement. She pauses and stares at the levers for a beat. Then she slowly reaches for them, pressing down and watching in awe as the metal parts way.

She takes a step over the threshold and I switch to the camera in the cellar where Brooks is secured.

"Ah, fuck, kitten."

I bolt down the hall and stairs and skid to a stop in the doorway to the cellar. Brooks's cold, gray eyes find mine briefly before he returns his attention to Harper, her back to me and her arms stretched out in front of her as her trembling hands aim the gun directly at Brooks.

I should go to her. I should scoop her up into my arms and get her the fuck out of here. But instead, I take a step back out of obvious view and watch in anticipation of how she chooses to handle this. Power and control are two things she's been stripped of since his assault, and this is her opportunity to recapture some of what he took from her. It'll cost her the remaining pieces of who she once was. It'll haunt her for the rest of her life. But me stealing it from her would be worse, because she'd never forgive me for denying her the satisfaction of watching her abuser take his last breath. This is how she'll free herself from the shackles of the trauma he caused her.

Thirty-Seven

Harper

Now that Zak's resting, I can do something I've been hoping to do since I first saw Cameron's face on that monitor.

Cameron hurt me. *Immensely.* He almost fucking killed me. Deep down, I knew this day would come, but now that it's here, I'm not entirely sure I'm strong enough to get through it. I should wake Zak and ask him to take me to him. I know he would because supporting me, even in the most unconventional of ways, is something he does without hesitation. Syphoning power and injecting it straight into my veins comes naturally to him. But I need to do this alone. I need to face Cameron and prove to myself that he didn't destroy me the way I thought he did.

Go get him, kitten.

Every cell in my body swells with a nauseating level of adrenaline when I take a step over the threshold and meet a set of stormy gray eyes, their whites tinged pink from blood and retinas burning a hole straight through my soul.

I open my mouth to speak, but all that comes out is a shaky breath.

Dried blood is crusted over Cameron's face, his blond facial hair stained brown and longer than usual. His typical military-style buzz cut has long since faded, short blond curls sprouting from his scalp. I didn't know his hair was naturally curly, nor do I care anymore. It simply proves how little I knew of the man I agreed to marry.

Cold, lifeless eyes rake over my body, fixating on my bare legs a moment too long. White hot rage that's been simmering on low finally bubbles to the surface and I lunge forward, screaming as I slam the butt of my gun over Cameron's head, his flesh splitting open and a fresh crimson oozing from the wound and splattering my face.

"I fucking hate you," I wail, the unforgiving metal of the gun cracking into his skull once more before I'm stumbling back and putting a safe distance between us again.

Every one of my limbs wobble uncontrollably as I lift the gun in front of my face, aiming it directly at the man I once loved. A man I once thought *loved me*.

"You raped me. You beat me. You left me for dead on the fucking doorstep of the man you thought I was sleeping with."

His brows pinch tight as his mouth opens and closes like a fish out of water.

"You deserve to rot in hell." I cock the hammer, my arms trembling and palms sweating profusely. "And those roses you sent ... You bastard."

"Harper," he rasps out. Fuck. I've almost forgotten what his voice sounds like. The same voice that used to comfort me now causes the hairs on the back of my neck to stand on end.

Shaking the gun threateningly, I spit out, "Don't fucking say my name." My voice cracks from the anger spilling into it. A manic laugh erupts from my chest and I take a step toward him. "Did you send the roses to my grandmother as well?" He blinks, and I have my answer. "You sick fuck," I sneer. "How dare you."

"Harp—"

"Shut up," I screech, taking another step forward. "You want to know what the best part is, Cameron? You thought I was fucking Zak when I wasn't. But now ... yeah. I am. And his cock is twice the size of yours. And he knows how to fucking use it."

Inhaling one final, deep breath, I slide my finger over the trigger and close my eyes. Cameron's pathetic pleas and woeful cries for forgiveness fade into the background, the whining and sobbing absorbed by the thick concrete walls surrounding us as I imagine a solid, warm body behind me. One that will never cause me pain in any way I don't crave on some deep, profound level. Strong, steady hands drift from my fingers and up my arms, adjusting my shoulders and hips just so, lining my body up into a proper shooting stance as the scent of sandalwood, gunpowder, and the woods waft around me, wrapping me up in its sweet, melancholic blanket.

Breathe, kitten.

Snapping my eyes open, I ready. I aim. *And I fucking fire.*

My hand makes one final swoop on Cameron's stomach, finishing off the tail end of the image I've painted. It's just the way he did to me before dumping me on Zak's doorstep. Except instead of *all yours*, I've decided on something else.

A single rose.

Stepping back, I admire my artistic abilities, smiling as Cam's head bobs limply from loss of blood. I hadn't aimed for his head. No. That would have been too easy. Instead, I aimed for his stomach and collected the blood from his wound.

"Kitten."

I startle, spinning around and finding Zak standing in the doorway, concern marring his handsome features.

"Zak," I say numbly. "He sent roses. I fucking hate roses."

"Jesus, Harper," he grates out, taking a step forward.

I match it with one step back. "Let me finish it, Zak. I have to finish it." He takes another step forward. "I never finish anything. Let me commit to this one thing. For once in my life. Please. I need to finish this."

His jaw slides as he studies me for a moment. He finally nods. But it's not without hesitation.

My shoulders relax as he circles me slowly, a familiar heat pressing into my backside as he nuzzles into my hair. "You want to paint this place red with his blood, kitten, then let's fucking do it."

He's going to let me do it. Zak's going to let me take Cameron's life. And he's going to stand behind me while I finally finish this thing once and for all.

Strong, steady hands drift up my arms, just the way I imagined when I shot Cameron in the stomach. I know I'm taking this from him. I know he wants to watch Cam suffer and be the one to end it all. But I need this more, and he knows that. Because right now, I'm spiraling faster than ever. Except now, I can see my rock bottom. And it's cold, lifeless, gray eyes are staring right back at me as I prepare to end his existence.

I can be that tether for you, kitten. I can hold you down until you're back on your feet again.

Zak's promise to be my tether, to be the stability I need while I figure it all out, plays on repeat in my head. I'm counting on him, and somehow I know he won't let me down.

"I've got you," he murmurs hotly in my ear as his hands skim down my body, adjusting my hips to the right angle the way he did when he was teaching me to shoot.

I release a held breath as one rough hand skates beneath the shirt I stole from his closet, heading north until he's cupping my bare breast and tweaking my nipple while the other sinks between my thighs, his middle finger finding my clit and circling it.

"You look incredible right now, kitten. His blood coating your hands. Fucking beautiful. *Powerful.*"

My knees buckle, but Zak's arm comes around my waist, holding me close as I aim the gun at Cameron's head. My hands are still shaking and my fingers are slick with the crimson essence of life, but now I'm quivering for an entirely different reason.

Warm, minty breath skates across my neck as Zak murmurs into my ear, "Take your freedom back from him, Harper." One long finger pushes inside me and I release a soft moan as I watch Cam's head bob limply. He's going to bleed out and die whether I do this or not. But something about finishing him like this—with Zak's hands and mouth on my body—is disturbingly satisfying. "Take back what he stole from you and give it to me instead."

Give it to me instead.

This time, I keep my eyes open. And I don't even hesitate applying pressure to the trigger. A shot sounds off and I feel the warm splatter of blood assault my face and arms.

Red. So much fucking red.

And there lay the remains of the man I promised to spend the rest of my life loving. To have and to hold. *Until death do us part.* The vows we would have exchanged someday. The ones we agreed on but never quite made it to.

Zak doesn't say a word as he gently guides the weapon lower, taking it from my hands and tucking it into his waistband while I stand stalk still, staring at Cameron's slack face, blood trickling from the gaping hole between his eyes. A steady hand appears in front of me, disrupting my view of the man I just murdered. He opens his palm, offering me a simple, solitaire diamond engagement ring. The one Cameron proposed to me with. The one Zak slipped off my finger before claiming me as his own in the pouring rain.

With trembling hands, I accept it and saunter forward, dropping the meaningless ring at Cameron's cold, dead feet, its thin band swallowed whole by the thickening puddle of blood.

Within a heartbeat, I'm scooped up into a pair of familiar arms and wisped away, every step away from Cameron's lifeless body allowing one more brick to be lifted from my soul. By the time we've made it to the bathroom, the weight is gone completely and my lungs begin to expand and contract as I breathe in the freedom I've been deprived of, the weight of Cameron's assault now gone, having suffocated me in more ways than I ever realized.

Setting me on my feet, Zak makes quick work of peeling the shirt over my head and removing his sweatpants. He pushes me roughly against the shower wall and seals his body to mine. Sticky blood smears between our bodies, bonding us in some sick, fucked-up way as warm, firm lips crush mine. My breath hitches as Zak's skilled fingers slide between my slick folds and circle my clit. His tongue sweeps into my mouth, tasting me like I'm the sweetest drug as I moan into his kiss. All tenderness has been tossed out the window like a used napkin, replaced by raw, unfiltered lust.

"Mine," he growls, his lips breaking free from mine and brushing over my neck and collarbone. He rolls my nipple beneath the pad of his thumb, eliciting a throaty moan from deep within my chest as his other hand continues its ministrations. "These tits are mine." His knuckles brush gently over the scar on my ribs. "Your pain is mine." He pushes two large fingers inside of me and I gasp from the sting of his intrusion. "All of you is mine, Harper."

Nodding eagerly, I breathe out, "Yes."

"I want to hear you say it. Tell me you're mine."

"I'm yours, Zak. *All yours.*"

Satisfaction rumbles from his chest and I grip the base of his thick cock, stroking the length of him and swiping my thumb over the bead of cum glistening on the tip.

He stops me with his hand around my throat, tilting my head back so I'm looking up at him. "You sore, kitten?"

"Yes," I rush out, my pussy still tender from when he fucked me on his desk in front of the monitors while Cameron listened from the basement. Then again in his bed before exhaustion finally took him from me.

"But you're going to let me fuck you anyways. Aren't you?"

I sink my teeth into my lip and nod. There's a fine line between pain and pleasure, and Zak knows how to expertly toe it.

My lip is tugged from between my teeth. "I want you in my bed. Now and every night. Got it?"

Words have literally escaped me, so I simply nod in agreement.

"Good girl."

Rough hands skate down the length of my body, cupping my ass and lifting me into his arms. My legs wrap around his hips and he lines himself up with my opening, pushing inside in one forceful thrust.

My breath hitches from the pain. But then the cold steel of his piercing hits my sweet spot and I feel myself relaxing around him.

My wet, naked back suctions to the tile wall as Zak's thrusts come hard and fast as the remnants of Cameron's blood is washed from our bodies, the water tinged pink and swirling down the drain at Zak's feet.

Just like that, a life has been smeared from the face of the planet, and I'm not sad about it.

"Fuck me like you hate me, Zak," I whisper in his ear, my nails biting into his skin and dragging across his back.

"I do hate you, Harper," he snarls, dragging his lips over my jawline and to my ear. "You're fucking wrecking me."

Filthy words echo off the shower walls as he drives wildly into me, stealing my breath and causing something dark and toxic to unfurl inside me.

"But if being wrecked is the price I have to pay to have you, then I'll fucking pay it. A million times over."

He takes what's his, dragging me with him as my own orgasm peaks and we tumble over the cliff together.

We come down from our highs, both panting and completely spent. Zak gently slides out of me and I wince from the sting of being railed so hard. He lowers me to my feet and shuts the shower off, snatching my hand in his and leading me back into his bedroom.

I yelp when I'm swiftly tossed onto my back on the mattress. Zak crawls between my thighs, his hips pressing into me and hard cock smashed between us.

Jesus Christ. The man's a machine.

"Zak—"

"Shut up, Harper," he murmurs against my mouth. His stamina is unmatched and I'm left gasping for air as his huge, wet body molds to mine, dwarfing me with his weight. He lowers himself onto his forearms on either side of my head.

"Zak," I repeat softly. "I'm ..." I swallow hard.

His expression sobers and he drops his forehead to mine after planting a chaste kiss on the tip of my nose. Our breath mingles as we inhale each other's oxygen the way we often do. He closes his eyes and calms his breathing as my hands explore the ridges and valleys of his muscular back and arms.

The desire to ask questions revs high in the back of my mind, but I won't push him for details right now. Because in this moment, the details don't really matter.

Our hearts beat wildly in our chests, exchanging power and feeding off each other. I can feel every pulse of the organ that keeps him breathing, relishing the way it picks up speed when I touch my lips to his.

Zak's affected by me just as much as I am him. And I've never been so grateful to be tethered to a man who knows exactly how much to give and take. He reads me like an open book, tapping into my mind in ways I can't explain and allowing me to be un-apologetically *me.*

Reluctantly, he rolls his large body off mine, snaking an arm around my waist and dragging me against his chest and weighing my legs down with one of his own. We lay like this for a while, just ... *being.*

"Truth or dare, kitten," he whispers in my ear, his warm breath causing my skin to pepper with goosebumps as he lazily drags his fingers up and down my spine.

"Truth," I respond sleepily, the adrenaline of the morning long gone and exhaustion kicking in.

"Why'd you sneak into my house while I was gone?"

Peeking up at Zak's handsome face, I feel a spark of something flicker to life inside me. It's my snark, and she's back with a vengeance. "Well, when you were gone, I wore my vibrator out and needed to retrieve the dildo I forgot to pack. It's this long." I lift my hands and hold them a foot and a half apart. "Maybe you've seen it somewhere?"

I yelp when he playfully nips at my shoulder.

"Fine," I sigh, rolling my eyes dramatically even though Zak can't see them. "I needed more batteries and knew where you kept them."

I let out a squeal when he flips me onto my stomach, grabbing my hips and roughly dragging me onto my knees. He delivers one harsh smack to my ass cheek.

"Zak," I screech. "That fucking hurt."

"Tell me, Harper. Does it make you wet running your mouth like that?"

"No. I'm dryer than the Sahara Desert right now."

"Liar," he hisses, skimming a finger up my seam to gather my juices, spreading them over the tight knot of my ass. I instantly clench, every muscle in my body rejecting his touch.

"I promised I'd fuck this ass, Harper. And you're making it incredibly difficult to refrain from driving my cock deep inside and tearing your tight little hole to shreds." He swats my ass again, then smooths the sting out with the palm of his hand. "Now are you going to be a good girl and tell me the truth? Or do I need to deliver on my promise?"

"I'll tell the truth. I'll tell the truth," I rush out, and he releases me.

I roll onto my back and tug the sheets over my naked body as Zak sits perched on his knees, staring down at me in the pitch black.

"The truth, kitten. *Now*."

"Okay. Okay. Jeez. If you must know … I couldn't sleep and thought maybe if I came here, that I could get some rest."

Awkward silence stretches on as Zak processes my admission. "Are you saying you're comfortable in my home?"

I shrug my shoulders and smack my lips. "I don't know. Your house isn't a *complete* dump, so yeah … I guess I'm comfortable here."

I don't need to see Zak's smile because I can *feel* it. His house is fucking beautiful. All natural wood and modern fixtures. The decor is minimal, but what artwork and detail there is, is high quality and tastefully done.

"And children …"

My chest cracks open. "Yeah." I've thought about this more than a few times since Zak told me he was snipped. And the truth is, it fucking hurts. But I'm not entirely sure in my fragile state of mind whether or not I can decide if having children is something I'm willing to forego in order to be with Zak.

He flops down beside me, pulling me into his arms and nuzzling into my hair. "Vasectomies can be reversed," he whispers against the shell of my ear. Wiggling in his embrace, I roll over and peek up at him, a thousand questions souring the tip of my tongue. He plants a kiss on my forehead and sighs. "Get some rest, kitten."

And that's exactly what I do.

Thirty-Eight

Zak

H ARPER'S MINE. SHE SAID the words willingly and nearly brought me to my knees in the process. This storm of a woman has destroyed every belief I've ever had. And I can't think of any other way I'd rather die than at the hands of the irritating little blonde that I can't get out of my head. Fuck. She's everywhere. She's in the air I breathe. She's in every shadow lurking in the dark. She's in my goddamn veins, rolling through me like some sort of lethal drug.

And right now, she's lying next to me. In my bed. And I never want to let her out of my sight again.

Her long lashes are fanned out across her cheeks as tiny puffs of air leave her barely parted lips. Her mouth hooks into a faint smile and I wonder what the hell she's dreaming about that has her so happy. Sweeping a lock of hair off her face, I study her features.

Sharp and angular, like a goddamn runway model. But those lips of hers ... so full and pouty with a sharp cupid's bow.

She's fucking beautiful.

"Stop watching me sleep," she whispers, her eyes still closed but her smirk deepening. "It's creepy."

"I love watching you sleep, kitten. It's the only time you're not running your mouth."

"Hmm," she hums, her blue eyes popping open and finding mine.

Up close, her irises are a vivid blue, like the clear waters of an island beach, but they're rimmed with a darker shade, like the deepest parts of the ocean. Those two blues have been my favorite colors for years. Perhaps the reason why I chose to be surrounded by them.

"You look tired. Did you sleep?" she asks sweetly.

"I did. But you snore like a lumberjack and kept waking me up." I grin down at her and lace our fingers on my chest, rubbing my thumb over her smooth knuckles.

She scowls and stares at our interconnected hands. "You look ..." Her throat bobs against my chest as she swallows, gathering her words carefully. "You look haunted, Zak."

My smile falters. "It comes with the job sometimes. Give me a few days and I'll be good as new." I won't be, but she doesn't need to bear that burden after what she's been through. The truth is, there are some missions that no matter how much therapy or time passes, they haunt each of us eternally.

Harper's shoulders sag in relief, but her eyes tell me she can see right through me. She props herself up on an elbow and I watch as the gears in her head slowly turn over.

"You should eat something."

Rolling her on top of me, I shift her into a straddling position. Her pert nipples graze my bare chest as her thick hair cascades around us.

"Hmmm. I'm hungry for a cute, innocent kitten." I drag the head of my cock up and down her seam, teasing her clit with my piercing, then thrust upward, easing inside of her. *Where I fucking belong.* She releases a sharp gasp and supports her weight with her palms on my chest, arching her back and giving me the most incredible view of her body.

It takes her a few adjustments, but she eventually accepts every inch of me into her.

She rolls her hips, grinding her wet pussy over me as she rides my cock slowly and sensually. I play with her tits and thumb her clit, her juices dripping down my balls as she comes hard around my cock. I meet her shortly after, filling her with my cum and kissing every inch of flesh I can get my greedy mouth on.

She rolls off me and we lay quietly with our limbs intertwined, staring at each other as though neither of us understand what's happening. This ride we're on—this wild roller coaster of ups and downs and stomach-churning loops—I never want to get off.

"I'm making you breakfast," she eventually says, prying herself from my embrace and slipping into one of my shirts and a pair of panties.

She swiftly disappears into the kitchen in a blur of wavy, blonde hair and long legs. I hear her rummaging around, pots and pans clanking and the fridge door opening and closing. Slipping out of bed, I take a quick shower, snatching my discarded fatigues and shirt off the floor. Something clatters against the tile at my feet and I glance down at the floor.

Snatching the familiar turquoise stone up, I hold it to the light and inspect it. I'm still finding these damn rocks everywhere. But for one to be inside the pocket of the fatigues I wore home from Colombia? Odd.

Tucking the stone into the pocket of my sweats, I find Harper in the kitchen, barefooted and sexy as fuck, whipping up a batch of scrambled eggs, bacon, pancakes, and French toast.

I pause and quirk a brow at her. "Take up cooking while I was gone?"

She flashes me a charming smile and returns to whisking batter for god-knows-what. I dump my dirty clothes into the washing machine and return to Harper, wrapping my arms around her waist and nuzzling into her hair.

Fuck, she smells good.

"I think your grandmother will be expecting a call shortly," I tell her, dropping gentle kisses up the length of her neck.

She shrugs and continues whisking. "Stella knows where I am now. I already sent her a text. But even if I hadn't, Nan would somehow know. She always knows ..."

Shaking my head, I murmur, "Crazy, old bird."

She spins around and throws her arms around my shoulders. "Be careful, Zak. The apple doesn't fall far from the tree. And I hear crazy girls are dangerous."

"You're not crazy, kitten. But you are dangerous."

She bats her long lashes at me, all innocent and full of mischief. "I couldn't hurt a fly."

I scoff, an image flickering behind my lids of Harper not even twelve hours ago, a psychotic look in her eyes while she painted Brooks's body with his blood. I've known this wildcat for over four years. I've watched her struggle through her chaotic little lifestyle, always flitting off to some foreign destination and flirting with unavailable men so she never has to commit to anything real. But never once have I seen her come undone the way she did in my cellar.

It was … incredible.

But she's different now that Brooks is dead. Like the wicked storm brewing in her soul has finally passed, leaving nothing but sunshine and clear skies.

We finish cooking breakfast together, then eat in comfortable silence at the island.

Harper disappears down the hall to call her grandmother while I clean up the kitchen. She returns a while later to find me sprawled on the couch, flipping through television channels. Her eyes dart to the remote with all new batteries and a flush of pink creeps into her cheeks.

"Something wrong?" I ask, a shit-eating grin stretching across my face.

She rolls her eyes and flops down beside me.

"Nan's happy to hear you're okay," she tells me, her hands rubbing up and down her thighs anxiously. I narrow my gaze on her and patiently wait for her to continue. "I told her Cameron has been ... *dealt with*. So she's requesting to go home now that the coast is clear."

Harper yelps when I grab her by the backs of the knees and drag her across the leather sofa, pulling her into my lap.

"Is that what you want? For her to go home now that everything's *dealt with*?"

Plump lips part as a set of vibrant blues scan my face. What it is she's searching for, I'm not entirely sure.

"I don't know. I mean ..." She begins anxiously gnawing on the inside of her cheek.

Adjusting her in my lap, I reach into my pocket and retrieve the turquoise stone I found, holding it out for Harper to take. "Is this one of yours?"

She inspects the stone, her eyes widening as recognition washes over her. She shivers, then closes her fist around the rock. "It's the one Nan sent with a note when I was still recovering. I ..." She shakes her head. "Why do you have it?"

"Somehow it made its way into the pocket of my fatigues."

"You had it with you the whole time you were gone?"

"Guess so."

Her head whips side to side as she huffs out a laugh. "Nan said you had a lucky charm with you. I just assumed she meant your coin."

"I don't take my coin on missions," I tell her.

Her perfectly groomed brows pinch tight. "Why not?"

I consider how to respond without making her emotional again, but decide it's best to just be honest. "It was my brother's coin that my grandfather passed down to him. Bran took that coin everywhere. Including when he was deployed and killed."

"So you think it's bad luck?" she asks, filling in the blanks.

I nod. "I'm not a superstitious person, but ..."

"But you'd rather not take a chance," she finishes for me. "I get it. Nan is always talking nonsense, but there's a part of me that wonders sometimes if maybe she's onto something." She hands me back the stone and I close my fist around it. "Keep it, Zak."

Tightening my arm around her, I whisper in her ear, "I'd rather keep you instead."

It's been a little over six weeks since Cameron Brooks's body was scrubbed from my basement. And Harper has finally agreed to see a therapist. The best of the best. One on Sweetwater's payroll. One who will take her secrets to the grave. It'll be a long road to recovery for her, but she's strong and resilient and will get through it like she seems to always do.

And Osmanov has dealt with the remaining pieces of the cartel, confirming Alvarez was detained and handled shortly after I came home from Colombia. The big, Russian bastard has proven himself a major asset. But I can feel it in my bones that it's going to come at a cost in the future. The way his gaze darkened as he undressed Sloane with his eyes ...

A shot pops off and I beam in pride. We're out at Mac's property again, Harper practicing her aim and getting damn good at hitting the target every single time. She's a natural and looks sexy as fuck wielding that much power.

"You're going to put me to shame if I keep letting you practice," I tell her, opening the cooler I packed and tossing a bottle of water at her.

She smiles all sweet and innocent and slugs back a few gulps. I used to force myself to look away from her mouth, but now I just stare, not giving a fuck that she knows I'm watching. *Or that it's making my dick hard.*

I take the gun and water bottle from her and set them on the picnic table. Harper's puzzled expression unfolds into anxiety as I stalk toward her, each step calculated and controlled as I approach like a hungry dog eyeing up a cute, fuzzy kitten.

I angle my head at her in question. "Are you afraid of me, Harper?"

She confidently snips out, "No."

"Then why are you retreating?"

Her blue eyes light with desire. "Because you're pursuing. Isn't that what prey do when being hunted by a predator?"

I let out a wry laugh. "Predator. Is that what I am?"

"You're the big, bad dog at the top of the food chain who preys on innocent little creatures like me. Isn't that what you once told me?"

"It is," I respond coolly, closing the space between us and grabbing her by the hips, spinning her so her ass is rubbing against the bulge in my jeans. Burying my face into her neck, I murmur, "Truth or dare."

Her heartbeat pulses against every inch of my body as I mold myself to her. It picks up speed the longer we stand there, her lithe frame fitting perfectly into mine like a puzzle piece. And I'd be willing to bet every dollar I own that she's considering making a run for it.

"Truth," she breathes out.

"Mmm," I hum thoughtfully. "Bold move. And here I thought you'd take the easy way out." She angles her head to peer up at me, those beautiful blue eyes shining so bright, she could light a thousand torches with just a glance. "Do you love me, Harper?"

Her jaw goes slack and she hesitates before spinning around and throwing her arms around my shoulders, lifting onto her tippy-toes to brush her soft lips against mine. "I hate that I do, but yes. I love you. It's stupid of me, because I know I'll only get hurt in the end."

Squeezing her tight, I drop my forehead to hers and speak slow and clear. "And what if I don't want it to end?"

She pulls back, her eyes darting between mine then down to my mouth. "You're Zak Shephard. It'll end eventually," she states matter-of-factly. "But I've accepted that."

Shaking my head, I step back from her, her words scoring deep into my heart, her razor blade tongue slicing and dicing.

"You still think that little of me, huh?" I begin to pace, perturbed by her shitty sense of judgment.

"What?" she snaps. "The big, bad dog can't handle the truth?"

Swiping a hand through my hair, I blow out a ragged breath, irritation swelling beneath a formidable layer of frustration. *This woman is infuriating.*

Stopping in front of her, I grab her by the upper arms and give her a gentle shake. "You still don't fucking get it," I snarl in her face. At first, she looks shocked, but then ... she looks fucking pissed.

She swats me away and glowers at me, her feet firmly planted in the soil and her little fists balled at her sides and ready to throw hands if I push my luck. I won't, considering what she's been through, but fuck if it wouldn't feel good to bend her over and fuck her until I'm permanently embedded inside her. Maybe then she'd understand.

"Get what, Zak?" she asks, her voice barely a whisper now, her words swept away by the light breeze rustling the trees around us.

"Truth or dare, Harper. And choose wisely."

She recoils, her spine stiffening as she stares back at the frustrated man before her. A man who would crawl on hands and knees to the edge of the world for her and she still doesn't fucking believe it.

"Zak," she whispers. "I don't—"

"Fuck, woman. Just choose."

She stands in silence for another moment before that magnetic pull takes hold and drags us toward each other. Her hand lays over my heart, her eyes blowing wide when she feels how hard it's beating. *For her.*

"Dare."

Reaching into my back pocket, I retrieve a small velvet box, popping it open in front of her. Her hand flies to her mouth as she stares down at the vivid blue diamond, its color rivaling that of Harper's irises and its cushion-cut edges encased in smaller black diamonds. They're some of the rarest on earth. Just like the woman herself. She's wild, untamed, and free spirited. A simple diamond just wouldn't suffice.

"I dare you to tether yourself to me for eternity."

"Zak. I—"

"You don't need to give me an answer right now." I huff out a wry laugh. "And I probably could have picked a better time to do this. But this chaotic, messy, unpredictable love we have … It's not going to end, Harper. There isn't a day goes by that I don't thank the universe for tethering us, even if it did happen in the most fucked way." Swiping a tear from her cheek with the pad of my thumb, I continue on. "I won't hurt you, kitten. Deep down, you know that." Her bottom lip wobbles. "Hurting you would mean assured destruction for me, because I'd rather die than be the one who causes you pain. I'll spend the rest of my life picking up your broken pieces and gluing them back together if I have to. If it means I get to keep you for myself." Her gaze swings back down to the ring. "Think about it, okay? Take your time."

Her cheeks expand as she blows out a ragged breath. Her eyelashes flutter before she lifts her wide gaze back to mine.

"It's gorgeous, Zak," she says softly. "That blue ..."

"Same color as your eyes but nowhere near as alluring."

Her mouth tilts into a shy smile. "Truth or dare, Zak. *And choose wisely.*"

"Dare," I respond confidently, my chest tightening with anxiety.

"I dare you to slide that ring onto my finger and kiss me."

Epilogue

Harper

I STAND IN FRONT of the long mirror, the frame encrusted with tiny rhinestones that reflect the sunlight beaming through the floor-to-ceiling windows of Zak's bedroom. *Our* bedroom.

The dress I chose fits my body perfectly, its chiffon bottom light and airy and comfortable so I can still dance and enjoy myself without feeling confined or weighed down by a mountain of heavy fabric. My hair is pulled back into a wide French braid, tiny jewels pinned throughout the length of it. My makeup is subtle, but my lips are painted a bold red with Zak's favorite lipstick.

"Oh my god, sweetie. You look incredible," Stella says from the doorway of the room, her hazel eyes welling with tears as she approaches me from behind.

I return my attention to my reflection and smile, tears pricking at the corners of my eyes.

"Don't cry. Don't cry. Don't cry," I chant, fanning my face with my hand and blinking away the tears before they have a chance to ruin my makeup.

"She's the most beautiful bride, isn't she?" Nan says from my side as she fusses with my bouquet, then hands it to me.

"Thanks, Nan." I lean down and kiss her, scrunching my nose when it leaves a small smudge of lipstick on her rosy cheek.

The door swings open again and in filter Sloane and Rachel, both dressed in the same satin dresses, the fabric a pale champagne that clings to both of their bodies in the most flattering of ways.

A low cat whistle comes next. "Your loser fiancé is one lucky man," Sloane says from behind me, staring at me in the mirror and popping her gum.

"Speaking of fiancé," Zak's deep voice filters from the doorway. Every pair of peepers in the room turn and glare at him. I can't help but smile and watch his reaction in the mirror. It begins with his warm, brown eyes bugging from his head, then moves to his tongue darting out and wetting his lips, then finally settles on something darker. Something ... dangerous.

He's dressed in a perfectly tailored black suit, the lines clean and crisp and his pocket adorned with a boutonniere that matches my bouquet. He's mouthwateringly delicious.

"No boys allowed," Sloane chirps. "Especially not you." She goes to shut the door but Zak shoulders past her and stares at me. "Jesus, kitten," he mutters lowly as I smooth my hands down my dress nervously.

All eyes bore into Zak as we wait for him to move or say something else. I've already decided today will be perfect, no matter what goes wrong. Because I'm marrying Zak Shephard, the bane of my existence and the man of my dreams. So breaking a little tradition doesn't bother me in the least. After all, it's not like we're a traditional couple. We're messy and fucked up and chaotic. And I wouldn't have it any other way.

"You got your look, now get the fuck out," Sloane says sharply, crossing her toned arms over her chest and glaring at her teammate. Zak ignores her completely and stands stalk still behind me, his eyes roaming hungrily over every inch of my body until a blush creeps into my cheeks.

He clears his throat and asks the group of appalled women, "Mind if I get a moment alone with my future wife?"

I glance around at all the eyes burning holes in Zak's face. "It's fine, girls. I'm sure this will be quick."

Everyone grumbles, Sloane punching Zak playfully in the shoulder on the way out and my nan stopping to wave a finger in his face in warning. The door clicks shut.

"You look ... Wow."

I spin around to face him. "What do you need, Zak?"

He wets his lips again and closes the space between us.

"I haven't seen you in two days, Harper," he points out, his tone laced with bad intentions as his gaze darkens to a rich, chocolate brown.

"Well, you have me now. So what is it that you want?"

He swipes his thumb over my bottom lip, then stares at the smudge of lipstick on his finger, planning something evil in that wicked mind of his.

"Truth or dare, kitten," he muses, his expression playful but a dark glimmer in his eyes.

"Zak. I don't have time to—"

He snakes an arm around my waist and drags me up against his solid body.

"Choose. Or I'll choose for you," he snarls into my ear, and I just know my lipstick is about to be destroyed.

Asshole.

Sighing dramatically, I say, "Dare."

He releases me. "On your knees."

"Fuck no. Absolu—" Strong hands grip my arm as he hauls me to my knees. I let out a yelp and immediately begin whining. "You're going to ruin my dress, Zak."

"Shut up, Harper, or I'll shred that pretty dress to bits with my teeth so you'll be forced to walk down the aisle in nothing but your underwear."

He makes quick work of unzipping his pants and freeing his cock right before my eyes and I can't help the pool of saliva that gathers in my mouth.

I don't have time to protest before he's gripping the back of my head and tugging me forward, his piercing clanking against my teeth as I open my mouth and he pushes himself all the way to the back of my throat.

"Ah, fuck, kitten," he hisses, his hips rocking and causing me to choke back tears as I grip his thighs for support. "Look at those beautiful red lips wrapped around my cock. Fuck, your mouth is perfect."

Saliva drips from the edges of my mouth, slipping down my neck and soaking into the sweetheart neckline of my gown. Tears track down my cheeks, mascara flooding my face and destroying the makeup I spent an hour applying. I slide my gaze to the mirror and take in the sight of a beautiful bride on her knees, her makeup destroyed and lips stretched around her fiancé's cock as he fucks her mouth and uses her for his own selfish satisfaction.

He pulls back enough to allow me to suck in a few panicked breaths through my nose before shoving back in, causing me to gag and sputter.

"You're beautiful, Harper. My sweet, innocent bride." He cups my jaw gently, caressing my cheek and swiping the mascara tears away before they have a chance to tumble to my dress and stain it. "I can't wait to fucking ruin you later."

I glare up at him as he stares admirably down at me, his eyes hooded and jaw slack as he slides his length in and out of my mouth, the steel balls of his piercing hitting the back of my throat.

I make googly eyes at him and lift my lips into a snarl, baring my teeth. I would never bite him, but he needs to know I don't take too kindly to this kind of behavior on my wedding day. This is my special day, and I deserve to be treated like a princess, not a fucking whore.

"I dare you. See what happens," he threatens, and I smirk around his cock.

He thrusts into me a few more times. "You're going to swallow every drop of my cum, aren't you?"

Nodding eagerly, I relax my throat as he pushes all the way inside and releases himself into the back of my throat. I do as I'm told, swallowing every last drop he gives me.

"Good girl. Now lick it clean," he orders.

I oblige, dragging the flat of my tongue up his thick cock and licking the remnants of his cum and my saliva clean. I teasingly flick my tongue over his sensitive tip, causing him to hiss and grab me by the throat and haul me to my feet.

"Such a filthy little bride," he growls in my face, tracing his thumb over my lip and swiping a drop of saliva and cum from the corner of my mouth and inserting it into his own mouth, sucking it clean.

"You're an ass," I spit out with a scowl.

"And you're perfect," Zak says sweetly, as if he didn't just force me to my knees and choke me on his dick. He sits patiently on the foot of the bed, allowing me all the time I need to fix my makeup and hair. But no matter how much effort I put in, it's pointless. I look like a woman who just sucked cock. He offers me his hand. "Ready to be tethered to me for all eternity?"

"Yes," I respond anxiously, taking his hand as he leads me out of the room and down the hall.

Leaning into him, I mutter, "Nan's going to know. You better sleep with one eye open for a while."

"Your sweet grandmother couldn't hurt a fly," he retorts. "Besides, once the granny flat is all finished this fall, she'll be out of the guest room and have her own space again. And we can make all the noise we want." He peers down at me and winks.

When Zak had insisted my nan come stay with us from now on, she had hummed and hawed for a while but eventually agreed to put her house up for sale with the promise I wouldn't send her to a retirement home. Then Zak surprised us when a contractor showed up with blueprints of the guesthouse he's having built on his property so she still has some independence but won't be far from me.

Warmth spreads in my chest at the thought of having everything I've ever wanted within reach.

Zak releases me, planting a chaste kiss on my cheek and backing away from the angry mob of women throwing invisible daggers his way.

"Catch you down the aisle, kitten," he says coolly stuffing his hands into his pockets and disappearing into the backyard.

"Oh, dear. You didn't ..." Nan rushes over and begins fussing over my hair and dress.

"Men," Sloane says dryly, rolling her eyes and shoving another appetizer from a serving platter on the island into her mouth. "They're all dogs."

Biting back a giggle, I say, "They are. And I've got a big, bad one."

The rest of the wedding goes off without a hitch. Zak and I exchange vows and we slide our wedding bands onto each other's fingers, kissing when the minister tells us it's safe to do so.

The only oops of the night is when the DJ mistakenly announces it's time for the father-daughter dance. It stings a little not having my dad here with me, but when Liam appears in front of me and holds out his hand, I choke back my tears and accept his offer. Liam pulls me into the middle of the dance floor and wraps one giant paw around mine, his other hand remaining firmly planted in the center of my back and never wandering lower.

"Thank you," I tell him, peeking up at his ruggedly handsome profile and watching as the scar slashing through his eyebrow crinkles from his frown.

"You're welcome," he responds gruffly.

I'm surprised to find that Liam is actually a good dancer, leading me confidently around the dance floor and ensuring I can keep up without tripping over my dress.

"So, Liam," I drawl. "That's two soldiers down. Looks like it's just you and Sloane left."

His brows furrow and he stares down at me with a warning look. There's zero romantic chemistry between Liam and Sloane. They're more like brother and sister. So I know they'll never become an item. But what I'm really curious about is why Liam is still single. He's rough around the edges. Like ... uber rough. And scary. But he's incredibly attractive and has a squishy spot inside of him that he likes to pretend doesn't exist.

"I don't have time for a woman, Harper. The job is—"

Rolling my eyes, I cut him off. "Yeah, yeah. I know. Yet somehow Joel and Zak have found a way to make it work."

His jaw ticks and I feel his posture stiffen in front of me.

I take that as my cue to change the topic. "Rachel seems really happy."

He nods once. "She is. She's excited about the job, too. She can work from home and go into the office when she feels up for human interaction. Gives her a little more control that way."

Someone clears their throat and Liam steps back. "Mind if I cut in?" a male voice says.

I turn to meet a set of familiar brown eyes, the skin around them weathered with age. If there's anything I'm certain of, it's that Zak is going to age like a fine wine. His father sure as hell did. Tuck Shephard is a silver fox.

Tuck leads me through the second half of the father-daughter dance, a solemn expression on his handsome face. I glance over his shoulder at his wife, Tillie, who's clutching her son's suit jacket and smiling with tears in her eyes as she watches her husband accept his new daughter-in-law with open arms.

"You make a beautiful bride, Harper. My son's a lucky man," he says curtly.

Zak's eyes remain glued to mine and I beam in pride. "I think I'm the lucky one. You raised an incredible man."

Zak and his father have a strained relationship, but it's not irreparable. I've learned that nothing is ever truly broken beyond repair.

"Thank you," he says quietly, averting his eyes as he holds me close like a father would. "I'd like to get to know him better. Wouldn't mind seeing him come around the house more often."

I feel a twinge of something in my gut. Excitement, I think. "I'd be happy to encourage that. As long as you can guarantee me you won't make him feel like any less of a man for the choices he's made."

Tuck pauses and peers down at me with pinched brows. "I don't think any less of him for those choices, honey. I just ..." He blows out a breath then begins shuffling his feet again. "Losing Brandon was rough. Don't know what I'd do if I lost Zak too."

"I think he needs to hear that from you."

Tuck nods in understanding and the song comes to an end. He kisses both of my cheeks then saunters off to stand with his wife.

Zak appears in front of me and gathers me into his arms.

"Tuck Shephard is a man of many words," I tell him with a smirk.

He chuckles softly. "Hard to get a word in with the guy," he retorts sarcastically.

"So ..." I drawl.

"So ..." he echoes.

"How does it feel to be a married man?"

He shrugs nonchalantly, but the twinkle in his eyes tells me he's happy. "Guess I'm stuck with you now. The old ball and chain."

That earns him a swift swat across the chest. But he just chuckles and shakes his head, then dips me low and kisses me. "Mrs. Shephard."

THE END

Acknowledgements

Wow. What an emotional rollercoaster this has been for me. From sobbing uncontrollably while writing scenes that touched me personally, to vibrating in excitement when I finished the first draft, I wouldn't have survived the ride without the love and support of so many incredible people. First, I would like to thank my editor, Kylie MacDougall, for being so patient and reliable. I would also like to thank my developmental editor, Kim Deacon, who worked tirelessly to ensure the story flowed and plot holes were filled.

But most of all, I'd like to thank my readers for their love and support. This journey would be entirely pointless without you.

If you enjoyed Written in Blood, please take a chance on Liam's story in Written in Flesh.

Author website: www.authoradwilde.com

About the Author

A.D. WILDE IS A Canadian author, born and raised in rural Ontario. When she's not reading or writing, she can be found hiking, road tripping to random North American destinations, or stuffing her face with carbs and wine.

Her favorite color is morally gray, her favorite MMCs are, at the very least, mildly psychotic and possessive, and her favorite FMCs are strong, stubborn and independent with a take-no-shit attitude.

A.D. is a mental health advocate, and encourages readers to always check the trigger/content warnings before diving in to any dark romance story.